The Firebird in Russian folklore is a fiery, illuminated bird; magical, iconic, coveted. Its feathers continue to glow when removed, and a single feather, it is said, can light up a room. Some who claim to have seen the Firebird say it even has glowing eyes. The Firebird is often the object of a quest. In one famous tale, the Firebird needs to be captured to prevent it from stealing the king's golden apples, a fruit bestowing youth and strength on those who partake of the fruit. But in other stories, the Firebird has another mission: it is always flying over the earth providing hope to any who may need it. In modern times and in the West, the Firebird has become part of world culture. In Igor Stravinsky's ballet *The Firebird,* it is a creature half-woman and half-bird, and the ballerina's role is considered by many to be the most demanding in the history of ballet.

The Overlook Press in the U.S. and Gerald Duckworth in the UK, in adopting the Firebird as the logo for its expanding Ardis publishing program, consider that this magical, glowing creature—in legend come to Russia from a faraway land—will play a role in bringing Russia and its literature closer to readers everywhere.

Mikhail Kuzmin, Portrait by K. Somov (1909).

Selected Prose & Poetry

Mikhail Kuzmin

Translated from the Russian and Edited by
Michael Green

ARDIS PUBLISHERS
NEW YORK, NY

This edition published in the United States and the United Kingdom in 2013 by
Ardis Publishers, an imprint of Peter Mayer Publishers, Inc.

NEW YORK:
The Overlook Press
Peter Mayer Publishers, Inc.
141 Wooster Street
New York, NY 10012
www.overlookpress.com
For bulk and special sales, please contact sales@overlookny.com

LONDON:
Gerald Duckworth Publishers Ltd.
90-93 Cowcross Street
London EC1M 6BF
www.ducknet.co.uk
info@duckworth-publishers.co.uk

Book design and type formatting by Bernard Schleifer
Printed in the United States of America
ISBN: 978-1-4683-0152-6

2   4   6   8   10   9   7   5   3   1

Go to **www.ardisbooks.com** to read or download the latest Ardis catalog.

Contents

INTRODUCTION

It is curious that the name of so remarkable a writer as Kuzmin should be at the present time so relatively little known. The present writer considers him to be one of the most interesting literary figures of our century. He was, as might be said of Pushkin, a great poet, an outstanding prose writer and a skilled and original playwright. Yet even writers of scholarly studies fail to mention him or dismiss him with a few inadequate and wretchedly stereotyped lines. What could be the reason for such obscurity, given the eagerness of the west to create such "sacred cows" (I use Vladimir Markov's expression) as Akhmatova and Pasternak, about whose smallest idiosyncrasies it is considered worthwhile to write at length? Two main reasons may be suggested, the first connected with Kuzmin's work, the second with his way of life.

The Russian poets of this century (an extraordinarily rich one) fall fairly neatly, by and large, into schools—they are Symbolists or Acmeists or Futurists or Imaginists. Kuzmin, almost alone among poets of his stature, cannot thus be neatly and conveniently categorized, and he himself loathed the idea of poetic "schools." Because of his early article "On Beautiful Clarity" he has sometimes been regarded as a predecessor of the Acmeists, or even as an Acmeist *tout court*. Kuzmin was also close to Symbolism, perhaps essentially closer to it than Acmeism; it was, after all, during the period when Symbolism dominated Russian poetry that Kuzmin's poetic personality was formed and that he published his first book of verse, *Nets* (1908), and the figure of the Guide which is such a dominant one throughout his poetry (a collection of 1918, perhaps his most spiritual, was actually called *The Guide*) can be regarded as a homosexual equivalent of Blok's Beautiful Lady.

This brings us to the second reason for the reluctance of the Soviet guardians of morality to admit Kuzmin into the sacred area they reserve for immortals, the reason that Kuzmin's diaries are still inaccessible to the western scholar (and what a treasure trove must be there). Kuzmin was homosexual, and not "discreetly" homosexual, but openly, even defiantly so. One cannot help feeling that the word "gay," so widely used in our day, and often so inappropriately, would have suited Kuzmin perfectly. Self-acceptance, cheerfulness, irony were essential ingredients of Kuzmin's "gayness." Kuzmin's sexual inclinations became well known, even notorious, early in his career (1906) when the Symbolist journal *The Scales* published his novel *Wings*, in essence a frank defence of the homosexual way of life. If we consider that an analogous American work, Gore Vidal's *The City and the Pillar*, was not published until more than forty years later (E. M. Forster had written his *Maurice*, but it was not published until after his death) we can appreciate something of the shock value a "gay novel" would have had at this time, and the courage needed to publish one. Homosexuality remained an important element of Kuzmin's poetry and fiction; it is not even absent from his theater; as I wrote some years ago apropos of *The Venetian Madcaps*, "the theme of a male partnership endangered by a female interloper which appears with such obsessive frequency in Kuzmin's work (…) is here, for once, brought to a tragic denouement."[1]

It is interesting and curious to what extent the art of prerevolutionary Russia was homosexual (I suppose one could say "the art of this century"—but that is material for another article, not to say a book): Diaghilev, the editor and guiding spirit of *The World of Art*, the enormously influential art journal of the day, as well as the organizer of the Ballets Russes, virtually the rebirth of ballet as an art, Somov, sadly little known in the west, the leading Russian painter of the period and the author of a very fine portrait of his friend Kuzmin.

Let us briefly examine the facts of Kuzmin's biography. Although 1875 is the date usually given in reference books for his birth, and indeed inscribed on the tombstone, a thing of exquisite simplicity (to use an expression all too often relied on as an adequate description of Kuzmin's verse) erected by a group of admirers in the '60s in the Volkovo Cemetery in Leningrad, it seems in reality, as John E. Malmstad demonstrates in his recent biography of the poet, to have been 1872. He was born on the Volga at Yaroslavl into a family of Old Believers. He developed an interest in the theater, something that was to remain with him all his life, by attending operettas in the local theater at Saratov. The Kuzmin family moved to St. Petersburg in 1885. A man who was to be an important influence on the young Kuzmin, and one who incidentally shared his sexual tastes, was Georgy Vasilevich Chicherin (1872-1936), later to be the first important Soviet diplomat, who attended the same gymnasium in St. Petersburg. Kuzmin looked up to Chicherin, a remarkably erudite young man, and was much influenced by him. Kuzmin's first love among the arts, and one that never ceased to be of central importance to him, was music. In August, 1891, he enrolled in the composition course of Rimsky-Korsakov at the St. Petersburg Conservatory. However, Kuzmin completed only three years of the full seven-year course. It was at this time, under Chicherin's influence, that he studied Italian and German. Even among the writers of a remarkably erudite period, Kuzmin is outstanding for his erudition. His knowledge of languages was to stand him in good stead during his Soviet years; he was able to keep body and soul together by translating works from Greek, Latin, French, German, Italian and English. The vastness of his erudition can also be sensed in his poetry, with its wide thematic range, its sometimes obscure literary references and the confidence with which it builds upon such recondite bases as Gnosticism.

In 1895 he went with his mother to Egypt; she returned to Russia, but he settled in Alexandria, where he remained until early 1896. It should not be forgotten in reading the Alexandrian Songs that the city was for him a real place he had experienced and not just a literary backdrop. This was a difficult time for the poet. We know that he had a religious crisis and a disastrous love affair; according to one biographer he actually attempted to commit suicide by taking poison.

In March, 1897, he left for Italy, and by July of the same year he had returned to St. Petersburg. The Italian experience was of immense importance to Kuzmin and Italy, as Vladimir Markov has pointed out in a recent article, pervades Kuzmin's verse. There can be no doubt that the Italian episode of *Wings* is largely autobiographical; the Catholic canon Mori, Signora Poldina and the Marquise Marati were actual acquaintances of Kuzmin in Fiesole, and he even used his real Florentine address for that of the Italian composer Orsini. Such was Mori's influence that Kuzmin very nearly became a convert to Catholicism, indeed he may even have done so for a short time. Closely connected with this mood of his was his interest in the early church Fathers, on whom he did much reading, and his work on a requiem.

Kuzmin's spiritual turmoil was not soon resolved. In late 1898 or early 1899 he set out for northern Russia, thus embarking on a period of his life about which we know virtually nothing. We are not even sure how long this period lasted—according to some, he was back in St. Petersburg in 1901, according to others, he did not take up residence in the capital again until 1903. Until the Kuzmin archive is opened, this period of his life will remain a mystery. We do know that he had a deep interest at this time in the Old Believers, even going so far as to make a serious study of their music and to live in a number of small monastic communities in Nizhny Novgorod and Kostroma regions. As Blok was the first to note, Kuzmin's "genealogy" was closely bound up with the Russian Schism. As far as Kuzmin's work is concerned, we can see traces of this experience in the second part of *Wings*, where the young hero Vanya lives with an Old Believer family;

there are too the spiritual verses published in the collection *Autumnal Lakes*, and in his work for the theater the three "Comedies" (one is tempted to call them "mysteries") of 1908 should not be forgotten.

On returning to St. Petersburg Kuzmin took up a number of abandoned projects. He was firmly resolved to be a composer and wrote a number of songs. It might be said of him that he came to poetry through music; the earliest "poems" he wrote were intended as texts for musical setting. It is significant too that Kuzmin's first published work, the "dramatic poem in eleven tableaux," *The History of the Knight d'Alessio*, was described by an acquaintance as a libretto. *The Green Miscellany*, an almanac containing work by various hands which appeared in 1905, also contained thirteen sonnets which are something of a compromise between Italian and Shakespearan in form, and which he had already set to music. None of this work is worthy of the mature Kuzmin, although as a storehouse of themes and motifs developed in later work it certainly repays study.

In 1904 Chicherin introduced Kuzmin to the World of Art circle. Diaghilev's journal had been appearing since 1899. It revolutionized the attitude to the visual arts in Russia (and eventually still further afield, since the Ballets Russes, with which Diaghilev occupied himself after its closing, may reasonably be regarded as the "offspring" of the World of Art). Although Kuzmin was not "formed" by the World of Art, being essentially what he was to be by the time he made the acquaintance of the group, there is no doubt that he found in it an immensely sympathetic milieu, and he was proud to describe himself as "un homme de Mir iskousstva." As well as esthetic sympathy, it was no doubt important for Kuzmin that, apart from Diaghilev, several members of the group (Nouvel and Somov, for example) were homosexual.

It was at this time that Kuzmin achieved fame and notoriety. Bryusov heard the poet-musician play and sing his Alexandrian Songs; much taken with them, especially with the texts, he published twelve of their number in the important Symbolist journal *The Scales*. Notoriety came when *The Scales* devoted an entire issue to *Wings* in November, 1906. *Wings* was undoubtedly the great literary scandal of its day; when the first edition sold out it immediately appeared in a separate edition, and when that edition sold out quickly it was immediately republished. It is curious that, while *Wings* was freely published, the censorship confiscated the little volume *Three Plays* which appeared in 1907. This was because one of the plays, *The Dangerous Precaution*, a "comedy with songs," is an adroit minuet of sexual identities which pokes fun at conventional morality. One wonders why *Wings* escaped a similar fate. Perhaps because the theater had a separate—and apparently stricter—censorship, or perhaps, as I have suggested elsewhere, "because the novel was a 'serious' treatment of 'the problem,' while the play cheerfully declines to recognize that a 'problem' exists."[2] The third issue of *The Scales* in 1907 contained the beautiful cycle of love poems *That Summer's Love*, which certainly deserves translation.

Kuzmin's association with the theater, with which he was to be concerned many years, began in 1906 with the production of Blok's *The Puppet Show*, for which he wrote music which was, to the ears of one contemporary listener, "piquant, highly-spiced, disturbing and voluptuous." *The Puppet Show* made a deep impression on Kuzmin: "On the subject of remuneration for the music to *The Puppet Show*, I simply don't know what to say to you," he wrote in a letter to Meyerhold dated December 22, 1906, "I'm so fond of this work of Alexander Alexandrovich, value your talents—his, your own and Nikolai Nikolayevich's [the artist Sapunov] so highly, am so genuinely devoted to your theater...." It would no doubt not be a mistake to see the figure of Finette in *The Venetian Madcaps* as a reflection of Columbina in *The Puppet Show*.

Kuzmin's association with the theater of Komissarzhevskaya is reflected in another work included in the present volume, the short story of 1907 "The House of Cards." The setting of this tale is certainly based on the life, onstage and off, of Komissarzhevskaya's troupe; the central figure, Demyanov, the composerpianist-poet who shares his first name and the initial of his patronymic with Kuzmin, is undoubtedly a self-portrait, while the sketch of a distinguished writer seriously offended Sologub and came close to destroying Kuzmin's good relations with him. Kuzmin's relations with another contemporary writer, Alexander Blok, were never other than excellent. The great Symbolist was highly pleased with the music that Kuzmin wrote for his play—he insisted on it being used in subsequent productions—and asked Kuzmin to write incidental music for his translation of Grillparzer's *Die Ahnfrau*, which was produced in 1909; most important of all from the point of view of this study, Blok had a profound appreciation of Kuzmin as a poet, saying to him in 1920, "There are few such poets as yourself in the world today."

The atmosphere surrounding the theater gave ideal opportunity to the roleplaying dandyism characteristic of Kuzmin at this period; he delighted in playing to the hilt roles which expressed certain aspects of his contradictory nature— the decadent dandy with the made-up eyes or the bearded, long-robed Old Believer.

At this time, in 1907, the St. Petersburg apartment of the poet Vyacheslav Ivanov and his second wife, Lydia Zinovieva-Annibal (incidentally the author of the first work in Russian, "Thirty-Three Freaks," to deal with lesbianism), the so-called "Tower," a name by which it was known because of its situation on the sixth floor of an apartment building, became the fashionable gathering place for writers and all those artistically or intellectually inclined. Kuzmin became a regular attender of the Ivanovs' "Wednesdays" in 1906. From being a frequent visitor to the "Tower," Kuzmin, who had a weakness for a congenial family atmosphere, was gradually transformed into a member of the household. The situation of two distinguished poets sharing a home is an intriguing one, and of course the question of whether one had any influence on the other inevitably arises. The answer seems to be in the negative; Ivanov was the most remote, learned and mystical of the Symbolists and Kuzmin a poet of a very different kind, though of course learning and even mysticism of a kind were by no means alien to him.

In 1908 Kuzmin wrote the three religious *Comedies*, much admired by Blok. Blok praised the "sparkling prose" and "airy verse" of *The Comedy of Eudoxia of Heliopolis*, pronouncing it "the most perfect creation in the field of lyrical drama in Russia," no small tribute from one poet to another. *Alexis* was written in the middle of 1907; Komissarzhevskaya, however, failed to share Blok's admiration; her reaction to *Alexis*, which Meyerhold, an admirer of Kuzmin's plays, wished to include in the theater's new seasons, was "an empty, quite useless picture in an exquisite frame." Komissarzhevskaya held stubbornly to her opinion, and none of Kuzmin's plays was ever produced at her theater. It was only some years after her death, during the First World War, that the actress' brother Fyodor Komissarzhevsky produced *Alexis* in the theater in Moscow that bore his sister's name.

At Bryusov's request, Kuzmin compiled his first collection of verse, *Nets*, which appeared in 1908. Blok's reaction to it, expressed in a letter to the poet, was: "God, what a poet you are and what a book this is! I'm in love with all of it, I understand every line and every letter and I press your hands long and hard, my dear, dear friend." "Alexandrian Songs" make up the fourth and last part of *Nets*, which is, in typically Kuzminian style, extremely varied in content, and Vladimir Markov has called this section of *Nets* "the finale of a great symphony, where themes and motifs which have previously sounded appear again, are combined, acquire universality—and where the initial lyrically autobiographical nature of the collection is overcome."[3] It is an odd coincidence that at the very time Kuzmin created his Alexandrian Songs, another poet, a native of Alexandria and a devotee of male beauty, Constantine Cavafy, was creating his own poetic myth of the city. There is no evidence that Cavafy and Kuzmin were acquainted either with each other or with each other's verse. Vladimir Markov has remarked of the Alexandrian Songs that they "astonished Kuzmin's contemporaries" by "the naturalness, the nonchalance even, with which he presented them with the first sizeable body of free verse in Russian,"[4] and there is no doubt that in this respect Kuzmin made an important technical innovation in Russian verse.

In 1909 Kuzmin gave a reading of his famous article, "On Beautiful Clarity," which he published in *Apollon* the following year. This brings us again to an important question which must be dealt with in a sketch of Kuzmin's career: was

Kuzmin an Acmeist, a predecessor of Acmeism or did he maintain an independent position in an age when poets were wont to wear labels? Certainly, "On Beautiful Clarity" was written at a time when Symbolism, the dominant poetic movement of the beginning of the century, had reached a crisis point. However, in the first place "On Beautiful Clarity" is subtitled "Notes on Prose" and is devoted exclusively to a discussion of prose and prose style; nor is the tone of the piece in the least "programmatic." The fact that Kuzmin chose never to republish the piece—one of his most famous—suggests that he became uncomfortable with the attempts to use it as a description of his own work, and still more as a kind of poetic "recipe." Nevertheless, one should not belittle the significance and the effect of such a piece at a time when the mystical and the metaphysical were expected qualities of a written work, the impact of its demand for clarity, logic and grace. And Kuzmin did offer his own name for the proposed new movement, one that never quite caught on—"Clarism." And there is no doubt that poets who were to become leaders of Acmeism saw Kuzmin as one of their own. Thus Bryusov in a letter to Kuzmin dated September 12, 1910: "Although (…) we have not chanced to come closer, I have become accustomed to considering you close, one of us." In the course of the years 1910-11 Kuzmin became quite close to the self-appointed leader of the Acmeists, Gumilev, even to the point of acting as a second in his duel with Voloshin. Gumilev had a high opinion of Kuzmin's verse: "Among contemporary poets M. A. Kuzmin occupies one of the first places;" however, Kuzmin would not have delivered himself of a similar opinion of his friend's verse, which he found depressingly mechanical and shallow.

In considering Kuzmin's relations with the Acmeists let us turn lastly to what remain the most puzzling and mysterious, those with Akhmatova. The poetess began to write with the encouragement of Kuzmin, and a copy of her first book of verse, *Evening* (1912), to which Kuzmin wrote a foreword, is inscribed to "My Wonderful Teacher." Yet later, for reasons that are mysterious, relations soured; there are negative references to Kuzmin in Akhmatova's memoirs, and a satirical and malignant portrait of him in *A Poem without a Hero*—itself curiously dependent on Kuzmin's masterpiece, *The Trout Breaks the Ice*.

Acmeism's attempt to prescribe a formula for the composition of poetry was deeply repugnant to Kuzmin. The words about Acmeism in "Fish-Scales in the Net," "Acmeism is so obtuse and absurd that the mirage of it will soon pass," may be regarded as an uncompromising statement of his final attitude to the movement. The famous "Manifesto" poem which begins the opening section of *Nets*, "Where shall I find a style to catch a stroll, / Chablis on ice, a crisply toasted roll…" has a distinctly revolutionary ring. There can be no doubt that in the context of Symbolism such an apotheosis of the small, the concrete and the frivolous must have seemed a deliberate flouting of orthodoxy, yet ultimately there is perhaps justice in Vladimir Markov's statement: "This striving to merge, to deepen and overstep limits yet again reminds us that Kuzmin is closer to Symbolism than he is to Acmeism."[5]

Kuzmin's life and productivity (though muted by the Revolution) also covers the years when Futurism was the dominant poetic school, and his attitude to that movement is worth considering here. It is typical of the breadth and generosity of Kuzmin's artistic sympathy that he did not reject a movement which must have repelled with its rejection of traditional culture. He enjoyed the respect of Mayakovsky, who regarded "Chablis on ice" as revolutionary, and Kuzmin dedicated his poem *The Hostile Sea* to him. Vladimir Markov has called Khlebnikov "Kuzmin's pupil in more senses than one,"[6] and Khlebnikov's "primitivism" appealed to Kuzmin. Khlebnikov insisted that Kuzmin's name be withdrawn from the Futurist manifesto "A Slap in the Face of Public Taste" and was deeply embarrassed when no withdrawal took place.

At this period Kuzmin was extremely active in the theater—as writer, composer and translator. It is no accident that a portrait of him painted by Golovin at this time shows him in the wings of a theater. To consider in the first place his translations: in 1910 he translated Boccaccio's *Fiametta*; in the field of opera he translated Strauss's *Elektra*, Gounod's *Faust*, Berlioz's *Benvenuto Cellini* and Johann Strauss's *Zigeunerbaron*. Meyerhold, after breaking with Komissarzhevskaya, had been made Director of the Imperial Theaters. In the guise of "Doctor Dapertutto," a pseudonym picked from Hoffmann for him by Kuzmin, he continued to direct the sharp, experimental productions close to his heart. These performances took place in the little theaters and cabarets which were such a feature of St. Petersburg life. There was the House of Interludes, the theater at Terioki on the north shore of the Gulf of Finland, the Stray Dog, in origin a "club" of poets, painters and actors, and its successor the Players' Rest. Meyerhold's first production as Doctor Dapertutto was at the House of Interludes in 1910, and the evening included a Kuzmin piece, *Dutch Liza*, a pastoral opera comique with an eighteenth-century setting. For the second cycle of these entertainments Kuzmin wrote lyrics and music to Znosko-Borovsky's charming comedy *The Transformed Prince* and music for Krylov's comic opera of 1786 *The Frenzied Family*.

In his article of 1911 entitled "Russian Dramatists," Meyerhold included Kuzmin (along with Blok, Bely, Sologub, Vyacheslav Ivanov and Znosko-Borovsky) among those playwrights whose work had contributed to the "new theater" in Russia, the aim of which was to "revive one feature or another of one of the truly theatrical epochs." Meyerhold credits Kuzmin with writing "plays in the spirit of medieval drama," as well as "reconstructing the French comic theater." Kuzmin's *The Venetian Madcaps* specifies as its setting "the Venice of Goldoni, Gozzi and Longhi;" Kuzmin wrote *Madcaps* in 1912, although it was not given until two years later. It could be said that the Venetian theme was "in the air" at the time; Blok, for example, was in 1913 contemplating a drama set in eighteenth-century Venice with "cards and candles," and there is, of course, Thomas Mann's famous novella of 1913 *Tod in Venedig*. Perhaps Venice had a special attraction for the citizens of St. Petersburg, another beautiful assemblage of buildings on water; Diaghilev and Stravinsky chose to be buried there.

In 1910 Kuzmin completed the play *The Prince from the Farm* and in 1921 produced what was to be one of the great successes of the season, the operetta *Maidens' Delight*. Other works of the same year were a short farce, *The Phenomenal American Girl* and a "mythological ballet" in one act called *Apollo and Daphne*.

However, Kuzmin's activity was not restricted to the theater. The short novel *The Journey of Sir John Fairfax*, set in seventeenth-century England, appeared in *Apollon* in 1910. In the same year he published two collections of narrative prose of varying length written between 1906 and 1909, the *First* and *Second Book of Tales*. To the translations dating from this period belong Remy de Gourmont's *Le Livre des masques*, in collaboration with B. M. Blinova, and two poems by Aubrey Beardsley, "The Three Musicians," and "The Ballad of a Barber"— which reminds one that if one wishes at all costs to attach Kuzmin to a movement, the movement in Russia to which he is most convincingly joined is Art Nouveau.

In the course of his life Kuzmin had two great loves, both of whom, curiously enough, were writers. It seems that in addition to what is usually sought in a lover—sexual and emotional satisfaction—Kuzmin felt the need for some kind of sharing of artistic ideals. Vsevolod Knyazev, the first of Kuzmin's great loves, was a minor poet whom Kuzmin seems to have encountered as a soldier in Riga some time in 1910. Knyazev is the "stripling with a bullet through his brain" who appears in the Second Prologue to *The Trout Breaks the Ice*, along with the painter Sapunov, who had been drowned when a rowing boat in which he had been going to Terioki with Kuzmin and some others had overturned (it was for this reason that *The Venetian Madcaps*, written in 1912, had not been produced until 1914; Sapunov had been working on the original sets).

These were difficult years for Kuzmin, perhaps the most difficult of his life. Knyazev began to drift away from him. He was bisexual and was seriously involved with the beautiful actress Olga Glebova-Sudeikina, a friend of Kuzmin; Glebova-Sudeikina played a role in *The Venetian Madcaps* and was the inseparable friend of Akhmatova. In 1913 Knyazev committed suicide. Fortunately, very soon after Knyazev's death Kuzmin met Yury Yurkun (the Mister Dorian of

The Trout Breaks the Ice), with whom he managed to maintain a relationship until his death in 1936.

Another event of this time which must have had a profoundly unsettling effect on Kuzmin was his break with Vyacheslav Ivanov, which not only deprived him of a good friend among the St. Petersburg poetic elect but also of the home he had made for himself in Ivanov's "Tower." The reasons for the quarrel are still not altogether clear, but it seems, as far as we can ascribe a cause to it, that Kuzmin was asked to marry Ivanov's stepdaughter as a "cover-up" for the fact that she was pregnant by Ivanov; he refused, and the friendship between the two poets was unable to survive Kuzmin's reluctance to act out a lie for the sake of convention.

He was now living at the apartment of the popular writer Evdokia Nagrodskaya on the Moika. Nagrodskaya is perhaps partly to blame for the massive output of not very distinguished prose by which he made a living at this period, publishing outside the exclusive literary journals in which his work had previously appeared. In 1915 Kuzmin set up a new apartment, his first independent home, together with Yurkun and "Yurochka's" mother, in which he lived until his death.

This was a period of intense productivity. The novel *Travellers by Land and Sea*, dealing with the intrigues around the writers' club The Stray Dog, of which Kuzmin was a leading member in its early years, was written in 1914. The following year he completed *The Quiet Guardian* and in 1916 *The Wondrous life of Joseph Balsamo Count Cagliostro*, intended as the first volume in a series to be entitled *The New Plutarch* which would treat the lives of historical figures in semi-fictionalized form. Apart from these large-scale works, Kuzmin turned out more than seventy stories between 1913 and 1917. To 1914 belongs the third and last of Kuzmin's large prerevolutionary collections, more a summary of past achievement than evidence of new departures, *Clay Pigeons*.

Preoccupation with writing did not keep the composer from his metier. *The Choice of a Bride*, a special favorite of St. Petersburg audiences, was produced at the Liteiny Theater in 1913 with choreography by Boris Romanov, who also choreographed *The Tryst*, produced at the same time. Another Kuzmin ballet produced at the Liteiny Theater was *The Enchanted Princess*, in addition to a play, *Alice Who Was Afraid of Mice*, which also dates from 1913. *The Fairy, the Bassoon and the Stagehand* was staged at Baliev's Moscow theater of light entertainment, as was *Everyone's Happy* (1917). The "mystery play" *The Knight Who Sold His Wife to the Devil* was also produced in 1917. Another establishment that staged works by Kuzmin was the Pavillion de Paris, which saw the staging of *The Bogus Thief*, written in 1914, and The Queen of Spades, where *The Phenomenal American Girl* (written in 1911) was staged. For the Kamerny Theater he wrote *Whit Monday in Toledo*, produced in 1915. Some half-dozen other pieces are mentioned in Kuzmin's theatrical list, but the texts of them have not survived. In 1916 The Players' Rest, decorated by Sudeikin in honor of "Carlo Gozzi and Ernst Theodor Hoffmann" (in honor of whom the central hall was named) took over from The Stray Dog as the artistic and bohemian center in St. Petersburg. It opened with a production of Kuzmin's "Arabian fairy-tale" *The Mirror of Maids*. It was here in October, 1916, that Kuzmin's friends organized a special ceremony to mark the tenth anniversary of Kuzmin's literary activity (*The Knight d'Alessio* of 1905 had clearly been forgotten).

This was a time, of course, when the tactless hand of history did not leave the creative artist undisturbed. St. Petersburg (or Petrograd as it was now called, a name Kuzmin heartily disliked) was not left untroubled by the First World War, and then in 1917 came the first of the Russian revolutions—the February Revolution. Kuzmin's first reaction, like that of many intellectuals, was positive and optimistic. In April 1917 he was elected, together with Blok, Mayakovsky and Punin, to one of four seats on the Praesidium of the new Association of Artists in Petrograd. This was a difficult time for him financially, since his income was solely derived from publishing and now, what with political instability and paper shortage, many journals were closing down and very few books were published. He had to sell off his collection of old books, his ikons and the many paintings he possessed by the contemporary artists who were his friends. These exhausted, he took to selling his own manuscripts. Because of the limited opportunity to publish, and perhaps because of the desperate nature of the times, most of what he wrote at this time was poetry, not prose.

Kuzmin, like his old friend Blok, whose reactions at this time were surprisingly like his, greeted the Bolshevik revolution with warm optimism. The fact that the Bolsheviks were outspokenly in favor of withdrawing from the war was no doubt a prime factor in attracting the war-weary poets. To this time belongs the cycle of openly—even blatantly—erotic poems *Pictures under Wraps*, published, according to the title page, in "Amsterdam," but really, of course, in Petrograd.

In September 1918, concerned with the desperate plight of those who made their living by the pen, Gorky and Lunacharsky, the Commissar of Public Education, set up an organization specializing in the translation of classics of world literature, called, appropriately, World Literature. Kuzmin took a keen and active interest in the enterprise. He participated in the planning of the French literature section and made translations for the selected works of Anatole France (how very high he placed France among writers of the period we can tell from "Fish-Scales in the Net," where he elevates the French novelist to the position of dominating writer of the age).

In October 1918 a new daily, *The Life of Art*, in the founding of which Kuzmin had played a central role, began to appear. Kuzmin was one of the four members of the paper's editorial board, another being Viktor Shklovsky. Kuzmin's field of specialization on *The Life of Art* was the theater, although he occasionally wrote reviews of music and books. The pieces he considered most significant he republished in his only collection of criticism, *Conventions* (1923).

But Kuzmin was not content to remain on the critical sidelines; he continued to be active in the theater. In October 1918 a cabaret at the Players' Rest contained a prologue and a "vaudeville," *The Dancingmaster from Kherson* with text and music by him. Kuzmin's special area of responsibility on the board was children's and puppet theater. The only play that Kuzmin wrote in 1918 was the "Chinese drama" *A Happy Day or The Two Brothers*, a children's play. Nor in the early days of the Soviet regime were Kuzmin's musical gifts denied recognition: he was appointed chief composer to the new Bolshoi Dramatic Theater.

Kuzmin's entanglement with the theater did not keep him from other work. There was a return to prose, although, alas, the productions of this period, almost certainly among Kuzmin's best, have only been partially published. Two chapters of a life of Virgil to be entitled *The Golden Sky* appeared in 1923. In the previous year two chapters had appeared from a Roman novel set in the reign of Marcus Aurelius, *Roman Wonders*. This work seems to have combined Kuzmin's main interests in a manner that came close to the ideal: the classical world, early Christianity and, in the Hadrian-Antinous relationship to which there is some reference, a legendary romance between two men. Kuzmin regarded *Roman Wonders* as his finest prose work, and the two published chapters give us reason to think he may well have been right. At this unfortunate period Kuzmin completed work on a novel *Veronica Lost* which never appeared in print at all. It was at this time that Kuzmin wrote what might well be considered his most enchanting short story, and one which demonstrates that his prose, at its best, vies with the finest of the age: "From the Notes of Tibertius Penzel," which was published in 1921. Nor was translation neglected; he continued his work on France with *Le Lys rouge*, he translated the libretto of Mozart's *Die entführung aus dem Serail* (not performed until 1925), he worked on Régnier, to whom, as we can tell from "Fish-Scales in the Net," he had grown somewhat cold. There were also translations of Venetian songs.

Kuzmin was not lucky in his most intimate relationships. His first great love had ended with the suicide of the beloved, his second—Yurkun—seemed threatened when that young man (like Knyazev, a bisexual) fell in love with a woman and married her. In 1921 Yurkun became the husband of Olga Arbenina. For a period, a dreadful one for Kuzmin, Yurkun moved out of the apartment he shared with the poet. However, he soon moved back, and a rather curious menage now formed the background of Kuzmin's life: in addition to the two men there was Yurkun's mother (who had never left the apartment) and Arbenina herself, who was not a permanent resident of the apartment but frequently stayed there.

The introduction of the New Economic Policy at this time somewhat eased the publishing situation, and in 1921 a new publishing house, Petropolis, issued a new collection of Kuzmin's verse, *Otherwordly Evenings*, and the little play, characteristically described as being for "live or wooden dolls," *Mary's Tuesday*, It is interesting, a sign that the grundyism characteristic of the Soviet period had not yet set in, that *Wings* was republished in 1923 (true, in Berlin, but under the auspices of Petropolis, a publishing house allowed to circulate its wares in the Soviet Union.) Another verse collection, *Echo*, appeared in 1921. The story "A Blue Nothing" appeared in the almanac *Petrograd* in 1923.

"Art is emotional and wise," Kuzmin had written in the course of a polemic with Marietta Shaginian, and "Emotionalism" was the name he chose for a new movement, if that is not too pretentious a word for any artistic impulse initiated by a writer so hostile to organized "movements." In October 1922 the group (Kuzmin was the only writer of any distinction it contained) issued the first number of an almanac, *Abraksas*, the third and last number of which contained a "Declaration of Emotionalism," clearly from the hand of Kuzmin, though it had two additional signatures. While "Emotionalism" does not offer anything further than generalizations based on Kuzmin's past practice, it clearly has much in common with Expressionism; Kuzmin was at this time passionately interested in this new movement in Germany, writing music for new German Expressionist plays and so taken with *The Cabinet of Dr. Caligari* that he was unable to keep it out of *The Trout Breaks the Ice*. Kuzmin's verse of 1921 and 1922 was published by the poet in December 1922 (although the date on the cover is 1923) under the title *Parabolas* (a title which in Russian makes play with a word meaning at once a geometrical figure and a "parable"). Since it was published by Petropolis in Berlin, it has remained the least known collection of Kuzmin's work in his native land, although the poet regarded it, together with *Nets* and *The Trout Breaks the Ice*, as his best work. It is difficult and avant-garde as the earlier verse had been sensuous, shapely and Art Nouveau.

It became increasingly difficult for such a man as Kuzmin to live under Soviet conditions. The journal *Abraksas* was closed because of its "unintelligibility" and "extremeness." The critics complained of the difficulty of his new work; he clearly had no place in the "new" society and it became ever more difficult for him to publish his work. In his *Literature and Revolution* Trotsky paired Kuzmin with Sologub as writers whose books are "completely and entirely superfluous to modern post-October man, like a glass bead to a soldier on a battlefield" and described them as "internal emigres." In 1926 and 1927 he managed to publish just a few poems in various periodicals, but after that he published no more. He was well on the way to becoming the non-person he was until very recently in the Soviet Union. The newspapers also became nervous of employing so incurably unsoviet a writer; no review appeared under his name in the Soviet press after 1926, though it is possible that some he wrote were published anonymously. In spite of lack of encouragement he continued to write. A play entitled *The Death of Nero* was written in 1929; it is a bold piece which mixes temporal planes quite ruthlessly, its twenty-eight scenes being divided among Rome in 1919, Saratov in 1914, Switzerland and the Rome of Nero. The piece remained unpublished until it appeared in 1977 in Volume Three of the Fink Verlag edition of Kuzmin's complete poetry.

In 1928 Kuzmin gave his last public reading, a curious, scandalous and touching occasion which deserves description here. The students of the Leningrad literary institutes had the idea of inviting virtually the last distinguished writer of his generation who was still alive and living in Leningrad. Kuzmin went, expecting the evening to be poorly attended, imagining himself to be a forgotten versifier. But when he arrived at the hall it was packed. The evening was clearly a rare success; Kuzmin read, among other things, the poem on which he had been working most recently, *The Trout Breaks the Ice*, and the audience grew ever more enthusiastic. But at last what the organizers of the event feared actually came to pass; the ticket system having broken down, there came crowding into the hall a mob of Leningrad homosexuals, many carrying flowers with which they showered the poet during the ovation that followed his reading. Kuzmin's delight equalled the alarm and horror of the affair's organizers; it was only by persuading the authorities that they were not party to the disgraceful events that they escaped serious trouble.

Encouraged by this reception, Kuzmin made one last attempt to find publishers for his last collection, and by something like a miracle (given the conditions prevailing in literature at the time) he succeeded; *The Trout Breaks the Ice*, a collection consisting of several cycles apart from the title narrative poem which is included here, appeared in March 1929. No agreement seems to exist among those who knew Kuzmin at this time concerning the amount of poetry he wrote during the last years of his life; it seems, at any rate, that there are two further long poems. It is doubtful whether any manuscripts survive, since Kuzmin was not at all careful in the preservation of this poetry, written purely for his pleasure; if someone liked a poem, he gave it to them.

Since Kuzmin could no longer make a living in journalism he became even more dependent on translation to keep body and soul together, and a list of the works he put into Russian at this period is simply breathtaking. In 1932 he translated the libretti of Verdi's *Don Carlo* and *Falstaff*. To a nine volume edition of the complete prose of Henri de Regnier he contributed versions of two novels.

He also translated a number of stories for the complete works of Mérimeé, Romain Rolland's life of Beethoven, Stendhal's life or Rossini (on which he worked with Innokenti Oksenov). He translated some poems by Heine and, together with S. Shervinsky, the *Westöstlicher Divan* of Goethe. From classical literature he translated *The Golden Ass* of Apuleius and some passages from the *Iliad*.

It is perhaps to Shakespeare that he paid deepest homage; of the plays he translated *King Lear, The Taming of the Shrew, The Two Gentlemen of Verona, Much Ado About Nothing, The Merry Wives of Windsor, Love's Labour's Lost, The Tempest* and the two parts of *Henry IV* (these last in collaboration with Vladimir Morits). Purely for himself he worked for many years on a complete version of the Sonnets, completing by the time of his death work on one hundred and ten. Unfortunately, all this work was lost during the Stalinist terror, when much of the Kuzmin archive was destroyed. Among other works of English he translated was Byron's *Don Juan*. But he did not devote himself entirely to "safe" classics, as is demonstrated by the version he made of the libretto of Berg's *Wozzeck*.

Kuzmin's health grew steadily worse and in late February, 1936 he entered the Kuibyshev Hospital in Leningrad, where he died on March I of pneumonia; though the Soviet press left his death virtually unmentioned, a great many Leningrad writers followed his coffin to its resting place in the Volkovo Cemetary. We may doubt whether Kuzmin, had he lived a year or two longer, would have had the privilege of a natural death. In 1938 Yurkun was arrested along with a number of other literary men and shot.

Are we on the brink of a Kuzmin revival? Will there come a time when his name will come as automatically to the lips of those speaking about post-revolutionary Russian poetry as those of Mandelstam, Pasternak and Akhmatova, whose equal he at least was? One hopes that the answer will be in the affirmative. Kuzmin's work has begun to be translated into English. In academe there are signs of interest—articles have begun to appear of which he is the subject. A Soviet edition of his poetry is still lacking, although one was announced some time ago; one assumes that Kuzmin's unmentionable sexual practices have hindered its appearance in print. However, as compensation for this there has recently appeared the splendid three volume set of Kuzmin's complete verse by Fink Verlag, under the editorship of John E. Malmstad and Vladimir Markov, the third volume of which contains an interesting biography of the poet by Malmstad to which the author of this introduction is most indebted. "Yu. Yu. goes about asking everyone who our leading poet is, thinking they will name me; no one does, though," Kuzmin noted, more in affectionate amusement, we may be sure, than wounded vanity. Perhaps Yurkun will finally not be disappointed with the answer given to his question.

NOTES

1. Michael Green, "Mikhail Kuzmin and the Theater," *Russian Literature Triquarterly* 7 (1973), 262.

2. Ibid., 253.

3. V. Markov, "Poeziia Mikhaila Kuzmina," M. A. Kuzmin, *Sobranie stikhov* III (Munich, 1977), 334.

4. Vladimir Markov, "Preface," *Wings, Prose and Poetry by Mikhail Kuzmin* (Ann Arbor: Ardis, 1972), xii.

5. V. Markov, "Poeziia Mikhaila Kuzmina," M. A. Kuzmin, *Sobranie stikhov* III (Munich, 1977), 373.

6. Vladimir Markov, "Preface," *Wings, Prose and Poetry by Mikhail Kuzmin*, xii.

WINGS

PART ONE

It was growing lighter in the railway car, which had emptied somewhat with the approach of morning; beyond the misted windows the eye took in the bright poison-green of fields undimmed by late August, sodden country roads, milkwomen's carts waiting at the lowered barrier, guardboxes, ladies down for the summer out strolling beneath gay umbrellas. New passengers, local people, got in with their briefcases at one drab station after another, and it was obvious that for them a train journey was not an epoch-making event or even an interesting episode in their lives, but merely part of their daily routine, and somehow the wooden seat occupied by Nikolay Ivanovich Smurov and Vanya seemed to possess a special solidity and importance. The sturdily bound trunks with their strapped-on cushions, the longhaired old gentleman sitting opposite with the old-fashioned traveling bag over his shoulder—everything told of long hours on the road, of a journey that was far from being an everyday event.

Glancing at the ruddy sunbeam which struggled through the engine's billowing steam, at Nikolay Ivanovich's face, foolish in sleep, Vanya recalled the squeaky voice of this cousin of his as it had sounded in the hallway of the house which now lay far behind—"home": "The money your mama left you is all gone; as you know, we're not rich ourselves, but since you're my cousin I'm prepared to help you; you've still got plenty of schooling ahead of you; I can't take you to live with me, but I'll arrange for you to live at Aleksey Vasilyevich's—I'll come and see you when I can; they're a lively crowd, and you'll have a chance to meet the right sort of people there. Make the best of things; Natasha and I would have been pleased to have you, but it's just out of the question I'm afraid; and anyway you'll be happier at the Kazanskis: the house is always crowded with young people. I'll pay for you, and when we come to settle up I'll deduct what you owe me." Sitting on the window ledge in the hall, Vanya had listened, not moving his eyes from the square of sunlight that lay across the chest, Nikolay Ivanovich's striped—lilac and gray—trousers, the painted floor. As the words flowed on he had thought of his mother's dying, how the house had suddenly filled with cluck-ing womenfolk, strangers, but all at once oddly close; he had remembered the ceaseless activity, the solemn requiems, the interment, the sudden emptiness and desolation when it was all over, and without looking at Nikolay Ivanovich he had repeated mechanically, "Yes, Uncle Kolya"—although Nikolay Ivanovich was only his cousin and not his uncle at all.

How odd it was to be traveling alone with this man he scarcely knew, to be sit-ting next to him for so long, to be discussing serious matters, making plans. And there was a faint feeling of disappointment—although he had known what to ex-pect—that they weren't entering Saint Petersburg through a great arch to find palaces and mighty edifices on every side and squares flooded with people, sun-shine and military music; that instead for miles there was nothing to see but nar-row vegetable plots behind gray palings, cemeteries which looked from afar like enchanted groves, dank six-storied workers' tenements hulking over tumbledown shacks, their outlines dimmed by smoke and soot. "So this is Petersburg!" thought Vanya, his disappointment mixed with curiosity as he gazed at the un-friendly faces of the porters.

*   *   *

"Have you finished, Kostya—may I?" said Anna Nikolayevna; she got up from the table and reached out long fingers, aglitter with cheap rings even at this early hour, to take a sheaf of Russian newspapers from Konstantin Vasilyevich.

"Yes; nothing of any interest."

"How can there be anything of interest in our newspapers? Now abroad—that's a different matter! They can write what they like there, and answer for it in a court of law if need be. The awful thing in this country is that you don't know what to believe. Official statements and reports are either unreliable or trivial; there's never any news here, apart from embezzlement trials and all the rumors the special correspondents feed us."

"But what do you get abroad, apart from sensational rumors? And it's non-sense to say they have to answer for their lies."

Koka and Boba lazily rattled their spoons in their glasses and munched bread smeared with rancid butter.

"Where are you off to today, Nata? Do you have things to do?" asked Anna Nikolayevna, trying to inject a note of motherly concern into her voice.

Nata—all freckles, vulgarly pouting lips and carroty hair—mumbled some-thing in reply through a mouthful of bun. Uncle Kostya, who had been a cashier

in a shady club until the day he was caught with his hand in the till, and who had
been living at his brother's without employment or occupation since his release
from prison, was waxing indignant over a misappropriation case.

"Now that the winds of change are blowing and new forces are being un-
leashed, everything is awakening," Aleksey Vasilyevich was fulminating.

"I'm by no means always in favor of awakenings; Sonya's aunt, for example, I
prefer asleep."

There was a constant coming and going of students and young men of no ap-
parent occupation who kept up a lively exchange of views, gleaned from the
newspapers, on the events of the latest race-meetings; Uncle Kostya called for
vodka; Anna Nikolayevna, her hat already perched on her head, stood drawing
on her gloves and talking about some exhibition, at the same time casting a dis-
approving eye on Uncle Kostya as he filled glasses with a shaky hand and said,
rolling kindly, somewhat bloodshot eyes, "A strike, my friends, why that's a, that's
a...."

"Larion Dmitrievich!" announced the maid, snatching up a tray of glasses and
a stained and rumpled tablecloth as she went briskly through to the kitchen.

Vanya turned from the window and saw the familiar tall figure in the baggy
suit—Larion Dmitrievich Stroop.

*   *   *

Of late Vanya had taken to brushing his hair and paying more attention to his toi-
lette. He examined his reflection in the little wall mirror, gazing indifferently at
the round, somewhat insignificant face, the red cheeks, the large gray eyes, the
beautifully formed mouth with its trace of a childish pout, the fair hair which, un-
curbed by the barber's shears, curled slightly. The tall, finely made, delicate-
browed boy in the black blouse neither pleased nor displeased him. Outside was
the yard with its wet flagstones, the windows of the outbuilding opposite, men
selling matches. It was a holiday and everyone was still asleep. Having risen early
by force of habit, Vanya sat down by the window to wait for morning tea, listening
to the pealing bells of the church nearby and the bustle of the maid, who was
tidying up in the next room. He called to mind holiday mornings at that faraway
place in the little old district town—"home," the clean, neat rooms with their
muslin curtains and icon lamps, morning service, the pie standing on the table
at lunchtime, everything simple and cheerful and cosy, and he was oppressed by
a tedium compounded of steady rain, barrel organs in backyards, newspapers
with morning tea, disorder and discomfort in dingy rooms.

Konstantin Vasilyevich, who occasionally looked in for a chat, poked his head
through the door.

"You alone, Vanya?"

"Yes, Uncle Kostya. Good morning! Anything the matter?"

"No, nothing. Waiting for tea?"

"Yes. Is Auntie up yet?"

"She's up all right, but she's staying in her room. She's in a temper about something—no money, I suppose. That's always the first sign—when she sits in her bedroom for two hours you can be sure there's no money. And what's the point? She'll have to come down sooner or later."

"Doesn't Uncle Aleksey Vasilyevich earn plenty of money then? Or don't you know?"

"Sometimes he does, sometimes he doesn't. And besides, what does 'plenty' mean? For a man no amount of money is ever plenty."

Konstantin Vasilyevich heaved a sigh and was silent for a while; Vanya too sat in silence, looking out of the window.

"What I wanted to ask you, Ivanushka," began Konstantin Vasilyevich again, "was if you have any money you could spare me until Wednesday. I'll let you have it back on Wednesday for sure."

"Where would I get money from? Of course I haven't got any."

"How should I know where from? Someone might have given you some...."

"What do you mean, Uncle? Who on earth would give me money?"

"So you haven't got any then?"

"No."

"Now that's too bad!"

"How much did you want?"

"Five roubles, say—a fleabite, a mere fleabite," Konstantin Vasilyevich perked up again. "Maybe you could manage it, eh? Just till Wednesday?!"

"I haven't got five roubles."

Konstantin Vasilyevich looked at Vanya with an expression in which disappointment mingled with cunning and said nothing for a while. Vanya's spirits sank still further.

"What's to be done? This rain looks as if it's never going to let up.... I tell you what, Ivanushka, how about getting some money for me from Larion Dmitrievich?"

"Stroop?"

"Yes—please do it for me, my dear boy!"

"Why don't you ask him yourself?"

"He wouldn't give it to me."

"Then why should he give it to me if he won't give it to you?"

"Take my word for it, he will; please, my dear boy—only don't let on that it's for me; pretend you need the twenty roubles yourself."

"I thought you said five!"

"Five, twenty—what difference does it make? Please, Vanya!"

"Oh all right. But suppose he asks what I want the money for?"

"He won't, he's not the sort to go asking silly questions."

"Only you will let him have it back, won't you?"

"Without fail, I promise."

"But Uncle, why are you so sure that Stroop will give me the money?"

"Because…!" And Konstantin Vasilyevich tiptoed out of the room smiling, at once delighted and embarrassed. Vanya stood at the window for a long time, his back to the streaming yard, and when he was called in to tea he paused before entering the dining room to stare again in the mirror at his flushed face with its gray eyes and delicately-drawn brows.

✻   ✻   ✻

In Greek class Vanya's attention was constantly diverted by Nikolayev and Szpilewski fidgeting and giggling in the front row. With holidays in the offing no one was in a mood to take school very seriously, and the teacher, diminutive and balding, sat with one leg curled up under him and discoursed on life in ancient Greece without asking for assignments; the windows were open, allowing a glimpse of red brickwork and treetops bursting into leaf. Every day deepened Vanya's longing to get away from Petersburg to the country—the further away the better. The brass handles of the doors and windows, the spittoons—everything brightly polished—the maps on the walls, the blackboard, the yellow waste paper basket, the backs of his classmates' heads—some cropped, some curly— all seemed insupportable to him.

"Sycophant—informer, spy: literally; 'fig-shewer'; in the days when the export of this product from Attica was forbidden under threat of fine, if one of these people—blackmailers we would call them—encountered a man who aroused his suspicions, he would produce a fig from under his cloak to warn him that if he didn't pay up…." And without getting down from his desk Daniil Ivanovich gave a vivid pantomime of it all—informer, victim, cloak, fig; then he bounded down and began to pace about the room with a preoccupied air, repeating some particular expression over and over again: "Sycophants…yes, sycophants…yes, sycophants," finding ever new and surprising inflections.

"Today I shall try to borrow some money from Stroop," thought Vanya, glancing out of the window.

Szpilewski stood up, blushing a fiery red:

"What does Nikolayev keep pestering me for?"

"Nikolayev, why are you pestering Szpilewski?"

"I'm not."

"What were you doing then?"

"Sit down. And as for you, Mr. Szpilewski, I advise you to be more precise in your choice of words. Bearing in mind the fact that you are not a young lady, Mr. Nikolayev can hardly be said to be pestering you, being of marriageable age and somewhat conventional ideas to boot.

❀   ❀   ❀

"This is how I see the question: if you want to work, work, if you don't, don't," Anna Nikolayevna was saying, with an air that suggested that the world was waiting with bated breath to hear how it was she saw the question. The drawing room, which was crammed from wall to wall with such period pieces as chairs resembling hip-baths, chaises longues and waste paper baskets, reverberated with the voices of the four women—Anna Nikolayevna, Nata and the Speier sisters, artists both.

"I'm very fond of this cupboard, but I don't care for the seat. I'd take the cupboard any day, given the choice."

"Even if you needed something to sit on?"

"Maids are always complaining that they're overworked; why, ours gets about more than any of us! Sometimes I don't leave the house for days on end, but our Annushka is always going out to the shops for all sorts of things—bread, boots, what have you. Just think of all the people she must meet! I must say I find all these complaints very exaggerated."

"Imagine, there's such a passion in his poses that the girls are afraid to sit too close. And he's an absolutely fascinating man—a Russian gypsy from Munich; he's been a high school teacher, a ballet dancer, an artist's model; and he has a fund of amusing little stories about Stuck!"[1]

"No, on a pink foulard it would be too bright. Pale green would be better, I think."

"Stroop's the one to ask about that."

"But Stroop left town yesterday, you poor dears—didn't you know?!" cried the elder of the Speier sisters.

"You can't mean it! Why? Where's he gone?"

"Well that I can't tell you—as usual, it's a secret."

"Who told you?"

"He told me himself; for three weeks, he said."

"Well that's not so very terrible!"

"You know, Vanya Smurov was asking today when Stroop would be coming to see us."

"What did he want to know for?"

[1] Franz von Stuck (1863-1928): German painter. From 1895 a professor at the Munich Academy of Fine Arts (Eds.).

"I don't know, some personal matter."

"Between Vanya and Stroop? Whatever next!"

"Well, Nata, we must be on our way," Anna Nikolayevna essayed an aristo-cratic twitter, and both ladies withdrew, skirts rustling, convinced that they bore a striking resemblance to the society ladies in the novels of Prévost and Ohnet,[2] which they read in translation.

❈   ❈   ❈

In April the renting of a summer cottage became a frequent topic of conversa-tion. Aleksey Vasilyevich was having to go into town almost everyday, Koka and Boba too, and the Volga trip planned by Anna Nikolayevna and Nata hung in the balance; anyway, if they couldn't get to Sestroretsk they could always go to nearby Terioki, and in the meantime the women busied themselves preparing their summer wardrobe as dust flew in through the wide-open windows, and with it the rattle of carriages and the jingle of horse-drawn trams.

Vanya sometimes went off by himself to the Summer Gardens to prepare his lesson or to read. Today he sat on one of the benches lining the path nearest to the Champ de Mars and, laying aside the open Taubner edition yellowish-pink cover upwards, he surveyed the people walking in the gardens and on the other side of the Lebyazha Canal. He seemed taller, and his spring tan had faded some-what. From the far end of the gardens came the laughter of children romping in the Krylov Playground, and Vanya did not hear the gravel crunching under Stroop's feet as he approached.

"Studying hard?" Stroop said, sitting down on the bench next to Vanya, who had intended to limit his greeting to a nod.

"I'm trying to, but if you only know how terribly boring it all is!"

"What is it? Homer?"

"Yes, Homer. Greek is the worst!"

"You don't care for Greek?"

"Does anyone?" Vanya smiled.

"That's a great pity!"

"What is?"

"That you don't care for languages."

"The modern ones I don't mind—at least you can find something worth read-ing—but who wants to read the Greeks, all that musty old stuff?"

"What a child you are, Vanya. A whole world, whole worlds lie beyond your ken; a world of beauty too, without a knowledge and love of which no man can call himself educated."

[2] Marcel Prévost (1862-1941) and George Ohnet (1848-1918): society novelists, im-mensely popular in their day (Eds.).

"Why waste all that time on grammar when you can read translations?"

Stroop gave him a look of infinite pity.

"Instead of a flesh-and-blood being who laughs and frowns, a being you can love, kiss or hate, a being with blood flowing in his veins, instinct with the natural grace of the naked body—instead of that you get a soulless doll, more often than not the work of some hack: that's your translation for you. And it really doesn't take much time to acquire the rudiments of grammar. All you have to do is read, read, read. Read looking up every word in the dictionary, as if you were cutting your way through a dense forest—you can't imagine what pleasure it will give you. You know, Vanya, I think you have it in you to become a completely transformed being."

Vanya remained sullenly silent.

"You live among people who have nothing to offer you—but perhaps that's for the best: at least you escape the prejudices of a life ordered by tradition, so that there's nothing to prevent you from becoming a truly free spirit, if only you wanted to," added Stroop after a silence.

"I don't know, I just want to get away from it all—from school; from Homer, from Anna Nikolayevna—that's all."

"And take refuge in the bosom of nature?"

"Exactly."

"But, my dear friend, if living in the bosom of nature means eating more, drinking milk, bathing and doing nothing—then of course it's all very simple; but it seems to me that enjoying nature is harder work than learning Greek grammar, and like all enjoyment it wearies one. I can't believe a man who lives in town without ever casting a glance at the loveliest things in nature's realm— water and sky—and then tells me he's going to look for nature on Montblanc; I refuse to believe that such a man loves nature."

¤　¤　¤

Uncle Kostya offered Vanya a ride in his cab as far as the school.

Summer's nearness could be sensed in the morning heat; half the streets were under repair. Uncle Kostya, whose bulk took up three quarters of the open droshky, sat squarely, feet planted wide apart.

"Uncle Kostya, if you'll just wait a moment I'll go and see if the chaplain's come today, and if he hasn't I'll ride with you to where you're going and walk back from there—it'll be better than sitting in school doing nothing."

"And what makes you think the chaplain won't be in today?"

"He's been away sick for a week now."

"All right then, go and find out."

A minute or so later Vanya came out, walked round the cab and got in the other side, next to Konstantin Vasilyevich.

"Our friend Larion Dmitrievich, my boy, must have got wind of our little plan—he's taken himself off and shows no sign of coming back."

"Maybe he has come back."

"In that case he'd surely have called on Anna Nikolayevna."

"What sort of man is he, Uncle Kostya?"

"What sort of man is who?"

"Larion Dmitrievich."

"He's Stroop, and when you've said that you've said everything. He's half English, wealthy, doesn't work, lives well, you might say in style, is highly cultured, extremely well-read—to tell you the truth, I don't really understand what he hangs round the Kazanskis for."

"He's not married is he, Uncle?"

"Quite the reverse, you might say—and if Nata thinks she's going to captivate him with her charms she's sadly mistaken; in fact it's beyond me what he finds to do at the Kazanskis. Yesterday was a laugh though: Anna Nikolayevna gave pitched battle to Aleksey!"

They crossed a bridge over the Fontanka. Peasants were standing on barges hauling fish from the hatches, steamboats puffed, and a crowd of idlers stood looking over the stone parapet. An icecream vendor trundled his sky-blue cart noisily past.

"Did someone tell you Stroop was back then? Or perhaps you've seen him yourself?" said Uncle Kostya as they parted.

"No, and anyway how could I if he's still out of town as you say?" said Vanya, reddening.

"Well, you said it wasn't hot, but you've gone as red as a beetroot all the same"—and Uncle Kostya's ponderous bulk disappeared into a doorway.

"Why didn't I tell him about my meeting Stroop?" Vanya asked himself, delighted to have a secret of his very own.

o   o   o

Tobacco smoke hung thick in the teacher's common room on the first floor, and glasses of weak tea gleamed faintly amber in the semidarkness. Entering, one had the impression of shapes moving about in an aquarium, an impression strengthened by the streaming rain outside the frosted windows. The buzz of voices and the tinkling teaspoons mingled with the subdued hubbub of midmorning break which carried from the hall and at times, more loudly, from the corridor outside.

"The sixth-formers are playing Orlov up again; the man's simply incapable of inspiring respect."

"Very well then, let's say you give him a 'D' and he stays where he is for another year—do you think that will do him any good?"

"I don't aim to do good, I simply try to give a fair evaluation of a boy's knowledge."

"The boys here would be horrified if they saw the syllabuses of French colleges, not to speak of their seminaries."

"Ivan Petrovich is hardly likely to be satisfied with that."

"Incomparable, I tell you, incomparable—and yesterday he was in marvelous voice."

"You're a fine one, going for a minor slam in clubs when all you've got is a king, a jack and a couple of low ones."

"Szpilewski is a young reprobate, and I can't understand what makes you stand up for him."

The shrill tenor of the school inspector, a Czech with a pince-nez and a gray pointed beard, cut through the other voices:

"So I do beg of you gentlemen to see that the ventilation windows are kept open; never let the temperature get above fourteen degrees—remember that a draft is ventilation too."

Gradually everyone dispersed, until only the soft bass of the teacher of Russian language, who was deep in conversation with the Greek, disturbed the silence of the common room:

"You get the most amazing types. In preparation for the entrance exam they were given a few things to read over the summer—well quite a bit in fact, including 'The Demon';[3] so you get an *ex abrupto* summary that goes something like: 'The Devil was flying over the earth and he saw a girl.'—'And what was the girl's name?'—'Liza.'—'How about Tamara?'—'That's it, Tamara.'—'Well, and then what?'—'He wanted to marry her, but her fiancé wouldn't let him; then the fiancé got killed by Tatars.'—'And so did the Demon marry Tamara after all?'— 'Oh no, an angel flew down and wouldn't let him get to her; and so the Devil remained a bachelor and hated everybody.'"

"I think that's wonderful...."

"Or take this comment on Rudin[4]; 'He was useless, he just talked and never did anything; then he got mixed up with a lot of good-for-nothings and ended by getting himself killed.'—'And why,' I asked, 'do you consider the workers, and indeed everyone who took part in the popular uprising in which Rudin died, to be good-for-nothings?'—'Yessir,' comes the answer, 'he died in the cause of truth.'"

"You were wasting your time trying to get from this young man a personal opinion of what he'd been reading. Military service, like monastic life, like most

---

[3] A narrative poem by Miokhail Lermontov (1814-1841), the arch-romantic among Russian poets (Eds.).

[4] The hero of Ivan Turgenev's novel of the same name, published in 1856 (Eds.).

elaborate dogmatic systems, is enormously attractive because it provides people with ready-made, clear-cut opinions on everything under the sun. For the weak that is a great support; the business of living becomes surprisingly easy when people are relieved of the necessity of forging their own ethical judgements."

Vanya was waiting for Daniil Ivanovich in the corridor.

"What can I do for you, Smurov?"

"Could I have a private talk with you, Daniil Ivanovich?"

"About what?"

"About Greek."

"But you're making satisfactory progress, aren't you?"

"Not exactly—I got 'C' plus."

"Well, that's nothing to worry about, is it?"

"That isn't what I wanted to see you about. I wanted to talk about Greek in general; please, Daniil Ivanovich, can I come and see you at home?"

"By all means, by all means. You know my address. Although I must say it's most unusual: a boy is making satisfactory progress and he wants to have a private talk about Greek! But come along by all means; I live alone and you'll always find me at your service between seven and eleven."

Daniil Ivanovich began to mount the narrow strip of matting that covered the stairs; he suddenly stopped, however, and called out after Vanya, "And don't go getting any ideas, Smurov: I'm at home after eleven as well, except that I'm in bed and available only for interviews of the most private nature, which I shouldn't imagine you'd be in need of."

❈   ❈   ❈

Vanya ran into Stroop in the Summer Gardens on more than one occasion, and almost unconsciously got into the habit of waiting for him, always choosing a bench along the same path; if Stroop failed to appear, he would leave reluctantly—the deliberate slowness of his steps belied by their youthful buoyancy—fixing a keen eye on any distant figure which bore any resemblance to Stroop. On one of these days when Stroop failed to appear he decided to take a walk in a part of the gardens he had not yet explored and ran into Koka, who was striding along, his overcoat unbuttoned to reveal his double-breasted jacket.

"So this is where you get to, Ivan! Out for a stroll?"

"Yes, I come here quite often. What of it?"

"How is it I never see you then? Do you sit round the other side somewhere or what?"

"Oh, I sit all over the place."

"It's funny, but I'm always running into Stroop here—I even suspect that we both come here for the same reason."

"Is Stroop back then?"

"He's been back some time. Nata knows, and so does everyone else; even if Nata is a little idiot I think it's pretty disgusting of him not to call on us, as if we were some kind of riff-raff."

"What's Nata got to do wtih it?"

"She's after Stroop—and if that isn't a waste of time I don't know what is: he's got no intention of marrying anyone, let alone Nata; I shouldn't think it's more than arty conversations even with Ida Holberg, so I'm probably getting worked up over nothing."

"You—worked up?"

"Well I'm in love, so it's only natural!" And forgetting for a moment that he was talking with someone who knew nothing of his private affairs, Koka grew animated: "She's a marvelous girl, cultured, musical, a stunner—and rolling in money too! Pity she's a bit lame though. And so I come here every day to catch a glimpse of her—she takes a stroll here every day between three and four. The only thing is that I'm afraid Stroop comes here for the same reason."

"You don't think Stroop's in love with her too?"

"Stroop? Not likely! He's a horse of a different color. It's just fine talk with him, while she almost worships the ground he walks on. Stroop and the tender passion—that's another matter, another matter entirely."

"You're just jealous, Koka…!"

"Bah!"

They had just turned by the beds of red geraniums when Koka exclaimed, "And there they are!" Vanya saw a tall girl with a pale, rather round face, ash-blond hair, the wide-set eyes of an Aphrodite—large gray eyes which the tumult of feeling had deepened to violet—and the kind of mouth that Botticelli loved to paint; she was wearing a dress of some dark material and walked with a limp, leaning on the arm of an elderly lady; Stroop, who was walking to the other side of her, was saying, "And men saw that beauty and love in all their forms are of the gods, and they became free and brave, and they grew wings…."

❀ ❀ ❀

Koka and Boba had managed to get a box for "Samson et Dalila." The premiere was postponed, however, and "Carmen" given instead; Nata, at whose insistence the whole venture had been undertaken in the hope of a meeting with Stroop on neutral ground, fretted and fumed, knowing that he would be unlikely to attend so popular a piece without some special reason. She gave up her seat in the box to Vanya, with the understanding that he go home if she arrived at the theater during the performance. Anna Nikolayevna, the Speier sisters and Aleksey Vasilyevich took cabs, the young people having set off earlier on foot.

Carmen and her friends were already kicking up their heels in Lillas Pastia's tavern when Nata, as if her intuition had whispered to her that Stroop was in the theater, arrived dressed from head to foot in pale blue, liberally powdered and in a state of some agitation.

"Well, Ivan, I'm afraid you'll have to make yourself scarce."

"I'll just sit the act through."

"Is Stroop here?" asked Nata in a whisper, sitting down beside Anna Niko-layevna, who silently moved her eyes in the direction of the box where Ida Hol-berg was sitting with an elderly lady, a very boyish-looking officer and Stroop.

"It was a premonition, a premonition!" said Nata, opening and shutting her fan.

"You poor foolish girl!" sighed Anna Nikolayevna.

At the interval Vanya was just about to leave when Nata invited him to take a turn about the foyer with her.

"Nata, Nata!" came Anna Nikolayevna's voice from the depths of the box, "Is this proper?"

Nata flew down the stairs, pulling Vanya after her. At the entrance to the foyer she stopped in front of the mirror to pat her hair in place, and then proceeded slowly into the still half-empty hall. They caught sight of Stroop; he was walking with the young officer they had seen in the box, deep in conversation. Before Vanya and Nata could attract his attention he had slipped into an anteroom where a crimped and curled female attendant languished behind a table spread with photographs.

"Let's go out, it's so stuffy in here!" said Nata, dragging Vanya after her in pursuit of Stroop.

"The other exit is nearer to our seats."

"What difference does it make?" yelled the girl, all but elbowing opera patrons aside in her haste.

Stroop saw them and suddenly became absorbed in the photographs. As they drew near Vanya called out, "Larion Dmitrievich!"

"Ah, Vanya!" Stroop turned: "Natalya Alekseyevna, forgive me, I didn't see you there."

"I never expected you to be here," began Nata.

"Why not? I'm very fond of "Carmen," I don't think I'll ever tire of it; it has the true pulse of life, everything in it is drenched with sunlight; I can understand Nietzsche being entranced by such music."

Nata listened in silence, fixing her gingery eyes on her quarry, and said delib-erately:

"It doesn't surprise me to run into you at "Carmen," but it does surprise me that you're back in St. Petersburg and haven't been to see us."

"Yes, I've been back a couple of weeks."

"Charming!"

They began to walk back and forth along the empty corridor, past dozing footmen, and Vanya, who was standing by the stairs, looked with interest at Nata's face as it grew mottled with angry red and at the darkening countenance of her cavalier. The interval came to an end, and Vanya had begun slowly to mount the stairs leading to the circle, intending to get his coat and leave, when Nata, almost running, a handkerchief pressed to her mouth, drew level with him.

"It's humiliating, do you hear Ivan, humiliating, the way that man speaks to me," she whispered to Vanya and ran on up the stairs. Vanya wanted to say good-bye to Stroop, and after waiting on the stairs for a bit went down to the lower corridor. Stroop and the officer were standing at the entrance to their box.

"I'd better say good-bye now, Larion Dmitrievich," said Vanya, pretending that he was on his way up to his box.

"Surely you're not going?"

"Yes, I wasn't in my seat, you see: Nata arrived and I was one too many."

"What nonsense, come and sit with us—we have seats to spare. The last act is one of the best."

"Are you sure they won't mind a complete stranger in their box?"

"Of course they won't; the Holbergs aren't the sort of people to stand on ceremony, and you're still a boy you know, Vanya."

As they went through to the box, Stroop leaned toward Vanya, who listened to him without turning his head:

"Another thing, Vanya: it may be that I won't be calling on the Kazanskis any more; and so, if you would like that, I'll always be very happy to see you at my place. You can say I'm helping you with your English, though I don't suppose anyone will ask you where you go and why. You will come Vanya, won't you?"

"All right. And have you really had a row with Nata? You're not going to marry her?" asked Vanya without turning his head.

"No," said Stroop seriously.

"You know, it's a very good thing you're not going to marry her because she's absolutely revolting, a perfect toad." Vanya, who had turned to look Stroop full in the face, suddenly burst out laughing and for some reason took hold of his hand.

o o o

"It's curious how we see only what we wish to see and find only what we came in search of. Take the way the Romans and the Latin peoples of the seventeenth century saw in Greek tragedy only the three unities, the eighteenth century rolling tirades and libertarian ideals, the Romantics feats of lofty heroism, and our own age the bright hues of the primordial and the Klinger-like[5] luminescence of distant horizons...."

Vanya listened, looking about the room, which was flooded with the sun's last radiance: walls lined to the ceiling with books in paper covers, books on tables and chairs, a thrush in a cage, a paralyzed kitten lying on the leather couch, and in the corner, standing apart—the penates of this dwelling—a small head of Antinous. Daniil Ivanovich was bustling about in felt slippers, making tea, bringing out from the iron stove cheese and butter wrapped in paper, while the kitten, without moving its head, followed its master's every movement with its green eyes. "What gave us the idea he was old? He's really quite young," thought Vanya, looking with surprise at the bald head of the little Greek.

"The Italians of the fifteenth century were firmly convinced that the friendship of Achilles for Patroclus and of Orestes for Pylades was nothing other than the love of Sodom, although there are no direct indications of this in Homer."

"Did the Italians make it up then?"

"No, they were right, but what matters is that love, whatever its nature, can never be depraved except in the eyes of a cynic. Do I act morally or immorally when I sneeze, dust the table or stroke the kitten? Nevertheless, these acts are potentially criminal—for example, suppose my sneeze tells a murderer that the time is ripe for his deed, and so forth. A man who commits murder calmly, without anger, takes away all ethical significance from the act; all that remains is the mystical bond linking murderer and victim, lover and lover, mother and child."

It had grown quite dark, and outside the roofs of houses and, in the distance, St. Isaac's Cathedral loomed against the grubby pink of the smoke-dimmed sky.

Vanya got ready to leave; the kitten, dislodged from its resting place on Vanya's cap, hobbled about on its crippled front paws.

"You must be a good man, Daniil Ivanovich, taking in the lame and the halt."

"He's a charming creature and I like to have him around. If being good means doing what gives one pleasure, then I suppose I am good."

"Tell me, Smurov," said Daniil Ivanovich as he shook Vanya's hand, "Was it your idea to come and see me for a Grecian chat?"

"Yes, except you might say someone put the idea in my head."

"May I ask who, if it isn't a secret?"

"No, why should it be? Only you don't know him."

"Perhaps I do."

· [5] Max Klinger (1857-1920): German painter, etcher and sculptor who specialized in allegorical subjects (Eds.).

"A man called Stroop."

"Larion Dmitrievich?"

"You mean you do know him?"

"You might even say I know him well," replied the Greek, raising a lamp to light Vanya downstairs.

❖   ❖   ❖

There wasn't a soul in the closed cabin of the little Finnish steamboat, but Nata, fearful of drafts and swollen glands, had nevertheless insisted on dragging the entire company there.

"There's not a decent summer cottage to be had, not a single one!" said Anna Nikolayevna wearily. "Everywhere nothing but filth—holes in the roof, drafts!"

"Cottages are always drafty—what do you expect? You've lived in one before!"

"Want one?" Koka proffered Boba his cigarette case, opened to reveal a naked lady.

"The awful thing about staying in the country isn't so much the place itself, but the feeling of living in a bivouac, so that everything seems disorganized and temporary—while in town you know what has to be done at what time."

"But what if you lived in the country all the time, winter and summer?"

"Then it wouldn't be so awful: I would establish a daily routine."

"It's true," put in Anna Nikolayevna, "you don't feel like settling in properly when you know it's just for a time. Take the summer before last—we wallpapered the place throughout, paid for everything out of our own pockets, and then we had to make the landlord a present of the lot; you couldn't very well scrape it off!"

"Are you sorry you didn't smear dirt all over it then?"

Screwing up her face, Nata looked through the glass at palace windows flaming in the sunset and at the rosy-golden waves that slid smoothly and unhurriedly past.

"And all those hordes of people—everyone knowing what everyone else has to eat, how much they pay their maids."

"The whole business makes you sick!"

"Why go then?"

"What do you mean, why? What else is there to do? Stay in town for heaven's sake?"

"Well and why not? At least when the sun's shining you can walk on the shady side of the street."

"Uncle Kostya is always having bright ideas."

"Mama darling," Nata turned round suddenly," let's go to the Volga; there are nice little towns there like Plyos and Vasilsursk where you can put up very reasonably. Varvara Nikolayevna Speier was telling me…. A whole group of them stayed in Plyos—Levitan[6] used to stay there too, you know; and they spent some time in Uglich as well."

"If I remember rightly they got kicked out of Uglich," put in Koka.

"All right, they got kicked out—and what of it? We won't be! Naturally enough their landlord said to them, 'Who knows what all you young ladies and gentlemen will be getting up to? Ours is a quiet town and we don't want any trouble; we're very sorry, but we'll have to ask you to leave.'"

They were approaching the Aleksandrovski Gardens; through the basement windows of the floating restaurant they caught a glimpse of a brightly lit kitchen with a blazing stove at the far end and a kitchen boy all in white, busy cleaning fish.

"Auntie, I think I'll go to Larion Dmitrievich's from here," said Vanya.

"What are you waiting for then? Go. A fine friend he's found for himself!" grumbled Anna Nikolayevna.

"Is there something wrong with him then?"

"I'm not saying there's anything wrong with him, just that he's no friend for you."

"He's helping me with my English."

"A sheer waste of time—you'd do better to prepare your lessons...."

"I think I'll go, Auntie, all the same."

"Go on then—who's stopping you?"

"Go and kiss your precious Stroop," added Nata.

"I jolly well will if I want to, and it's nobody else's business either."

"On the contrary...." began Boba, only to break off as Vanya pounced on Nata:

"You wouldn't mind kissing him yourself, but he doesn't want to because you're a ginger-haired toad, because you're an idiot! So there!"

"Ivan, that'll do!" Aleksey Ivanovich's voice rang out.

"Well what have they got their claws into me for? What's it got to do with them where I go? Am I a baby or something? I'll write to Uncle Kolya tomorrow...."

"Ivan, I said that's enough," exclaimed Aleksey Vasilyevich a tone higher.

"The snotty-nosed brat, the little guttersnipe, behaving like this!" stormed Anna Nikolayevna.

"And Stroop will never marry you, never, never!" Vanya blurted out, beside himself with rage.

Nata quieted down at once and, strangely composed, said in a low voice:

"And will he marry Ida Holberg?"

"I don't know," replied Vanya, no less simply and softly, "I should think it's pretty unlikely," he added, almost gently.

[6] Russian landscape painter (1861-1900) (Eds.).

"And now just listen to them!" cried Anna Nikolayevna. "Don't tell me you take the brat seriously?"

"Maybe I do," Nata muttered, turning to the window.

"Ivan, don't you believe they're such idiots as they're trying to make out," said Boba reasonably: "they're as pleased as punch to have you to keep them in touch with Stroop and feed them tidbits about the Holberg girl; only if you're truly attached to Larion Dmitrievich be a bit more careful in the future, don't give yourself away."

"How do you mean?" asked Vanya, surprised.

"Has my advice born fruit so quickly?!" Boba burst out laughing and stepped out onto the quay.

⚹ ⚹ ⚹

Vanya entered Stroop's apartment to be greeted by singing and the sound of a piano. Instead of going straight through to the drawing room, he stole into the study to the left of the hall and stood listening. An unfamiliar male voice was singing:

> "The twilight enshrouding the warm sea at evening,
> The beacons that flame to the darkening heavens,
> The drift of verbena when feasting is done with,
> The freshness of dawn after nights spent unsleeping,
> The shouting and laughter of womenfolk bathing,
> The peacocks of Juno that walk in her temple,
> The vendors of violets, pomegranates and lemons,
> The moaning of doves and the dazzle of sunlight—
> O when shall I see thee, adorable city?"

And the piano's sonorous chords veiled the voice's yearning phrases as in a mist. Then came the sound of men's voices in lazy conversation, and Vanya went through to the drawing room. How he loved this spacious room with its translucent greens, haunted by echoes of Rameau and Debussy, and these friends of Stroop, so unlike the people he met at the Kazanskis; these arguments; these late bachelor suppers, convivial with wine and lighthearted talk; this study lined with books from floor to ceiling, where they read Marlowe and Swinburne, this bedroom with its toilet stand and its garland of terracotta fauns dancing on a background of bright green; this dining room with its coppery hues; these tales of Italy, Egypt, India; this ardent responsiveness to all poignantly lovely things, whatever age or clime had brought them forth; these strolls about the Islands; these discussions which at once fascinated and disturbed; this smile transfiguring an ugly face; this all-pervasive odor of *peau d'Espagne* with its hint of decay; these lean, strong fingers, barbaric with rings, these shoes with their oddly thick soles—how he loved all this, without knowing what it was that drew him to it.

* * *

"We are Hellenes: the intolerant monotheism of the Hebrews is alien to us—their rejection of the visual arts, their slavish attachment to the flesh, to the getting of heirs, to seed. In the whole of the Bible there is not a single indication of a belief in bliss beyond the grave, and the only reward mentioned in the Commandments (and that, be it noted, for showing respect to those who gave us life) is 'that thy days may be long upon the land.' According to the Jews a sterile marriage is a stigma and a curse, and those bound in such a union forfeit the right to worship in the temple; yet it is a Jewish legend which tells us that childbirth and toil are a punishment for sin, not the purpose of life. And as human beings put sin behind them, so will they put behind them childbearing and toil. The Christians have some inkling of this: according to them a woman must purify herself with prayer not after marriage, but after giving birth, while a man is released from all such observances. Love needs no justification outside itself; nature too is without trace of the idea of finality. The laws of nature are of an order quite different from the laws of God, so called, and the laws of man. The law of nature does not say that a given tree must bear fruit; it says that in certain conditions the tree will bear fruit and that in other conditions it will not only fail to bear fruit, but will wither and die just as simply and naturally as it would have born fruit. That a heart will stop beating if it is pierced with a dagger—there's no finality, no good or evil in that. And the only man capable of breaking the law of nature is he who can kiss his own eyes without tearing them from their sockets, and see the back of his own head without a mirror. And when they say to you 'unnatural,' be content to look at the blind fool who has said such a thing and go your way, not behaving as do those sparrows which fly up at the sight of a scarecrow in a vegetable garden. People go about like the blind, like the dead, when they might create for themselves a life burning with intensity in every moment, a life in which pleasure would be as poignant as if you had just come into the world and might die before the day were done. It is with such greed that we must fling ourselves upon life. Miracles crowd upon us at every step: there are muscles, sinews in the human body which one cannot look upon without a tremor! And those who would bind the idea of beauty to the beauty of a woman seen through the eyes of a man—they reveal only vulgar lust and are furthest of all from the true idea of beauty. We are Hellenes, lovers of the beautiful, the bacchants of the coming day. Like the visions of Tannhäuser in Venus' Grotto, like the inspired revelations of Klinger and Thoma,[7] somewhere lies our ancient kingdom, full of sunlight and freedom, of beautiful and courageous people, and thither we sail,

[7] Hans Thoma (1839-1924): German painter of mythological and religious subjects (Eds.).

my argonauts, over many a sea, through mist and darkness. And in things yet un-
heard we shall descry ancient roots, in glittering visions yet unseen we shall know
our own dear land!"

❊   ❊   ❊

"Vanya, would you mind looking in the dining room and telling me what the time
is," said Ida Holberg, letting her embroidery fall to her lap.

The large room in the new house resembled a sunlit cabin on a ship's deck and
was furnished sparsely and simply; yellow curtains hung the length of an entire
wall, covering the room's three windows and causing an uneasy yellow light to fall
on the leather trunks, the brass-studded suitcases waiting to be packed, the box
of late-blooming hyacinths. Vanya put down the Dante he had been reading from
and went into the next room.

"Half past five," he said, reappearing. "Larion Dmitrievich is a long time," he
offered, as if in answer to the girl's unspoken thoughts. "Have we done enough
for today?"

"It's not worth starting a new canto, Vanya. And so:

> 'e vidi che con riso
> Udito havenan l'ultimo construtto;
> Poi a la bella donna tornai il viso.'

'And saw that they had smiling heard the final declaration, then turned him to
the lady fair.'"

"The lady fair—do you think she really symbolizes the contemplation of the
active life?"

"You can't believe everything the commentators say, Vanya, apart from the
historical information they provide; to understand simply and beautifully—that's
all that matters, otherwise instead of Dante you get some kind of mathematics."

She put aside her work and seemed to be waiting for something as she sat
there, tapping the gleaming arm of her chair with a paper-knife.

"I'm sure Larion Dmitrievich will be here soon," declared Vanya in a faintly
patronizing tone, again catching the girl's thought.

"Did you see him yesterday?"

"No, I didn't see him either yesterday or the day before. Yesterday he went
to Tsarskoye in the afternoon and spent the evening at his club, and the day before he went to the Vyborg Side—I don't know where exactly," reported Vanya
with mingled deference and pride.

"To see whom?"

"I don't know—he had some business there."

"You don't know what exactly?"

"No."

"Listen, Vanya," began the girl, not raising her eyes from the paper-knife, "I beg of you—not just for my sake, but for your own and Larion Dmitrievich's, for the sake of all of us—to find out what this address is. It's very important, very important for all three of us"—and she held out a scrap of paper on which was written in Stroop's scrawling, angular hand: "Vyborg Side, 36 Simbirskaya Street, Apt. 103, Fyodor Vasilyevich Solovyov."

✲   ✲   ✲

Nobody was particularly surprised when Stroop added Russian antiquities to his other enthusiasms and began to receive visits from dealers—some smooth-tongued and dressed city-fashion, some in long caftans, venerable and full of holy texts, but rogues to a man—eager to sell him manuscripts, icons, ancient stuffs, bronzes of doubtful provenance; when he began to take an interest in ancient choral music, to read Smolenski, Razumovski and Metallov,[8] to visit Niko-layevskaya from time to time to listen to the choir, and, at last, to master the ancient musical notation under the tutelage of a pock-marked chorister. "I never suspected the existence of this secluded corner of the *Weltgeist*," said Stroop, trying to communicate this new enthusiasm to Vanya, who, to his surprise proved, for once, somewhat recalcitrant.

One day Stroop announced as they were drinking tea:

"Now this is something you really must see, Vanya: an authentic Old Believer from the Volga, the old-fashioned kind—just imagine, eighteen years old and goes about in a long peasant *poddyovka*, doesn't drink tea; his sisters are in a sectarian nunnery somewhere in the wilds; his parents have a house on the Volga with a high fence and watchdogs on chains, and the whole household goes to bed at nine—it's like something out of Pecherski,[9] but not so treacly. You must see him for yourself. Let's go to Zasadin's tomorrow, there's an 'Assumption' of his I want to see; our man will be there and I'll introduce you to him. Oh, and you'd better write down the address just in case; I may well drive straight there from the exhibition, and then you'll have to find the place by yourself." And without looking in his address book, as if it were something long familiar, Stroop dictated: "'36 Simbirskaya Street, Apt. 103'—there's a sign saying furnished rooms—ask there."

✲   ✲   ✲

[8] Stepan Vasilyevich Smolenski (1848-1909), Dimitri Vasilyevich Razumovski (1818-1889), Vasili Mikhaylovich Metallov (1862-1926): Russian musicologists whose work contributed to the revival of interest in Russia's ancient church music (Eds.).

[9] Vasili Mikhaylovich Metallov (1862-1926): Russian musicologists whose work contributed to the revival of interest in Russia's ancient church music (Eds.).

On the other side of the wall two voices could be heard in muffled conversation; a weight clock ticked quietly; tables, chairs and window ledges were stacked and strewn with blackened icons and books in leather-covered boards; the air was stale and dust-laden, and from the passageway, through the fanlight, crept the moldy smell of sour cabbage soup. Zasadin was standing in front of Vanya and saying as he put on his caftan:

"It'll be a good forty minutes before Larion Dmitrievich gets here, maybe as long as an hour; I have to go out now and pick up an icon—so what shall we do? Do you want to wait here, or is there somewhere you'd rather go?"

"I'll wait here."

"Good, good. I won't be long. Perhaps you'd like to have a look at this in the meantime"—and Zasadin handed Vanya a dusty "Lives of the Holy Fathers" and hurried out; the smell of cabbage soup drifted ever more pungently through the doorway. Standing by the window, Vanya opened the book at a tale which told how a certain hermit was visited by a woman who lived alone in the same wilderness and afterwards was sore vexed with carnal thoughts, dwelling always on this same woman; able to contain himself no longer, he took up his staff and in the scorching heat of the day bent his steps toward the place where the woman abode, staggering in his lust as one blind; and in perturbation of spirit he saw that the earth had yawned, and lo, in the pit lay three rotting corpses—a woman, a man and a child; and there came a voice saying: "Behold this woman, this man, this child—who can now distinguish between them? Go work thy lust." All, all are equal before death, love and beauty, all bodies are equally fair, and lust alone drives men in pursuit of women and causes women to hunger after men.

Behind the wall a youthful, rather husky voice was saying:

"I'll be on my way then, Uncle Yermolay—what do you keep on scolding me for?"

"Don't you give me good reason to, you good-for-nothing? I know all about the little tricks you've been getting up to."

"But how do you know Vaska wasn't telling you a pack of lies? What do you have to go and listen to him for?"

"Why should Vaska lie? Let's hear it from you then—have you been getting up to tricks or haven't you?"

"All right, so I have—and what of it? Doesn't Vaska? Come to think of it, everyone here does except maybe for Dmitri Pavlovich"—and the speaker's laughter sounded through the wall. After a moment's silence, he began again in a more confiding tone, dropping his voice: "Vaska showed me the ropes himself; one day a young gent comes and says to Dmitri Pavlovich, 'I want to be bathed by the one who let me in'—me that was—and Dmitri Pavlovich, knowing this gent liked to get up to tricks and that Vasili had always looked after him before, says, 'I'm sorry, your honor, but he can't go along by himself; he's not one of the regulars and doesn't know what it's all about.'—'To hell with you then, let me have the two of them together, him and Vasili!' Then Vasili butts in and says, 'How much do we get?'—'Ten roubles on top of your beer.' But the way we've got it fixed, you see—if the curtains are pulled over the door it means there's going to be hanky panky, and you can't be giving the attendant less than five roubles to turn a blind eye; so Vasili says, 'No, your honor, that doesn't suit us.' So he promises us another ten. Vasya goes out to get the water ready, and I begin undressing, and the gent says, 'What's that on your cheek, Fyodor—a birthmark? Or is it dirt?—and he laughs and reaches out his hand. So there's me standing there like an idiot, not knowing myself if I've got a birthmark on my cheek or not. But then Vasili comes back—real sore about something he is—and says to the gent, 'If you're ready, sir'—and off we all go."

"Does Matvey live here now?"

"No, he's got himself a position."

"Who with? The colonel?"

"That's right; thirty roubles he gives him and all found."

"So he did, and his boss gave him the money for the wedding too, and had a coat made for him—eighty roubles it cost. His wife lives in the country though—you couldn't go living with a woman in that sort of job. As a matter of fact I'm thinking of taking a position myself," said the speaker after a short silence.

"One like Matvey's you mean?"

"Nice gentleman he is, lives by himself—and I'll be getting thirty roubles too, like Matvey."

"You'll be in trouble, Fedya, if you don't watch out."

"And maybe I won't."

"And who is this gentleman? Friend of yours?"

"He lives here on Furstadt Street—you know, where Dmitri's a junior footman—on the second floor. And he comes here too sometimes to see Stepan Stepanovich."

"Is he an Old Believer then?"

"No, nothing like that. They say he's not even Russian. English or something."

"Is he well spoken of?"

"Yes, they say he's a nice kind gentleman."

"Well then, I wish you luck."

"Good-bye, Uncle Yermolay, thanks for everything."

"Come round any time, Fedya."

"I will"—and banging the door behind him, Fyodor set off down the passageway with a light, ringing step. Driven by an obscure impulse, Vanya stepped quickly out of the room and called out after the retreating figure of a lad wearing a jacket over a belted Russian-style blouse—the belt tassels hung down below the jacket—patent-leather ankle boots and a cap pushed back at a rakish angle: "Excuse me, do you know when Stepan Stepanovich Zasadin will be back?"

The lad turned, and in the light from the room behind him, Vanya glimpsed a pair of quick, mischievous gray eyes set in a face whose pallor suggested a life spent behind closed doors or amid perpetual steam, dark hair cut in a fringe and a firm, beautiful mouth. In spite of a certain coarseness of feature, there was a softness about the face, and although Vanya could not but feel antipathy as he looked at the mischievous, caressing eyes and the insolently mocking mouth, there was something in the face, in the slender form whose easy grace the jacket could not hide, that captivated and disturbed him.

"Are you waiting for him then, sir?"

"Yes, and it's almost seven."

"Half past six," Fyodor corrected him, taking out his pocket watch, "and there was us thinking there was nobody in his room.... He'll be back soon, I should think," he added, for the sake of something to say.

"I see. Thank you—excuse me for troubling you." said Vanya, not moving from the spot.

"Not at all," replied the other with a smirk.

A bell rang, and in came Stroop, followed by Zasadin and a tall young man in a *poddyovka*. Stroop glanced quickly at Fyodor and Vanya, who stood facing one another.

"Forgive me for making you wait," he said to Vanya, while Fyodor ran foward to take his coat.

All this Vanya saw as if in a dream; it seemed to him that a mist was closing in on everything and that he was slipping into a gaping pit.

❖   ❖   ❖

When Vanya entered the dining room, Anna Nikolayevna was just finishing what she was saying: "And it's really a shame that such a man should compromise himself like that." Konstantin Vasilyevich silently moved his eyes in the direction of Vanya, who had picked up a book and taken a chair by the window, and said:

"People say 'recherché, unnatural, useless,' but if we put our bodies only to uses considered 'natural' then we'd still be using our hands to tear raw meat and cram it into our mouths or to belabor our enemies; our feet we'd be employing to chase hares or run away from wolves and so forth. It reminds me of a story from the 'Thousand and One Nights' which tells how a little girl, tormented by the notion of finality, kept asking her mother for what purpose this, that and the other was intended. And when she asked about a certain part of the anatomy, her mother gave her a good whipping, saying 'Now you see what it was meant for.' One can't deny that the good woman gave sensible proof of the correctness of her explanation, but it can hardly be said to exhaust the possibilities of the said part. All attempts to draw some kind of moral boundary between what is natural and what is not add up in the end to the same thing—that a man's nose was created for the express purpose of being coated with green paint. A man must develop every capacity of mind and body to the utmost and search untiringly for new outlets if he doesn't wish to remain a Caliban."

"Well, gymnasts walk on their heads...."

"At any rate that's a new accomplishment, and—who knows?—walking on one's head may be very pleasant, or so Larion Dmitrievich would say"—and Uncle Kostya threw a challenging glance in the direction of Vanya, who continued to be absorbed in his book.

"What has Larion Dmitrievich got to do with it?" even Anna Nikolayevna felt compelled to ask.

"Surely you don't imagine that I was expressing my own views?"

"I'll go and see how Nata is," announced Anna Nikolayevna, getting up.

"Isn't she well then? I never seem to see her," said Vanya, as though the thought had suddenly struck him.

"That's not surprising. You disappear for days at a time."

"Where do I disappear to?"

"That's something we ought to ask you," sniffed his aunt as she left the room.

Uncle Kostya sat drinking the remains of his coffee, cold by now; there was a strong smell of napthalene in the room.

"Were you talking about Stroop when I came in, Uncle Kostya?" ventured Vanya.

"About Stroop?—I really don't remember. Annette was telling me something or other."

"I thought it was about him."

"No, why should the two of us be discussing Stroop?"

"Do you really think Stroop has opinions like you said?"

"That's the way his reasoning goes, at least; about his actions I know nothing—and another man's beliefs are a very dark and delicate matter."

"Surely you don't think he says one thing and does another?"

"I don't know; I don't know anything about his affairs—and besides, it isn't always possible to act in accordance with one's wishes. For example, we were intending to be down in the country long ago, while as you see...."

"Uncle, this Old Believer Sorokin I told you about has invited me down to the Volga to stay with his family: 'Come and see us,' he says, 'Dad's a good sort; come and see how folk live in our part of the world, if that would interest you.' I don't know why, but he seemed to take to me at once."

"Sounds like a good idea. Why not go?"

"Auntie won't give me any money, and it's not worth it anyway."

"Why not?"

"Everything's horrible, horrible!"

"And why is everything horrible all of a sudden?"

"I don't know, I really don't," said Vanya, burying his face in his hands.

Konstantin Vasilyevich glanced at Vanya's bowed head and quietly left the room.

❀   ❀   ❀

The hall porter was not to be seen; the doors leading to the stairs were open, and from the closed study came the sound of a voice raised in anger, followed by a hush in which could be heard the subdued murmur of what seemed to be a woman's voice. Vanya stood motionless in the hall without taking off his coat and cap; the knob of one of the double doors leading to the study turned, and the door half-opened to reveal a hand resting on the knob and the red sleeve of a Russian-style blouse. Stroop's words were clearly audible: "I won't allow any-one—let alone a woman—to touch on that subject. I forbid you—forbid you, do you hear?—to talk about it!" The door closed and the voices became indistinct; filled with foreboding, Vanya examined the familiar hall: electric lights in front of the mirror and over the table, coats on hangers; a pair of lady's gloves had been left on the table, but there was no sign of a hat and coat. The doors were again flung open with a crash, and Stroop, white with anger, strode through to the passage without noticing Vanya; he was followed a moment later by Fyodor, almost running, his red silk blouse unbelted, a decanter in his hand. "What can I do for you?"—he addressed himself to Vanya, evidently not recognizing him. Fyodor's face had a hectic flush, as if he had been either at the bottle or the rouge jar; his blouse was unbelted, his hair carefully combed, and, by the look of it, slightly curled, and he smelt strongly of Stroop's cologne.

"What can I do for you?" he again asked Vanya, who was staring at him wide-eyed.

"Can I see Larion Dmitrievich?"

"He's not at home."

"How was it I just saw him then?"

"I'm afraid he's very busy and can't see anyone at the moment."

"Well go and tell him I'm here anyway."

"No really, you'd better come by some other time; it's just not possible for him to see you now. He's not alone," Fyodor lowered his voice.

"Fyodor!" called Stroop from the depths of the passage, and the lad dashed off on noiseless feet.

Vanya stood there for a few minutes before going out onto the stairs, pulling the door to behind him; on the other side angry but muffled voices could be heard. In the porter's room, adjusting her veil in front of the mirror, stood a lady of medium height wearing a gray-green dress with a black top. As he passed behind her Vanya caught a clear glimpse of her face in the mirror: it was Nata. Having adjusted her veil to her satisfaction, she mounted the stairs unhurriedly and rang the bell to Stroop's apartment, while the porter arrived just in time to let Vanya out into the street.

❂   ❂   ❂

"What's all this about?"—Aleksey Vasilyevich paused in his reading of the morning paper: "Mysterious suicide. Yesterday, the 21st of May, at the Furstadt Street apartment of L. D. Stroop, a British subject, Ida Holberg, a girl in the full bloom of youth, settled her account with life. The youthful suicide left a note in which she asked that no one should be blamed for her death, but the circumstances of this sad occurrence point to a romantic involvement. According to the owner of the apartment, in the course of an angry scene the deceased scribbled something on a scrap of paper, seized a revolver which lay out in readiness for his, Stroop's, forthcoming journey, and before those present could do anything to prevent her discharged it into her right temple. The mystery is further complicated by the fact that Mr. Stroop's servant, Fyodor Vasilyevich Solovyov, a peasant from Oryol Province, disappeared without trace on the same day, and that it has not been possible to identify a lady who arrived at Stroop's apartment half an hour before the fatal occurrence, or to determine what, if any, influence she had on the tragic turn of events. An investigation is under way."

No one at the tea-table said a word; the room smelt of napthalene; the clock ticked.

"What could have happened? Nata? Nata? Do you know?" said Vanya at length in a voice he hardly recognized as his own. But Nata went on tracing patterns on her empty plate with her fork and made no reply.

PART TWO

"Just imagine, Vanya, the strangeness of it—another person, a being quite separate from yourself, with different legs, different skin, different eyes; and he's yours, all yours, to gaze at, to kiss, to touch—every hidden mark on his body, the golden down on his arms, every little mole, every little dimple of that loving flesh. And there's nothing about him you don't know—the way he walks and eats and sleeps, the way his face wrinkles when he smiles, the workings of his mind, the smell of his body. And somehow you no longer seem to belong to yourself, as if you and he were a single being: flesh cleaves to flesh, and if love fills your life, Vanya, there is no greater bliss on earth—but without love life is unbearable, unendurable! And let me tell you this, Vanya—there's less pain in loving without possessing than in possessing without loving. Marriage, marriage! The priest gives his blessing and the children are born, but that's not the holy mystery of it— why, that cat over there litters four times a year: no, the holy mystery of it is that the soul burns to yield itself to another being and to take him utterly unto itself, be it for a week, be it for a day; and if two souls burn with a mutual flame then God has united them. To make love coldheartedly, calculatingly is sinful, but he who is touched by the hand of fire will remain pure in the eyes of the Lord whatever he may do. Whatever he may do, whomsoever the flaming spirit has touched, all will be forgiven him, for he has gone out of himself, he is a man possessed, a man clothed in the spirit...."

And Marya Dmitrievna, too agitated to remain seated, got up, paced from apple tree to apple tree and then sat down again on the bench beside Vanya; before them lay the Volga with the neverending forest of its far bank, and over to the right a white village church.

"And it is terrible, Vanya, to feel love's hand upon you; it's as if you were flying and all the time falling, or as if you were dying—just like in a dream; and wherever you go you are haunted by some poignantly remembered feature of the beloved—his hair, his eyes, his way of walking. And it's really very strange—what is so special about this face after all? A nose in the middle, a mouth, two eyes. What is it that so moves you, so entrances you? After all, you see plenty of beautiful faces and you admire them, as you would a flower or a piece of brocade, and then along comes this special face—perhaps not even beautiful—but this face and no other plunges your soul, and yours alone, in turmoil. Why should this be? And another thing:"—the speaker hesitated—"well, of course men love women and women love men; but sometimes, they say, it can happen that a woman loves a woman and a man a man; it happens, they say, and I've read about it myself in the *Lives of the Saints:* there was the blessed Eugenia, and there was Nifont, and Pafnuti Borovski; and what about Tsar Ivan Vasilyevich? You know, such things aren't hard to believe; mightn't God have implanted this thorn in the human heart among so many others? And it's hard, Vanya, to deny the heart's longings—and sinful too maybe."

The sun had almost disappeared behind the jagged crests of the distant pines, and the Volga, curving in three great bends below them, was transmuted by the rosy-golden light. Marya Dmitrievna gazed in silence at the dark woods on the far shore and at the wan purple of the evening sky; Vanya too was silent, his lips parted, as if he were still listening to his companion with his whole being; suddenly he remarked, half sadly, half censoriously:

"But a lot of people just sin out of curiosity, out of pride, out of greed."

"Yes, a lot of people do, I know—but then the sin is on their own heads," admitted Marya Dmitrievna, crestfallen; she remained still, not turning to look at Vanya: "But it is hard, Vanya, so hard for those in whose hearts such longings have been implanted! I don't mean to complain—for others life is easy, but there seems to be no point to it. It's like cabbage soup without salt—filling but flavorless."

❀   ❀   ❀

Luncheon was eaten successively in the dining room, on the balcony, in the hall, out in the yard under the apple trees, before being at last transferred to the cellar. The cellar was dark, and there was a smell of malt and cabbages mingled with a faint odor of mice, but it was thought to be cooler than the rest of the house and free of flies; to catch what light there was, the table was placed opposite the doorway, but when Malanya, having all but run across the yard with the food, paused in the entrance before descending the dark stairway, the gloom deepened yet further, and the cook would invariably grumble, "Merciful heavens, you can't see your hand in front of your face! I'd like to know what put it into their heads to come down here!" Sometimes they grew tired of waiting for Malanya, and curly-headed Sergey, the lad from the shop, who always ate at the house with Ivan Osipovich, would go running to fetch the meal. He would come galloping back across the yard with the dish held triumphantly above his head, while the cook scurried along behind him waving a fork or a spoon and yelling, "Did you think I wasn't going to bring it or something? Why make Sergey run around? I wouldn't have been a minute...."

"You wouldn't have been a minute, but we want it right now!" Sergey would riposte, banging crockery down in front of Arina Dmitrievna with a flourish and smirking as he took his seat between Ivan Osipovich and Sasha.

"What did God make this hot weather for?" asked Sergey. "It's no good to anyone: water dries up, trees burn down—everyone has a hard time...."

"For the rye, I suppose."

"But it doesn't help the rye much either if there's too much and at the wrong time. But right time or wrong, God still sends it."

"If it comes at the wrong time, then it's a punishment for our sins."

"But what about this?" put in Ivan Osipovich. "One of our old men died of sunstroke; he hadn't done anyone any harm and he was on his way to church, but the heat struck him down all the same. How do you explain that?" Sergey sat in silent triumph.

"Well he must have suffered for the sins of others, not for his own," decided Prokhor Nikitich somewhat hesitantly.

"How can that be? You mean to say others can get drunk and gad about and the Lord kills innocent old men for their sins?"

"Or, if you'll excuse the example, what if you didn't pay your debts and I got sent to the clink instead of you? Would that be fair?" added Sergey.

"You'd do better to get your soup down instead of talking nonsense; 'what's this for, what's that for?'—what are you for, come to that? You think there's no point to the heat, Seryozha, but it may well be the heat thinks there's no point to you."

Having eaten their fill, they sat diligently imbibing tea, some with apples, some with jam. Undaunted, Sergey returned to his philosophizing:

"There are times when I find it hard to make sense of things; take this, for instance: a soldier kills—I kill; he gets the St. George Medal and I get hard labor. Why's that?"

"How can you be expected to understand such things? Let's put it like this: a married man lives with his wife and a bachelor gets mixed up with some woman; there are people who say it comes to the same thing, but there's a great difference. And where does that difference lie?"

"Don't ask me!" responded Sergey, staring at him wide-eyed.

"In the imagination. In the first case," said Prokhor Nikitich, as if he were searching for ideas as much as for words, "in the first place, a married man has dealings with one woman only—that's one thing; another thing is that they live in peace and quiet, they're used to each other's ways and the husband loves his wife in the same way that he eats porridge or gives his clerks a dressing-down, while with the others it's all foolishness, ha-ha this and hee-hee that, no constancy, no sobriety—and that's why one is deemed lawful and the other fornication. Sin doesn't lie in the act itself, but in its relation to other things."

"But after all, if you don't mind me saying so, it's not unknown for a husband to worship the ground his wife walks on, while another man will have grown so used to his mistress that kissing her means no more to him than swatting a gnat; in such a case, who's to say which is lawful and which is fornication?"

"To do those things without love is an abomination!" Marya Dmitrievna burst out.

"You say 'abomination,' but you shouldn't use words without knowing their underlying meaning. What does 'abomination' mean? Bowing to graven images, that's what—and eating the flesh of hares, if you like. What we're talking about, though, is fornication."

"Fornication, fornication—is that all you can talk about? I ask you, what a subject to discuss in front of the boys!" cried Arina Dmitrievna.

"Well and why not? They understand perfectly well—isn't that right, Ivan Petrovich?" said old Sorokin, turning to Vanya.

"Excuse me?" Vanya was taken by surprise.

"What's your opinion on the subject?"

"Well you know, I think it's very hard to pass judgement on other people's affairs."

"Quite right, Vanechka,"—Arina Dmitrievna was delighted. "And never judge; that's what the Bible says: 'Judge not, that ye be not judged.'"

"Well, there are some that don't judge, but have judgement passed on them all the same," said Sorokin, pushing his way out from behind the table.

❀   ❀   ❀

The only people remaining on the wooden pier and the landing stage were market-women with their rolls, Caspian roach, raspberries and salted cucumbers; deckhands in brightly-colored shirts stood leaning on the boatrail, spitting into the water. Arina Dmitrievna, having seen old Sorokin safely aboard the steamship, sat down on a broad plank beside Marya Dmitrievna.

"How could we have forgotten the oatcakes, Mashenka? You know how Prokhor Nikitich loves them with his tea."

"And do you know, I put them out specially where I couldn't help but see them—and it still didn't help."

"You might have reminded us, Parfen."

"What's it got to do with me? If you'd have left them outside somewhere, of course I'd have given a shout, but I had no reason to go looking around inside," the old workman defended himself.

"Ivan Petrovich! Sasha! Where are you off to?" Arina Dmitrievna called out to the boys, who were already scrambling up the hill.

"We're walking, mama—the path's quicker, you'll see."

"Well get along with you then—your legs are young and strong. Are you sure you wouldn't like to ride, Ivan Petrovich?" she coaxed.

"No really, it's all right, thank you—we'll walk," Vanya shouted from halfway up the hill.

"See over there, the Lyubimov boat's just come in," exclaimed Sasha, pulling off his cap and turning his flushed and sweating face to the wind.

"Will Prokhor Nikitich be gone long?"

"No, he'll be back from Unzha before Saint Peter's day—he just wants to have a look at things there, that's all."

"Don't you ever go along with your father, Sasha?"

"Oh yes, always—but this time you were staying with us, so I decided not to go."

"You shouldn't have done that. You musn't let me be in the way."

Sasha put on his cap again, pulling it down over his black wind-blown hair, smiled and said:

"There's no question of you getting in anyone's way, Vanechka—I'm really very glad to stay behind with you. Of course, if it was just mama and auntie I'd get bored, but the way things are I'm very glad." He fell silent for a while, then continued, as if speaking his thoughts aloud, "You know, you can go to Unzha, to Vetluga, to Moscow and see nothing beside the business in hand— it's almost like being blind. All the time it's timber—timber this and timber that: how much does it cost, how much will transport be, how many planks and beams will it make—nothing else. That's the way dad is, and that's the way he's bringing me up to be. Wherever we go it's always the same old round— woodsmen, taverns—and always the same old talk. It gets boring, you know. Imagine a builder who built nothing but churches, and not whole churches ei- ther, but just the cornices—he'd go around the world and see nothing but church cornices; he wouldn't take the slightest interest in all the different people, how they lived and thought and prayed and loved, he wouldn't see the trees and the flowers—he'd only have eyes for his precious cornices. A man ought to be like a river or a mirror—whatever is reflected in him he should make part of himself; then he'll be like the Volga—there'll be sun in him, and stormclouds and forests and high mountains and towns with churches; nothing should seem to him more important than anything else, and then everything will be joined together inside him. But if just one thing gets hold of a man it'll gobble him up—particularly if it's greed for material possessions or godliness."

"What do you mean by 'godliness?'"

"Well, religion, that sort of thing. For people who think and read only about that it's hard to understand anything else."

"But after all there are bishops who don't hold themselves aloof from worldly things, even some of yours—Bishop Inokenti, for example."

"Of course there are, and do you know, in my opinion that's a very bad thing: it's not possible to place equal value on everything and to be a good bishop or a good officer or a good merchant. And that's why I envy you from the bottom of my heart, Vanya—you're not being forced to follow one single path, and you know everything and understand everything, not like me, even though we are the same age."

"Oh really, how can you say I know everything? They don't teach us anything at school!"

"All the same, you're much more likely to understand everything knowing nothing, than you are knowing only one thing."

Below them droshky wheels clattered faintly and from the river came the sound of loud swearing and the plash of oars.

"They're taking a long time."

"They must have dropped in on Loginov," decided Sasha, sitting down on the grass beside Vanya.

"Are we really the same age?" asked Vanya, gazing beyond the Volga, where shadows of clouds fled across the meadows.

"Oh yes, we were born almost within a month of each other—I asked Larion Dmitrievich."

"Do you know Larion Dmitrievich well, Sasha?"

"Not that well; we haven't known each other very long; and then he's not the sort of person you get to know all at once."

"You heard about what happened?"

"Yes, I was still in Petersburg at the time; it's all a lot of nonsense, that's what I think."

"What is?"

"All that about the lady's death not being suicide. I saw her once—Larion Dmitrievich pointed her out to me in the gardens: something very strange about her, there was. I said to Larion Dmitrievich at the time, 'Mark my words, that young lady will come to a bad end.' She was a bit touched in the head, that's what I think."

"Yes, but you can be the cause of a death without firing the shot yourself."

"No, Vanechka, if a person gets upset by something that doesn't concern him and kills himself, no one's to blame."

"But don't you think that Stroop was in some way responsible for her death?"

"Well, you tell me why she killed herself."

"I think you know very well already."

"Fyodor, you mean?"

"That's how it seems to me," replied Vanya uncomfortably.

Sasha made no answer for some time, and when Vanya lifted his eyes he saw that his companion was gazing at the road with a blank, even slightly cross, expression; the droshky, with Parfen on the box, had at last come in sight.

"Why don't you answer me, Sasha?"

Glancing quickly at Vanya, Sasha said simply, and with some heat:

"Fyodor's a simple soul, a peasant—why should anyone shoot themselves because of him? If you followed that line of reasoning Larion Dmitrievich would have to do without a coachman for his horses and a porter to open the door to visitors; why, he wouldn't even be able to go to the dentist when his teeth ached. In order for there to be no Fyodor, there'd have to...."

"Are you sitting here waiting for us?" cried Arina Dmitrievna, getting down from the droshky; Parfen and Marya Dmitrievna busied themselves with bags and bundles, while the black yard dog scampered about barking.

* * *

On the Feast of Saint Peter they planned to visit an Old Believers' monastery forty versts beyond the Volga, as it seemed fitting that they should stand through a mass on so important a holiday; they also wanted to visit Anna Nikanorovna, a distant relative of the Sorokins, who lived on her bee-garden near the monastery; a trip to Cheremshany, where Prokhor Nikitich's daughters lived, was postponed until the Feast of the Prophet Elijah; in this way they would be able to stay until the end of the fair, which Vanya too was eager to see. In September they were all to return home—the women from Cheremshany and the men from Nizhni Novgorod, while Vanya was to travel straight on to Petersburg at the end of August, without stopping off for a final visit. Four days before their departure they were all sitting over evening tea—they'd almost finished packing—and discussing for the umpteenth time who was going where, and for how long, when two letters addressed to Vanya, who had not had a single letter since his arrival, came in the evening mail. One was from Anna Nikolayevna, asking him to look around for a small summer cottage in Vasilsursk at a rent of about sixty roubles, as Nata had now become so listless and droopy that she couldn't face the thought of spending the summer near Petersburg; Koka had gone to Notenthal, near Hangö, to forget his woes, while Aleksey Vasilyevich, Uncle Kostya and Boba were quite happy to stay in town. The other letter was from Koka himself; in it he spoke at some length of his grief "at the loss of that divine creature, driven to her death by a scoundrel," and reported that there was a kursaal right next door, hordes of girls, and that he was spending whole days at a time riding about on his bicycle—and so on and so forth.

"Why is he telling all this to me?" thought Vanya, folding the letter. "Doesn't he have anyone else to confide in?"

"My aunt and cousin want me to look for a summer cottage for them—they'd like to stay here for a while."

"That's soon settled; I think Germanikha's is empty—some people from As-trakhan wanted to rent it, but for some reason they haven't turned up. It would be close to you, too."

"Could you please find out for me if she'd let them have it for sixty roubles, Arina Dmitrievna—and anything else you think they ought to know?"

"She'll let them have it for fifty—don't you worry, I'll settle everything."

Alone in his room, Vanya sat for a long while at the window, without lighting the candles; Petersburg, the Kazanskis, Stroop, Stroop's apartment, and, most in-sistently for some reason, Fyodor as he had last seen him, the sash of his red silk blouse undone, a smile on the flushed face that was unusually so pale, a decanter in his hand: all came crowding into his mind. Lighting a candle, he took out a small volume of Shakespeare, the one with *Romeo and Juliet*, and tried to read; he had no dictionary, and without Stroop's help he understood little, but all at once he was filled as never before with a sense of beauty and pulsating life, as if something long-unglimpsed, half-forgotten, yet infinitely dear, had risen up and clasped him in a warm embrace. Someone knocked softly at the door.

"Who is it?"

"It's me. May I come in?"

"Of course."

"I'm sorry to bother you," said Marya Dmitrievna as she entered, "I brought you one of our rosaries—put it in your bag with your things."

"Oh—thank you."

"What was that you were reading?" asked Marya Dmitrievna, in no hurry to leave. "I was wondering whether you mightn't have picked up the *Lives of the Saints*."

"No, it's just a play, an English play."

"Ah, and I was thinking it might be the *Lives*—I couldn't make out the words, but it sounded as if you were chanting."

"Was I reading aloud?" asked Vanya, surprised.

"But of course you were…. I'll put the rosary here on the shelf…. Good night."

"Good night."

And, having straightened the icon lamp, Marya Dmitrievna left the room without a sound, closing the door gently but firmly behind her. Vanya stared be-musedly, as if he'd suddenly been woken up, at the saints in the icon case, the lamp, the iron-bound chest in the corner, the neatly-made bed, the sturdy table by the white-curtained window, beyond which lay the garden and the starry sky, and, closing the book, he blew out the candle.

❁   ❁   ❁

"Just look at all those forget-me-nots!" Marya Dmitrievna kept exclaiming as they rode by a marshy patch overgrown with pale blue flowers and tall water grass which shimmered with the gleaming wings and emerald bodies of many dragonflies. She and Vanya made their way at a leisurely pace, while the buggy with Arina Dmitrievna and Sasha went ahead; she seemed brimming over with high spirits, now jumping down from the wagon to walk along the road which edged marsh and forest, now climbing up again, now picking flowers, now humming a tune, and all the while talking to Vanya as if to herself—intoxicated, it seemed, by forest and sun, blue sky and blue flowers. Vanya gazed with a faintly patronizing indulgence at the glowing, suddenly boyish face of this thirty year old woman.

"Moscow we had a lovely garden; we lived in Zamoskvorechye[1]—we had apple trees there and lilacs, there was a spring in one corner and a black-currant bush. In the summer we never used to go anywhere, and I used to spend every day in the garden; I even used to make jam there.... What I like, Vanya, is to walk barefoot on the hot earth or bathe in the river; you can see your body through the water, little glints of sunlight dancing over it, and if you dive under and open your eyes, everything's green, so green, and you see the fish darting by; and afterwards you lie down on the hot sand to dry off, you feel the breeze—it's wonderful! It's even better lying there alone, without any of your friends around. And it's not true what the old women say—that the body is sinful. Isn't it all the Lord's handiwork—water, trees, bodies? The only sin is to resist God's will; when, say, someone is marked out for something and yearns after it with his whole being, and other people say, 'You musn't,' 'It's not allowed'—'that's sinful!' And there's so little time, Vanya, so little time! Just like a good housewife who lays in stores of cabbages and cucumbers knowing that they'll be scarce later on, we should look and love our fill, Vanya, and fill our lungs with the sweet air while we can! Our day is soon done, youth flies, and a moment that's past will never come again—we should always remember that, and then life would be as sweet to us as it is to a newborn baby or to one who is dying."

In the distance they could hear the voices of Arina Dmitrievna and Sasha; behind them Parfen's wagon rattled over the log road; flies buzzed, and all around it smelled of grass, marsh and flowers; it was hot, and Marya Dmitrievna in her black dress and loosened white kerchief, pale with fatigue and heat, dark eyes shining, sat next to Vanya, hunched slightly forward, sorting the flowers she had picked.

"When I talk to you, Vanya, it's like talking to myself—that's because your heart's as pure as a newborn babe's."

[1] The area of Moscow across the Moskva River from the Kremlin, formerly the stronghold of Moscow merchants (Eds.).

They rounded a bend to come upon a broad clearing in which a number of buildings stood clustered together, their entrances facing away from the road; many of them looked like barns, windowless, or with windows cut in the upper story; with no street to order them, they stood in a cluster, gray with time. There was not a soul to be seen, and only the barking of dogs from the monastery greeted the buggy as it drove up with Arina Dmitrievna and Sasha in a cloud of dust.

◦   ◦   ◦

After the service, Vanya went along with the Sorokins to visit the hermit Leonti, who lived in his bee garden half a verst from the monastery. As they made their way hurriedly through a shady copse to a small clearing, where somewhere among tall grass and flowers, water could be heard gurgling in a wooden trough, Arina Dmitrievna told Vanya about the hermit Leonti:

"It's a long time since he left the Great Russian Church for the true faith— must be thirty years now, and he wasn't so young then. He's a hale old fellow though, one of the Lord's stalwarts; four times he's been dragged through the courts—he did two years in Suzdal; he's a great one for fasting, and he prays like a man on fire—once he starts, there's no stopping him! And the future's an open book to him.… Don't go telling him right off that you're Orthodox, Vanechka, he might not like it."

"Perhaps he might be able to give me more useful advice."

"No really, I wouldn't tell him.…"

"All right, all right," said Vanya absently, gazing with curiosity at the low-roofed hut set about with pink hollyhocks, and at the gray haired old man with the long, straggly beard and merry, twinkling eyes who sat on the earthen ledge in front of the hut, dressed in a white shirt, dark blue breeches and a skullcap.

"So he comes up to my place, this priest, goes straight over to the table, picks up my Bible and starts thumbing through it. 'Good thing it's the authorized edition or I'd have to take it—and these pictures and any manuscripts you have I'm taking for sure': My room had portraits of Semyon Denisov,[2] Pyotr Filippov and some others hanging on the wall. Well, that was a long time ago, and I still had plenty of strength in me—so I says, 'We'll see about that, Reverend.' The sacristan—drunk he was, and wailing the whole time—says 'Leave him be, Father!' The priest throws me down on the bed and keeps trying to sprinkle me with tea from a saucer—he thought I was in need of baptizing—but I gave a heave and threw him off. 'Good-bye,' says he, 'I'll be talking to you again—and when I went to show them out, he goes and kicks me down the hill."

[2] Semyon Denisov (1862-1741): founder of the Vyzhski Monastery, which became a center of the schism within the Orthodox Church (Eds.).

And with the air of one repeating an oft-told tale, the old man began to tell how he had been with the Nekrasovites[3] in Turkey, how he had almost been killed, how he had been in prison in Suzdal, and how he had been saved each time by a cross containing holy relics, and, stooping as he passed through the doorway of the hut, he brought out a hollow cross whose copper mounting bore the embossed inscription: "Relics of St. Pyotr, Metropolitan of Moscow, Worker of Miracles, of the Sainted Princess Fevronia of Murom, of the Holy Prophet Jonah, of the Sainted Tsarevich Dmitri, and of our Blessed Mother, Mary of Egypt."

Through the windows of the hut they glimpsed icons on shelves, the reddish flames of icon lamps and candles, window ledges and tables covered with books, and a bare bench with a log for a pillow. Turning to Vanya, the hermit intoned, his eyes twinkling with a merriment which seemed hardly in keeping with his words:

"Be firm in the true faith, my son, for what can be mightier than the true faith? It takes away all our sins and leads us to the abode of eternal light. It is meet that we love the eternal light of our Lord Jesus Christ above all things. What is eternal, what is incorruptible save the Kingdom of Heaven, the soul's salvation? A flower delights you today—tomorrow it fades. You give your heart today to one who must die tomorrow. Your bright eyes will become hollow and dim, your rosy cheeks will grow withered, your hair and teeth will go, and every part of you will be food for worms. Walking corpses—that's what people are in this world."

"Things will be easier for you now—you'll be able to build churches, to worship openly," said Vanya, trying to divert the old man's thoughts.

"Seek not after that which is easily gained, but strive after that which must be won with pain! Ease, freedom and riches bring whole nations to destruction, while grievous suffering serves only to strengthen their faith. The enemy of mankind is cunning, and his wiles are hidden in darkness—often he seeks to lead us astray with seeming mercies."

"I don't understand why he's so bitter," said Vanya as they left the bee garden.

"Yes, and can people help that they have to die?" Marya Dmitrievna supported him, "I would love something all the more if I knew that tomorrow it was doomed to perish."

"Love as much as you like, but don't give your heart to one single thing, or it will gobble you up," observed Sasha, who had been silent until now.

[3] Nekrasovites: a dissenting sect which took its name from Ignati Nekrasov. After the failure of the Don Cossack revolt of 1707-08 Nekrasov and his followers sought refuge in Turkey, where their descendants preserved their faith and their hatred of the Russian Empire (Eds.).

"Not another philosopher!" sniffed his aunt.

"Wasn't I given a brain to think with?"

"Strange that he didn't realize you were Orthodox. But perhaps, my dear, he foresaw that one day you would come to the true faith," mused Arina Dmitrievna, gazing fondly at Vanya.

✿   ✿   ✿

A single icon lamp flickered in the darkness of the room; outside, the rich red of the sunset, tinged at the edges with yellow, threw the black pines beyond the clearing into bold relief. Sasha Sorokin, dark against the glowing window, was saying:

"It's hard to reconcile these things. As a member of our faith once said, 'How can you offer up prayers to Jesus after coming from the theater? Praying after killing a man would be easier.' That's just it: you can be of any faith and kill, steal and fornicate, but to understand *Faust* and say your rosary as if you meant it, Lord knows what would be—flirting with the devil; no, it's unthinkable. But then, if a man commits no sins and keeps God's law, but without believing that they are the road to salvation, then it's worse than if he didn't keep them, but believed. And how are you to believe when everything in you rejects belief? How can you help knowing what you know, remembering what you remember? And it's no good thinking that you can say: this makes sense, this I'll observe, but that's unimportant and can be ignored. Who's set you up as a judge? Until the Church says otherwise, we must observe all the laws, not only that—we must shun secular arts and not allow ourselves to be treated by doctors of another faith and strictly observe all fast days. Only old men living in the woods can keep up the old faith. How can I call myself what I'm not, and don't even consider it necessary to be. And how can I believe that only our little group is going to be saved, and that the rest of the world is wallowing in sin? And if I don't think like this, how can I consider myself to be an Old Believer? And it would be just as painful to embrace any other faith or way of life which held others to be inferior; on the other hand, if you understand all of them, you can't be a true adherent of any one."

Sasha's voice faded into silence only to start up again when no reply came from Vanya, who was lying on the bed in the darkness.

"Perhaps you, as an observer, can see and understand our way of life, our faith, our rites, better than we can ourselves; you may be able to understand our people, but they'll never understand you—perhaps dad or some of the old folk might be able to understand some part of you, but not the most important part—and you'd always be a stranger, an outsider. That can't be helped. Even I, Vanechka, fond as I am of you and much as I respect you, I'm always conscious of something in you that weighs on me and makes me feel uncomfortable. Our fathers, and their fathers before them, lived, thought and understood things differently; we're still a long way from you—sooner or later the difference will out, and there's nothing we can do about it."

Sasha again fell silent, and for a long time there was no sound, save the chanting which came to them faintly through the open doors of the chapel.

"And what about Marya Dmitrievna?"

"What about her?"

"How does she see things? Does she fit in?"

"It's hard to make her out—she's devout, misses her husband a lot."

"Has he been dead long?"

"Yes, it's been eight years; I was just a little boy then."

"She's awfully nice."

"She's all right—not that her ideas aren't pretty limited too," said Sasha, closing the window.

❧   ❧   ❧

Another cartload of guests drove up to the gates; Arina Dmitrievna, who had just taken her place at the table, ran to greet them, and from the porch could be heard welcoming shouts and hearty bussings. It was noisy and hot in the great room, where a dozen or so men sat eating; barefoot Froska, who had been brought in to lend Malanya a hand, was kept busy running to the cellar with a large glass pitcher, which she would bring back bubbling to the brim with cold kvass. In the room where the women ate, Marya Dmitrievna was sitting in the chair usually occupied by the lady of the house, who was kept constantly on her feet, bustling from table to table, darting into the kitchen and running to greet ever newly-arriving guests. Anna Nikolayevna sat there too with five other guests, who kept mopping their faces with sweat-soaked handkerchiefs, while course after course was served, quantities of Madeira and home-made brandy were downed, and flies crawled in and out of dirty glasses and settled in swarms on the whitewashed walls and crumb-strewn tablecloth. The men had taken off their jackets, and sat in their vests and brightly-colored shirts, red-faced and glassy-eyed, talking, hiccoughing and laughing uproariously. Sunlight streamed through the open door, glinting on the glass of the china cabinet, the brightly burning icon lamps and the painted bird cages in the next room; aroused by the general commotion, the canaries were singing their heads off. Dogs crept in from the yard, only to be chased out again, and the weighted door, held open for a moment by Froska's bare foot, kept slamming and screeching. The house smelled of raspberries, pies, wine and sweat.

"Now what would you do? I gave him strict orders to telegraph his answer to Samara—and not a word out of him!"

"Just soak it in alcohol, and after you've let it sit overnight in the cellar, boil it with oak bark—it comes out very tasty."

"You should have heard the sermon Father Vasili from Gromov gave on Ascension Day: 'Blessed are the peacemakers, and therefore I counsel you to make your peace with the Chubykinskaya alms house—forgive the warden his debts and don't call him to account!' What a joke!…"

"I tell him thirty-five roubles, and he offers me fifteen.…"

"Pale blue, a beautiful pale blue, with a design in pink," came a voice from the women's room.

"Your health, Arina Dmitrievna! Your health!" shouted the men to the lady of the house as she went rushing through on her way to the kitchen.

As if at a given signal, there was a scraping of chairs, and, turning toward the icons in the corner, they all began crossing themselves in silence; Froska was already dragging in the samovar, and Arina Dmitrievna was doing her energetic best to ensure that the guests didn't stray too far before tea.

"Don't tell me this kind of life appeals to you," said Nata to Vanya, who had volunteered to see them safely past the Sorokin's yard dogs.

"Not particularly, but I can think of worse ways of living."

"I find that hard to believe," remarked Anna Nikolayevna, opening the wicker gate again to free the snared hem of her gray silk dress.

❊   ❊   ❊

"Let's sit here, Nata. I'd like to talk to you."

"All right. What did you want to talk to me about?" asked the girl, sitting down beside Vanya on a bench shaded by tall birch trees. The sound of chanting came to their ears: the painters who were decorating the church nearby had been forbidden by the priest to sing secular songs at their work. The church porch was hidden by spiraea bushes which grew thickly on all sides, but every word came floating clearly through the open doors onto the evening air; somewhere, far off, cattle lowed as they returned from pasture.

"What was it you wanted to talk to me about?"

"Perhaps I oughtn't to bring back painful and unpleasant memories.…"

"I suppose you want to talk about that awful business," said Nata after a silence.

"Yes, if there's anything you can tell me about it, I'd be grateful."

"You're mistaken if you think I know more about it than anyone else; all I know is that Ida Holberg shot herself—why she did it, I have no idea."

"But you were there when it happened?"

"Yes, but I didn't get there half an hour before—more like ten minutes; and most of the time I was standing alone in the hall."

"Did you see her shoot herself?"

"No, it wasn't until I heard the shot that I ran into the study."

"And she was already dead?"

Inside the church painters were intoning, "Lord, hear my prayer."

"Take your hands off me, you beast! What d'you think you're doing! Stop it!"

"E-e-e!"—from the church porch came the sound of a woman's voice raised in simulated alarm; her unseen partner preferred to go about his business in silence.

"E-e-e!"—this time the cry was more piercing, as if someone were drowning, and although there was no wind, a violent tremor passed through the spiraea bushes.

"...Thy evening sacrifice!"—the singing within ended on a conciliatory note.

"There was a decanter or a soda siphon on the table—something made of glass anyway—and a bottle of brandy; a man in a red shirt was sitting on a leather couch near the table—he seemed to be busy with something; Stroop was standing to the right, and Ida was sitting at the desk with her head thrown back against the spine of the chair...."

"And she was already dead?"

"Yes, I think so. As soon as I entered the room, he began shouting at me, 'What are you doing here? For your own safety, for your own peace of mind, leave! Leave this minute, I beg of you!' The man who was sitting on the couch got up, and I noticed that he was unbelted, and that he was very handsome; his face was fiery-red, and his hair was long and curly. He looked drunk to me. Then Stroop said, 'Fyodor, show the lady out.'"

"Thy will be done,"—they were singing something else now; from the church porch came murmurs of reconciliation; a woman, it seemed, was crying softly.

"All the same, it's terrible," muttered Vanya.

"Terrible," echoed Nata, "and all the more so for me—I loved him so much," and she began to cry.

Vanya looked at the girl with distaste—at the pouting mouth, the freckles which had now coalesced in brownish blotches, the mop of ginger hair; she seemed to have aged, to have grown flaccid.

"Were you really in love with Larion Dmitrievich?"

She nodded; they were both silent, then she asked, her voice oddly gentle:

"Do you ever write to him now, Vanya?"

"No, I don't even know his address—he gave up his Petersburg apartment, you know."

"He shouldn't be hard to find."

"And suppose I were corresponding with him?"

"Oh, nothing."

A dashing young fellow in a jacket and cap stepped quietly out of the bushes and, as he drew level with them, bowed to Vanya. It was Sergey.

"Who's that?" asked Nata.

"Sorokin's assistant."

"He must have been the hero of that little episode," added Nata with something approaching a leer.

"What episode?"

"On the church porch—don't tell me you didn't hear anything."

"I heard some women yelling, but I didn't pay any attention."

✿   ✿   ✿

Vanya almost stumbled over a man who was sleeping on the shady slope of the river bank. Dressed in a white suit, the man lay with his hands folded under his head; the cap of his teacher's uniform, which should have shielded his face, had slid down onto the grass. There was something familiar about the bald spot, the upturned nose, the sparse, reddish beard, about the whole diminutive figure: with a start Vanya recognized his Greek teacher.

"Is it really you, Daniil Ivanovich?"—Vanya was too amazed for polite greetings.

"None other! But why so surprised? After all, you found your way here, and you're from Petersburg."

"How is it I haven't run into you before?"

"That's easily answered—I only got here yesterday. Are you here with your family?" asked the Greek, sitting up and mopping his bald spot with a red-bordered handkerchief. "Why don't you sit down—it's shady here, and there's a breeze."

"Yes, my aunt and my cousin are here too, but I'm staying with the Sorokins—maybe you've heard of them?"

"I'm afraid not. It's really not bad here, not bad at all—the Volga, the orchards and all that."

"Where's your kitten and your thrush—did you bring them with you?"

"No, I expect to be traveling for quite some time, you see…."

And, growing animated, he began to explain how, having come unexpectedly into a modest inheritance, he had taken leave of absence with the intention of fulfilling a long-cherished dream—a journey to Athens, Alexandria and Rome. However, he had decided to wait for cooler weather before venturing into southern climes, and in the meantime, equipped with a small suitcase and a few favorite books, he was making his way down the Volga, stopping at any place that took his fancy.

"There are some very interesting excavations going on now in Rome and Pompeii, and in Asia too—long lost works by ancient writers are turning up all the time." And throwing off his cap in shining-eyed abandon, the Greek poured out his dreams, his enthusiasms, his plans, while Vanya gazed wistfully at that ugly face aglow with overflowing vitality.

"Yes, that's interesting, that's very interesting," he murmured thoughtfully when his companion finished speaking and lit a cigarette.

"Will you be here till the fall?" Daniil Ivanovich suddenly remembered to ask.

"Probably. I'm going to Nizhni Novgorod for the fair, and I'll go straight home from there," said Vanya, ashamed that his plans were so unimpressive.

"Well, are you happy here then? These Sorokins—are they interesting people?"

"They're very simple, but kind and warmhearted," answered Vanya, feeling only cold indifference as he thought of these people, now suddenly so alien. "I'm bored here, bored to tears! There's no one here to fire the imagination, no one to understand what can't be put into words," Vanya suddenly burst out—"No one—not here, not even in Petersburg."

The Greek gave him a sharp look.

"Smurov," he began, not without solemnity, "you do have a friend who values your heart's noblest aspirations, who will never deny you his understanding and affection."

"I'm very grateful, Daniil Ivanovich," said Vanya, reaching out his hand.

"You needn't be," responded the Greek, "I wasn't speaking of myself, as a matter of fact."

"Who then?"

"Larion Dmitrievich."

"Stroop?"

"Yes.... Wait, don't interrupt me, I know Larion Dmitrievich very well indeed; I saw him after that unfortunate affair, and can assure you that he is no more guilty than you would be if, say, I were to drown myself because you have fair hair. Of course, it's a matter of the utmost indifference to Larion Dmitrievich what people say about him, but he did express regret that certain people he held dear should have changed in their feelings toward him—and among others he mentioned you. You might keep that in mind; you might also keep in mind that he's in Munich and can be reached at the Four Seasons Hotel."

"I'm not judging him, but I don't need his address—and if you came here to give it to me, your efforts have been wasted."

"Beware of vanity, my friend. Would someone of my advanced years stop off at Vasilsursk on his way from Petersburg to Rome just to give Stroop's address to Vanya Smurov? I didn't even know you were here. You're upset, you're not well, and all I'm doing is being a good doctor and prescribing what you need— the kind of life that Stroop represents."

* * *

"How well-formed you are, Vanechka!" Sasha paused in his undressing to look at Vanya, who stood naked on the dry bank, leaning forward to splash water on his face and under his arms before wading in. Vanya looked down at the widening circles and saw the undulating reflection of the long, lissome body, tanned by sun and swimming, the narrow hips and slender legs, the blond curls clustering about the graceful neck, the large eyes set in a face that seemed leaner, though not without a touch of boyish roundness, and, smiling to himself, he stepped into the cold water. Sasha, who was shortlegged for his height, white-skinned and fleshy, found a deep spot and plunged in with a splash.

The entire river bank, as far as the grazing herd of cattle, was covered with young bathers, who ran up and down yelling and splashing in the shallows; red shirts and underclothing lay about in scattered heaps, while on the high ground further off the rosy bodies of children and adolescents could be glimpsed beneath the willows, against the bright green of new-mown grass, bring to mind Thoma's visions of paradise. With voluptuous exhilaration, Vanya felt his body cleave the cold depths and writhe, fish-like, to churn the warmer surface. Tired at last, he floated on his back, seeing only the radiance above him, arms motionless at his sides, content to drift with the current. Cries of alarm, ever more urgent, brought him to himself; a dredger had been at work near the spot where the cattle were grazing, and the voices seemed to be moving in that direction. The two boys pulled on their shirts as they ran, and were met with shouts of, "They got him, they got him, they fished him out!"

"What's going on?"

"A boy who drowned last spring—they've only just found him. He got snagged on a log—couldn't swim out," came in breathless snatches from boys racing by them.

A woman in a white kercheif and a red dress came running down the hill, sobbing loudly; reaching the spot where the body lay stretched out on a length of bast matting, she flung herself downward in the sand and began keening, her body racked with sobs.

"It's Arina…his mother!"—a whisper ran through the crowd.

"Don't you remember, I was telling you his story?" Sergey, who had come running up from somewhere, was saying, as Vanya stood staring with horror at the swollen, slimy corpse—could that shapeless flesh have been a face? Naked except for a pair of boots, the corpse lay there, loathsome and terrible in the bright sunlight, surrounded by noisy and curious boys, whose rosy bodies could be glimpsed through their unbuttoned shirts. "He was an only son, he always wanted to be a monk—ran away three times, but every time they brought him back; they even used to beat him, but there was no changing his mind; the other boys would be buying cakes, but he'd spend everything on candles; got mixed up with a skirt—worthless bitch she was— not realizing what he'd let himself in for, and when he did realize it, he went for a swim with the lads and drowned, just like that; he was only sixteen...." It seemed to Vanya that a wall of water lay between him and Sergey's words.

"Vanya, Vanya!" the woman shrieked, lifting herself to her knees, and again falling forward into the sand at the sight of the swollen, slimy corpse.

Overcome with horror, Vanya turned and fled up the hill. Brambles and net-tles tore his flesh as he stumbled on, not daring to glance behind, as if pursuers were on his heels. Heart pounding, temples throbbing, he halted at last in the Sorokin's garden. Apples hung on the wide-spaced apple trees, forests gloomed beyond the tranquil Volga, grasshoppers chirred in the grass, and in the air hung the smell of honey and calomile.

❋ ❋ ❋

"There are muscles, sinews in the human body which one cannot look upon with-out a tremor,"—Stroop's words came to Vanya as he stared in the mirror at the pale, haunted face, the delicately-drawn brows, the gray eyes, the red mouth, the curls falling about the slender neck. He showed no surprise when, at this late hour, Marya Dmitrievna came silently into the room and closed the door firmly and softly behind her.

"No, no, I can't bear it! What does it all mean?"—he flung himself toward her, "My cheeks will fall in, turn waxen, my body will swell and be covered with slime, my eyes will be eaten by worms—my body will be nothing but a heap of bones! And there are muscles, sinews in the human body which one cannot look upon without a tremor! Nothing lasts, nothing escapes destruction! And there's so much I don't know, so much I haven't seen—and I want, I want.... There's blood in my veins, I'm not a stone; and I know now that I'm beautiful. It's hor-rible, horrible! Who will save me?"

There was no surprise in Marya Dmitrievna's eyes, only joy, as she looked at Vanya.

"Vanechka, my darling boy, I'm so sorry for you, so sorry! I've long feared this moment, but I see that the Lord has willed that it should come to pass," and un-hurriedly blowing out the candle, she embraced Vanya and began covering his mouth, his eyes, his cheeks with kisses, pressing him more and more tightly to her bosom. Vanya sobered at once and attempted to free himself from this hot, unwelcome and uncomfortable embrace, mumbling over and over again, "Marya Dmitrievna, Marya Dmitrievna, what's the matter with you? Let me go. Don't." But she clasped him ever more fervently to her, covering his cheeks, his mouth, his eyes with quick, light kisses, and whispering, "Vanechka, my darling, my joy."

"Let me go, you disgusting bitch!" shouted Vanya at last, and exerting all his strength, he broke from the woman's embrace and ran out of the room, slamming the door behind him.

*   *   *

"What am I to do now?" Vanya asked Daniil Ivanovich, to whom he had come in the middle of the night in search of refuge.

"It seems to me that you'd better leave," said his host, who was wearing slippers and a dressing gown over his underclothes.

"But where can I go? I suppose there's Petersburg—but they'd ask why I'd come back, and besides, I'd be bored there."

"Yes, that would be awkward—but you can't possibly stay here in the state you're in."

"What am I to do?" said Vanya, gazing helplessly at the Greek, who sat drumming his fingers on the table.

"Having no idea of your personal resources and obligations, I can't presume to suggest a long journey; and besides, you couldn't travel alone."

"What am I to do?"

"If I could be sure you'd trust my good intentions and not start getting all sorts of foolish ideas, Smurov, I'd propose that you come along with me."

"Where to?"

"Abroad."

"I haven't got any money."

"We'd have enough; one day you'll be able to settle up with me; we could go as far as Rome together, and make up our minds there whom you were coming back with and where I was going on to. That would be the best thing."

"Are you really serious, Daniil Ivanovich?"

"Of course I'm serious."

"Is it really possible—me in Rome?"

"More than possible," smiled the Greek.

"I can't believe it," gasped Vanya.

The Greek smoked his cigarette in silence, his eyes twinkling as they rested on Vanya.

"You're so good, so kind!" the boy burst forth.

"It'll be very pleasant for me not to have to travel alone; of course, we'll have to economize—stay at the local inns instead of smart hotels."

"Oh that'll be even more fun," said Vanya enthusiastically.

"All right, I'll speak to your aunt in the morning."

And morning found them still discussing the trip, the cities and towns they would include in their itinerary, planning excursions. Emerging into the bright sunlight, Vanya stood for a moment in the street with its grassy cobbles; could he really be in Vasilsursk, and was that really the Volga with its gloomy forests?

*   *   *

PART THREE

"Tannhäuser" was over, and the three of them were sitting together in a cafe on the Corso. The imminence of parting contributed to the conviviality of their mood, and the half-unintelligible Italian chatter, the clink of plates and ice cream glasses and the remote strains of the string orchestra which floated through the tobacco haze all lent the occasion a feeling which bordered on the intimate. At the next table, an officer with a whole rooster's wing on his cap and two ladies in dresses which, though black, contrived to be showy, did not so much as glance their way, and through the open window with its net curtains they could glimpse street lights, passing carriages and pedestrians who trod both sidewalk and street; a fountain plashed in the square nearby.

In his dark suit, which, though perfectly commonplace, somehow suggested the dandy, Vanya looked more of a schoolboy than ever—tall, slender and very pale. Daniil Ivanovich, who accompanied his friend everywhere in the office of "the traveling prince's tutor," as he laughingly put it, was now engaging his charge and Ugo Orsini in conversation with an air of benevolent patronage.

"Whenever I hear that opening scene in the second version—the one written by the Wagner of 'Tristan'—I feel an unspeakable rapture, a prophetic tremor, just as I do with Klinger's paintings or D'Annunzio's poetry. Those dancing fauns and nymphs, those visions of Leda and Europa in an antique landscape which suddenly opens before one, shining, radiant, breath-taking, yet somehow profoundly familiar, familiar to the point of pain; those cupids who take aim from the trees, as they do in Botticelli's 'Primavera,' at dancing fauns who freeze in languorous poses when the arrows strike them; and all this in the presence of Venus, who keeps watch over the sleeping Tannhäuser with more than mortal love and tenderness—it's like the breath of a new spring, of a new passion for life, for the sun, surging up from the darkest depths of being," and Orsini passed a handkerchief over his pale, smooth-shaven face, which was just beginning to show signs of fleshiness; his eyes were black and lusterless, his mouth sinuous and finely-chiselled.

"You know, that was the only time Wagner ventured into classical antiquity," remarked Daniil Ivanovich, "but I've heard the opera many times without the re-worked Venusberg scene, and I've always thought that it stood next to 'Parsifal'—the idea of which it shares—as Wagner's profoundest conception. But I can't understand or accept the way he resolves these works. Why this renunciation? Why this asceticism? Neither the nature of Wagner's genius nor anything else can justify such endings!"

"Musically, the scene doesn't fit in very well with what he wrote earlier—
Venus is a little too close to Isolde."

"As a musician, you're in a better position to know that. But meaning and
idea—these are the proper domain of the poet and philosopher."

"Asceticism is essentially a highly unnatural phenomenon, and the supposed
continence of certain animals is pure fiction."

They were served with richly-flavored ice cream and water in large, long-
stemmed goblets. The cafe was emptying somewhat, and the musicians had already begun to run through their repertoire for the second time.

"You're leaving tomorrow?" Ugo enquired, straightening the red carnation in
his buttonhole.

"I wouldn't mind saying goodbye to Rome if it meant not splitting up with
Daniil Ivanovich for a little longer," said Vanya.

"You're off to Naples and Sicily, aren't you? But where are you going?"

"To Florence in the company of a canon we know."

"Mori?"

"That's right."

"How do you come to know him?"

"We met at Bossi Gaetano's—you know, the archaeologist?"

"The one who lives on the Via Nazionale?"

"Yes. He's such a nice little canon, you know."

"Well, I can truthfully say: Now lettest thou thy servant depart in peace—I'm
entrusting you to the Monsignor's keeping."

Vanya smiled affectionately.

"Are you really so weary of me?"

"Terribly!" joked Daniil Ivanovich.

"We'll probably meet in Florence; I'll be there in a week's time: my quartet
is being given there."

"That would be nice. You can always find the Monsignor at the cathedral, you
know. He'll be able to give you my address."

"And I'll be staying at the Marchesa Moratti's in Borgo Santi Apostoli. Please
don't stand on ceremony—the Marchesa lives alone and is always glad of visitors.
She is my aunt, and I am her heir."

A smile of insidious sweetness played for a moment on the finely-chiselled
mouth and glinted in the black, lusterless eyes, and the rings glittered on the
sinewy musicians fingers with their closely trimmed nails.

"That Ugo looks like a poisoner, don't you think?" asked Vanya of his companion as they walked home up the Corso.

"What a fancy! He's just an awfully nice man, that's all."

✿   ✿   ✿

Although rain was streaming down the sidewalk outside, the coolness of the museum was pleasant and refreshing. After a last-minute visit to the forums, the Coliseum and the Palatine Hill, they found themselves almost alone in a small gallery before the "Running Youth."

"Only the 'Ilioneus' torso can rival this in the way it conveys the vitality and beauty of the youthful male body. What does it matter to us now that he is armless and headless? We can still feel the crimson blood pulsing beneath the white skin, and every muscle fills us with a heady rapture. The body itself, the physical substance, will perish, and perhaps even the creations of art—Phidias, Mozart, Shakespeare—will perish, but the idea, the form of beauty contained in them cannot perish, and this, perhaps, is the only thing of value in the changing and transient diversity of life. And these ideas are divine and pure, no matter how rude their embodiment. Did not the forms of religion clothe the highest ideals of asceticism in symbolic rites, which, though savage and fanatical, were nevertheless illuminated by the symbol within, and therefore divine?"

Offering some final precepts before parting, Daniil Ivanovich said:

"Listen to me, Smurov: if you should find yourself in need of spiritual consolation or help in settling yourself in cheap lodgings, then go to the Monsignor; but if you should find yourself completely out of funds or in need of wise, intelligent counsel, then go to Larion Dmitrievich. I'll give you his address. Is that agreed? Do you promise me?"

"Isn't there anyone else? I'd be very reluctant to go to him."

"I can suggest no one more reliable. If that's how it is, I'm afraid you'll have to find someone on your own."

"And Ugo? Wouldn't he help?"

"Hardly; it's not often that he has any money. And I just can't understand the grudge you have against Larion Dmitrievich, even to the point of refusing to write to him. What could have happened to warrant such a change?"

Vanya stared at a bust of the youthful Marcus Aurelius for a long time without replying. At last he began in a slow monotone:

"I'm not accusing him of anything, nor do I consider that I have any right to be angry, but to my bitter, regret, having involuntarily made certain discoveries, I can no longer feel about Stroop as I did before; and this prevents me from seeing in him the guide and friend I need."

"What romanticism—if only it didn't sound as if it had been learnt by rote! You're like one of those 'transcendental' young ladies who used to imagine that their admirers saw them as beings who didn't eat, or drink, or sleep, or snore or blow their noses. Every man has his natural functions which in no way degrade him, no matter how unpleasant they might appear to others. To be jealous of Fyodor means to admit yourself his equal, having the same significance and purpose as he has. But even that—silly though it would be—would be better than this romantic squeamishness."

"Let's not talk about it any more; if there's no other way, I'll write to Stroop."

"And you'll do well to do so, my little Cato."

"But it was you who taught me to despise Cato."

"Without much success, apparently."

❋   ❋   ❋

The path to the terrace took them across a lawn dotted with clumps of flowers, which glimmered softly in the twilight; a delicate whitish mist was spreading, moving swiftly, as though in pursuit of them; somewhere owlets were hooting; in the east a shaggy star gleamed fitfully in the mist, now tinged with pink, and the lattice-windows of the old house before them flamed strangely as they caught the first light of the morning sky. Ugo had finished whistling his quartet and was smoking a cigarette in silence. As they were passing the terrace, their heads not quite reaching the balustrade, Vanya stopped abruptly; someone was speaking what was unmistakably Russian.

"So you'll be in Italy for some time yet?"

"I don't know; you can see how weak Mama is; after Naples we'll go on to Lugano, but for how long, I don't know."

"Then I'll be deprived of the opportunity of seeing you, of hearing your voice...." the man's voice began.

"Four months or so," the woman's voice hastily interrupted him.

"Four months!" echoed the first speaker.

"I'm sure you won't be bored...."

Hearing the steps of Vanya and Orsini on the stairs, they fell silent, and all that could be made out in the dim morning light were the shapes of a seated woman and of the rather short man who was standing beside her.

As they entered the hall, to be enveloped by the warm stuffiness of a crowded room, Vanya asked Ugo:

"Who were those Russians?"

"Anna Blonskaya and one of your artists—I don't recall his name."

"He seems to be in love with her."

"Oh, that's no secret—and neither is his dissolute way of life."

"Is she beautiful?" asked Vanya, still rather naively.

"See for yourself."

Vanya turned around: making her entrance was a pale, fragile girl with smooth, dark hair combed low over her ears; her face was fine-featured, with a rather large mouth and blue eyes. She was followed, after an interval of some five minutes, by a man of about twenty-six, who entered hurriedly with a stooping gait; he had a small pointed beard, curly hair, pale, bulging eyes beneath thick brows the color of old gold, and his ears were pointed like a faun's.

"Yes, he loves her too much to treat her like a woman. These odd Russian notions!" added the Italian.

The company was dispersing, and a portly cleric was rolling his eyes and saying over and over again:

"His Holiness gets so tired, so terribly tired...."

Caught by a sunbeam, the windows flashed dazzlingly, and the muffled sound of carriages being brought up could be heard.

"Until we meet again in Florence, then," said Orsini, shaking Vanya's hand.

"Yes, I'm leaving tomorrow."

❀   ❀   ❀

They were all lying on gaily-colored quilted mattresses set in the window ledges: Signoras Poldina and Filomena in one window and Signora Scolastica with the cook Santina in the other, when the Monsignor led Vanya along the narrow, dark and cool street to the old house with an iron ring on the door instead of a bell. After the first burst of noise, when the shrieks and exclamations had died down, Signora Poldina continued to hold forth alone:

"Ullise says: 'I'm bringing a Russian *signore*, he'll be staying with us,'—'Ullise,' I say, 'you're joking, no one has ever stayed with us; a prince, a Russian barin—how will we be able to look after him?'—but whatever my brother has a mind to do, he does. We thought that a Russian *signore* would be a great big tall man, like that Mr. Buturlin we saw, but this one is such a little boy, so skinny, such a darling, such a little cherub," and Signora Poldina's elderly quaver subsided in melting cadences.

The Monsignor took Vanya to see the library and the sisters dispersed to their rooms and to the kitchen. Hitching up his soutane, the Monsignor began to mount the stairs, displaying thick calves sheathed in black home-knitted stockings and the sturdiest of shoes. In priestly fashion, he loudly intoned the titles of books which, in his opinion, would be of interest to Vanya, passing over the others in silence—stocky and red-cheeked, for all his sixty-five years, and of a cheerful, obstinate and narrowly didactic disposition. The shelves were full of books in Italian, Latin, French, Spanish, English and Greek, some standing, some lying flat—Thomas Aquinas beside Don Quixote, Shakespeare next to odd volumes of saints' lives, Seneca side by side with Anacreon.

"A confiscated book," explained the canon, noticing Vanya's look of surprise and pushing a small illustrated volume of Anacreon a little further to one side. "There are many books here confiscated from my spiritual children. They can't do me any harm."

"This is your room!" declared Mori, leading Vanya into a large, square, paleblue room hung with white curtains and with a curtained bed in the middle; the somewhat bare walls with engravings of saints and a Madonna of Good Counsel, the rude table, the shelf of edifying books, the painted wax figurine of St. Luigi Gonzaga[1] dressed in a hand-sewn choirboy costume, which stood under a glass dome on the chest of drawers, the stoup of holy water by the door—all lent the room the appearance of a monastery cell; only the piano by the balcony door and the toilet stand by the window prevented the resemblance from being complete.

"Shoo puss, shoo, shoo!" Poldina fell upon a plump white tomcat which had appeared in the hall to add the finishing touch to the occasion.

"Why are you chasing him away? I'm very fond of cats," remarked Vanya.

"The *signore* is fond of cats! Oh what a poppet! Oh what a darling! Filomena, bring Micina and her kittens to show the *signore*.... Oh what a darling!"

❀   ❀   ❀

They had been walking around Florence since morning, the Monsignor ranging in a sonorous sing-song from the fourteenth century to the twentieth, informative, discursive and anecdotal by turn, relaying with equal relish present-day scandal and incidents out of Vasari; he would stop in the middle of busy side-streets to develop his eloquent and, more often than not, censorious periods, would address himself to passers-by, to horses and dogs, would laugh uproariously and sing to himself, spreading about him an atmosphere of homely courtesy and rough tact, as guilelessly didactic as it was good-humored—an atmosphere reminiscent of Sacchetti's *novelle*.[2] Sometimes, when his store of tales ran short of the need he had to speak—to speak in vivid images, declaiming and waving his arms, to make of conversation a primitive work of art—he would turn to the hoariest plots of the *novelliere* and retell them with naive eloquence and conviction. He knew everybody and everything, and not a corner, not a stone of his native Tuscany and his beloved Florence was without its legends and time-honored anecdotes. Vanya's visit provided him with an excuse, of which he took full advantage, to pay all kinds of calls. Vanya met ruined *marchesi* and counts who lived in dilapidated palaces and quarreled with their servants over cards; he met engineers and doctors, merchants who lived the frugal, sequestered lives that their fathers had before them; he met budding composers who yearned for

[1] St. Luigi Gonzaga (1568—1591): canonized (1726) as St. Aloysius Gonzaga. Noted for his intense love of chastity, he became the patron saint of youth (Eds.).

[2] Franco Sacchetti (c. 1335-c. 1400): after Boccaccio, the most popular storyteller of his age. His *Novelle* are based on real incidents in Florentine life, both public and private, and throw interesting light on the manners of the time (Eds.).

Puccini's fame, aping him with their neckties and fat, beardless faces; he met the Persian consul, fat, solemn and benign, who lived near San Miniato with his six nieces; he met apothecaries; he met young men who were vaguely described as errand boys, English ladies who had gone over to Catholicism and, finally, Mme. Monier, an aesthetic and artistic lady who lived in Fiesole with a whole company of guests in a villa decorated with charming allegories of spring and commanding a view of Florence and the Valley of the Arno. Invariably cheerful and eternally a-twitter, she was tiny, ginger-haired and quite hideous.

※　※　※

They had remained sitting at a table out on the terrace; in the approaching twilight, the plates, which were of a uniform deep red, gleamed richly against the roseate table cloth, like pools of blood. The smell of cigars, wild strawberries and the wine left in the glasses mingled with the scent of garden flowers. From the house came the sound of a woman's voice singing some ancient air, punctuated every now and then by a brief silence or by a burst of chattering and laughter; and when the lamps were lit inside, the view from the terrace, almost dark by this time, was reminiscent of the set for Maeterlinck's *L'intérieur*.[3] Ugo Orsini, pale and beardless, red carnation in lapel, was speaking:

"You can't imagine the sort of woman he's wasting himself on. If a man is not an ascetic, there is no greater crime than a chaste love. Just look where this love of his for Blonskaya has landed him: all that's attractive about Cibo are those depraved mermaiden eyes of hers in that pale face. Her mouth—ugh, her mouth!—just listen to the way she talks; nothing is too tasteless for her to repeat, every word she utters is a vulgarity! Like the girl in the fairy tale, every time she opens her mouth, out pops a mouse or a toad. That's the truth! And she won't let him go. He'll forget Blonskaya and his talent and the whole world for the sake of this woman. He'll soon be as good as dead as a man, let alone as an artist."

"And you think that if Blonskaya…if he loved her in a different way, he would be able to break with Cibo?"

"Yes, I do."

After a silence, Vanya began timidly:

"And do you really consider him incapable of a chaste love?"

"Can't you see what has come of it? One look at his face is enough. I'm not laying down any law—one can never be certain of anything in this world—but I can see that he's being destroyed and I can see what's destroying him, and it in-

---

[3] Maeterlinck's play *L'intérieur* was staged by the Moscow Art Theater in 1904 as part of an evening of one-act plays by Maeterlinck (the others being *L'intruse* and *Les aveugles*) (Eds.).

furiates me because I have a great deal of affection and a great deal of admiration for him. That's why I look upon Cibo and Blonskaya with equal detestation."

Orsini finished his cigarette and went into the house, and Vanya, left alone, kept thinking of the young artist with his fair curly hair and pointed beard, and his pale eyes, at once mocking and sad. And for some reason his thoughts turned to Stroop.

From the drawing room came the voice of Mme. Monier, bird-like and affected:

"Do you remember in Segantini's[4] painting, that genius with enormous wings who sits above the lovers by the mountain spring? It is the lovers themselves who should have wings—and all who are bold and free and not afraid to love."

"A letter from Ivan Strannik;[5] such a dear woman! She says that Anatole France greets us and sends us his blessing. I kiss thy name, great teacher!"

"It's your own? To words by D'Annunzio? But of course, by all means—why didn't you tell us about it before?"

The noise of chairs being pushed back was succeeded by a couple of loud, imperious chords on the piano, and Orsini's voice launched with somewhat crude ardor into a broad melody which bordered on the banal.

"Oh, I'm so glad! His uncle, you say? Splendid!" twittered Mme. Monier, running out onto the terrace; with her ginger hair and long pink dress, she looked at once hideous and delectable.

"Ah, there you are," she exclaimed, stumbling upon Vanya, "I've news for you! A fellow-countryman of yours has arrived. But he's not a Russian, even though he's from St. Petersburg; he's a great friend of mine; an Englishman. Well? What do you say to that?" she rattled on, not waiting for an answer, and vanished down the garden's broad driveway, silvery now in the moonlight, to greet the new arrivals.

"For heaven's sake, let's go. I'm afraid; I don't want this to happen—let's leave without saying goodbye, right now, this instant," Vanya urged the canon, who was sitting over his ice cream and looking at Vanya wide-eyed.

"Certainly, my child, certainly, but I don't understand what you're so worked up about. Very well then—I just have to get my hat."

"Quickly, quickly, *cher père!*" wailed Vanya, overcome by an unaccountable

---

[4] Giovanni Segantini (1858-1899): Italian painter, influenced by the French Impressionists. The painting referred to, completed in 1896, is entitled "L'amore alla fonte della vita" (Eds.).

[5] Ivan Strannik: pen name of Anna Mitrofanovna Anichkova (1868-1935); Russian writer living in Paris. She wrote novels in both French and Russian, and was the author of the study *La penseé russe contemporaine* (1903) (Eds.).

terror. "They're coming, they're coming!" he cried, veering off the main road, which echoed with the clatter of hooves and carriage wheels. Then, at a bend ahead of them, quite unexpectedly, Mme. Monier and several of her guests emerged from a narrow path, having taken a short cut around; and with them, quite unmistakable in the moonlight, was Stroop.

"Let's stay," whispered Vanya, squeezing the canon's hand. Even the light of the moon was enough to reveal the deep flush which had risen to the boy's smiling, excited face.

∗   ∗   ∗

It was a thirteenth century house with a well in the second-floor dining room in case of siege, a fireplace big enough to hold a shepherd's hut, a library, family portraits and a chapel. They drove out of the main gate in four donkey-drawn gigs; some wraps and blankets had been sent on with provisions, but the servants brought out some more in case of cold during the ascent. Leaving Florence, they had travelled by train as far as Borgo San Lorenzo, and then by carriage past Scarperia with its castle and wrought iron, past Sant' Agata; and now they made a hasty breakfast in order to get back from the mountains before dark. In the absence of conversation, the only sound to be heard was the clatter of knives and forks and the tinkle of coffee spoons. Leaving behind vineyards and farms embowered amidst chestnut trees, they climbed ever higher up the narrow, winding road, the leading carriage sometimes finding itself perched directly above the hindermost one. The flora of the south gave way to birches, pines, lichens and violets, and clouds hung suspended below them. Still short of the summit of il Giogo, from which both the Mediterranean and the Adriatic are said to be visible, they rounded a bend to view Firenzuola lying beneath them like a handful of reddish-grey pebbles on the winding ribbon of the Faenza road, along which an old-fashioned stagecoach was moving in their direction. The coach halted to allow one of the female passengers to alight and relieve herself; in the meantime, the driver sat perched on his box, calmly smoking and waiting until they could get under way again.

"Isn't that just like something out of Goldoni! What delightful simplicity!" gushed Mme. Monier as she cracked her red-handled whip. In a smoke-blackened tavern which called to mind a bandits' hideaway, they were offered fried eggs, cheese, chianti and salami. The proprietress, a suntanned woman with one eye, sat listening, her cheek pressed against the back of a wooden chair, as a man in a green felt hat and shirtsleeves, bold of eye and black of brow, told the ladies and gentlemen about her:

"Everybody knew that Beppo was coming here at night…. So the *carabinieri* say to her, 'Auntie Pasca, you needn't be squeamish about taking our money, we'll get Beppo any way sooner or later.' She thought it over, but she couldn't make up her mind...she's an honest woman, as is plain to see.... But there's no getting away from fate; one night he comes back from a kinsman's wedding—he's had a drop too much, and he goes straight to bed.... Pasca's told the *carabinieri* to be ready, and so she gives them a whistle—and of course she's taken Beppo's knives and gun away from him. What could he do? He's only human, *signori*...."

"How he did curse! Tied up, he was, but he kicked this bench here over, threw himself on the floor and started threshing about!" said Pasca huskily. Her white teeth flashed in a smile and her solitary eye twinkled, as if she were recounting the pleasantest things imaginable.

"Yes, she's a fine woman, our Pasca, and no doubt about it—even if she has only got one eye. How about another little glass?" spoke up a bearded man, slapping the hostess on the shoulder.

"Smurov, Orsini, run back up there for me; I've forgotten my parasol. You're the last ones, we'll wait for you! Eh? What's that? Parasol, parasol!" shouted Mme. Monier from the front carriage, reining in the donkeys and turning her face toward them, hideous, pink and smiling, and framed in wind-blown gingery locks.

The tavern was empty; the uncleared table, the pushed-back benches and chairs bore witness to the recently departed visitors, and from a curtained recess which hid a bed came sighs and muffled whispering.

"Is anyone there?" shouted Orsini from the threshold, "The *signora* left her parasol behind. Have you seen it?"

There were whispers behind the curtain; then Pasca emerged, still straightening her grubby skirt; divested of kerchief and bodice, bony and tanned, she seemed, for all her youth, a creature of terrifying antiquity. Without a word, she pointed to a white-handled parasol of frothy lace edged with a faint yellow design which stood in a corner of the room. From behind the curtain, a man's voice shouted, "Pasca, hey, Pasca, are you coming? Have they gone now?"

"Just a minute," the woman answered hoarsely and, going up to the broken piece of mirror which adorned the wall, she pushed into her dishevelled hair the red carnation left behind by Orsini.

* * *

They were almost the only ones in the theater to be so engrossed in Isolde's outpourings to Brangane that they failed to notice the royal party's entrance into the box directly facing the stage. Responding to the welcoming huzzas of the audience with an awkward bow, the king lowered himself into a chair in the front of the box with a bored, official look; a small man with a large head and a moustache, he wore an expression at once sentimental and cruel. Performance or no, the house was brightly lit; ladies in décolletage with necklaces of precious stones sat with their backs half-turned to the stage, exchanging smiles and gossip, while their escorts, flowers in their button-holes, languid and irreproachably correct, went from box to box paying visits. Ice cream was brought round, and middle-aged gentlemen sat in the depths of their boxes reading newspapers held open in front of them.

Sitting between Stroop and Orsini, Vanya was unaware of the whispering and commotion around him, so completely were his thoughts taken up with Isolde as she imagined the sound of hunting horns in the rustling of leaves.[6]

"There's the apotheosis of love for you! Take away night and death, and it would be the greatest of all songs of passion; the melodic line and the conception of the entire scene have such a feeling of ritual about them—it's like some marvelous hymn!" said Ugo to Vanya, who had turned deathly pale.

Stroop kept his opera glasses fixed on the box across from them. There, in intimate proximity, sat the fair-haired artist and a small woman with hair of a brilliant black, which fell in waves about her pallid, unrouged face; her large mouth was painted a bright red, her eyes, enormous and almost colorless, were like standing pools. Dressed in a bright yellow gown trimmed with gold, she looked flashy and pretentious; the insane audacity of the woman was evident in the very angle of her upturned chin. And Vanya listened mechanically to tales of the adventures of this Veronica Cibo—an interweaving of the names of the men and women who had perished because of her.

"She's an utterly unprincipled woman!" Ugo's voice carried through the din, "She'd have been at home in the sixteenth century."

"Oh, that's too fancy for her—call her a trollop and have done with it!" and the coarsest names fell from the lips of the irreproachably correct gentlemen as they stared lustfully at the yellow gown and the depraved mermaiden eyes.

Whenever Vanya had occasion to turn to Stroop with some innocuous question, he would blush and smile; it was as if he were uttering the first conciliatory words after a stormy quarrel or speaking with someone just recovering from a long illness.

"I keep thinking of Tristan and Isolde," said Vanya, strolling with Orsini along the corridor. "It's supposed to be the ideal portrayal of love, the apotheosis of passion, but really, if you look at it objectively and think how it ends, doesn't it come to much the same as that episode in the tavern at il Giogo?"

"I'm not sure I understand what you mean. Does the presentation of carnal union embarrass you?"

---

[6] In Wagner's opera (Act II, Scene I), it is Brägane who hears the huntsmen's horns, while Isolde, in ecstatic anticipation of Tristan's arrival, insists that it is only the rustling of leaves (Eds.).

"No, but in any real-life action there's always something ludicrous and base. Didn't Tristan and Isolde have to unbutton their clothes and take them off? And weren't capes and hose as lacking in poetry in those days as jackets are now?"

"Oh, what thoughts the boy has! That's really funny!" Orsini stared at Vanya and burst out laughing. "That's how it always is; I don't see what's troubling you."

"If the basic act is always the same, what difference does it make how you arrive at it—through universal love or animal impulse?"

"What are you saying? Can this be Canon Mori's friend talking? It goes without saying that facts in themselves, mere physical occurrences, are unimportant; it's one's attitude to them that's important—and the most mortifying fact, the most unlikely situation can be justified and purified by one's attitude toward it," said Orsini earnestly, almost as if he were delivering a lecture.

"Perhaps that's true, even if it does sound a bit didactic," remarked Vanya with a smile, and sitting down beside Stroop, he gave him a searching sidelong glance.

*   *   *

They arrived rather early at the station to see off Mme. Monier, who was planning to spend a couple of weeks in Brittany before going on to Paris. The globes of the electric street lamps glowed white against the pale yellow sky, cries of *"pronti, partenza"* rang out, passengers were fussing to get seats on the earlier trains, and from the buffet came a neverending din of shouted orders and tinkling spoons. They drank coffee as they waited for the train to come in; a bouquet of Gloire de Dijon roses lay on an open *Figaro*, next to Mme. Monier's gloves. The lady herself was sitting calmly in a maize-colored dress adorned with pale yellow ribbons, while her escorts traded witticisms about the political news which they had just read, when Veronica Cibo appeared at a neighboring table. She was dressed for a journey and her face was hidden by a green veil. With her was the artist, valise in hand, followed by porters carrying luggage.

"Look, they're leaving! There's no hope for him now!" said Ugo, retreating to his party after greeting the artist.

"Where are they going? Is the man blind? She's vile, utterly vile!"

Cibo lifted her veil, pale and defiant, and without a word indicated where the porter should set their things down. The hand which she laid on her companion's sleeve seemed to claim him as her property.

"Look—there's Blonskaya. How did she find out? I don't envy her or Cibo either," whispered Mme. Monier, as another woman, dressed in grey from head to toe, walked quickly toward the artist, who was sitting with his back to her, while his companion fixed the newcomer with a blank, unflinching stare. She went up to him and began quietly in Russian:

"Seryozha, where are you going? And why have you kept this from me, from all of us? Aren't we your friends? This will be the end for you—I know it. Is it something I've done? Is there some way I can make amends?"

"What is there to make amends for?"

Cibo continued to stare fixedly at Blonskaya, as if she were looking right through her.

"Will you stay if I agree to marry you? You know that I love you."

"No, I don't want anything!"—the surly reply was snapped out, as if the speaker were afraid of weakening.

"Is there nothing to be done? Is this your last word?"

"Perhaps. Things often happen too late."

"Seryozha, take hold of yourself! Come back with me, or you'll lose every-thing—your art, everything!"

"What's the good of talking? It's too late to set things to rights, and besides, this is what I want!"—the artist suddenly raised his voice to a near-shout. Cibo shifted her gaze to him.

"No, this isn't what you want," said Blonskaya.

"Do you think I don't know my own mind?"

"No, you don't. You're just like a little boy, Seryozha!"

Cibo rose to follow the porter who was carrying her luggage and turned silently to her companion; he got up and put on his coat without answering Blon-skaya.

"So you're really leaving then, Seryozha?"

Mme. Monier, twittering excitedly, had bade her friends goodbye, and her gingery head could now be seen through the car window, nodding behind her bouquet of Gloire de Dijon roses. On their way back they saw Blonskaya as she hurried past, a gray figure, leaning heavily on her parasol.

"It was like being at a funeral," remarked Vanya.

"There are people who seem forever to be attending their own funerals," an-swered Stroop, staring straight ahead.

"When an artist is lost, it's a tragic thing."

"There are others, artists of life, whose loss is no less tragic."

"And sometimes there are things which it is too late to do," added Vanya.

"Yes, sometimes there are things which it is too late to do," repeated Stroop.

◊ ◊ ◊

They entered a low-ceilinged, cell-like room illuminated only by the light which streamed through the open door. Inside, the old cobbler sat hunched over a boot, his round spectacles perched on the end of his nose, like a painting by Dou. It was pleasantly cool inside after the sunny street, and the smell of leather mingled with that of jasmine, a bottle containing several sprigs of which stood on the top shelf of a cupboard lined with boots, just below the ceiling. The cobbler's apprentice stared at the canon, who sat with feet spread wide, mopping the sweat from his brow with a silk handkercheif, while old Giuseppe held forth good-naturedly in his lilting voice:

"What am I, gentlemen? Just a poor craftsman—but some of us are artists, real artists! Oh, it's not as easy as you might think to sew boots according to the rules of art. You've got to study and know the foot you're sewing for; you've got to know where the bone is broader and where it's narrower, where the corns are, where the arch is higher than it ought to be. No man's foot is like another's, you know, and only an ignoramous would say that a boot's a boot and good for any foot. Ah, you should just see some feet, *signori!* And all of them have to walk somehow. All the Good Lord said was that feet should have five toes and a heel, and the rest can be as it likes, do you get me? And even if someone's got six toes, or four, the Good Lord gave him feet like that, and he has to walk on them, just like other folk walk on theirs. A master cobbler's got to know that and help as best he can."

The canon noisily gulped chianti from a sturdy glass and kept flapping his broad-brimmed black hat to drive away the flies which continually alighted on his sweat-beaded brow; the apprentice never took his eyes off him, while Giuseppe's words flowed over them, smooth and lilting, inducing drowsiness.

As they were crossing the cathedral square on their way to Giotto's, a restaurant frequented by the clergy, they encountered old Count Guidetti, rouged and be-wigged, supported on either side by a young girl of modest, even staid, appearance. Vanya recalled the stories he had heard about this decrepit creature and his so-called "nieces," and about the stimulants needed to titillate the jaded senses of this old profligate with his cadaverous, painted face and eyes which sparkled with wit and intelligence. He remembered the old man's talk, the never-ending stream of paradoxes, witticisms and anecdotes, the vanishing legacy of an irrecoverable past, which poured from the old man's mumbling lips, and he seemed to hear Giuseppe saying, "And if someone's got six toes, or four, the Good Lord gave him feet like that, and he has to walk on them, just like other folk walk on theirs."

"The walls, the very stones blushed when the count was on trial," said Mori, turning left to enter a room filled with black-clad figures and a scattering of laity—those who wished to observe the Friday fast. A middle-aged Englishwoman was speaking to a beardless youth in strongly-accented French:

"We converts have a greater love for, a more conscious understanding of the beauty and attraction of the Catholic faith—of its rites, its dogmas and its disciplines."

"The poor woman," explained the canon, placing his hat on the wooden bench next to him, "she's from a family of wealth and position—and now she lives in poverty and has to go round giving lessons because she has come to know the true faith and everyone has washed their hands of her."

"Risotto! Three portions!"

"There were more than three hundred of us when we left Pontassieve— there's never any lack of pilgrims going to the Annunziata."

"Saint George! With him and the Archangel Michael and the Holy Virgin— with such protectors as that—one need have no fear of anything!"—the Englishwoman's accented speech faded into the general hubbub.

✧   ✧   ✧

"He was a native of Bithynia; Bithynia—the Switzerland of Asia Minor, with its verdant mountains, alpine streams and pastures; he had been a shepherd there before Hadrian took him to live with him. He travelled everywhere with his emperor, and it was on one such journey that he died in Egypt. There were vague rumors that he had drowned himself in the Nile as a sacrifice to the gods for the life of his protector; others asserted that he drowned while trying to save Hadrian. At the hour of his death, the astronomers discovered a new star in the heavens. His death, with its aura of mystery, and his remarkable beauty, which had breathed life into a decaying art, had an effect which was not limited to the court. The inconsolable emperor, wishing to do homage to his favorite, elevated him to the pantheon of the gods, instituted games, built palaestrae and temples in his honor, and oracula where he himself, in the early days, wrote responses in archaic verse. But it would be a mistake to think that the new cult was disseminated by force and only among those attached to the court, that it was a mere official observance which died with its founder. Even centuries later we find sects dedicated to Diana and Antinous; as well as conducting modest religious rites, a sect would bury its members and arrange communal feasts. The members of these sects—prototypes of the earliest Christian communities—belonged to the poorest class; the charter of one of these groups has come down to us in full. Thus, with the passing of time the deified favorite of the emperor took on the aspect of a nocturnal deity associated with the afterlife, and, while not as widespread as the cult of Mithras, the worship of Antinous has remained one of the most powerful manifestations of the religion of the deified man."

The canon closed his notebook, and, peering at Vanya over his spectacles, remarked:

"The morals of the pagan emperors do not concern us, my child, but I cannot conceal from you that Hadrian's relationship with Antinous was far from being one of paternal devotion."

"What made you decide to write about Antinous?" asked Vanya, without looking at the canon; his thoughts were elsewhere, and the question was perfunctory.

"I read to you what I wrote this morning; the Roman caesars are my field of study."

It struck Vanya as funny that the canon might find himself writing about Tiberius' life on Capri; unable to restrain himself, he asked:

"Have you written about Tiberius, *cher père?*"

"Of course."

"And about his life on Capri—you remember how Suetonius describes it?"

Touched on a sore spot, Mori began heatedly:

"You're right, my friend, that was terrible, terrible! Only Christianity, only that sacred teaching, could have saved mankind from perdition and dragged it out of that cesspool."

"But your attitude to the Emperor Hadrian is more favorable?"

"That's a different matter, my friend; there was something noble in that, although I must emphasize that it was a terrible perversion of feeling—one, however, which even those enlightened by baptism were not always able to resist."

"But isn't it all essentially one and the same thing?"

"You're laboring under a terrible delusion, my son. What is important in every action is one's attitude toward it, its aim and also the reasons behind it; actions in themselves are merely the mechanical movements of our bodies and cannot offend anyone, much less the Good Lord," and he again opened his notebook at the place held by his fat thumb.

✿   ✿   ✿

They were walking along the road which followed the far side of the Cascine; through the trees they could see meadows dotted with farms and a range of low mountains beyond. They passed a restaurant, deserted at that time of day, and walked on through a region which grew ever more rustic. Here and there, a shiny-buttoned watchman would be sitting on a bench, and in the distance boys in cassocks frolicked under the watchful eye of a plump abbot.

"I'm so grateful that you agreed to come," said Stroop, lowering himself to a bench.

"If we're going to talk, we'd better do it walking: I think better that way," observed Vanya.

"An excellent idea."

And they began to walk, now pausing, now moving forward again through the trees.

"Why did you deprive me of your friendship? Was it because you thought me to blame for the death of Ida Holberg?"

"No."

"Why then? I'd like an honest answer."

"You shall have it: it was because of your affair with Fyodor."

"Is that it?"

"I know what was going on—you can't deny it."

"I admit I can't."

"Now, perhaps, my attitude would be quite different, but at the time I didn't know very much and had given things very little thought. It was very painful for me, I must confess, because I thought I was losing you forever, and with you, the path to the beautiful in life."

Circling a glade, they continued to follow the same path, and the laughter of children playing ball came to them remotely.

"Tomorrow I'm supposed to be going to Bari, but I could stay; it depends on you: if your answer is no, send me a note saying 'go'; if it's yes, then write 'stay.' "

"What do you mean, 'no' or 'yes?' " asked Vanya.

"Would you like me to spell it out for you?"

"No, don't, I understand; but is this really necessary?"

"It has become unavoidable. I'll wait until one o'clock."

"I'll give you my answer, one way or the other."

"Just one more little effort and you'll grow wings. I can see them already."

"Perhaps—but the growing can be very painful," said Vanya with a wry grin.

✿   ✿   ✿

They sat talking late on the balcony. Vanya was surprised to find himself listening to Ugo with carefree attention, as if it were not the next day that he had to let Stroop have his answer. The unsettled nature of the situation, of his feelings and ties, held a certain pleasure for him, a kind of airy desperation. Ugo was speaking fervently:

"It doesn't have a name yet. The first scene: a gray sea, cliffs, a golden sky beckoning from afar, the argonauts in quest of the golden fleece—everything will be startling in its boldness and originality, but at the same time you will know it as the dear and timeless land of your longing. The second scene—Prometheus, condemned to his chains: 'None shall penetrate nature's mysteries and break her laws unpunished, and only the incestuous parricide shall guess the riddle of the sphinx.' Pasiphae appears, blinded with lust for the bull, terrible, and prophetic: 'I see neither the diversity of chaotic existence nor the harmony of divine visions!' All recoil in horror. Then the third: the Elysian Fields, with scenes from the Metamorphoses—the gods assuming all sorts of shapes for the sake of love. Icarus falls, and Phaethon after him; Ganymede speaks: 'My poor brothers, of all who sought to fly up to the heavens and only I have remained, for it was pride and childish curiosity which lured you toward the sun, while I was lifted up in the beating wings of a love beyond mortal ken.' Great fiery, visionary blooms burst open; birds and beasts go two by two, and through a palpitating rosy mist we see the forty-eight positions of human coupling from the Indian *manuels érotiques*. And everything begins spinning in a double orbit, each in its own sphere, in ever-widening circles, faster and faster, until all outlines merge into one and the whole whirling mass takes shape, becoming suddenly still above the glistening sea and the treeless, yellow, sun-beaten cliffs as the colossal, radiant figure of Zeus-Dionysus-Helios!"

After a sleepless night, he got up exhausted and with an aching head. He washed and dressed with studied deliberation. Without opening the blind, he went over to the desk, upon which stood a glass of flowers, and slowly traced the word "go"; after a moment's thought, still with the same sleepy expression, he added, "and take me with you." Then he threw open the window onto a street flooded with sunlight.

✻   ✻   ✻

STORIES

AUNT SONYA'S SOFA

I dedicate this true story to my sister.

It's so long that I've been standing in the storeroom, surrounded by all kinds of junk, that I have only the dimmest recollections of my young days, when the Turk with a pipe and the shepherdess with a little dog scratching itself for fleas, hind leg raised, all of them embroidered on my spine, gleamed in bright hues—yellow, pink and sky-blue—as yet unfaded and undimmed by dust; and so what occupies my thoughts now more than anything else are the events to which I was witness before once more being consigned to oblivion, this time, I fear, for ever. They had me covered in a wine-colored silken material, stood me in the passageway and threw over my arm a shawl with a pattern of bright roses, as if some beauty from the days of my youth, disturbed at a tender tryst, had left it behind in her flight. I should add that this shawl was always carefully draped in exactly the same way, and if the General, or his sister, Aunt Pavla, happened to disturb it, Kostya, who had arranged this part of the house to his own taste, would restore the folds of the soft, gaily-colored stuff to their former exquisite casualness. Aunt Pavla protested against my disinterment from the storeroom, saying that poor Sophie had died on me, that someone or other's wedding had been upset because of me, that I brought the family misfortune; however, not only was I defended by Kostya, his student friends and the other young people, but even the General himself said:

"That's all prejudice, Pavla Petrovna! If that old monstrosity ever had any magic power in it, sixty years in the storeroom should have taken care of that; besides, it's standing in the passageway—no one's likely to die or propose on it there!"

Although I wasn't very flattered to be called a "monstrosity," and the General proved to be less than a prophet, I did at any rate establish myself as part of the passageway with the greenish wallpaper, where I stood faced by a china cabinet, over which hung an old round mirror, dimly reflecting my occasional visitors.

There lived in General Gambakov's house, in addition to his sister Pavla and his son Kostya, his daughter Nastya, a student at the institute for young ladies.

✻   ✻   ✻

The next room had a westerly outlook, and so admitted into my passageway the long rays of the evening sun; they would strike the rose-patterned shawl, making it glint and shimmer more enchantingly than ever. At this moment, these rays were falling across the face and dress of Nastya, who was sitting on me; she seemed so fragile that I almost thought it strange that the ruddy light did not pass through her body, which hardly seemed a sufficient obstacle to it, and fall on her companion. She was talking to her brother about the Christmas theatricals, as part of which they were planning to put on an act from "Esther;" it seemed, however, that the girl's thoughts were far from the subject of the conversation. Kostya remarked:

"I think we could use Seryozha too—his accent is pretty good."

"Are you suggesting that Sergey Pavlovich should play a young Israelite girl—one of my handmaidens?"

"Why that? I can't bear *travesti* roles—not that he wouldn't look good in a woman's costume."

"Well, what other part is there for him to play?"

I knew at once that they were talking about Sergey Pavlovich Pavilikin, young Gambakov's friend. To me he had always seemed an insignificant boy, in spite of his striking good looks. His close-cropped dark hair emphasized the fullness of his round, strangely bloodless face; he had a pleasing mouth and large, pale-gray eyes. His height enabled him to carry off an inclination to plumpness, but he was certainly very heavy, always collapsing onto me and scattering me with ash from the *papirosy* with very long mouthpieces which he smoked one after another; and nothing could have been more empty-headed than his conversation. He came to the house almost every day, notwithstanding the displeasure of Pavla Petrovna, who could not abide him.

After a silence the young lady began hesitantly:

"Do you know Pavilikin well, Kostya?"

"What a question! He's my best friend!"

"Is he?...But you haven't been friends all that long, have you?"

"Ever since I began attending university this year. But what difference does that make?"

"None, of course. I just asked because I wanted to know...."

"Why do you find our friendship so interesting?"

"I would like to know whether one can trust him.... I'd like to...."

Kostya's laughter interrupted her.

"It depends what with! In monetary affairs I wouldn't advise it!…All the same, he's a good friend, and no skinflint when he's in funds—but you know he's poor.…"

Nastya said after a pause:

"No, I didn't mean that at all—I meant in matters of feeling, affection."

"What nonsense! What on earth do they put into your heads at those institutes? How should I know?!.. Have you fallen for Seryozha or something?"

The young lady continued without answering:

"I want you to do something for me. Will you?"

"Is it to do with Sergey Pavlovich?"

"Perhaps."

"Well, all right—though you'd better not forget that he's not much of a one for wasting time on young ladies."

"No, Kostya, you have to promise me!…"

"I've said I'll do it, haven't I? Well?"

"I'll tell you this evening," announced Nastya solemnly, looking into her brother's uneasily shifting eyes, eyes which, like hers, were hazel flecked with gold.

"Whenever you like—now, this evening," said the young man unconcernedly, as he got up and readjusted the rose-patterned shawl which the girl had released as she too rose.

But no ray of the evening sun gleamed on the tender roses because Nastya had gone into the next room and taken up a position at the window, as impenetrable to the ruddy light as before; she stood there gazing at the snow-covered street until the electric lights were lit.

❊ ❊ ❊

Today I simply haven't had a moment's quiet—such comings and goings all day, and all through my passageway! And what's the point of all these amateur theatricals—that's what I'd like to know. A swarm of young misses and young men—lord knows who they all are—bustling about, yelling, running, calling for some peasants or other to saw through something or other, dragging about furniture, cushions, lengths of cloth; it's a mercy they didn't start taking things from the passage—why, they might even have carried off my shawl! At last things quieted down and a piano began to play somewhere far off. The General and Pavla Petrovna emerged cautiously and sat down beside each other; the old maid was saying:

"If she falls in love with him, it will be a family misfortune. Just think of it— a mere boy, and worse than that—with no name, no fortune, absolutely nothing to offer!…"

"It seems to me you're very much exaggerating all this—I haven't noticed anything...."

"When did men ever notice such things? But I, for one, will fight against it to the bitter end."

"I shouldn't think things will ever reach the point where you have to be for or against."

"And he has absolutely no morals at all: do you know what they say about him? I'm convinced that he's corrupting Kostya too. Nastya's a child, she doesn't understand anything," fulminated the old lady.

"Well, my dear, and whom don't they talk about? You should hear the gossip about Kostya! And it wouldn't surprise me if some of these fairy tales didn't have a grain of truth in them. Only age can protect you from gossip—as the two of us ought to know!..."

Pavla Petrovna blushed crimson and said curtly:

"You do as you wish; at least I've warned you. And *I* shall certainly be on my guard—Nastya is my blood too, you know!"

At this moment Nastya herself entered, already dressed in her costume for the play—pale blue with yellow stripes, with a yellow turban.

"Papa," she began breathlessly, turning to the General, "why aren't you watching the rehearsals?"—and without waiting for a reply she rushed on, "What about lending our emperor your ring? It has such a huge emerald!"

"You mean this one?" asked the old man in surprise, showing an antique ring of rare workmanship, set with a dark emerald the size of a large gooseberry.

"Yes, that one!" answered the young lady, not at all disconcerted.

"Nastya, you don't know what you're asking!" her aunt intervened. "A family heirloom which Maksim never parts with, and you want him to let you take it to that madhouse of yours where you'll lose it in no time? You know your father never takes it off his finger!"

"Well, it's only once or twice, and even if someone does drop it, it's sure to be somewhere in the room...."

"No, Maksim, I absolutely forbid you to take it off!"

"You see, Aunt Pavla won't let me!" said the old General with an embarrassed laugh.

Nastya stalked out crossly without the ring, and Pavla Petrovna set about comforting her brother, who was upset to see his daughter disappointed.

And again there was hubbub, rushing about, changing of clothes, leavetaking.

Mr. Pavilikin remained in the house a long time. When he and Kostya came into my passageway it was nearly four o'clock in the morning. Coming to a standstill, they kissed each other good-bye. Sergey Pavlovich said in an embarrassed voice:

"You don't know how happy I am, Kostya! But I feel so uncomfortable that this should have happened today of all days, after you had let me have that money! Lord knows what awful things you might think...."

Kostya, pale, his eyes shining with happiness, his hair rumpled, again kissed his friend, and said:

"I won't think anything at all, you idiot! It's simply coincidence, chance—something that could happen to anyone."

"Yes, but I feel awkward, so awkward...."

"Don't say another word about it, please—you can let me have it back in the spring...."

"It was just that I needed those six hundred roubles desperately...."

Kostya made no rejoinder. After a little while he said:

"Good-bye, then. Don't forget you're going to "Manon" with me tomorrow."

"Yes, of course!..."

"And not with Petya Klimov?"

"O, *tempi passati!* Good-bye!"

"Close the door gently, and tread softly when you go past Aunt Pavla's bedroom: she didn't see you come back, and you know she doesn't much care for you. Good-bye!"

The young men embraced once more; as I said before, it was nearly four o'clock in the morning.

✿　✿　✿

Without taking off her rose-trimmed fur hat after the ride, Nastya sat down on the edge of the chair, while her escort kept pacing up and down the room, his cheeks faintly pink from the frost. The girl was chattering gaily away, but underneath the bird-like twitter there lurked a certain unease.

"Wasn't that a glorious ride! Frost and sunshine—that's so nice! I adore the embankment!..."

"Yes."

"I love to go horseriding—in the summer I disappear for days on end. You've never visited our place at Svyataya Krucha, have you?"

"No. I prefer to ride in a car."

"You do have bad taste.... You know, don't you, that Svyataya Krucha, Alekseyevskoye and Lgovka are all my personal property—I'm a very good match. And then Auntie Pavla Petrovna is going to leave me everything. You see—I'm advising you to think things over."

"The likes of us mustn't be getting ideas above our station!"

"Where do you pick up these gems of shop-assistants' wisdom?"

Seryozha shrugged and continued his steady pacing back and forth. The young lady made one or two more attempts to start up her twittering, but each time more halfheartedly, like a broken toy, until she at last fell silent; when she spoke again, it was in a sad, gentle voice. Without taking off her hat, she sank back in the chair; as she spoke in the darkened room, she seemed to be addressing a plaint to herself:

"How long it's been since we put on our play! Do you remember? Your entrance.... What a lot has changed since then! You've changed too—I have, everyone has.... I didn't really know you then. You've no idea how much better I understand you than Kostya does! You don't believe it? Why do you pretend to be so slow on the uptake? Would it give you pleasure if I came out and said what is considered humiliating for a woman to say first? You're tormenting me, Sergey Pavlovich!"

"How dreadfully you exaggerate everything, Nastasya Maksimovna—my dimness of wit, my pride, and even, perhaps, your feelings for me...."

She stood up and said almost soundlessly:

"Do I? Perhaps...."

"Are you going?"—he was suddenly alert.

"Yes, I have to change for dinner. You're not dining with us?"

"No, I'm invited somewhere."

"With Kostya?"

"No. Why do you ask that?"

She was standing by the table with the magazines, reluctant to leave the room.

"Are you going to him now?"

"No, I'm leaving straight away."

"Are you? Good-bye, then! And I love you—there!" she added suddenly, turning away. No word came from him in the darkness which hid his face from her, and she threw in laughingly (or that was the effect she intended), "Well, are you satisfied now?"

"Surely you don't think that's the word I would choose?" he said, bending over her hand.

"Good-bye. Go now,"—the words came from her as she left the room.

Seryozha turned on the light and began walking in the direction of Kostya's room, whistling cheerfully.

❀   ❀   ❀

The General was pacing about holding a newspaper; he seemed very upset about something. Pavla Petrovna was following him about the room in a rustle of black silk.

"You mustn't let it upset you, Maksim! It happens so often these days that you almost get used to it. Of course, it's dreadful, but what can we do about it? It's no good kicking against the pricks, as they say."

"It's no good, Pavla, I just can't reconcile myself to the thought of it: all that was left was his cap and a mess of blood and brains on the wall. Poor Lev Ivanovich!"

"Don't think about it, brother! Tomorrow we'll have a funeral mass said for him at Udely. Put it out of your mind, think of your own well-being—you have a son and daughter of your own to worry about."

The General, red in the face, sank down onto me, letting fall his newspaper; the old lady, nimbly picking it up and placing it out of her brother's reach, made haste to change the subject:

"Well, did you find the ring?"

The General again displayed signs of uneasiness:

"No, no, I haven't. That's another thing I'm terribly worried about."

"When do you last remember having it?"

"I showed it to Sergey Pavlovich this morning on this very sofa; he seemed most interested…. Then I dozed off—when I woke up it had gone, I remember that…."

"Did you take it off?"

"Yes…."

"That was ill-advised of you. Quite apart from it's cash value, as a family heirloom it's priceless."

"I'm sure it means some misfortune is in store for us."

"Let's hope that Lev Ivanovich's death is misfortune enough for the time being."

The General heaved a deep sigh. Pavla Petrovna pressed on relentlessly:

"Did Pavilikin take it with him, I wonder. That's just the sort of thing I'd expect of him."

"Why should he have? He had such a good look at it—and he asked how much a dealer would give for it and all that."

"Well, perhaps he just took it."

"Stole it—is that what you're trying to say?"

Pavla Petrovna had no chance to reply: the conversation was interrupted by Nastya, who came rushing excitedly into the room.

"Papa!" she cried, "Sergey Pavlovich has proposed to me; I hope you're not opposed to the idea?"

"Not now, not now!"—the General waved her away.

"And why not? Why put it off? You know him pretty well by now," said Nastya, reddening.

Pavla Petrovna rose to her feet:

"I have a voice in this matter too, and I am opposed to the match under any circumstances; at the very least I demand that we postpone this discussion until Maksim's ring is found."

"What has papa's ring to do with my fiancé?" asked the girl haughtily.

"We think Sergey Pavlovich has the ring."

"You think he has committed a theft?"

"You could put it like that."

Nastya turned to the General without answering her aunt, and said:

"And do you believe this fairy tale?"

Her father said nothing, redder in the face than ever.

The girl again turned to Pavla:

"Why are you standing between us? You hate Seryozha—Sergey Pavlovich—and you invent all sorts of nonsense! And you're trying to set father against Kostya too. What is it you want from us?"

"Nastya, don't you dare, I forbid you!…" said her father, gasping for breath.

Nastya paid him no attention.

"What are you getting in such a rage about? Why can't you wait until the matter is cleared up? Can't you see that it's a matter of principle?"

"I can see that where my fiancé is concerned no one should dare even to suspect such a thing!" shouted Nastya. The General sat in silence, turning redder and redder.

"You're afraid—that's the truth isn't it?"

"There can only be one truth, and I know what it is. And I advise you not to oppose our marriage—or it'll be the worse for you!"

"You think so?"

"I know!"

Pavla gave her a searching look.

"Is there any reason for this hurry?"

"What a nasty mind you have! Kostya!"—Nastya threw herself toward her brother, who had just entered, "Kostya darling, you be the judge! Sergey Pavlovich has proposed to me, and father—Aunt Pavla has him completely under her thumb—won't give his consent until we clear up this business about his ring."

"What the devil is all this?! Do you mean to tell me you're accusing Pavilikin of theft?"

"Yes!" hissed the old lady. "Of course you'll stand up for him, you'll even redeem the ring. There are a few things I could tell about you too! I can hear the doors squeaking from my room when your friend leaves and what you say to each other. Be grateful for my silence!"

Never in all my life have I heard such an uproar, such a scandal, such a torrent of abuse. Kostya banged with his fist and shouted; Pavla appealed for respect to be shown to years; Nastya screamed hysterically…. But all at once everyone fell silent: all the voices, the noise and the shouting, were pierced by the strange animal-like sound emitted by the General, who, silent to this moment, had suddenly risen to his feet. Then he sank back heavily, his face between red and blue, and began to wheeze. Pavla threw herself toward him:

"What's the matter? Maksim, Maksim?"

The General only wheezed and rolled the whites of his eyes, now completely blue in the face.

"Water! Water! He's dying—it's a stroke!" whispered the aunt, but Nastya pushed her aside with the words:

"Let me see to him—I'll undo his collar!" and sank down on her knees before me.

❀   ❀   ❀

Even the passageway was not free of the pervasive smell of incense from the old General's funeral mass; the sound of chanting too could be faintly heard. More than once I had the feeling that they were singing a farewell to me. Ah, how close I was to the truth!

The young men came in, deep in conversation; Pavilikin was saying:

"And then today I received the following note from Pavla Petrovna"—and taking a letter from his pocket, he read it aloud:

"Dear Sir, for reasons which I trust there is no need to go into here, I find your visits at this time, a time so painful to our family, to be undesirable, and I hope that you will not refuse to comport yourself in accordance with our general wish. The future will show whether former relations can be resumed, but in the meantime, I can assure you that Anastasia Maksimovna, my niece, is fully in agreement with me on this matter. Yours, etc."

He looked inquiringly at Kostya, who remarked:

"You know, from her point of view my aunt is right, and I really don't know what my sister will have to say to you."

"But, I mean to say, all because of such a little thing!…"

"Is that what you call papa's death?"

"But it wasn't my fault!"

"Of course it wasn't.… You know, not long ago I read a story in the 'Thousand and One Nights': a man is throwing date stones—a perfectly harmless occupation—and happens to hit a Genii's son in the eye, thus bringing down on his head a whole series of misfortunes. Who can predict the results of our most trivial actions?"

"But the two of us will still see each other, won't we?"

"Oh certainly! I shan't be living with the family any more, and I'm always delighted to see you. What's between us is a bit more permanent than a schoolgirl crush."

"And doesn't have to be afraid of date stones?"

"Precisely...."

Seryozha put his arm round young Gambakov, and they went out of the room together. I was never to see Pavilikin again, as I was to see little of any of the people I had grown familiar with during my final period of grace.

*   *   *

Early next morning some peasants came tramping in; "This one here?" they asked Pavla Petrovna, and set about lifting me. The oldest of them lingered, trying to find out if there was anything else to be sold, but on being assured that there wasn't, he went out after the others.

When they turned me on my side to get me through the doorway, something struck the floor (the carpets having already been taken up in anticipation of summer). One of my bearers picked up the fallen object and handed it to the old lady, saying:

"Now there's a fine ring for you, ma'am. Someone must have dropped it on this here couch, and it must have gone and rolled down inside the covers."

"Good. I'm very much obliged to you!" said Aunt Pavla, turning pale; hastily dropping into her reticule a ring with an emerald like a large gooseberry, she left the room.

June, 1907

A HUNTER'S REPAST

June 4th.

Wouldn't Marie, Claudia, Pyotr Ivanovich and the good baron, to say nothing of the rest of my friends, be surprised if they could see me now? I have a room on the mezzanine with old-fashioned furniture covered in motley chintz. The windows look out onto a large sunny yard surrounded by red stone outbuildings and overgrown with grass. The only things to remind me of myself are the writing paper and envelopes on the desk and a copy of the latest yellow-backed novel. It's so hot I can't move, I don't know why I carted all my dresses here—who is there to show them to? Sergey Ivanovich or Kostya? Alas, the former I find profoundly uninteresting, while the latter is a perfect child, and besides, he gets on my nerves with those decadent airs of his. Country diversions hold little attraction for me, and I occupy my leisure by rummaging through the odds and ends in the library; I've picked out a pile of books, but I'm not likely to get around to reading them. I'm positively stupefied with the heat. I think I'll wear my amethyst brooch to dinner today.

June 7th.

Every mail brings me a letter from Paul. He writes that he's bored without me, but one really can't take him too seriously. I judge by myself: so far I'm perfectly happy, and I think I could live here for a long time without sadness and without joy, without intrigues and dramas, without flirtations and earth-shaking passions. The country has a decidedly calming effect.

June 15th.

I can't understand how Nastya can bear to live in such a hole all the year round, and with a husband like Sergey Ivanovich into the bargain. He's a fine enough figure of a man, and he has beautiful eyes—but what a bear! Besides, how can one love a man who gets up at the crack of dawn and is always busy with his farming, who spends his leisure wandering about the woods with a gun and goes to bed hardly later than ten? Well, of course he does get up at five.

June 16th.

Today I had a long talk with Nastya about the old days when her father was alive and they lived in Petersburg. It seems as though a dozen years have passed since then, but actually it's only been two. Time doesn't fly at nearly such a rate as people say. I think Nastya isn't as bright as she used to be—there's no other way I can explain her devotion to Sergey Ivanovich. Such an anxious note creeps into her voice whenever she speaks of him. I do hope Nastya doesn't think she has cause to be afraid of me. Kostya went riding; he's a pretty fellow and looks younger than his twenty-four years; and there's no denying that boots and breeches do wonders for a man's figure. It must be a week since I last wrote to Paul; it's horrid of me, I know, but somehow I've let things slide lately. Sometimes I can't even be bothered to change for dinner.

June 25th.

Marvelous! Sergey Ivanovich is apparently not indifferent to me. At least yesterday, when we were all turning in for the night and I had just started up the stairs to my mezzanine room, he came after me and whispered, "Sofia Nikolayevna, can't you see how I'm suffering?"

He had the most absurd whipped-dog look—and he was breathing so heavily that the candle I was holding almost went out. At first I honestly didn't understand what he meant, and asked in all sincerity, "Whatever is the matter?" He buried his face in his hands and mumbled, "Can't you see I'm hopelessly in love with you, like a foolish boy?" "What are you saying?" I exclaimed, hastily mounting the stairs. Leaving the lamp unlit, I sat down at the window; going over the past few days in my mind, I became convinced that it was only my lack of attentiveness which had prevented me from noticing Sergey Ivanovich's feelings. Lately, whenever he's at home, he's always at my side, he pays me all kinds of little attentions, never takes his eyes off me, and, busy as he is, occasionally takes a stroll with me in the garden as far as the pond and back again. Who would have thought that such a bear-like exterior could conceal such a tender heart! Catching the sound of heavy foot-steps in the bushes under my window, I put my head out into the bushes under my window, I put my head out into the darkness and whispered, "Is that you, Vasili?" Vasili was their gardener; of course I knew very well that it wasn't Vasili who was moving about in the garden, and my supposition was correct, because Sergey Ivanovich's voice rang out in reply to my whisper. Leaning out, I said with gentle firmness, "Go to bed, my friend. You see, I'm not angry with you—I'm worried about you." With a shout of joy, he leapt toward the window, but I slammed it shut and blew out the candle, so that the darkness became impenetrable…Well, isn't that just like a chapter out of a novel?

June 29th.

Lately, we've been behaving as though we'd had a quarrel: we never look each other in the eye, we avoid being left alone together, we are constrained and hardly ever speak, so that every word, every gesture, takes on a new significance. I've been taking a close look at him. There's no arguing that Sergey Ivanovich has his own special kind of charm. Actually, it's the boyishness and naive goodheartedness of this grown-up child that amaze me most. It's almost timidity. He wouldn't think twice about stopping a runaway troika at full gallop, but he blushes and shuffles his feet like a schoolboy whenever he's obliged to pass me a cup or plate at the table. I don't think his tender feelings have gone unnoticed—Kostya has already begun dropping transparent hints. This is all the more unpleasant for me because Kostya is an incredible chatterbox, and the last thing I would want is for Nastya to guess what's going on inside her husband. I'll have to have a talk with the boy tomorrow and see if I can't play the coquette with him. On second thoughts, that might spoil everything, as if I were making too much of the whole affair. I'll leave everything in God's hands and won't breathe a word. I've forgotten when I last wrote to Paul. You'd think I'd fallen in love myself.

June 30th.

Today the whole household went over to a neighbor's to finish up the nameday party leftovers. I'm no great devotee of such amusements, and I'd intended to let this cup pass, picturing to myself how I would spend the whole day on my own, curled up on the sofa with a book. But Sergey Ivanovich gave me such a piteous, pleading look, that I couldn't bring myself to gratify my wish. Perhaps that was stupid of me, all the more since, as it turned out, my act of self-sacrifice was insufficiently appreciated. I rode with Kostya. Every now and then the other carriage would pass us, and through the cloud of dust I would catch a glimpse of Nastya's big hat and her husband's happy, smiling face. I had no idea that the countryside around here was so beautiful. Of course, I'm making it all sound too idyllic, but our drive along the edge of the forest, following the steep green bank of a swirling stream, with villages, meadows and hills (burial mounds, perhaps) beyond, produced a decidedly pleasant impression. My companion kept me entertained with literary and social chat. I must confess that in large doses I find this of little interest, and besides, none of our writers really knows how to write— it's as if they were aiming their stuff at schoolgirls and midwives. In the theater it's as much as you can do to sit a play through, and when the impulse to put a book down is so easily yielded to, it's no wonder that I never finish a single modern book. It was an old house with old-fashioned furniture—but I've had my fill of that lately. Well, of course they plied us with food and drink until we were bursting at the seams. They gave us a tour of the cattlesheds and the greenhouses; we had to go and listen to "the echo" and look at "poet's dell"; we ate wild strawberries with milk. When evening came, the men sat down to cards, while the women got down to domestic tittle-tattle and confidences. I could have predicted the entire program, down to the smallest detail. On the way home, though, I rode with Sergey Ivanovich. The night was as black as pitch; living in Petersburg, one can have no conception of such blackness. All the same, we drove fast, causing birds to flap up from the rye fields in alarm. Sergey Ivanovich gave me his impressions of the evening; he talked animatedly and a note of joy sounded in his voice. At last, having exhausted these reminiscences, he fell silent and heaved a sigh. I pretended not to hear and sat there in silence, when suddenly there came a muffled whisper:

"Well, Sofia Nikolayevna?"

"What do you mean, 'well?'"

"What do you intend to do?"

"About what or who?"

"Well, about your…that is, about my feelings for you?"

"I don't understand what you mean."

"You know how I love you; but what about you—do you love me?"

I said nothing. After waiting a few minutes he repeated his question. My reply was barely audible:

"Yes."

He said, "Thank you," and kissed my hand; in the darkness I felt him embrace me and press his lips to my cheek. I drew away gently and said, "Darling, you mustn't." I remember this evening and our conversation to the last word, to the smallest detail.

They were waiting for us when we got home: the rooms were lit and the samovar was steaming. Without taking off my hat, I began in a loud, cheerful voice:

"Well, Nastya, I have to hand it to that husband of yours! He kept me entertained all the way home with his retelling of the day's events. It was like living through everything twice."

"Now that's not quite fair. I presented everything in a revised and supplemented version," said Sergey, in a voice no less loud and cheerful.

"I never even noticed!" I joked, throwing off my canvas wrap.

Nastya smiled faintly and murmured:

"So you weren't bored."

I gave her a smacking kiss, and we all went in to tea.

July 1st.

What can I say? The inevitable has happened. But why go on about it? I'm terribly happy and have no regrets whatever. I supposed I'm a bit to blame where Nastya is concerned, but it's her fault if she doesn't know how to keep her husband's love. The only thing that bothers me is that Kostya seems to have got wind of something. At least his smiles and ironic glances, his hints and little jokes, make it quite clear that he knows something, but is keeping it to himself out of a sort of disdainful benevolence. At last, I couldn't stand it any longer, and, seizing an opportune moment, I said to him:

"Look here, Konstantin Maksimovich, I've had enough of this."

"Of what, precisely?"

"Of your behavior."

"My behavior?"

"You know very well what I mean."

Kostya shrugged his shoulders and murmured:

"Really, Sofia Nikolayevna, I haven't the slightest notion of what you're talking about."

"Exactly—and that's why I'm asking you not to be so eager to show the world how you feel about something you don't understand."

But of course, we didn't quarrel—it's really rather difficult to quarrel with Kostya Gambakov. He's a good sort at heart, but a frightful tattler and as giddy as they come.

July 4th.

I decided after all to warn Sergey to be more careful. I'm afraid he's terribly thoughtless, and is all for casting discretion to the winds. He gave Kostya a fearful scolding, and he keeps saying awful things about his wife. I put a stop to that, but deep down I was flattered. And besides, I find such rashness difficult to resist.

July 6th.

Today, as we were retiring for the night, Nastya stopped me and said:

"Let's go to your room for a minute; I must talk to you."

"All right," I said, overcome with confusion.

Nastya went into the room and stood with her back to the stove. After what seemed a rather long silence she came right out with it:

"Is Sergey Ivanovich in love with you?"

"In love? With me? I've no idea…Why should he be in love with me?"

"Has Sergey been unfaithful to me?"

"How should I know? Why don't you ask him? What have I to do with it?"

Then she fell to her knees in front of me, and the words came tumbling out:

"Sonya, tell me, I beg of you—has he ever made you a declaration of love? Has he kissed you? Has he made you any promises?"

She was clasping me about the knees and weeping as she gazed up into my eyes. I summoned all my courage and petted and comforted her as best I could. When she had calmed down a little, I said:

"Nastya, do you trust me?"

"Yes," came her barely audible reply.

"Well then, I give you my word that Sergey Ivanovich has said nothing to me, has made me no declaration, hasn't even hinted at anything. I swear to you that as soon as I notice signs of anything even faintly resembling love on his part with regard to myself, I'll tell you about it and be on my way. Now you can sleep soundly."

"Thank you, Sonya, you're a true friend," said Nastya, rising to her feet and kissing me.

I felt utterly crushed and didn't get a wink of sleep all night. When Sergey found out about it all, he flew into a terrible rage and began treating Nastya in a manner which was positively offensive; he never says a civil word to her now. All my remonstrances only make things worse.

July 15th.

It's been more than a week since I've touched this notebook. Nothing has changed: I'm becoming more and more attached to Sergey; he's behaving like a madman; Nastya suffers, but trusts me absolutely; Kostya is bored and spends his time wandering about the garden. Today, as I watched the red calico sunset behind the mill, it occurred to me how much cruelty there is at the heart of every happiness.

July 20th.

Today for the first time the horizon stood out sharp and clear: autumn is approaching. No doubt it's still a good way off and the warm haze will return tomorrow, but the first sign, the first warning of autumn has been given. Sergey and his steward left yesterday evening to go hunting. This is a masculine passion I don't entirely comprehend: to fight your way through thickets, spend the night in a peasant hut, drink vodka and shoot a few miserable ducks—what's so interesting about that? We had breakfast and dinner without Sergey. I was sitting on the garden swing when he returned. Paying no attention to Kostya, who was sitting close by, and throwing caution to the winds, I ran to the back porch in time to meet the returning hunters. He was covered from head to toe in mud, dust and slime, and the crimson blood had already caked on the speckled birds which dangled head downwards from his belt. After a barely mumbled greeting, he shouted for dinner to be served and went off to clean himself up.

He ate alone, as the rest of us had already dined, which did not prevent the entire household from being present at the table; you'd have thought Sergey had just returned from America. I can't stand all this fuss about nothing, and so I sat reading a novel in the next room, acting as if there were nothing out of the ordinary. But Nastya came in and begged me to come and listen to Sergey's stories in such a sweet and touching way that I relented. Hunting tales! I ask you! I burned with shame for Sergey, all the more as Kostya was there too, listening attentively to all that was said and every so often casting a triumphant glance in my direction. I felt like a cat on hot bricks; never have I suffered so. Sergey had evidently worked up quite an appetite—he devoured a chicken, picking it up and tearing the meat from the bone, and then licking his none too clean fingers. Apparently he was not aware of anything untoward, to judge by the way he flung his napkin down on the table, leaned back in his chair, and with a sigh of satisfaction, delivered himself of: "God gave us to eat, our thanks shall be meet—and now, time for beddie-byes."

Nastya gazed adoringly at her husband, delighted that he was out of his sullen mood.

It looks to me as though he's beginning to develop a paunch. My God! My God!

Kostya whispered:

"I understand...Poor Sophie!"

"Leave me alone!" I shouted, not caring who heard.

"What's this? Quarreling?" asked Sergey indifferently as he scraped back his chair and set off for bed.

My God, how humiliating!

July 21st.

This evening I said to Nastya:

"Nastya, let's go into the garden and have a talk."

"What do you have to tell me?" she said anxiously.

"I'm leaving at dawn tomorrow."

"What's the matter? Why?"

"Do you remember the conversation we had?"

"Oh. So that's it?"

"Yes, the time has come."

"How strange that it should happen now, just when I'd begun to set my mind at rest and was least expecting it."

"One can never foresee when these things will happen. Do you think it's easier for me?"

"Forgive me, I was thinking only of myself. You're a saint, Sophie, a real saint, and you have a truly noble heart."

"Enough of that—a fine saint I'd make. Besides, it's about time I was leaving anyway, so this was a happy coincidence—if happy is the right word."

"But you aren't in love with Sergey?"

"No."

"I'll never forget this, Sophie. I'll tell the children to pray for you…"

And bending down, she kissed my hand before I could withdraw it.

July 22nd.

I'm on my way. No one knows I'm leaving, no one is seeing me off. It's as if I were escaping. I'm trying to drive all thoughts of Sergey out of my head. Even when autumn does arrive, I'll still be ashamed to tell people how I was taken in. How could anyone be so naive at twenty-four?

March, 1910

THE HOUSE OF CARDS

CHAPTER ONE

"Who was the third to come in?"

"No one: there are two of us."

"My sweet Mania, emotion is making you see double."

The two gentlemen who had entered and were dressed in identical suits in spite of the difference in color, were caught in the light of five small lamps, bright for the small room with the look of a corridor with four mirrors, in the talk, the shouting, the powder floating in the air, the smoke of cigarettes.

Sitting in front of the mirror, where a little icon of the Holy Virgin hung suspended on a pink ribbon, as if at a young girl's bedside, she cried out into space, not turning her head and applying dark-blue paint to her eyelids.

"Pelageya Petrovna, my sweet, is the pilgrim girl ready for 'The Vain Journey?' Hurry up!"

From somewhere behind the wall, a good way off, voices were raised in response. Artificially enthusiastic voices, not accustomed to these modest premises, again twittered in chorus to greet a tall blond woman with a beautiful, dry, unremarkable face.

"Nadia! What an eternity since we saw each other! You're abandoning us—is it true? You don't play any more?"

"Nadezhda Vasilevna is pleased to be capricious," remarked a gentleman with a long nose and a bored face.

"Not at all. You don't know, Oleg Felixovich, how it all went. You remember the beginning of the scene: I enter with the words: Good evening, good Frau Thekla. Varvara Mikhailovna told me herself…"

"If they've taken the role from me at the dress rehearsal, I just don't know, I'll throw myself into the Moika!" hysterically announced the woman sitting in front of the mirror.

Bells rang out in the corridor, where the noise was quietening down, the curtains swelled.

"Yesterday we drove down from the mountains, and I didn't notice how frostbitten my ear was; it was only when I got home that I found out that it was twenty-three degrees."

"Why are you looking such a birthday boy?"

"I received the very pleasant news that my good friend Myatlev will shortly be coming here from Moscow."

"Really? And soon?"

"Very soon. I'm expecting him tomorrow."

"Are you very pleased?"

"Of course. I'm a great friend of his."

"It's funny, but I already had the idea today that three of you had come to see me."

"That brings to mind the old aria," remarked the elder of the two, who wore a yellow jacket:

"'If we meet a loving couple,
We meet them together with a third.
Who's the third? Love itself'."

"Surely you're not in love?"

"Of course, invariably, only not with each other."

She was already running down the stairs, not listening and singing: "Myatlev's coming, Myatlev's coming."

"Quiet! They're ringing up the curtain!" the assistant poked his head out.

It grew quiet in the wings, and from the stage the voice of the leading actress came strangely to their ears, at once commonplace and thrilling: "If you only knew how blissfully, how uncontrollably the voice of love draws me!.."

The two gentlemen dressed identically, in spite of the difference in the color of their suits, went quietly into the dark pit, which was half empty.

CHAPTER 2

The gray pages of thick letter-paper were quickly covered unceasingly with small, uneven writing. In the large, almost empty room with only books lining the walls, with a window consisting of a single uncurtained pane of glass, in the uncertain light of two candles standing on a small table, two men sat in silence, and only the scraping of a pen reverberated in the air, where dark blue rings floated from the cigarette of the second man.

Pressing a seal with the head of Antinous to the lilac sealing-wax on the engraved envelope, the writer continued to be silent, gazing ahead.

"It's finished; a letter breaking things off," said Demyanov hesitantly and not at once.

"You like taking decisive steps. Tell me, do you never regret them?"

"I'm not taking any steps, everything is happening of its own accord, and like the Egyptians I am inclined to consider regret a mortal sin."

"But I'm very sorry about this spring and summer!"

"Yes," said the first thoughtfully, "How long ago that was!"

"Do you remember our journey to the park?"

"That was when I was temporarily living at your place, and Nalimov was always with us!"

"The trip to the 'Slavyanka'…"

"We came back once; there were four of us, I think, in the one and only cab…"

"And we bought roses on the bridge."

"They were rather faded and shed their petals all over the stairs, along the corridor, in the room, as if strewing our path."

"The next day you were in Sestroretsk."

"That was ages ago, we went swimming twice, but that was without you."

"And then with me."

"There we drank Chablis Mouton Desmoulins."

"We often played *Figaro*…"

"And my departure?"

"Did you suffer very much on the Volga?"

"Dreadfully; do you remember the desperate letter, telegrams, my early arrival?"

"You were very hard to bear with your enamoured egotism."

"Surely you don't prefer me the way I am now—free and lighthearted?"

"For how long?"

"Who knows? Intensity of suffering is a sure sign of love coming to an end; it's some kind of birthpangs, for me personally, of course."

"You've cooled down completely now?"

"I preserve a tender memory, and I know that this body is beautiful, but I'm not in love. And then, I can't want the impossible."

"That's rationalization."

"It's part of my nature. Love comes and goes independently of my will and all at once mercifully pulls the arrow from my heart."

"That's very poetical."

"It's very true and very mysterious."

A maidservant knocked at the door and entered to announce: "For you, Mikhail Alexandrovich."

"Who is it?" asked Demyanov, getting up.

"Petya Smetanin."

Guest and master of the house exchanged glances, and the latter made haste to hide the letter which had just been written, where stood the words: To Pyotr Ivanovich Smetanin. The tall fairhaired young man with a straight, somewhat retrousse nose who entered began to greet them with awkward familiarity.

CHAPTER 3

"If you find it amusing when Matilda sits on your stomach and says she's a chimera, when in one evening you have ten of the silliest tête-á-têtes of the most compromising kind, when you listen to as many as twenty poets—then we've had a very good time. But, between ourselves, all that has palled to a considerable degree."

"Yes, it's very boring."

The gray sunless day fell evenly through the four windows of the big blue-green room. At the big writing table, bent over it, sat Andrei Ivanovich Nalimov, thoughtfully and with concentration putting together some kind of dust-jacket for a new book. Demyanov stood by the window, beyond which was visible a canal which was still not frozen over, infrequent passers-by, a row of old houses on the opposite bank. On the open grand piano lay the score of a work by Grétry. They were silent, like people who were close and accustomed to each other, forgetful of the tea growing cold on the low table.

"You're ungrateful, Nalimov, you don't know how to live."

"That's true, and I'm very weighed down by it, but you—are you really happy?"

"Often—very happy, I'm not now, because I'm not busy with anything."

"You're amazingly frivolous."

"I'm devilishly faithful, while I'm being faithful, but suddenly one wakes up with the feeling that the things one is attached to are utterly alien, remote, unloved."

Nalimov took off his glasses, having finished his work, and listened indifferently, fixing his eyes, sad and intelligent like those of a dog, before him. It was getting more and more dark, and the friends, now sitting on the couch, were hardly visible in the light of the street lamp through the window.

"What boredom!"

"You don't see Petya Smetanin any more?"

"Why shouldn't I? He drops by occasionally. What made you ask that?"

"Nothing in particular. You used to enjoy being with him before."

"Yes."

"You're very unfaithful to your friends."

"A hint with regard to Temirov?"

"You're going to have lunch with us, aren't you? Just father and me, there'll be no outsiders."

"I don't know"—Demyanov's answer came from somewhere right out of the darkness.

A loud ring of the bell forced them to turn on the electricity, which clearly and coldly lit up the two men getting up to greet a young man in uniform, with a fine-drawn face with something unpleasant about it, narrow eyes and large locks of curling hair. They exchanged greetings; clearing his throat a little, he immediately sank down in an armchair in an unattractively languid posture. Interrupting himself, he began several pieces of news, jumping from one thing to another without finishing, hurrying and tiring himself. The two who had been there before listened with a smile to the guttural, agitated speech.

"Where have you come from?" asked Demyanov indifferently. "From them? From the little actresses?"

"What a ghastly thought. Not at all, I was at Matilda Petrovna's about the affairs of the club."

"What has Matilda Petrovna got to do with the club?"

"Oh, how is it that you don't understand? I was on business at first, then at the Sachs woman's."

"What are you mixing things up for?"

"Oh, you're just finding fault. Did you know that Matveyev has arrived? Well, what a victory that is, I congratulate you!"

"What nonsense! And over whom?"

"But you know that Matilda Petrovna is in love with you like…"

"Like a snake?"

CHAPTER 4

In the depths of the long hall decorated with camelias in tubs, gray-green canvasses and pale blue lanterns, on a couch which looked as though it had been prepared for Venus or the Empress Cleopatra, lay the semi-recumbent figure of a gray-haired man proclaiming in a slow, elderly voice, like an archimandrite on Holy Thursday:

"Dear Empress, our Alceste, the entreaties of your sleepless nights have been heard by the gods, the blooming, joyous health of your spouse, the Emperor Admetus, will return."

"Why have you prepared such a poetical couch for him?"

"Well, I didn't know of what age or appearance he was."

Suppressed laughter and whispering resounded from the doorway, where crowded the actresses, not wishing to occupy for a long time seats in front of the honored guests.

Turning his pale face with a glossy forehead such as a corpse has for a moment in the direction of the whispering, turning a page noisily and unhurriedly, the man sitting on the couch began once more.

Past Demyanov, who was also standing by the door, gently pushing the public aside, came a young man with a very pale round unbearded face, dark hair with a rather English look about it; he glanced about himself briefly and sharply with eyes that seemed oddly sightless, and then, pretending to be held up by the crowd, once again turned his round face, which seemed deathly pale in the light of the blue lantern, on Demyanov.

"Who is that?" asked the latter, turning to Nalimov, who was standing beside him.

"I don't know, I'm here for the first time, some actor or other. Ask Temirov."

"Temirov isn't here, you know."

"'Spring', play 'Spring'!" "Mikhail Alexandrovich, your turn"—two actresses of some sort with billowing skirts like the angels of Berlandalo flew past.

The lead actress sat surrounded by poets, smiling nicely when she didn't understand what was said to her by a tall, pink-complexioned man in a pince-nez with an aureole of golden hair, rocking back and forth, now raising himself on tiptoe, now sinking down once more, as if he were performing some dance.

As he played, Demyanov kept seeing, over the heads of others, the pale, round face with seemingly sightless eyes fixed on him. This embarrassed and angered him, and hurriedly finishing a ditty to his own sentimental and frivolous words, he hurriedly went out into the neighboring hall, where those not interested in the reading and music were having a bite of something to eat and chatting.

"May I congratulate you on your success?" called little Wolfram Grigorevich Dachsel from some distance away, munching a sandwich; Demyanov absent-mindedly put something on a plate without answering. The other did not withdraw.

"What's wrong with you, are you mad, or have you had an escapade today? Why are you so *absorbi*?"

"You don't know who that pale gentleman is who was standing by the second window while I was playing, do you?"

"I wasn't in there, you know. Which one? Not that one there?" asked Dachsel, twisting and lifting up his nose, and pointing to a young man with a round face, dark hair, and gray, apparently unseeing eyes, who was pushing his way through the crowd.

"We haven't been introduced. Myatlev, a great admirer of yours," the man said, as if choking, as he came up to Demyanov.

"Really? I'm delighted—Demyanov," he replied, turning somewhat pale.

CHAPTER 5

The newly fallen snow was melting, and a warm, deceptively spring-like day gave the impression of Lent at the cemetery.

On the church portico beggars crowded, and soft, sad singing wafted from the door opened by those entering. Demyanov was following two women over the narrow bridges between the thick-clustered monuments on the right, to a tomb on the left, when suddenly he was brought to a halt by familiar voices, which reached him from a cross-path. Three actresses, still wearing winter gowns, talking exaggeratedly loudly, were making their way through awkwardly, escorted by two men. Mikhail Alexandrovich, hidden by a large monument, heard their incoherent and affected conversation.

"I just adore Chaikovsky's 'Credo'."

"And ever since then they spend all their time in the studio, the two of them together."

"Maybe it's just gossip."

"My dear Manya, not gossip, I assure you, not gossip."

"But was it long ago that he arrived? And such intimacy so soon."

"I think one has to be completely ignorant of Myatlev's reputation to see any danger in this," interjected the masculine voice of a passer-by somewhere on the left.

Demyanov located his ladies behind the grating of a tomb. Raisa was eating a wafer of communion bread on her spread-out dress, while Tatyana Ilinishna was speaking rather softly in a singsong voice: "And what happened then, Rayechka, I'll tell you." Catching sight of the approaching man, she smiled at him without changing the conversation, tucking in her dress so as to clear a space. Raisa listened indifferently, as if to something she knew already, concentratedly munching her communion wafer. She was skinny and unattractive, and had a pointed nose.

"Margarita Ivanovna, Arkady Ilich's widow, was the one she loved most, and the one she treated most gently; and the morning she was to die I'm sitting there in the bedroom, the blinds are down, only the icon lamps are glimmering. Margarita comes in affectionately, asks after her health, about this and that—and there's nothing in reply, she just looks straight ahead and doesn't say anything. Margarita calls out to her: 'What's the matter, dear aunt, don't you recognize me? I'm Margarita, the late Arkady Ilich's widow. Or don't you love me any more?' She suddenly answers quietly: 'I see that you are Margarita, the late Arkady Ilich's widow, and I hear what you are saying, but as for loving, to tell the truth, I don't love you.' Margarita darted toward her: 'What are you saying, auntie? What have I done, how am I at fault?' 'You haven't done anything, you're not at fault in any way, but love is from the Lord; it comes and it goes like a thief in the night. I love Semyonushka now.' We can't believe our ears. We've never had a Semyonushka, apart from the shop boy, and his granny, I remember, had never seen him. In the evening Senka was summoned to his granny, and she didn't so much as glance at him—and that night she died."

After a moment's silence, Raisa observed: "And Klavdia Gubova fell out of love suddenly too, out of love with her fiancé, and she couldn't bear the sight of him, while before that she could not get enough of him. But I think that all that is only illusion, surely it's not possible to stop loving one fine morning, just like that?"

"I don't think it's as impossible as it seems," remarked Demyanov, who had remained silent up to now.

"Mikhail Alexandrovich, you be sure to celebrate the day of your Angel at hour house, together with Mishenka, yes indeed," added the old woman Kurmasheva, getting up to leave.

"Thank you, only I'd like to invite one or two of my friends."

"Well? Our house is your house, don't forget that."

CHAPTER 6

A bell ringing out in the corridor forced four people in a tiny dressing room with flowers on its unpainted table to lower voices that were already talking in subdued tones. Oleg Felixovich was chatting with some fellow with a narrow beard and shaggy hair, a fellow whose velvet breeches recalled a type of artist that has already gone out of fashion.

"…you have to feel the mood of this thing, its gray-blue shade of a suffering feminine soul…right? We'll all keep this in mind, won't we? It might turn out all right."

The other, shaking his curls, said: "I have some ideas for a costume for Varvara Mikhailovna! The color of grubby crushed strawberries, and like this: a skirt, then another one of the same color, falling over it in a dirty brick red; above, a *tailleur* in bright Veronese green, a white waistcoat…how about that? It's a pity that the setting is Norway, because I have a wonderful sketch of some palms."

"That doesn't matter. What's important is the mood of the thing. The setting can be shifted—show us your palms. When Komissarzhevskaya was acting once they shifted *Zobeida* from Persia to Tiflis, and instead of a Persian costume they gave her a Hebrew one."

"I believe they shifted the second act there not to Tiflis, but to the private room from the erstwhile *Alkazar*…" remarked Demyanov, smiling.

Allowing the artist to leave, Temirov turned to the director, who was sitting at the table with a preoccupied air.

"Would it be an embarrassing question, dear Oleg Felixovich, if I asked you what's running at your theater—is it a Scandinavian miracle play with palm trees, or Sudermann's *Heimat?*"

"*Heimat?* Where did you hear that?" he said with a start.

"Calm down, people from our circle—Vasya the painter who is mounting the Sudermann, I think. In society they talk only about the Scandinavian thing."

"That's tactics, Nikolai Pavlovich, we have to arouse interest…You'll never understand that…"

"Yes, but the device of spreading rumors hardly works when it's repeated several times…"

Valentin, who had just come in, interrupted the conversation, lowering himself onto a bench with a sigh after shaking hands.

"Are you tired?" asked Demyanov. "Well, how was it yesterday? I don't know precisely who you're in love with, but yesterday all the candidates were certainly here, do you remember?"

"It was already morning when we came back, went into the cathedral to buy communion bread, and ate it with milk in a dairy. She's beautiful, she has wonderful deep eyes and an angelic smile. Oh, all right, I won't go on," he lost his temper, noticing the smiles of his listeners.

"I'm listening with the livliest attention," interjected Demyanov, who had somehow suddenly become gloomy, lighting a cigarette. " Tell me, Temirov, will Mstislav mind it at all if I dedicate my latest piece to him? When I was working on it I kept thinking of him…of his art. It will be well deserved."

"Oh, he'll be wild with enthusiasm, he raves about you, and is just looking for a chance to get acquainted."

"That's so easy to do," said Mikhail Alexandrovich. "He wouldn't agree to come with us tomorrow as a fourth?"

"I'll let him know; probably yes. Well, time for me to go," Temirov took his leave, leading the director away by the arm.

After a silence, Valentin quietly observed, as if to himself: "They say there's no believing Myatlev."

Demyanov looked at the youth questioningly.

"They say he's conceited and vain."

"What kind of attack is this? Why fly has bitten you? Is he your rival with Ovinova or something?"

"No."

"Well, what's the matter then? You don't know him."

"What are you getting excited about? How could you know him either? Perhaps I'm concerned about you."

"About me! What an idea!"

"It's not completely a matter of indifference to me to see you made a fool of."

"You know, what you say is very vulgar, it's a bad French play."

They both fell silent, and the bell which again rang in the corridor did not make them change their pose of angry smokers lost in concentration.

CHAPTER 7

It was pleasant after prolonged journeying, now rapid, now at a trot, after long snow-covered roads past fenced-off dachas, abandoned old theaters, frozen rivers, after frost, a moonlit night, empty clearings at the edges of islands—it was pleasant, having passed yard-keepers in the rather narrow yard, to enter, their fur coats and hats covered with powder, the broad, bright, warm passage from which issued the shrill sounds of Rumanians.

"We asked for something dry, didn't we? Pieper Heidsiek brut?" said Demyanov, sinking down next to Petya Smetanin opposite Myatlev, who was sitting by Temirov.

The old tapestry depicted Priam in the tent of Achilles, the walls with their dark oaken panelling were reminiscent of dining rooms in old-fashioned houses, old servants with the faces of eunuchs silently observed the group of almost their sole customers. They were already eating the cheese, and at the unoccupied table next to them blue flames licked the sides of the porcelain coffee-pot. Petya was humming a maxixe to the musicians, holding a wineglass between two fingers, affectedly sticking out his little finger. They recalled past trips, funny incidents, trifles, people they had talked with, wine labels; the hall filled somewhat with late visitors, music raged; Demyanov did not take his eyes off Matveyev's pale face, trying to find some answer in the quick, apparently unseeing glances he was casting all this time. They fell silent, having exhausted their conversation, and having smoked their last cigarettes without any particular impulse to do so.

Once more the straight road, the dachas flashing by, the snow on the trees brought on sleepiness, and Petya slept, pressing softly against Demyanov's shoulder. In the moonlight eyes grew strangely dark in exaggeratedly white faces.

"I feel as if I'm ready to reply truthfully to any question at all now," announced Myatlev, as if making a challenge. "And the first thing I shall say is that no one's art has moved me as much as yours!"

"Well, are you in love with Mikhail Alexandrovich?" asked Temirov.

"Oh yes."

"In what way?"

"In any way you like."

"In every possible way?"

"In every possible way."

"And do you think that I love you?" Demyanov himself now ventured to ask.

"Oh yes."

"When did you first think that?" continued the questioner, his voice somehow trembling.

"From our first meeting."

"You didn't think I would tell you that?"

"Oh no, if you didn't say it, I'd say it."

"First?"

"First."

"Will you remember our words of today tomorrow?"

"Do you think I'm drunk?"

"Do you know how important what we're saying is?"

"Yes."

"What destruction, or what a dawning of art, of feeling for life, can come out of this conversation?"

Myatlev, with a quick smile, repeated:

"Oh yes!"

"How strange this is, as if in a dream; doesn't the whole trip, this whole conversation seem somehow fantastic to you?" broke in Temirov, who had apparently been dozing up to this point.

They were already crossing the embankment; Petya woke up and yawned, making an effort to sing something. The others kept their silence, something on their minds. Having kissed Petya and Temirov good-bye, Demyanov restricted himself to a handshake with Myatlev, who stared at him unblinkingly with his seemingly unseeing eyes.

CHAPTER 8

The clatter of a broken cup betrayed Rayechka's emotion when she noticed Myatlev entering the room arm in arm with Demyanov, a room already filled with dressed-up girls, two or three students and rosy-cheeked young men wearing jackets. Blushing, the girl remained motionless, with the hand that had let the cup fall extended, while Tatiana Ilinisha said, shaking her head:

"Oh Rayechka, what a person you are—so careless."

"This is my friend, Myatlev the artist, auntie," said Demyanov, leading the bowing youth up to them.

"We're delighted, delighted, Mikahil Alexandrovich's friends are our friends. My daughter Raisa," added old Kurmysheva, indicating the girl who had not yet regained her composure.

"I've heard a lot about you from my brother, from Valentin...I never dreamed...I'm so glad to see you here..." she muttered, dropping her restless eyes.

"The oracle! The oracle! Your forfeit, Valentin Petrovich, there's no hiding it, if you don't mind," twittered a flock of young ladies in light-colored dresses, comically resembling each other, appearing on the threshold of the large room next door.

"Let's go too," whispered Myatlev to Mikhail Alexandrovich, moving toward Valentin, who was sitting under a large plaid. "A couple," squeaked someone, when from different directions they each placed a finger on the head which represented the oracle.

And they looked at each other attentively and smilingly beneath the searching gaze of those present, until the disguised, mock-solemn voice of the sooth-sayer rang out: "These two will soon belong to each other."

The loud laughter which greeted the prophecy was not shared only by Raisa, who followed what was happening with fearfully held breath.

"Couldn't I go and wash my hands somewhere?" Myatlev turned rather breathlessly to Demyanov.

"Right now! Let's go through to Tatyana Ilinishna's bedroom, it's nearest."

"There it is," he said, pointing to a washbasin which was clearly visible in the light of the icon lamps in front of what was practically a whole iconostasis of ancient icons.

"I don't need it," whispered Myatlev, locking the door with a key. "Surely you understand?"

"Can it really be true? Why now? Here?" muttered Demyanov, sinking down on Tatyana Ilinishna's bed as if his legs had collapsed beneath him.

"This is what's necessary, this is what I want," said the other, suddenly kissing him strongly and slowly.

Demyanov crossed himself broadly, and sinking onto the floor kissed Myatlev's shoes.

"What are you doing?" the latter said, somewhat embarrassed.

"I am thinking our icons for sending you here, and I kiss your feet which have brought you here for my happiness, for my joy."

CHAPTER 9

To settle accounts with life
I have become an architect,
And I draw and draw and draw—
I draw nothing but hearts.

The women who greeted the sentimental and absurd little song with loud laughter and applause had all agreed to wear multicolored costumes of a single design, made out of fine paper, held together by delicate little colored ribbons, and half-masks; they were mysterious, fresh and young in the light of the colored lanterns They danced, whirled about, sat down on the floor, sang, drank the wine which gleamed red in long wine-glasses, making merry somehow gently and noiselessly in the half-lit room; in dark corners sat couples, conversing tenderly and lovingly. Emerging into the neighboring room, Demyanov caught sight of Valentin sitting with his face buried in his hands. He stood next to the youth, putting a hand on his shoulder.

"This is stupid; why torment yourself? Why suffer? Shouldn't love be a joy?" he began somewhat artificially.

"Why do you utter empty words? You know yourself that it isn't true." He replied without taking away his hand.

After a moment's silence, Demyanov began again: "Is that Ovinova—the one you love?"

Valentin nodded in silence.

"Have you talked to her about it?"

"No."

"Why not? Didn't you have the nerve? If you like, I'll talk to her?"

"No…I tell you what, though, if you want to do me a favor, you'd do better to talk to Myatlev."

"To Myatlev? About what?"

"Still about her."

Demyanov said restrainedly: "It seems to me that you're making a mistake in considering him to have some connection with her."

"Talk to him, I beg you, it's all the same to him, but so important to her and to me."

"All right, I'll talk to him; some sort of trifling nonsense, I suppose."

"Quiet, they're coming into the anteroom," whispered Valentin, and they froze, while the voices of those who came into the anteroom could be heard clearly against the soft music from the hall.

"You know," Nadia Ovinova's voice could be heard, "when you go, I'll leave the theater, because you're the only one who has interested me here. It's very silly to tell you this, but you've treated me so coldly, drily, hardly saying anything to me of late, that I decided to tell you this now, on the last day."

Myatlev's voice answered rather hoarsely: "Nadezhda Vasilevna, you yourself have avoided meetings and I haven't changed toward you in the least."

"Why deceive me?" exclaimed the girl piteously. "Do you think I don't see? Do you think I don't feel? And I'll tell you how long you've been this way and why. Do you want me to? Shall I say it?"

"Say it," answered Myatlev with a grimace.

"Very well!" And she said something softly which fell short of the ears of the troubled listeners.

The silence lasted several seconds, not broken by even a whisper, then Myatlev said in a still hoarser voice: "You know, if a man had said that to me, I'd slap him!" He went out, slamming the door.

The lengthy silence that settled again was broken by Demyanov:

"You see that I was right."

"I see how much she loves him, and I see that neither you, nor Myatlev, nor I—no one can do anything about it."

"Why take everything so tragically?"

"I'm simply saying what is."

And Valentin, not glancing at Demyanov, who stayed behind, went quickly into the hall, where Temirov was beginning the same absurd and sentimental song all over again.

CHAPTER 10

"Une belle lettre d'amour!" said Nalimov coldly, with two fingers holding out the folded note to Myatlev; the latter stood next to Demyanov, radiant and rosy from the light of the sunset through the uncurtained windows; the camelias gleamed still redder in the same light, and a lady with a tall powdered coiffure stood out alone and unexpected on the already darkening wall. He had come up joyful and animated, as though not before a parting. Nalimov smiled and added:

"Mikhail Alexandrovich loves letters and knows how to write them, and what you have just been kind enough to show me is not the best specimen."

"Why did you do that?" asked Demyanov, emerging with Myatlev onto the deserted canal bank. The latter, taking a quick look about him, smiled joyfully and triumphantly:

"I'm proud of your friendship, I'm ready to shout about it, to trumpet it forth to the whole world. Just wait, I'll come soon and we'll be together inseparably, eternally, I'll go with you everywhere, to the houses of strangers and friends, to the theater, to concerts."

"I'll send you my sketches, write letters every day—several times a day."

"How I'll look forward to them. All the time, every hour, I'll be thinking of you, of your immediate arrival, every line of verse, every note will belong to you."

"What happiness, what unexpected happiness."

"What unexpected happiness!" repeated Demyanov, like an echo.

"And if I stay in Moscow for long, you'll come and see us, won't you? We have an amusing lilac-colored house with a courtyard entrance, a private residence, the yellow gates always locked, you have to knock, there are warm staircases inside; we have two dogs, in my room I have an excellent washstand, there's a cupboard, an apple tree, just one, outside; the trees in the park are visible, it's beautiful in spring."

"My dear friend," said Demyanov very quickly, pressing his companion's elbow with his hand. They were walking with light, seemingly winged steps, the people they passed seemed sweet, well-dressed, without care in the early, still radiant twilight, they went inside to eat pies, laughing for no reason, staring at each other.

"I'll take you to the station, do you have a ticket?"

"Not yet, and please don't worry yourself; I'll call in for my things, perhaps...."

"Perhaps what?"

"Perhaps I won't manage to go today...."

"What? Surely that isn't still possible?"

"Why does it disturb you? It doesn't make any difference, does it?"

"No, it doesn't matter, I don't know why I was worried myself, it's nonsense of course."

They kissed lightly, as if parting for an hour, and Myatlev waved his hat for a long time when Demyanov's cab drove away, then he sat in a different sleigh and set off in the opposite direction from the place where he lived. Climbing the dark staircase in the courtyard to the door whereon was inscribed: "Elena Ivanovna Borisova," he rang the bell and the door was opened by a serving maid with a candle, who said that the mistress was home and let him into a narrow and dark hallway.

CHAPTER 11

Valentin's face grew sadder and sadder as Demyanov spoke consoling words to him uncertainly and at length. Eventually, fixing his eyes, which up to this time had been cast down directly on his interlocutor, he said meaningfully:

"It is not unknown to you, of course, that Myatlev came back here again yesterday, having spent only two weeks in Moscow."

Reddening, Demyanov answered restrainedly: "Perhaps."

"Why hide things? With your closeness you would have to have known earlier that he would be here."

"Perhaps," repeated Demyanov soundlessly.

"And you know, you must know, that his renewed appearance deprives me of the peace of mind I have hardly regained."

"Are you sure that Myatlev has really arrived?"

Valentin shrugged his shoulders without answering.

"You've seen Pavel Ivanovich, of course?" Oleg Felixovich came up to the speaker.

"Possibly," answered Demyanov with a smile, feeling that the whole room was starting to go around.

"Enough of discretion; rumors are even going around that he didn't dream of going to Moscow and spent all this time at your place."

"What nonsense! Who does he have to hide from?"

"You're leaving already? So early?"

"Yes, I'm leaving, an awful headache."

"He's arrived, he's arrived—and I find it out third hand! Two weeks of silence, not to warn me of his coming, not to let me know about his arrival! There's friendship for you, there's love! And how have I deserved this?"

In his emotion Mikhail Alexandrovich got out of the cab, walked some distance on foot, got in again and drove off with a burning head and a heart that was somehow empty, sinking.

"You have been asked to hand over the little house and the card," said a sleeply porter, opening the door to Demyanov and rummaging about on the table in the hall.

"What little house? Who was it?"

"Well, a toy, I was even surprised myself. A young gentleman, he often visited you before, I think he's called Myatlev. Here it is…" He found Myatlev's card.

There was nothing written on the back of it.

"Did he call himself?"

"Himself."

"Late?"

"At nine o'clock."

The little house was the kind peddlars sell before christmas, made of thick cardboard with cut-out doors and windows with sashes on both floors; red and green transparent paper was inserted in the windows, so as to shine gaily when a candle was lit inside the house.

THE DOUBLE CONFIDANT

ONE

As yet "unsaved," Marguerite was flinging her prayer even higher into the heavens, Mephistopheles was still unlit by the red glare of the hell beneath the boards, Faust had still not given up hope of persuading the enamored infanticide to flee, when Modest Brandt, clumsily picking a way through strange legs, emerged into the foyer of the theater.

Hastening past the mirrors, he caught a fleeting glimpse of sidewhiskers, round, wandering eyes, high forehead, narrow, twisted mouth, uniform.

A tall lady in furs stopped him with the furtive touch of an ungloved hand to his elbow, in the manner of an intimate.

"I expect you tomorrow, my friend."

"Surely it's not Thursday tomorrow," he exclaimed in a whisper.

"No, but don't be afraid; I think they were all there last week, only our own people will be there…There's a great deal I have to tell you," she added after a silence; she sought out an old gentleman in a top hat with her whitish eyes and moved away with a slow, slightly limping gait.

Emerging into snow and moonlight, he quickly set off to visit Fortov—Viktor Andreyevich—who lived a short walk along the silent, still canal. His friend would be expecting him, as they had agreed earlier.

Striding along the narrow, deserted embankment, he thought of Rebecca's whitish, enormous eyes, her invariably black, invariably silken dress, her gatherings, her somehow mysterious, somehow seductive words, her warm, rather plump arms, at once seductive and maternal, her slow, limping gait.

Stars, sharp and tiny, glittered like pins.

Viktor Andreyevich himself opened the large red doors with their copper fittings, embraced him and helped him out of his coat. He talked gaily and maliciously of people they knew in the theater, himself pouring tea into cups of deep blue, wine into glasses, and serving slices of apricot tart. They were tête-à-tête, as agreed.

Taking the wine with them, they moved to the study, and pacing the parquet floor and smoking more than his wont, Viktor Andreyevich, his rubicund face flushing a deeper red, spoke with a smile, as if he were continuing something the beginning of which was known to his listener.

"Modest, don't be surprised if I tell of a new love affair."

"Of yours? Why should I be surprised?"

"Naturally of mine, or rather with regard to me. A certain girl has fallen in love with me, a girl whom, quite seriously, I think extremely highly of. The beginning was terribly banal, but not without a romantic touch: an exchange of letters, secret trysts in the garden, scenes, tears, kisses, benedictions."

Modest Karlovich listened, from time to time throwing a glance at the speaker, who, regaining his composure, spoke gaily and confidently.

"Yes, she knows everything. It may be that she has the idea of saving me. That amuses me, all the more as to put on a show of pure love is not in the least difficult as far as she is concerned."

"Is she beautiful?"

"Yes, undoubtedly, in my opinion."

"Why do you only tell me about this now?"

"I don't know. I was entertained by this romance of tears and high passion in the manner of Balzac, and your mocking laughter would have spoiled it for me."

"Has she written to your herself, come to see you?"

"Yes, she came to see me herself. Just imagine: Pavel didn't want to let her in at first."

The young man's account lasted a long time, while the other listened to him distractedly, twisting a white knife in his hands; the wine in the half-emptied glasses gleamed yellow, like the pale dawn in the windows. Modest rose at last and asked:

"Who is she then—or is that secret?"

Viktor Andreyevich nodded that it was. Smiling, the other observed:

"You're changing: secretiveness already."

The raconteur said hastily:

"You don't know her anyway, but her name's Nastasia; poetical, don't you think?"

"Nastasia? Yes, not bad."

TWO

Even before stepping out of the elevator, Modest heard the sounds of a piano from the floor occupied by Rebecca Weltmann. Sinking into a chair by the door without greeting his hostess, he listened to the loud and affected playing of a tall clean-shaven young man wearing a large mauve tie.

In the distance, Rebecca threw a welcoming nod, screwing up her whitish eyes. On the floor at her feet sat a fair-haired girl in black, scarcely visible in the semidarkness; eight or ten shadowy presences lurked in the corners, on sofas; the samovar was smoking by the thickly shaded lamp. A young man, little more than a boy, sitting at his side, whispered: "Rebecca Mikhailovna is probably having one of her visions; look how she's sitting. She told me amazing things about the fourth sonata—did you know?"

"Has Adventov read his poems yet?" asked Modest, who knew the evening's program in advance.

"Not yet: first of all I think he's going to talk with Rebecca Mikhailovna; the origin of his 'The Leader' is a great mystery," said his neighbor, blushing and excited, with the pride of someone in the know.

Next to Rebecca, who sat with her great head with its casque of flaxen hair flung back, was ensconced a small, thin man in black with a bald spot and eyes set lower than was proper.

She started up at his approach, flapped the gray wings of her eyes, lighting up with a smile, and said softly: "I have to talk with you, my friend; follow me up to my room later. Dearest, dearest."

Wafting a sweet perfume, she passed through the salon, limping noiselessly over the soft carpets. The girl remained on the floor, kissing her hand as she left. The music fell silent, and the soft hum of conversation in the corners became distinct in the sudden quiet.

"From the rose-pierced heart the blue blood streams!"—the words of the poet overrode the other exclamations.

The kneeling girl straightened without getting up, prepared to listen. Young men with buttonholes talked about the ballet, laughing. Emerging into the wide corridor, Modest heard the sound of Admetov's voice, at once wooden and disturbing.

The corridor was formed by bends leading to quarters unguessed by visitors. His knock was met with a "come in," and the door shut soundlessly behind him of itself. Rebecca was difficult to make out at first in the deep leather armchair behind pots of lilies that made the head spin with their cloying scent. A portrait of a man with a long beard stood between tall candles on a little table in one corner. In the small heated cell there was a smell of incense, there was stillness and languor.

"Sit down," she said.

He sat down close to her knees, feeling drowsiness creeping upon him.

"What a long time since I've seen you—greetings!"

The kiss she gave him was sweeter and more protracted than a sisterly one, as she wound her warm plump arms about him.

"Well, how are you? Are you doing as I told you?"

"Yes," he responded soundlessly, as if letting the words drop into water.

"Don't think that these things are silly trifles. They do so much to form a man, his soul, do you understand? And don't stake money at three o'clock. I've thought about you such a lot these last few days; didn't you feel it?"

Not the words, but the voice, the perfume, the dim light filled him with a delicious languor, the gaze of the enormous whitish eyes seemed to drink his body. He shifted so as not to fall asleep. The voice was already murmuring of other things: of Viktor. Was he not unhappy, should he not be approached, helped, shown the way? She said that he had fallen in love, that she had seen the girl.

"A little dark-haired thing, with a bold look about her, but unripe, quite unripe, without perturbation of spirit, you know what I mean? Hardly the type to save him. You talk to him; he's fond of you; no harm in that, for the cause everything is permissible. It won't deprive you of me, you understand that? There can be no general rule for everyone, everything *ad hominem*. I'll bless you, if you like. The main thing is that he shouldn't be lost to us...."

From a hidden cupboard she produced a black rosary, unfastened a cross, and giving them to him, said:

"These are for him; let him pray and gain strength."

Again she began to kiss him, and white lightnings flashed from one pair of eyes to another. Imperceptibly she drew him toward the sofa; freeing himself, he said:

"No, not today; I know it would be wrong now."

"Yes, yes, yes, you're right," mumbled Rebecca, confused, maternal, with unextinguished summer lightnings in her whitish eyes.

He left alone, without going into the drawing room, where a vague hum of voices could be heard.

The fresh frosty air was so consoling, so consoling.

THREE

Meeting almost constantly, as before, the friends confined their conversation to Viktor's love for Nastia. Without weariness, without irritation, Modest listened to these tales of trysts which only one in love could have distinguished one from another; these reported words of love he found neither insipid nor cloying, weaving a habit out of sweet declarations. Not noticing a certain banality in his friend's descriptions, he himself, drawing on a cigarette, pictured scene after scene in his mind and, at home, as he prepared for bed, tried to guess what was in store for him tomorrow: what kisses, embraces and tears would be related to him by Fortov's scarlet lips.

Did Viktor Andreyevich tell how she came into the garden in a lambskin jacket, rosy-faced, with a rose in her hair; did he recount how in childish joy she had flung her arms around his neck, whispering: "Dearest, dearest"; did he convey the tender sternness of his beloved as she gave her blessing to his vow of chastity—Modest accepted his friend's confessions with equal readiness, his heart drinking in words of a love not his own.

Was it of his own love that the rubicund speaker was telling?

When she saw Brandt, Rebecca would demand an account of the student and Nastia, informing of her dissatisfaction that all was not going as she, the all-wise sybil, would have wished. She would reproach him for his indolence and failure to act.

Whether they encountered each other at tedious gatherings or sat in their warm and languorous retreat, met in passing in the crowded streets—they always talked about the same thing, as if forgetting for a time that there were other things in life.

And gazing at the garden below, roseate in the sunset glow, the officer listened to the same softly insistent words of honeyed power. Rebecca Mikhailovna moved from one armchair to another, never ceasing to weave toils needed for someone.

"But how can this be? Was it not you I chose to lead Fortov? Was it not you who was to draw him away from a destructive passion—and what happens? You all but egg him on in this vulgar affair?"

"It isn't as vulgar as you think—which is true of many things."

"Very well, very well, but all the same this young miss, Vetkina, can never be one of us."

"Who knows?" he ventured, hoping to justify himself.

"But does Viktor Andreyevich lover her, at least?"

"She loves more than he."

"Thank heaven for that, but how then are we to explain this strange and comic business?"

After a silence, she asked:

"Did you give him the cross?"

"Yes, yes," he said, remembering that he had forgotten to do so.

"At seven o'clock on Friday?" .

"Yes," he affirmed, blushing in the semi-darkness.

Covering her eyelids with the palms of her hands, flinging back her head, her face suddenly of a vatic pallor, Rebecca fell silent, her plump body straining upward. Lowering his eyes, Modest waited until, with a deep sigh, she lifted the veil, as it were, from her eyes and announced:

"I saw—a green clearing—Viktor flying on a single wing, my cross clutched in his hand. It is time he set forth."

He got up quickly, straightening his uniform, fingering the undelivered cross in his pocket and lowering his wandering gaze, and through his thin lips articulated:

"It will be arranged...he will leave."

And that evening, once more drawing on a cigarette in Fortov's old house on the quiet canal, he barely remembered, utterly captivated by highly colored tales, the injunctions of wise, whitish-eyed Rebecca.

"Perhaps you should go away?" he said with assumed indolence.

"I was thinking that myself," said the younger man simply.

They wrote a letter to Nastia together, as previously they had together thought out the steps, words and deeds of one of the loving pair:

"For the first time it feels like a game of chess, like war, but at the same time you have to remain utterly cold. It's amusing."

"That's not the only novelty for you in all this."

Thoughtfully the other said: "Hm? Well *that* novelty isn't terribly interesting!" And again they set to considering phrases for the letter of leavetaking.

"The day after tomorrow I'll be leaving for my sister's; shall we see each other again?"

"Undoubtedly."

They embraced and parted. The double confidant hastened at once to the high-ceilinged retreat to convey tidings of the impending departure.

He posted the letter, which he knew by heart, himself. He thought with boredom of the warm, plump arms of his motherly inamorata.

FOUR

Having indifferently accepted the "good-bye" with a parting "write!" from the carriage doorway, passing those who had come to see others off and were in no hurry to leave, knowing the hour to be late for the theater and early for sleep, Brandt made his way to a restaurant far from the station and house, moderating with the measured step of military gait the desolation that suddenly overcame him. And what for?

Fortov's cheeks glowed a tender pink in the swarthy oval of his face and his eyes lost none of their dark glitter as the train carried him away from his new love and his old friend. The frosty stars gleamed down from a greater height than in summer.

Cramped and smoky, the restaurant was already emptying. There was no music, and, unadorned, the drunken clamor emerged in all its pitifulness and squalor. Modest sat alone as he ate and drank, thinking that he must soon leave, fearing that he would not be able to sleep at home, conscious again of the resounding emptiness in his dead, which walking had seemed to mitigate.

From a neighboring table, a stray "Fortov" caused him to raise his head. Probably he had misheard. There were four people there: two students, a goat-bearded monk and a boyish civilian; others came over to them and went away again, sat down with them, drank, or simply greeted them with a bow, spoke at length; the group of four remained. He listened intently; again what seemed to be foreign speech struck his ear. They were speaking of someone with abuse and laughter, someone didn't like someone else's amorous intrigue, calling him a "scoundrel, good-for-nothing, corrupter, mercenary." Again "Fortov" flashed by. Or had he misheard?

"That Nastasia's a fool," said the old man, "a pitiful, dangerous fool. How could she fail to see, how could she fail to hear about what kind of a man it was she was flinging herself at? And what could she have seen in him? A chocolate box cherub…"

"Perhaps she wants to save him, to lead him out on the path of righteousness, to perform a service for all her sex; After all, the rogue is handsome," sniggered one of the students.

"But what can she do? Everything's upside-down these days: si la jeunesse pouvait, si la vieillesse savait!" the gray-bearded one announced with secret pride. The boys exchanged glances smilingly. One of the students blurted out, leaning back in his chair and rocking back and forth:

"In my opinion, Miss Vetkina is entirely worthy of her partner. They put their heads together in order to raise the gentleman's reputation in certain eyes!" Having spoken, he looked around, as if seeking objections.

Modest got up, went over quietly to their table and said sternly:

"Are you speaking of Mr. Fortov?"

"Perhaps we are—what's it to you?"

"He is my best friend."

"Congratulations!"

"My name is Brandt, and I forbid you to speak in this manner."

The old fellow went into a bustle of conciliation.

"Of course it's no reproach to the lad. It's all that Nastia up to her cunning tricks, the bitch.

Modest said quietly:

"Anastasia Maximovna is a person of the utmost purity, and I will not permit you to speak in this way!"

Blinking, the old man tried to continue.

"Only your nearness to the grave prevents me from calling your behavior by its right name. As for you," Modest turned to the student, who had frozen in a pose at once embarrassed and insolent, "my friends will be calling on you tomorrow."

"Do you imagine that I'm going to fight a duel with every fool I happen to run into?" he yelled after the retreating officer, who was making his way through the crowd of belated pleasure-seekers and lackeys.

The drunken quarrel came to nothing; having sobered up, the student came round to apologize, awkward in his embarrassment. He was called Razhak.

The next morning Modest received a narrow envelope written in a strange hand.

"Dear Mr. Brandt, not having the pleasure of being acquainted with you personally, I venture to convey my gratitude for your noble expression of friendship for Viktor Andreyevich Fortov. I shake your hand. Respectfully yours,

A.M. Vetkina"

How had it become known? He remembered that he had seen the boy in civilian clothes at Madam Weltmann's, when his eyes fell on that vatic lady's uneven handwriting on the other envelope.

"What do I hear," she wrote, "Tavern brawls, duels over Miss Vetkina? Is your knightly ardor appropriate? I await information from you, dear brother. Come as soon as you can.

Yours, Rebecca"

All these winter days, sunny or sunless (with wintry, brief and, ah, sweet sunshine) Modest stayed home. Fortov wrote that he had arrived at his sister's in the country, the kind of long letter filled with trivia that people write at their leisure in some remote spot.

"If you were to come, you would see our old house with a lot of rooms furnished back in the 1820s, ramshackle and charming. The stoves crackle of a morning. Waking up, I hear the grumbling of Leonid who originally came from here and who is unused to looking after stoves and who won't let fat Martha into my room. Having read newspapers and letters, and waiting to have breakfast with my sister, who has been busying herself with domestic chores, I go out for a sleigh ride alone; it's so comforting, so peaceful and mournful in the fields in winter! I never noticed that before. In the evening my sister and I play old piano duet music, I read to her aloud, we drink tea, chat about the town, which she hasn't seen for eight years. In spite of the difference between us in years, she is very interested in my affairs, even those of the heart, being so utterly unprejudiced that my romance with Nastya touched her less than the others. Looking after the household, rising before dawn, she keeps her interest in everything and reads Bryusov without batting an eye, let alone the French. We don't see much of the neighbors—the characters here would be a treasure trove for a Sologub or a Remizov. I've made friends with a member of the Corps of Pages who came here for the holidays, and I often go to see him. Send me the books that are on order but not yet collected at Wolf's, three pounds of candied ginger and three jars of English chocolate liqueurs. I'll be here for another month or so. How are you all? How is Rebecca Mikhailovna? How go the "orgies" on the English Embankment? Petya Klimov? Our dear friends? Send me the proofs of my latest poems as soon as they come out. Pavel will let you have them. I embrace you. Regards to all."

FIVE

Day followed day for Modest, monotonous in their diversity. It was as if the lamp in the yard had been snuffed out and everything had gone dark. The same friends, acquaintances, theaters, gossip and books, the same way of life for some reason suddenly palled and became wearisome. And more often than before he passed the dark mornings, the sunless days, the quiet evenings at home in the company of his old father, or quietly strolling at times ill-suited to strolling. He grew thin. "As if I were in love," he thought mockingly to himself, but he was not in love, the old ties that bound him to Rebecca were weakening. So it seemed. Out of habit, he kept thinking of Viktor's affair with Nastya, now left to his imagination alone. In the same way he pictured scene after scene, as if the stories had come flying in a merry swarm from Fortov's scarlet lips. The pictures he drew grew ever gloomier: Nastya, in these fantasies, was insulted by all, even his friend had deserted the wretched girl, while he, Modest, in reconciling them consoled her and became her shield. He saw her so clearly that he seemed to be acquainted with her and to know her personally. Letters from the country arrived often enough, but little of town affairs was said in those letters.

One day, a friend who was walking with Brandt near the Champ de Mars observed indifferently:

"That's Vetkina over there!"

Without so much as a start, Modest lifted his eyes to a girl going out into the snow from a doorway, and dropped them again: that was not the way she was in his story, Nastya.

A young lady, not tall, but not short either, was getting into a sleigh in the white snow, turning toward the passing officers her dark, rather round face, unsmiling, fashionably coiffeured under her hat. She nodded in answer to their bow, not glancing at Modest. Shielding her eyes and nose from the white snow with her muff, she quickly drove off.

"Is that Vetkina, Nastasya Maximovna?"

"Yes. Do you know her?"

"By name. Not personally."

They talked of other things: about the army, the theater, so that Modest almost forgot Vetkina's face. But the other Nastya also grew dim, and no longer came so willingly and lightly to his call in his stories. She became a pale, radiant blank. He conceived a desire to test his memory, remembering the street and the house from which the girl had gone out into the snow on that occasion.

The thaw had set in; from afar the wind wafted a false spring from the sea; it was dark and warm, gray and damp.

Standing by the church on the opposite side of the street, he waited for the door under the porch to open, like any other door, and for a girl, not tall, in a lambskin jacket, like any other girl, to come out. The pigeons cooed loudly to welcome the warm weather, there came a fine trickling of water from pipes, horses splashed as they stepped deep in the dun-colored slush. But she did not come out. He had not realized that this would upset him so much. Having penned a refusal to Rebecca's letter, he stayed to drink tea with his father, even putting on slippers. The old man suddenly asked, as if he had not seen him for a long time:

"Why have you got so thin, Modya? Are you ill or something? You must look after yourself, you must look after yourself."

"There's nothing wrong with me, papa," his son replied.

The old man shuffled to his room to cough away the night.

Modest sat frowning in an armchair by the stove, slipper dangling, not calling to mind that his friend had not written to him for a long time, he pulled down the yellow blind over the bewept window panes, and sank into thought. The whitish eyes, the malty smell of scent, the plump arms swam up momentarily. He slumped down. "What is this, O Lord?!" Again he fell to thinking, warmed by the heat, until his sleepy nanny clinked cup against cup and said:

"You should go to bed, Modest Karlovich, instead of dozing out here."

That night he kept having dreams. How long it lasted! Who had made minutes seem like hours?

The next day he went again; a more successful day.

Nastya came out and was going somewhere on foot; she was taller than she had seemed before and taller than Rebecca had said. Decorously and hurriedly, she walked across the frozen puddles, not turning round toward Modest. Reaching for money to give to a beggar, she let fall her umbrella. He picked it up, she said "Thank you" without glancing at him; she seemed pale; her voice was toneless, flat, low.

He walked further, sometimes seeing her, sometimes not, accepting her in his thoughts as she was, not knowing how he could have thought her otherwise.

Fortov wrote of his not very imminent return, of a life of involuntary exile in the delightful backwoods, of a new friendship, of books, of Petersburg gossip—of Nastya, of love, not a word. Modest reserve, no doubt.

Rebecca kept summoning him in order to talk about Viktor Andreyevich, how he was doing, what he was doing and what it was he needed. "But he doesn't need anything!" Modest would try to say, and the lady, muttering a conciliatory "yes, yes, yes, you're right" for a moment, an hour later would again be worrying about Fortov, how he was doing, what he was doing and what it was he needed. There was no dampening her.

SIX

The momentary silence of the lecturer gave Modest a better possibility of hearing what Rebecca, who was sitting beside him, was saying. The same old things about herself, and other things too.

Above the table, where ecclesiastics and laymen with an ecclesiastical air were sitting, hung strange landscapes of mysterious sunlit lands. A number of pictures hung about the walls of the residence, which at other times served as an exhibition hall. One speech succeeded another, fading into the air—beards alternated with clean-shaven chins, long hair with cropped craniums, words from quiet temples sounded alongside words from the tribune. "Christ," "Christianity," "progress," "prayer," "evolution," "socialism" merged in a stupefying din. A venerable monk was lisping on about marriage and children born out of wedlock. A politician was chewing his liberal oration like a man chewing bast in his sleep. A bald Jew in black heatedly pronounced his "Vs" as "Ds" as he fulminated against Christianity. They got up, they sat down. It was hot. Rebecca whispered:

"It's been a week—I came here for a special reason. Do you think I need all this rubbish? You can, if you like, cease to love me, but you cannot abandon the cause."

A beardless student, lisping in his childish voice, said, looking at the priest, that he was hardly likely to be a Christian, referring to him as "Alexei Petrovich" instead of "Father Alexei." The latter, turning red, clutched at the cross on his breast. Adventov, accompanied by a cadet taller than he, came in through the entrance, clicking his heels. Rebecca whispered:

"Desertion is unthinkable; to go so far—and then, as you know, we are bound so closely—it was predestined that our souls should be as one—dearest, dearest." Members of the audience were now speaking. A tall grayhaired officer stood up and shouted, crossing himself, that the name of the Evil One was uttered more often here than that of Christ. Someone else, another student, demanded that they should all be quiet:

"Pray; play politics, but don't chatter. What has driven you together here? Emptiness, poverty and idleness. Priest, why are you not taking care of the ladies of the night? Men, why are you not in your studies? Wives, why are you not with your children? Pray, if you believe, but don't chatter idly. Christ is alive, don't make him into an abstraction of ingenious thought!"

His voice broke off, like that of a young cock; everyone fell silent, lowering their eyes; a philosopher in black, stout as a deacon, began a speech, his handsome face twitching every now and then.

Modest looked steadily into Rebecca's eyes and said deliberately: "But I don't love you any more, Rebecca Mikhailovna."

As she remained silent, he repeated:

"But I don't love you any more."

She emitted a strange, hoarse sound, and again was silent.

"I love another," he said, not quite conscious of what he was saying.

"Whom?" he guessed by the movement of her lips rather than heard.

"Vetkina," someone said for him. Surely he couldn't have said it! And a sudden light entered into his soul, as if a lamp had been carried into a cellar. That was it. The truth. And he repeated loudly, joyfully:

"I love Vetkina, I love Vetkina."

Rebecca, bringing her face close to his, gripping his hand, forgetful of other eyes and ears, gave a strangled cry:

"Come to your senses, Modest! Modest, you didn't say that! That's dreadful!"

"I love Vetkina," he said with stubborn joy.

"You don't know what the consequences of this will be. Give it up, come to your senses."

"I love Vetkina."

"As your teacher, I forbid it. You know how tolerant I am, but this I forbid, and I have the right to do so."

The officer smiled and said nothing.

The meeting was breaking up. The monk, surrounded by his stepdaughters and sisters-in-law, was still lisping on about children born out of wedlock.

"What happened to your dog?" someone asked.

"I had to have it shot."

"You've given up this fantasy of yours, haven't you, my friend?" said the vatic lady, taking the silent Modest's hand.

"I love Vetkina," he repeated distinctly. Throwing back her head with its flaxen casque of hair, stretching out the cloak she had already cast about her, she cried out in grief and rage:

"Wretch! I curse you, I excommunicate you, I give you over to Satan. In three days you will die a pitiful death, spiritually you have already perished. Be warned. Remember. In three days you will die. I now call death down upon you!"

She breathed upon him with her whole being, her whitish eyes, her breast and her broad face. She went out. Modest smiled.

SEVEN

But in three days the condemned man didn't die, and didn't even give a thought to the sentence that had been passed on him. A great radiant emptiness entered his soul, like a chamber that had been illuminated by a cool and luminous radiance. As if another had said to him: "You love Nastya Vetkina," and everything had become clear to him, but without joy. It was also without joy because in a few days Viktor Andreyevich would be arriving, and Modest didn't know how he would greet this new development, which was as yet unknown to his new beloved herself. He had not been at the station since seeing off Fortov, and remembered all the more vividly the evening of his friend's departure four months before, the first evening that he had risen to the defense of a girl with whom he was unacquainted. Fortov seemed a little thinner when he emerged, but he had not lost the roses that bloomed in his swarthy cheeks. With the tenderness of friendship, as if he were the elder of the two, he enfolded Modest in a generous and manly embrace; Modest guiltily allowed himself to be squeezed, not knowing whether to throw himself forlornly on his neck or to push him away. In the radiant happiness of openhanded youth, Fortov did not notice his friend's hesitation. He smiled magnificently, seeming to become even taller, straighter, younger. In a ringing, cheerful voice he gave orders to his servant, while the latter bustled about cheerfully but not excessively, without noise. "Victorious Viktor," thought Brandt without envy, captivated afresh by the dark eyes and smiles of his excessively youthful friend; he tried to be as gay as he with the determination of affection, talked louder, stepped out more boldly, keeping pace with him along the platform to the carriage waiting in the darkness. In the old house on the canal everything was as it had been before; with quick steps, having hurriedly taken off his coat, Viktor went through all the rooms, greeting each object with a rapid glance. They sat down to tea that had already been prepared; only then did they start to speak of news unmentioned in their letters. Fortov spoke at length of a new friendship, of his quiet life with his sister on a country estate in winter, of plans, writings, dreams. His level voice throbbed with relentlessly burgeoning life; the temple of his solitary love seemed a wretched and desolate barn. For the time being he concealed his secret, asking simply: "And what about your love affair?"

"Wonderful, marvelous, we'll see a lot of each other in town as well, live close to each other, in the summer we'll all go somewhere together, I'll introduce you."

"What do you mean, in town as well?!" exclaimed his companion. "You're thinking of something else; I was talking about Nastasya Maximovna"—he cried out in his love, forgetting to hide that he knew more than her name.

"Oh, yes, Nastya Vetkina," said Viktor, cruelly not bothering to hide the secret of her surname, and frowning for the first time.

"Yes, you're right. I did write to her, she wrote to me too," he added in a somewhat subdued tone.

"Has something happened then?"

"Nothing at all."

"Then have your feelings changed?"

"There is nothing that does not change. You're like a child. I love her."

An awkward silence crept into the joyful chatter of friendly reunion. Words fell like stones into water, Fortov's face, youthful as ever, suddenly set in an expression of annoyance. Modest regretted that he had begun his questioning, driving away the thoughts, "Why, why? Should I tell him?"

"She wrote to me that you had stepped forward as her champion in a tavern?" the younger one said mockingly. "I believe she wrote you a letter? You really should have introduced yourself: I'm not jealous, and you could have done me a friendly service."

He spoke as if he were driving in nails, the scarlet mouth became dry and mocking.

"I could do that. Why not?"

The words died, meeting no response.

"And what about Rebecca Mikhailovna?" he tried again.

"We've parted."

"How could that have happened? Have your feelings changed then?" Fortov asked the same question Modest had earlier.

Modest flushed crimson and observed:

"What's the matter with you? How can you compare that?"

He must have understood, for he answered:

"And why not, knight of the 'Unknown Lady'?"

He began to pace up and down, they talked further, for a moment friendship spread its wings and flew off. Pausing, Viktor Andreevich said:

"I'm tired of your lectures, Modest. I love Vetkina, or maybe, if you like, I don't love her. She was never in any sense mine, if that's what you want to hear, and I don't want her to be. If you've fallen in love with her, so much the better—I grant you complete freedom of action, and even my help if you want it."

"Why is he too talking to me of love?" thought Modest, and said:

"I don't know her."

Casting a pitying glance at him, his friend said:

"A pity."

Once again someone else began to beat with life within Modest, who shouted in the face of the other, the victorious, the dazzling:

"I know her, I know her address, and her house, and how she dresses. I've seen her, and spoken to her, I've had a tryst with her and I've kissed her!…"

"So much the better for you," said Fortov, knitting his brows, unsmiling. All at once he shrank, softened, broke.

"It's all lies, Viktor—forgive me; I don't know her, I'm not well."

"You're not," said the other drily. "You're not well because you love her without knowing her; you're a romantic of the purest water, my dear—I hadn't suspected that."

He saw him out, affectionately once more, in the generosity of his dazzling youth.

EIGHT

Love and vexation smoldered within him, laying waste his soul. What if it were base, dishonorable: he wrote a letter to Nastya, with the ostensible purpose of opening her eyes to Viktor, concealing his own affliction. Probably she would not yet have forgotten his name. He wrote it, and, sinking back in his chair, he looked at the address for a long time without any thoughts, except for one: "I've done it, I've taken the step." He sent it by messenger, hastening to have a decision and a reply to his request for a meeting. Everything seemed to have come to a standstill, except for expectation. He went from one window to another, from door to door, picking one book from the shelf and then another, pretending to read. A knock at the door without a ring. He rushed to open it; whitish eyes gazed at him from behind a black veil.

"You?!" he exclaimed, starting back.

She limped over to the couch, without removing her hat and without answering; she sat down and began speaking brokenly to Modest, who stood at a distance:

"I had to see you…You have acted badly, very badly, not with regard to me…"

He gave a start, thinking only of one thing.

The lady continued, not looking at him, but determinedly.

"But you have so much strength, and much that would be unpardonable in others must be pardoned in you. You don't know yourself what you're doing, but you are guided by another, who knows better than I and better than you what is necessary for the salvation and good of our brothers…"

She rose and asked loudly:

"Do you still maintain that you love Nastasya Maximovna?"

He nodded silently, without moving. She continued:

"So be it, then, but remain with us—that's what I have to say to you. Remain as you were and do not abandon us."

She concluded in a softer tone, suddenly sweeping him with the white beams of her eyes. He understood; very quietly he said:

"I don't believe you."

"What, dearest?" she asked tenderly, deceived by the quietness of his speech.

"I don't believe you," he whispered even more quietly, and added: "What's the point of all this? It's sinful, everything's so confused…My God, you're forty-seven years old!" He was babbling as if in a dream. She started to say: "Yes, yes," then, "What's that, what's that?", fell silent, sitting down once more on the couch. Without speaking, she put on her hat, lowered her veil and said, delaying her departure:

"Can I ask one thing of you as a man of decency?"

"Tell me what it is."

"Let nobody know what has passed between us. No one must know of it, whatever your opinion of me."

"Yes, of course. That's how it would be without your asking."

She went out. A servant, hurrying in to give him a note, began, with a look of surprise, to hand the lady her coat. The paper burned in his hand like a coal. Smiling, Rebecca said:

"Don't bother about me, go and read it: perhaps it's something urgent."

"Miss Vetkina expects you at eight o'clock this evening, sir," interjected the servant. In the mirror he saw the lightnings, as if from the hand of Jove the Thunderer, flare and die in the white abysses of her eyes. Why was she dawdling? Why was she suddenly swaying, bowing? With her whole weight she sank back in his hastily extended arms, looking down with a gaze of unbearable radiance. She drank some water brought by the servant and went away for ever.

"Thank you for the cruel service you have rendered, I am glad, seeing in you a friend; I must speak with you; if you can, this evening at eight, if not—choose your own time.

A. Vetkina"

NINE

He didn't see the street he knew so well, where she lived, he didn't see the entrance, didn't see the room, the furniture—he didn't see anything, almost didn't see her standing in the small room in her black dress. Her voice was subdued, low. She gave him a sharp look as he came in, as if trying to remember him; not remembering him, she said: "I'm grateful to you for the letter, although I don't altogether comprehend what it was that moved you to write it. Considering you to be a friend of Viktor Andreevich, and not being acquainted with you, I'm rather at a loss. I believe you, and I'm grateful, but what was it that moved you to do me this service?"

"Friendship for you."

"That does not yet exist," Nastya interrupted him hurriedly and somewhat coldly.

"On my part only, on my part. I'm not speaking of the future, I'm not thrusting myself on you."

"I didn't mean to say that, and then you have the right to speak in that way. But this is what I want to know: all that you write about Fortov, does it apply to the past, even the most recent past, or to the present?"

"To the present."

"Yes, of course—otherwise your action would make no sense; but what am I to make of his behavior toward me?"

She began to walk up and down the room, forgetting to put on the light, listening to what Modest said softly and incoherently from his corner. Impossible to convey what he said, his words were apparently aimless, but in response to each a thought rose within her, sometimes completely unexpected and not connected with a given sound. Whether they talked for long in this manner she did not know. At last there came to Modest's ears: "To be led by the nose in this way, to be so deceived!" And she sank down in an armchair; then he approached her, and bending over her, began to speak of his love. Silently and patiently as before she listened to this hardly more coherent speech. At last she rose and said, almost angrily:

"Listen, your love might arouse in me distrust of what you have to say of other matters, but—alas!—it's too much like the truth, too convincing. I shall say to you what I would not say to anyone but a close friend. He—that man— no longer exists for me, he is dead, he is nothing, but there are no further consequences of this change in my feelings. I don't love you in the least. Goodbye."

Seeing that he still lingered, she added:

"And I don't think that I would ever grow to love you," and she got up, without offering him her hand.

July-August 1908

From the Letters of Maiden Clara Valmont to Rosalie Tutelmaier

27 July 172...

Forgive me, dear auntie, for not having written to you for so long, but this moving has made everyone go out of his mind; everything is now getting just a little in order, and yesterday they even got round to putting up a sign; Papa does all the bustling about himself, gets cross with us and swears at us, and yesterday got to the point of putting on his waistcoat back to front. Mama sends you her warmest regards; I have a room separate from hers but next door, and I leave the doors open at night, still being a terrible little coward. Apart from Jeanne and Pierre, still no more than a boy, Papa has Jacques Mobert, who joined us not long ago, a native of these parts, it seems. And he is such an odd fellow—came to get hired right in the middle of the night, when we were getting ready for bed; Papa almost chased him away without so much as talking to him, but everything was settled. There is plenty of work, thank goodness, so that Papa gets rather tired; but what is to be done, we have to keep body and soul together somehow. What shall I tell you of Lachaise-Dieu? It's a very small town with an old monastery rather like a fortress, and mountains visible in the distance. We may find it very boring here, although we have already made the acquaintance of one or two people. As it is, there is still no time to do anything because of getting settled. Goodbye, dear aunt; forgive me for not writing very much—there is terrible little time, and it is so hot as well that my whole back is wet. I kiss you, etc.

Your loving niece,
Clara Valmont

15 September 172...

I thank you, dear auntie, for the fur coat that you sent. Really you are too prudent, sending your delightful gift now, when we are still going for walks wearing no more than dresses. I recognized dear Aunt Rosalie both in this carefulness and in the choice of material! Where did you manage to find such wonderful material? Above all, with such a pattern? Those brilliant roses, green leaves on a golden-yellow background, are the object of surprise among all our friends, who come to see us especially to have a look at your gift, and I am waiting impatiently for the cold weather in order to put on this miracle for the first time. We are all in good health, although we live modestly and do not go anywhere. Jacques keeps us very much amused at home; he is a very entertaining, sweet young man, gifted and hardworking, so that Papa cannot praise him highly enough. Mama doesn't like his not going to church and dislike of pious conversation. It is bad, of course, but youth can be forgiven this failing, all the more as Jacques is, generally speaking, a very modest young man: not an idler, not a gambler, not a drunkard. Once more I thank you, dear aunt, for the fur coat, and I remain your loving niece

> Clara Valmont

2 October 172...

Dear aunt, I felicitate you with all my heart on your birthday (we must not forget that you are now entering your sixty-ninth year!) and I would like to greet it in a less troubled, less confused state than that in which I now find myself. Oh auntie, auntie. I'm so used to writing you everything that it is far easier to make my confessions to you than to Father Vitalius, our priest, whom I have known for only a few months. How shall I begin? With what? I am trembling like a little girl, and only the memory of your dear, kind face, the awarness that for Aunt Rosalie I am still the same little Clara, give me courage. You remember that I wrote to you about Jacques Mobert, well, auntie, I have grown to love him. Remember your own youth, Regensburg, young Heinrich von Mondschein and don't be too strict with your poor little Clara, who has not been able to withstand love's enchantments...He promises to confide in Father and marry me after Christmas, but nobody suspects anything at home, and you must not give me away, please. How much easier I feel for confiding in you. I particularly love his eyes, which are so enormous when we kiss, and then he has a way of rubbing his eyebrows against my cheeks, which is enchantingly delightful. Forgive me, dear aunt, and don't be angry with your poor

> Clara Valmont

By the way, Jacques is not from these parts at all, and no one in Lachaise-Dieu knows him—we were quite wrong in imagining such a thing. But what does it matter really? Isnt that true?..

3 December 172…

It's true that misfortune never comes alone! Mama noticed my waist yesterday, began to question me, and I confessed everything. You can imagine Mama's grief, Papa's anger. He struck me in the face and said: "I never thought to have a trollop for a daughter," and went out, banging the door. Mama, weeping, comforted me as best she could. But how much I needed you, dear aunt, your tenderness, your advice. I don't go anywhere now, and I won't need to put on your coat. But the most terrible thing is that Jacques has deserted us. I'm certain that he has set off for his own town to ask his parents' blessing; but whatever is happening there, he just isn't here, and my boredom, my anguish are made still worse by his absence. I have the impression that everyone knows of my shame, and I'm afraid of going to the window; I sew without a pause, although now it is rather difficult to sit bent over for a long time. Yes, evil days have befallen me. As the song has it:

> Love's pleasures last a single moment,
> Love's suffering lasts a lengthy age.

Goodbye, and forgive your loving
Clara

2 June 172…

You probably thought, auntie, that I am already dead, not having received any letters from me for so many months. Unfortunately, I am alive. I shall tell you calmly all that happened. Jacques is no longer alive, and may God forgive him his evil as He has spared us from the wiles of Satan. On May 22nd I was delivered of a child, a boy. But, merciful God, what a child it was: covered in hair, without eyes and with unmistakable little horns on its head. They feared for my life, when I should set eyes on my child. My child, what horror! Nevertheless, they decided to christen it according to the rites of the holy Catholic Church. During the ceremony, water, prepared for pouring, suddenly began to let off steam, there arose a terrible stench and when the priests were able to open their eyes after the pungent steam, they saw in the font instead of the baby a large black horseradish. Heaven preserve us from the wiles of Satan. You can imagine all the sorrow, all the horror, and the joy that we were not utterly ruined. When I was told everything that had happened in the church, I became like a madwoman. We held a service, and every day they sprinkle holy water. They have read me prayers to drive out evil spirits. Father Vitalius advised that my organism be cleansed of the evil seed...You wouldn't recognize me, dear aunt, so much have I altered during this time. Such a misfortune does not fall to everyone's lot. But God will preserve all those who trust in Him.

Goodbye, etc., Your Loving
Clara Valmont

21 June 172...

I am writing to you again, dear aunt, thinking that you must be very worried by our affairs. After my cleansing, the local people began to root out the remaining traces of the evil spirit from among themselves. They remembered all the various work done by Jacques Mobert (although it would be better to call him the fiend Beelzebub): boots, ladies' shoes, slippers and jackboots, and, piling everything in the square in front of the abbey, they burned it all. Only the old watchmaker Limosius refused to hand over his boots, saying that solid boots were more important to him than stupid superstitions. But of course he was a Jew and a godless man, taking no trouble for the salvation of his immortal soul. Goodbye, dear aunt, etc.

I remain your loving
Clara Valmont

THE SHADE OF PHYLLIS

I

Whe old Nektaneb lifted his eyes from the nets that had been flung over him, his attention caught by a sharp cry that floated alone in the cool of the evening, he caught sight of a small boat in the pillar of the sinking sun's reflection, and an individual making vain efforts to escape by swimming. To ride over, throwing his nets where he had seen someone drowning, to fling himself into the water and back into the boat, already carrying the one he had rescued, was a matter of a few minutes. The girl had been deprived of her senses, and, the natural high color having fled her cheeks, the artificial paint emerged more distinctly on her thin, rather long face. Only when the old man had laid her carefully upon the matting in his hut—for he was no more than a poor fisherman—did the rescued woman open her eyes and sigh, as if aroused from a deep sleep, and, together with the first signs of life, her sorrow returned, because tears ran abundantly from her pale hazel eyes, and she began to toss about as if in a fever, loudly and bitterly bewailing her lot. From her incoherent words and exclamations, Nektaneb discovered her to be a wealthy heiress, an orphan, rejected by some heartless youth and attempting in a fit of despair to bury her grief in the river's flow. He also discovered that she was called Phyllis. But anyway, he could have guessed that without her words, for the house of her parents, now deceased, was situated close to the river's bank, where boats were moored to be taken out and for any other needs their owners might have. She wept as she spoke, entwining her arms about the old fisherman's neck and pressing herself against him, as a baby presses against its wetnurse, while he stroked her hair and comforted her as best he could.

II

Morning and deep sleep brought the calm that had not come with gentle words. Happier thoughts, more cheerful plans arose in tender Phyllis's head. She told

Nektaneb clearly how to find his way to the house of the cruel Pancratius, how
to invent a deceiving tale about her death, which allegedly had already taken
place, observing, in order to make report to her, how his handsome face, which
always wore an expression of boredom, changed when, to confirm his tale, he
should hand over a note, allegedly found in the folds of the drowned woman's
clothes together with a striped coverlet. She clapped her hands, having written
a letter of farewell, and tried to hurry the old man, full of excitement and joy. The
messenger had to go through quite a few streets before he reached Pancratius's
small but comfortable country house. The young master was occupied in playing
ball with a tall boy in light, paleblue clothes when the old fisherman was brought
to him. Learning that there was a letter from Phyllis, whose garden stretched to
the river, he asked, without breaking the seal and running a hand through his
dark curly locks: "Did the lady send you herself?"

"No, but it was her wish to see this letter in your hands."

"The writing is certainly hers; let's see what this dear letter brings us."

A smile was still on the young man's lips when he began to read the girl's final
letter, but gradually his brow folded in a frown, his eyebrows rose, his lips con-
tracted, and his voice sounded grim and fearful when he asked, hiding the letter
in his clothes:"Is what is written in this letter true?"

"I don't know what the poor mistress wrote, but this is what I saw with my own
eyes"—and then followed a tale cleverly invented, but of course half true, of
Phyllis's alleged death. The coverlet, known to Pancratius as the girl's undoubted
property, finally convinced him of the truth of the sad invention, and sending
the fisherman away with a reward, he absently renewed his ballgame with the tall
boy, a game with which he always occupied himself between his bath and lunch.

I I I

Seven or eight times the rejected Phyllis forced herself to listen to details of the
meeting with Pancratius. She wanted to know both what he had said at first and
what he had said later, and how he had been dressed and how he had looked: had
he been sad or indifferent, pale or healthy-looking—and Nektaneb made vain attempts to strain his old memory in order to answer the girl's tumultuous and incoherent questions.

The next morning he said: "What do you think, mistress? Shouldn't you go
back to your house, seeing that you are among the living?"

"Go home? Not for anything in the world! Then everyone would find out that
I am alive; you're forgetting that I am one of the departed."

And Phyllis burst into loud laughter, the brightness of her eyes and cheeks
making her joking inventions all the funnier.

"I'll stay with you: by day, when you go into town, I'll lie among the vegetable beds, and I won't be noticed among the ripe melons, and in the evening you'll tell me about what you saw during the day."

At last the fisherman persuaded the young mistress to tell everything to her old wet-nurse, who lived on a farm not far from Alexandria, to tell her everything frankly and to wait there for what time and fate would reveal. Himself, he promised to give her a daily report of the activities of Pancratius which had any kind of bearing upon the girl who loved him.

"How am I to get there?"

"I'll take you across myself in my boat."

"Through the whole town? A living corpse?"

"No, you'll be lying on the bottom, under a cloth."

"The guards will come and arrest you as a thief."

"I'll cover you on top with matting."

Being a complete orphan, Phyllis was easily able to hide her disappearance and to live peacefully on old Manto's farm, trying to guess by the flowers from morning to night whether her distant young man would ever grow to love her, now tearing off one petal after another, now slapping down leaves impatiently, angry at an unfavorable answer, or responding with childlike pleasure to the opposite kind. Since the emotion of love did not deprive her of her appetite and the modest farm lunch did not satisfy her taste, grown capricious from inactivity, the secret of her life soon became known to the woman who managed her house in town, who sent every day through the old fisherman now a sweet pastry with ginger, now some skillfully prepared game, now a cockscomb pie, now a fragrant melon boiled in tender honey.

I V

With much ado Nektaneb's old legs hastened in the wake of the rapid and youthful steps of Pancratius and his companion. It was already evening, and the smell of salt and grass came from the sea, the large lantern had been lit in the drawing rooms and music could be heard, across the street walked sailors in groups of four and more, hands joined, and our companions penetrated further and further into the town's dark run-down quarters. At last, pushing back a reed curtain, they went into a house with the look of a thieves den or a low inn for the harbor crowd. Nektaneb lingered in going after them, so as not to draw their attention, and waited for other visitors in order to make his way in unnoticed. At last he noticed five sailors, the youngest of whom was saying: "And she put a sponge in his chest instead of a heart; in the morning he started boozing, the sponge fell out—and he died."

The fisherman, who went in with them, was unable to make anything out for some minutes, having been broken by poverty and age of the habit of visiting such places. Noise, shouting, the rattle of clay mugs, singing and the sound of a drum pierced the suffocatingly stuffy air. Women singers sat by the curtain, wiping away sweat and trickling rouge with their hands. On the table, among mugs full of wine, a naked ten-year-old Nubian girl brought her head close to the customers' heels in a skillful winding motion. A trained dog aroused enthusiasm, guessing the amount of money in the vistors' purses by means of numbers crudely cut out of wood. Pancratius sat by the exit with his companion, pulling his caracalla still lower over his eyes, which made them seem glittering and changed. He stopped the old man, who was making his way through, saying: "Listen, was it you who brought me news of the death of the unfortunate Phyllis? I was looking for you, I am Pancratius the rhetorician, but keep it quiet…Come and see me tomorrow after midday; there's something I want to tell you: the woman who died won't let me rest." He spoke in a half-whisper, was pale, and behind his hood his eyes seemed glittering and changed.

V

Phyllis sat on the threshold of the house, reading some scrolls Nektaneb had just brought; in the hand of the copyist was written: "Elegy of Phyllis, the Unhappy Daughter of Palemon." She sat bending over, not hearing the slaves passing through with tubs of gleaming milk, the gardener clipping the flowers, the little dog barking as it chased leaping frogs, and in the distance the reapers sang a plaintive song. The lines grew blurred before her, and the memory of past anxieties again clouded her untroubled gaze.

> Parents, O parents,
> My father and mother,
> Bright-colored clothes
> Have you left me,
> Horses of white,
> Bracelets fine woven,
> But most dearly I love
> The shawl of rich crimson
> With the full-throated phoenixes.
> Parents, O parents,
> My father and mother,
> Much have you left me
> In lands and in cattle.

Goats with strong legs,
Sheep with strong brows,
Cows with strong horns,
Oxen and mules—
But what I love most
Is the white dove, brown-spotted:
She was called "Catamite."
Parents, O parents,
My father and mother,
Many true servants
Have you bequeathed me:
Growers of marrows, growers of flowers,
Weavers and spinners,
Brewers of mead, bakers of bread,
Tumblers and players of pipes—
Yet most dearly I love
The crone deep in age
Who has been my nanny.
Dear to me is my nanny,
Dear is my dove,
Dear is my shawl,
But my garden's still dearer.
It sinks, it sinks
To the river, our garden,
On the land by the river,
Lives my friend.
I cannot send,
Cannot send him a flower,
But with the rowers I'll send
A bow, a deep bow.

And further was written:

In the morning my nanny said to me
—No reason to hide things from an old woman—
"You spend the whole day telling fortunes from flowers,
But you can't tell a quince from an apple,
You sew, but you do not embroider,
You tenderly kiss your gay-colored dove,
And at night you whisper: "Pancratius.""

And further was written:

> What shall I choose, dear friends:
> To a friend that's cruel
> Shall I again confess all?
> Or throw myself into
> A fast-flowing river?
> Both paths are hard,
> But the first is the hardest—
> Such blushing, such stammering.

And further was written:

> The blushing sun will rise in the morning,
> You will go and attend to your business,
> Those passing will see you,
> They will think: "Cruel Pancratius"—
> But pale Phyllis will be no more!
> You'll walk along the alleyways,
> Read Phylonus with your friends,
> Throw the discus and run to catch it—
> Everyone will say: "Handsome Pancratius"—
> And pale Phyllis will be no more!
> You will return to your cool house,
> You will take a fragrant bath,
> You will play ball with a boy,
> And you'll fall asleep calmly before morning
> Thinking: "Happy Pancratius"—
> But pale Phyllis will be no more!

And much more was written besides, and so the girl read until evening, sighing and weeping over her own words.

VI

Pancratius did not now play ball with the boy, did not sit down to lunch, but walked through the small inner garden along the bed of stock, with the look of a man tormented with anxiety. Immediately upon greeting he began: "The dead girl gives me no peace; I see her in my sleep, and she beckons me somewhere, smiling with her pale face."

The old man, knowing Phyllis to be among the living, remarked:

"There are deceiving dreams, sir, do not let them worry you."

"They cannot but worry me; perhaps, after all, I am the innocent cause of her death."

"Consider her to be alive, if that would bring back your peace of mind."

"But did she not die?"

"That which we consider to be dead is dead, and which we consider to be alive lives."

"It seems that you are getting close to what I wanted to talk about with you. Promise me that you won't breathe a word."

"You have my promise."

"Do you know an exorcist who would summon the shade of Phyllis for me?"

"The shade of Phyllis?"

"Yes, the shade of the dead Phyllis. Can that seem strange to you?"

Controlling himself, Nektaneb replied:

"No, it doesn't seem strange to me, and I even know the man you need, only do you believe in the power of magic yourself?"

"Why should I ask you otherwise? And what have my beliefs to do with it?"

"He lives not far from me, and I can arrange a time for us to meet."

"Please do so. You have helped me greatly with your words 'that which we consider to be dead is dead,' and the opposite."

"Enough, sir, those are empty words, thoughtlessly dropped by an uneducated old fisherman, which is what I am."

"You yourself do not know the entire meaning of those words. For me, Phyllis is as if she were alive. Arrange the thing we talked about as soon as possible."

The youth gave the fisherman some money, and the old man, taking a long path to the farm, was occupied with many different thoughts, leading to one clearer and propitious one, so that Phyllis, who had not slept and herself opened the gate for him, saw him smiling and as if bearing news of good fortune.

VII

Nektaneb's plan was met by the girl's astonished exclamations.

"You think so? Is that possible? Won't that be sacrilege? Think of it; magical invocations have the power to call forth the souls of the dead—but how shall I, a living being, deceive him whom I love? Will not the dog-headed goddess punish me?"

"We offer no outrage to sacred rites; you're not dead, and were not so; we will make use of the external form of the incantation to calm Pancratius's unquiet spirit."

"Has he come to love me now, and wants to see me?"

"Yes."

"To see me dead! Dead!"

"But you will be alive."

"They will dress me in funeral clothes, a dead girl's wreath! I will speak through the smoke from sulphur, which will make the image of me a dead one!"

"I don't know in what guise you will have to represent the spirit. If you don't wish to do that, it could be avoided."

"How?"

"By refusing to answer the summons."

"Not to see him! No, no."

"It will be possible to say that the exorcist finds this quarter of the moon unfavorable."

"And then?"

"Then Pancratius will calm down by himself and forget everything."

"He'll calm down, you say? When will Parrasius come so that we can make the agreement and he can teach me what to do?"

"When you wish: tomorrow, the day after."

"Today. All right?"

Left by herself, Phyllis sat motionless for a long time, then plucked a flower, and receiving a "yes" to her constant question, was about to smile, but straightaway turned pale again and whispered: "You have been given the happiness of love not as a living being, wretched Phyllis!" But the morning sun, the singing of the grasshoppers in the dew, the quiet river, the short list of the years she had lived through, the dream of a now loving Pancratius quickly brought back the laughter to the crimson lips of the merry and faithful Phyllis.

VIII

When the harp sounded softly in answer to the magic formula and a vague shadow was thrown on the curtain, Pancratius did not recognize Phyllis; her eyes were covered, her cheeks pale, her lips compressed, her hands folded on her breast in a bandage, all of which gave her a strong resemblance to a corpse. When she halted, opening her eyes and lifting her bound hands weakly, Pancratius asked the exorcist's permission and addressed her, sinking to his knees, thus:

"Are you the shade of Phyllis?"

"I am Phyllis herself," came in response.

"Do you forgive me?"

"We are all subject to fate; you could not have acted other than you have."

"Did you return to earth willingly?"

"I could do nothing but obey the incantation."

"Do you love me?"

"You see my love now; I have ventured on a terrible crime, perhaps, in summoning you. Do you believe that I love you?"

"Dead?"

"Yes. Could you come closer to me? Give me your hand? Respond to my kisses? I will warm you and make your heart beat again."

"I can approach you, give you my hand, respond to your kisses. I have come to you for that."

She took a step toward him, while he rushed toward her; he did not notice that her hands were warmer than his own, that her heart was beating against his own, that her eyes were gleaming, gazing into his darkened glance. Pushing him away, Phyllis said: "I'm jealous of you."

"Jealous of whom?" he whispered, languishing.

"The living Phyllis. You loved her and tolerate me."

"Oh, I do not know, do not ask me. You alone, you alone I love!"

Phyllis said no more, not responding to the kisses and holding herself aloof; at last, when he threw himself upon the floor in desperation, weeping like a boy and saying: "You do not love me," Phyllis said slowly: "You yourself do not know what I have done," and going up to him, she locked him in an embrace and began to kiss him passionately and sweetly on the lips. Himself redoubling his tenderness, he did not notice how the girl grew weaker, and suddenly exclaimed: "Phyllis, what is the matter with you?" and let her free of his embrace, and she fell soundlessly at his feet. It did not surprise him that her hands were cold, that her heart was not beating, but the silence which suddenly descended on the chamber filled him with inexplicable fear. He cried out loudly, and the slaves and the exorcist who came in saw in the torchlight a dead girl in tangled burial robes, a discarded bandage and a wreath of delicate golden leaves. Pancratius again cried out loudly, seeing lifeless one who had just responded to his caresses, and stumbling to the doors whispered in horror: "Look: the decay of three weeks is upon her brow! Oh! Oh!"

The exorcist, who had come up, said: "The term given by magic has expired, and once more death has gained possession of the girl who returned temporarily to life"—and he made a sign for the slaves to carry out the corpse of the pale Phyllis, daughter of Palemon.

Florus the Bandit

I

Each time that Florus Emilius quickly reached the opposite wall, made of the same red, gleaming stone, he would so impetuously swing round his face, which had turned pale, and his steps were so very ringing, so unlike his usual lightness of gait, that the old slave and the dumb boy sitting on the floor would give a start every time and screw up their eyes when the edge of the master's pale blue robes would brush lightly against them as he turned.

As if tired of the throwing, he sent forth the old man, shaking his head with closed eyes in a sign of refusal to listen to business reports. The boy, creeping up to the sleeping man, kissed him on the knee, gazing into his eyes. Giving a whistle to the big retriever, all three of them went through to the garden, where they walked in each other's wake once more: the master, silent and with big steps, the mute boy minced along, the retriever, shaking his large head, hurriedly strode behind them.

Calmed by his second tiredness, Florus entered the house continuing to read an epistle he had already begun:

"…what I am going to say will seem childish to you, but this trifle deprives me of peace and spiritual calm, essential to all those who hold man's dignity dear. The other day I met a simple fellow whom I had never seen before, but with a glance so familiar that if I shared the teaching of Brahmins concerning metempsychosis, I would have thought that the two of us had met in a former life. And what is stranger still is that the memory of this meeting has been growing stronger in my head, as beans swell when they are strewn in water for the night, and doesn't let me rest, and I'm prepared to go and look for this man myself, not caring to entrust others with the task, ashamed of my own weakness. Perhaps all this is the result of the imperfect state of my health: frequent dizziness, sleeplessness, melancholy and needless fear do not allow it to be considered satisfactory. The man I met had gray eyes of unusual brightness, with swarthy skin and dark hair.

In height and build he was like me. Greetings to Calpurnius, a kiss for the children; I sent the amphoras to your house in town long ago now. Once more I wish you health."

I I

After a moment's silence, the physician asked: "To what condition does your own bear the most resemblance, sir?"

"I have not experienced the situation of a man locked in a dungeon, but I believe that the state in which I find myself is closest of all to such a case. For some time my movements have been hindered, even my willpower seems limited; I want to walk and I can't; I want to breathe and I gasp for air; vague unrest and melancholy exert their power over me."

Florus fell silent, as if weary of talking; turning pale, he began once more:

"Perhaps my idea of a dungeon is influenced by a dream I had before my illness."

"You had a dream?"

"Yes, such a vivid one, so clear! And the strange thing is that it continues as if to this time, as if I wanted to (I'm convinced of it) I could spend my whole life in it, and treat you, my friend, as a phantom."

"It doesn't disturb you to tell me about it?"

"No, not at all!" replied Emilius hurriedly, wiping away the drops of sweat that had broken out on his pale forehead. He began, as if calling things to mind with an effort, brokenly, in a voice that would suddenly rise to a shout then fall to a murmuring whisper.

"Don't tell anyone what you will hear…swear…perhaps this is the very truth. I don't know…I killed—don't think…it was there, in my dream. I ran away, wandered about for a long time, feeding on berries (I remember: wild cherries), stealing bread, milk from the udders of cows in the fields, directly. Oh, the sun burned, and the bogs made me drunk! Making my way through the harbor gates, I was seized, like someone who had stolen a knife. A tall red-haired shopkeeper (yes, they shouted "Titus" at him) held me fast, weak and confused as I was; a red-haired woman was laughing loudly, a red-haired dog was squealing between my legs, carnations lay about on the pavement, soldiers marched, armored in bronze…they hit me…the sun was scorching. Then darkness and a stifling cool. Oh, coolness of gardens, bright springs, mountain wind, where are you?…"

And Florus, in a state of collapse, fell silent and sank forward. The physician said "Go to sleep," and went out to the manager to talk about the sick man. The dumb boy listened, opening his eyes and mouth greedily. Toward evening Florus summoned his old nanny. Squatting on her haunches, the old woman, having run out of fairytales and childhood recollections, spoke disconnectedly of what her wrinkled eyes had seen and what her deaf ears had heard. Wrapping herself tightly in her shawl, the nanny mumbled:

"Sonny, the other day at the Havana Gates I saw a murderer: he had a knife in his hands, but his face wasn't terrible; his eyes were bright, oh how bright, he had dark hair, a boy by the look of him. My son-in-law, the shopkeeper Titus, got hold of him…"

Florus shouted, seizing her by the arm:

"Don't talk! Don't talk! Go away! Titus, you say? Titus is a magician?"

Frightened, the boy ran into the chamber at the shouting.

I I I

Many more days passed in this struggle, and the sick man said more than once: "I can't carry on any more: it's more than my strength!" and from pale he somehow turned black, gnawed by a secret illness. Dark circles fringed his eyes, and his voice seemed to emerge from a dried-up throat. Every night he did not sleep, tormenting the dumb boy with fear.

One morning, getting up before dawn, he asked for his hat and shawl, as if preparing to set out on a journey. The old man refrained from asking questions, and it was only in answer to his glance that Florus said:

"You will follow me!"

The young master's gait was light and easy once more; and color returned to the crimson roses of his cheeks. The windings of the streets and squares led them far from the house, giving the slave no answers to the riddle. At last he ventured to ask, when they were tired, as if having reached their destination:

"Will you go in here, master?"

"Yes."

Florus's voice rang out carelessly. They entered a prison. As Florus Emilius was known to be rich and noble, he was able without difficulty, although for a price, to see whether his slave, who, it appeared, had fled not long ago, was not to be found among the prisoners. Quickly, with a vigilant eye, he searched the prison down to the last cellar, as if looking for those who had earlier been familiar to his gaze. Out of breath, he asked:

"Are all the prisoners here? Are there no more?"

"No more, sir. One escaped yesterday…"

"Escaped?.. His name?.."

"Malchus."

"Malchus?" he responded, seemingly pricking up his ears. "Bright eyes, swarthy, black hair?" asked Florus in delight.

"Yes, you're right, sir," the warder nodded his head.

Gay as never before was Emilius Florus as he emerged from the building; he spoke like a child, and his eyes, which had not lost their dark rings, gleamed.

"My old Mummius, look: was the sky ever so soft, the trees and the grass ever so friendly? We'll go to my farm on foot; I'll eat wild cherries and drink milk straight from cows' udders. How gently the day flows by! You'll get me a girl smelling of grass, goat and just faintly of onion; we won't take dumb Lucus to the country. Oh, old Mummius, aren't I healthier than ever before? The clouds are high, as if it were spring, as if it were spring!"

IV

In the morning Florus made joyful preparations for the road, leaving his comfortable estate house to go for a long walk along both broad and narrow roads. Gorgo, who had been found for him, was gentle, silent, submissive and simple, like a heifer; she gave her swarthy body lightly and purely; she waited in the house, singing songs from the old days.

Dumb Lucus, who had come running to join them of his own accord, accompanied his master everywhere, rejoicing with sad eyes and tired, boyish face. He watched in silence, not leaving Florus for a moment with his suddenly returned cheerfulness. Always to walk along the mountain paths, to lie on the grass, bright with flowers, to lie on one's back and gaze into the pale blue firmament, to sing simple village songs untiringly, making people purse their lips for a little into their double flutes! In a quiet herd, the white, dazzlingly white, blindingly white clouds stood above grove and river; they were waiting. With milk-stains on his lips, unshaven, Florus kissed Gorgo with his red mouth, forgetting his city languor, disregarding the smell of onion. Dumb Lucus cried in the corner. Day followed upon day, like flower after flower entwined in a wreath.

One evening, in the midst of careless play, Florus seemed bedimmed by sadness or seized by an invisible enemy. Becoming suddenly hoarse, he said: "What is this? Where is this darkness coming from? This captivity?" He lay down on a low bed, turned to the wall and sighed in silence. Gorgo came softly and embraced him without looking at him. Florus pushed her away, saying: "Who are you? I don't know you. It isn't time: take care lest the rumbling of the fortress awakens the sleeping guard." She withdrew in silence, and the dumb boy again crept in, like a dog, kissing the dangling hand.

It was a stuffy night for the servants dozing at the entrance to Florus's bedchamber. Lucus alone remained with his master, dumb and devoted. For a long time only the steps of Emilius walking back and forth could be heard. Near morning, just before dawn, the servants sank into a light sleep. Suddenly the air was pierced with a shriek in a voice that did not seem human. It seemed that the unearthly thing cried out "Death!", awakening an immediate echo.

After a pause, the servants knocking at the door were let in by the dumb boy, his face unrecognizable from fright. "Death, death!" he repeated in a wild voice not accustomed to pronouncing words. Not even amazed by the sounds from the dumb man, the servants rushed to the bed, upon which, his blackened head flung back, lay the master, motionless. Lucus returned to Florus's bed as to an abandoned place, and stretched out on the floor, which collapsed quickly and noiselessly.

They quickly follwed the physician and manager out, bearing the ominous news.

The dumb boy unceasingly repeated "death," as if the power of speech had been given to him again only for that one word.

Florus lay there, his blackened face and lifeless hand flung back. The physician, having examined the body and pronounced death to be certain, with amazement revealed to the manager the dark, narrow and swollen bruise on the dead man's neck, which could not be explained at all. The sole witness of the death of Florus Emilius, dumb Lucus, overcoming the heaven-sent twisted speech of his miraculous fear, the gift of speech having returned to him, said:

"Death! Death! Again he's imprisoned...he walked, he walked: lay down on the bed, as if he was tired...not a word did he say to me; toward morning he started to wheeze, disturbed; I rushed over to him; he fluttered his eyes at me, began moving them around, wheezing. Ye gods! Morning gleamed red in the window. Florus didn't move, he'd turned black..."

Lucus was forgotten in grief and funeral bustle.

The next morning it was barely light when a bare-footed and ragged old fellow made his way in, begging to see Florus; no one knew who he was. The manager came out, thinking to find some explanation of his master's death. The newcomer was stubborn and simpleminded by the look of him. Packs of dogs howled around.

"You didn't know that Florus Emilius had died?"

"No. It doesn't make any difference. I have done what was ordered me."

"By whom?"

"Malchus."

"Who is he?"

"He is not with us now."

"He died?"

"Yesterday morning he was hanged."

"Did he know the master?"

"No. He sent him, a man he did not know, his love and news of his death. The dumb will begin speaking among you."

"They are speaking already," said Lucus, who had come up, bending over the old man's dirty hand.

"You won't take a look at the dead man?"

"What for? Has his face changed very much?"

"Very much."

"The noose changed that one too. He has a big mark on his neck…"

"Is there much you want to say?"

"No, I'm going."

"I'm coming with you!" said Lucus to the unknown man gently.

The sun had already tinted the yard with rose, and hired women let forth piercing howls to the heavens, laying bare their bony breasts.

THE STORY OF XANTHOS

THE COOK OF THE EMPEROR ALEXANDER,
AND HIS WIFE KALLA

O n all his lengthy campaigns, the great Alexander was accompanied by
old Xanthos, who was in charge of the imperial kitchen. It was not easy
for the old man to make difficult crossings over deserts and mountains,
but the emperor would not part with his old cook, having grown accustomed to
him and fearing poison in the case of the food being prepared by other, less devoted hands. Xanthos loved Alexander, having known him since his birth, as he
was very old and had been in the service as a cook since the time of the king's
grandfather. Xanthos's wife was also a woman deep in years, but she did not stray
from her husband, nor from the Macedonian hero, who in her eyes still remained
a child. She followed behind the troops in a covered carriage and baked Alexander fish pie as no one else was able to, using old recipes, and in her sleepless
hours she would sometimes invite herself to the emperor's tent to sing Thessalian
songs and tell fairytales.

Thus they traveled from country to country, from region to region, passing
mountains, rivers, deserts and boundless marshes.

After one of his victories, Alexander halted in a remote canyon and expressed
the wish to eat his favorite fish pie; Kalla immediately set about cooking, and in
order to make the business go more quickly sent her husband to the stream to
clean fish while she herself kneaded the rich dough. The cook cut the fish up
with a knife and began washing it in a mountain stream, but as soon as the stream
touched the ripped-open fish, they suddenly came to life and slipped from the
hands of the astonished Xanthos; and not only were the fish themselves resur-
rected, but even the roe, which had been thrown away and lay on the shore and
on which the scattered waves of the stream fell, turned into fishlets and merrily
jumped into the babbling water. The old man remained motionless in the position he was, on his knees; regaining his composure, he uttered thanks to the merciful nymphs who had shown him such a miracle, secretly told everything that
had happened to Kalla, and they returned to the stream with large pitchers in

order to gather the miraculous water, baked pie with the new fish, which had been washed at another source, this time an ordinary one. The old married couple did not say anything to anybody of the magical power of the life-giving water, but each morning they drank a few mouthfuls from a hidden vessel. And their former youth began to enter the decrepit bodies, their wrinkles disappeared, their cheeks took on high color, their hair thickened, their eyes began to gleam, their gait grew lighter, their voices ringing. This wonderful transformation did not escape the eyes of Alexander, when one day instead of a decrepit crone there came to him an elderly woman of about forty, in whom, without difficulty but with great surprise, he recognized Xanthos' wife Kalla. With a sharp glance at the newly entered woman, he said distinctly: "Do I see the spouse of my cook, old Xanthos, or are demons deceiving me with visions? Or has my old childhood returned to me and I am lying in my swaddling clothes? Who has relieved your shoulders of thirty long years, good mother?"

The cook's wife at first denied everything, but then, exacting a terrible oath from the emperor, she revealed everything to him as it had been. Alexander said nothing in reply, but he ordered Xanthos to be summoned at once to his presence. And he entered with the firm gait of an elderly man, but one full of strength and power. Throwing a rapid glance in his direction, the king shouted: "Confess, deceiver, that you concealed from me the source of the life-giving water in order to make use of it alone. Madman, do you think that immortality can be achieved by simple mortals? Or when you get home will you pour out your water into small vessels and go and sell it in the marketplace to all who want it? The gods alone give us the power of immortality, neither will, nor chance give the heavenly gift to us. You will see what a mistake you have made." Alexander ordered the cook and the now much younger-looking Kalla to be bound, and to be put in a wooden cage so as to be pulled in the wake of the troops until he decided what to do with them. The rumor about the miraculous water spread through the camp, and everyone came hurrying to see the revived people. The king himself asked every morning how the captives were; of course he had loved Xanthos and Kalla since his childhood, and for that reason he coped with the situation, but for some reason he always turned pale and frowned at the answer, "They're getting younger all the time," and almost as soon as the early pre-dawn light forced him to open his eyes, he would already be shouting "How are the prisoners?" — "They're getting younger still" was the invariable reply, and each time the emperor's countenance grew still paler and more severe. And the imprisoned old folk, hiding under the clothes on their breasts flasks with the living water, gazed ever more clearly with their newly young eyes, their cheeks became ever smoother and softer, their bodies themselves became more lithe and shapely, and when Kalla sang Thessalian songs, her voice sounded as it had fifty years earlier, when she had run, a mere girl, through the mountain valleys, gathering red poppies. In their cage the youthful married pair laughed, joked, played with pebbles, as if forgetting their imprisonment, like carefree birds. The freshness of long before returned to their very kisses, as though at the first declaration of timid love.

Thus did the emperor march forward, and behind the troops followed the cart with the carefree prisoners. Eventually a flat, shining sea gleamed before them beyond a yellow sandbank. Alexander assembled his soldiers and ordered them to lead out Xanthos and Kalla to the center. They came running like school children, laughing and throwing a ball back and forth, and the king, pale, leaned on the shoulder of Haephestion so as to hide his emotion. He began in a hoarse voice: "Friends and brothers-in-arms, now you will see with your own eyes whether mortals not born of the gods may attain sweet immortality here." Then he gave orders for the cook and his wife to be seated in a boat, to sail out into the deep and, stones being tied about their necks, to be thrown into the sea; himself mounting a lonely hill, he looked on, surrounded by friends, as his commands were carried out. And only when the splashing waves had calmed, closing once more over the cast-down bodies, did Alexander say loudly, raising high toward the heavens the vessels with miraculous water which had been taken away from the old folk, in a voice that carried far along the seashore: "Men and brothers, have you seen with your own eyes where the pride of human self-will leads, where leads a path not indicated by Heaven? We are mortal and must die; only the children of the gods, only the sons of Ammon may venture upon immortality." He threw the vessels to the ground, and the sound made by their fragments was drowned in the cries of the crowd: "Glory to the son of Ammon, to the hero Alexander the immortal!" But from the sea came a childish howl in a thin voice like the whisper of rushes: "Alexander, Alexander, look about you, admit your guilt and repent!"

And there, cutting the low waves, sped a triton and a naiad with the faces of Xanthos and Kalla; the former blew upon a twisted horn, and the other, winding herself about her friend's neck, shouted, opening her mouth wide: "Alexander, our thanks to you for casting us into the sea, now you can no longer reach us, and we do not fear death or tedious senility. I am Kalla, and Xanthos is at my side. And you, emperor, will die a cruel death in Babylon. Remember, remember." And gleaming with radiant spray, they disappeared in the distance, where the sun was sinking behind a flat cape. On the bank, the emperor and his troops were silent for a long time, but at a given signal trumpets roared, shields clanked, carts creaked and the whole enormous throng turned away from the sea and slowly began to move back in the gathering twilight. Alexander ordered a youth to take aim at a low-flying gull and, gathering up the fallen bird, to march in front of the troops together with him, in order to test every stream, to see whether it was not the life-giving source.

But in vain did they dip the gull in all the streams and rivers; it only got wet, but life did not return to it. When it began to rot, the youth threw it away and took aim at another.

In this way they marched over mountains and valleys, past lakes and boundless marshes: the emperor in front, at his side the bowman with the dead bird in his hands, behind them the colonels, and behind them the troops followed on like a heavy stormcloud, and in the rear the squeaking carts filled the air with dust.

For a long time they wandered in this way, not finding the miraculous mountain valley, until Alexander gave the order to abandon the birds and not to shoot new ones.

He came out to the troops and again tried to convince them of the obvious impossibility of immorality, even in his, Alexander's, divine guise. His voice was firm and ringing, his eyes shone and his cheeks glowed with color because on this occasion the son of Philippa had berouged them, in order not to disturb the hearts of the weak with imperial doubt.

THE EDUCATION OF NISA

I

Nisa had close-cropped hair, like a girl from an orphanage, and she never understood why she couldn't play with the boys in the yard. Katya and Manya, who already had plaits, threw up their hands and exclaimed squeakily:

"Nisa, you shameless girl! How can you possibly play with boys?!"

The little girl looked at them in perplexity. They burst our laughing and both began to whisper at once:

"You can't even go up to boys! They're fighters and nogoods. They're hooligans. If there's a lot of us and there's one boy, and there's no one around, then you can give him a licking — and that's it!"

"Do you remember how we gave Petka from the laundry a pinching? We threw his hat in the rubbish heap, tore his shirt to bits!.."

"How could you do that?" Nisa was surprised and interested.

"And how he yelled!" recalled Katya enthusiastically, not answering Nisa's question.

"How could you do that to him?" the girl repeated.

Manya replied.

"We just did. because he was a boy. What's the point of looking at them? If you look at them, they'll sit on your neck, and they'll give you a hiding when they hand you something to drink."

She answered seriously and thoughtfully, like a grown-up woman, and her face suddenly became female, dried-up and housewifely. But Katya somehow abandoned herself more joyously and lyrically to memories.

"He started whining, clenched his fists, and we took him by the arms and by the cheeks, yes, by the cheeks. Two girls are holding him, and two are thrashing him. But then he was such a scoundrel, he began kicking with his legs, biting. However, the yardkeeper arrived at this point with a broom, we all ran away, and he, the yardkeeper, rapped Petka in the back of the neck with the broom!"

Nisa wanted to ask something else, but into the room came two older seamstresses, and the girls became quiet. Mrs. Smolyakova's establishment was situated on the first floor, and the passing public could be seen very well. It was snowing, and it was somewhat dark for working, the seamstresses sewed unwillingly, yawning and shaking with sleepiness and from the cold. Nisa did no more than pull the threads from what had been sewn and which were left behind in the tacking. Sometimes young men would stop at the window with collars turned up and their hands in their pockets. The seamstresses bowed to a few of them, trying to prevent Madam from noticing, Madam who was bustling about in the next room. A conversation was struck up lazily from remarks about the young men in the street. At first Nisa didn't understand anything, as if the seamstresses had been speaking Finnish, but she listened attentively, as did the two other girls.

They poured abuse on some Kolya or other, who had not obtained tickets to the theater, had given the money to his brother, had not bought himself a new overcoat — in general had conducted himself quite differently from what Mrs. Smolyakova's seamstresses, whose opinion he obviously valued highly, would have liked. Valerian, who, judging from the conversation, worked in a barber's shop, also caught it in passing. They laughed at some Dmitry Petrovich, vowed to squeeze another three hundred rubles out of him, threatening that in the reverse case they would write to his wife about all his carryings-on. But they did not abuse him, only laughed. Apparently he was a wealthy and naive individual whom it was amusing to make a fool of. They condemned a Klavdia Nikanorovna unknown to Nisa, who stood on ceremony with her railroad engineer.

"Another worthless scoundrel! Hasn't got a penny to call his own, but turns it on, turns on the feelings. I wouldn't have let him past my threshold for a long time. What's the point of looking at them! Klavdia's a fool! Yes, just a fool!.."

Suddenly the speaker noticed that the little girl was listening and looking so closely that she had even stopped pulling out the basting.

"What are you looking at me for, little mouse? Don't you understand anything, is that it?"

"No, I understand!.." babbled Nisa.

"Yes, a lot you understand! If people understood everything at your age, then there'd be no women in the world to make fools of themselves."

"Like me and you!" another seamstress took her up, adding after a moment's silence:

"Learn, Anisia, learn and be sensible. Listen to what your elders say."

But the elders had no chance to say any more, as the doorbell jangled, and through the glass door a tall lady could be seen entering the shop, brushing the snow from her capacious red coat. Half an hour later, Mme. Smolyakova herself called by the workroom and addressed herself to Nisa:

"Nisa, get dressed and go to Miss Kadnikova's house. You'll take a visiting card and get forty rubles. Come back on foot or you'll have the money snaffled from you on the tram. It's not far, on Kazanskaya Street. You know the way? Look lively then."

I I

At the Kadnikovs they were already waiting, and even, apparently, with impatience, for Zinaida Petrovna, an older lady, although she had been absent only for about forty minutes. In the course of this time a lady friend had managed to come and see her sister, Elena Petrovna, to convey some amazing news concerning Leonid Grigorevich Surov and go away leaving the ladies in utter confusion, Lenochka was crying sullenly in the dining room, the mother, Maria Mikhailovna, was walking from room to room, looking through all the windows to see whether Zina, the most energetic and resourceful of the three girls, would be coming back soon, in the kitchen the situation of Alyona Petrovna, who had at this moment been transformed into a sort of model, immediately familiar in every detail, was being hotly discussed.

"We were waiting for you so impatiently, Zina!" burst out Maria Mikhailovna, without giving her daughter time to take off her coat.

"What's happened?" her daughter asked somewhat drily and knitted her brows. In general, she often frowned, at which her face would become older and more unpleasant.

"What's happened indeed! What might have been expected. Leonid parades himself about and behaves goodness knows how! Everyone notices it, it strikes everybody, even Liza Vlasovna, and she's such a dumb chick, doesn't notice anything any more."

Zina shrugged a shoulder, as if she disagreed with such a definition of Liza.

"She came running in here this morning, all excited — she's a good girl…from a good family…not a gossip…she's not some kind of Mme. Pernod. And even she was indignant…Then what will others be saying? Yesterday Leonid was at the theater again with the same woman, sat in a box…Everyone saw them. Everyone knows that he's Lenochka's fiancé, and everyone knows that's his girlfriend. She's some kind of Russian woman…a tailoress or a chambermaid…I was even told her name, *nom de guerre*, but I don't remember it. It's a scandal. Everyone's sorry for Lena, but they're all laughing at us in their hearts. And all this is because you have some idiotic ideas of your own about men and about love. I'm sure that if I were young such incidents would never happen to me, and if they did happen, they wouldn't affect me so painfully!…"

"I completely share your views, mama. Perhaps I don't formulate them quite as you do, but I think in almost the same way."

Maria Mikhailovna nodded her head and began to speak in an almost doctrinaire manner, as if she was accustomed to expressing her views and did it with pleasure:

"Man is the eternal enemy of woman, we are constantly at enmity. Love is a duel. Whoever loves is vanquished. I'm not closing my eyes, I understand that there are cases of attraction, we still have too much of the animal in us…But that I could love a man as I love you, for example, that's nonsense! Here everything is one's own, related, feminine, but there, but there — it's hostile. Yes, struggle, curiosity (rather nasty curiosity), instinct, but not love! I can better understand a Negress, a Chinese woman, than my own husband. I laugh when they talk about friendship between a man and a woman. Of course, in war all weapons are fit to be used. Fools may be assured of the existence of this fiction, but among ourselves we know that it's only a fiction. Then there are the equal rights of women! It's absurd. We are sovereigns, always were and always will be, and then what equal rights are there between us and our slaves? They sense this, believe me, and avenge themselves, avenge themselves crudely and stupidly. At first I thought that women who talked about women's rights were degenerates, but then I was convinced that their minds are in the right place, they're not so stupid at all. It's only a device. To speak clearly it is necessary to speak crudely. Men and women are two camps, no truces and war to the knife. Of course it's all nonsense what the little Jew wrote (and he at least had the tact to shoot himself) about M and F! It's even indecent."

Maria Mikhailovna fell silent, grew thoughtful and suddenly smiled, obviously remembering something very amusing, Zina listened indifferently, obviously not for the first time, to her mother's reasoning. She finished thoughtfully:

"Not long ago I saw in a shop window a book called 'The Intermediate Sex.' What perversity! What are the police looking at? I even talked in this connection with Father Alexander, but though he's a member of the clergy and my confessor, he's a man all the same and understands absolutely nothing."

"All this is very fine, but what am I to do?" a voice rang out, and into the room stepped a girl of about twenty, quite unlike Zinaida Petrovna, a little blonde with a round face and pale blue eyes, now tear-stained.

"Throw all the nonsense out of your head and spit in his face, if you can't make him behave himself decently!" shouted Maria Mikhailovna and fanned herself with a handkerchief. Elena Petrovna dropped her eyes and, it seemed, was ready to weep. Her mother looked at her in silence, then exclaimed:

"Ugh, what a silly female you are! Be a woman, Lena, and remember your dignity. You just don't have any pride."

"But I love him!" burbled Elena Petrovna.

Maria Mikhailovna threw up her hands and prepared to pounce on her daughter, but was forestalled by Zina. She began to speak softly but impressively, knitting her thick brows continuously:

"Of course it's a great pity, Lenochka, but you will have to give up the thought of Leonid Grigoryevich. I understand that it's difficult for you, but we will help you. Judge for yourself, if he loved you he wouldn't put you in such unpleasant, difficult and ridiculous situations. Surely it can't be pleasing to you that every empty-headed rattle such as Liza Vlasovna comes running to you with sympathy, advice and indignation? You'll hardly reform Surov, you don't have a strong enough character for that. In that case, what's to be done? What will your life be like afterwards? You know how much I love you, I wouldn't wish you any harm. And my advice is: it's better to put an end to this business right now, because later it will be even more difficult, perhaps even impossible, and sooner or later you'll have to do it. Mama, of course, exaggerates, but essentially she's right. You mustn't idealize love and consider it impossible to resist. We'll go abroad in the spring, you'll enjoy yourself, gain new impressions, perhaps fall in love with someone else (of course masses of people will fall in love with you) — and everything will be settled. I'm boring when I talk because I don't know how to talk in any other way, but when it comes down to it, all this will be much nicer and more fun. Believe me, my friend! And also believe that there is no one who will love you as mama and I do."

Zinaida Petrovna embraced her sister and stroked her hair, kissing her now and then on her closed eyes. Maria Mikhailovna nodded approvingly in time to Zinaida's words and Elena Petrovna's breast rose and fell more and more calmly. At last she lifted her eyes, threw herself on her sister's neck and started to weep, but more easily now, as if she had decided to do something. Zina said tenderly:

"I'll write him a letter for you and we'll send it to him right now."

"Right now?"

"Yes, of course, what's the point of dragging it out? If a thing has to be done, do it."

Elena Petrovna sighed and replied barely audibly but calmly:

"Very well then, write it. But afterwards show me what you write."

"Of course."

"There's no need to insult him."

"It would be worth giving him a good lecture!" muttered Maria Mikhailovna, but didn't insist, catching sight of Lenochka's imploring gaze. Zinaida got up from the floor, to which she had sunk during her conversation with her sister, and going through the hallway suddenly caught sight of the waiting Nisa:

"Oh, I'd completely forgotten about you, my girl!"

The elder Kadnikova had an idea of some kind. Standing there for a moment, she asked the little seamstress:

"Will you be missed in the workshop if you don't go back there for half an hour?"

"I don't know. No, I don't think so."

"In that case wait a little and when you go home take a letter to Konyushen-naya Street, it'll be on your way."

Zinaida Petrovna went out to write the letter, and Maria Mikhailovna discussed with the waiting Elena Petrovna, now fully composed, how convenient it might be to have a male servant. Mama was against it.

"A great pleasure: a big peasant hangs about the room, rattles scissors, smokes, drinks vodka — faugh!"

"But then it's more convenient for parcels. And then, mama, it is a pleasure in my opinion. Though he may be a peasant, he's a man all the same, and you have the right to humiliate him in all sorts of ways, yell at him, shout curses at him, force him to do the dirty work, to appear before him almost undressed — and he can't either say or do anything. He's offended, tormented, perhaps even falls in love, but he doesn't dare say anything. In my view, that's entertaining."

'Maria Mikhailovna looked at Lenochka in surprise.

"The thought of that never came into my head!"

Then she kissed her daughter, muttering:

"In some matters you're not so stupid, my friend!"

The letter was ready, and Nisa immediately read on the envelope: To Leonid Grigorevich Surov.

III

The door was opened for Nisa by a tall young woman wearing curl-papers and housecoat. She said that Leonid Grigorevich wasn't at home right now, took the letter Nisa handed to her hesitatingly and, taking a glance at the envelope, exclaimed:

"You're from Mme. Smolyakova?"

"Yes, I'm studying there."

"How is Madam then? Lusha and Klasha?"

"Thank you. Do you know them?"

"Good heavens, how could I not know them when I worked for them nigh on four years. Yes I did! Well, in that case we'll go and have a cup of coffee and you can tell me all about it."

Nisa thought that she was going to be taken to the kitchen, but the young woman invited her into a small dining room where a coffee set stood in one corner, a tart that had been started on, cookies, honey and sausage in wrapping.

"Well there you are, be my guest. What's your name?"

"Anisia — Nisa."

"Wonderful. And I'm called Nastasia Alekseyevna. My surname is Solomina."

Nisa's new acquaintance had a pleasant face with somewhat high cheekbones, dark puffy eyes and a large mouth. Her cheeks were thickly berouged and her neck, visible through her broad collar, was rather dirty. The girl was afraid and sat nervously on the leather-covered chair, thinking that at any moment the owner would come and chase them into the kitchen; but Nastasia Alekseyevna pressed a button and into the room came another girl with pitted skin and wearing an apron. Solomina talked to her like a lady. At last Nisa asked cautiously:

"Is this the apartment of Mr. Surov, Leonid Grigorevich?"

"Yes, his. Why do you ask? Oh yes, you've brought a letter, haven't you. Where's this letter from? From the workshop's accounting office, is that it?"

"No, from Miss Kadnikova."

"From Miss Kadnikova? What the devil! Yes, and you're a fine one, my girl! You're still a little thing and you're already carrying love letters around!"

And Nastasia promptly grabbed the envelope, tore it open, and taking out a small sheet of paper began to read it, holding it away from her eyes and a little to one side. Finishing it, she burst out laughing and, slapping Nisa on the nape of the neck, said gaily:

"Bravo, Nisa, deliver letters like that every day if you like! Leonid Grigorevich has been given a good dressing down—serves him right, I'll always say it serves him right! Now he'll lose his head. If only the young lady doesn't come riding out to the person in question — they're a feeble race, these young ladies!"

Nastasia burst out laughing again and twisted her little shoulders. Nisa was growing to like her more and more.

"Wouldn't you like to have a smoke? Well, you shouldn't, you really shouldn't. We'll have more left. Isn't that right?"

Although Nisa enjoyed listening to Nastasia, there was a great deal that made her feel uncomfortable. In the first place, why had she read a letter not addressed to her; in the second place, what was the position of Solomina herself in Surov's apartment; in the third place, wouldn't they be driven out of the dining room? But she didn't dare ask, all the same, she refused a third cup of coffee just in case. For her part, after the letter Nastasia Alekseyevna was in absolute high spirits and chattered away with the little girl as if she were a grown-up, asking about the seamstresses, their doings and affairs of the heart. She took the girl to see the apartment, consisting of four bachelor's rooms furnished, or so it seemed to Nisa, unusually well. She was particularly struck by the gramophone and the cage with the gray parrot.

"Do you live here?"

"No. Surov lives here, I only come here on visits."

Having teased the parrot, Solomina continued lazily:

"But I'm fed up with him. And now that things have been broken off with his fiancée I'll give him up if he doesn't marry me."

"But don't you love him then?"

Nastasia gave her a sidelong look and answered, taking her time:

"What do you mean by 'love?' He gives me to drink, feeds me,, clothes me, keeps me amused — and that's how I live. And I'm lazy, my dear, too lazy to go looking for someone else. And love?! It isn't always interesting to kiss, it's just wearing your lips out."

"Is he young?"

"Young."

"Pretty?"

Nastasia Alekseyevna, shouting with laughter, sat down in the chair so that it shook. The parrot flapped its wings, called out "Fool," and began furiously pecking at its wire.

"You kill me, Nisa! I ask you, when can men be said to be pretty? I'm not bad-looking, but a man…no, it's too much! What a crazy girl you are! And then what do they need beauty for? They're not loved for their beauty, are they?"

"But what for then?"

"You're too little to understand. The main thing for him is that he should have someone to bully, that's why they let people approach them. To bully and to insult — and that's it. Of course, there are old women too who love to beslobber each other, but that's not the essence of the thing. Man is woman's main enemy, let me tell you that. He should be knocked out and humiliated, and then you can fondle him a bit so that he has a chance to recover. But sometimes I'm ready to tear the heads off all those rascals."

"But why did you read the letter?"

"What letter?"

"From Miss Kadnikova."

"Oh that! I just read it. Nothing lasts long. Why should I look at him? I've got used to him a bit now, but before I used to look at him buttoning up his collar, flattening his hair with a brush, buttoning his suspenders — and could have hit him or run for my life. But with my woman friends it's not at all like that. They spend all their time dressing, there's nothing interesting, sometimes you can even make a joke of it. But with him, all his things are alien, hostile, unclean! Don't think I don't love him then, but the male spirit doesn't smell sweet to our kind, whatever we say, whatever sentimental songs we sing."

As if coming to her senses, Solomina began to hurry Nisa home, fearing that she would get lost and extracting a promise from her that she would come and visit her without fail. In fact, Nisa was grumbled at, but everybody was so interested in news of the Misses Kandinkova and Nastya that Nisa's fault went almost unnoticed.

IV

Five months went by. Nisa had already done up her hair in a little plait, she no longer played with the boys, didn't even talk to them. There came rumors that Elena Petrovna had gone abroad and was preparing to marry a young man from the embassy. There was no news of Nastasia Alekseyevna, and Nisa couldn't make up her mind to visit her a second time. At last, one Sunday, she set off to see her acquaintance, whom she had liked so much on her first visit. But she was not to be found in the house that Solomina had indicated to her. The yardkeeper said that she had moved to Zakharevskaya Street, and added:

"Soon Nastasia Alekseyevna will become a general's wife."

"How is that?"

"Some old fellow is going to marry her."

"What old fellow¾"

"Well, General Palchikov."

Nisa was ashamed of asking questions—as if she were less well acquainted with her friend's business than the yardkeeper, and she remarked casually:

"Oh yes. Nastya said something to me about Palchikov. He's an old man, isn't he?"

"Old. A widower. His son's a big boy, nineteen years old. Nastasia Alekseyevna shouldn't get bored, whatever happens."

And the yardkeeper smiled meaningfully.

The girl glanced at him sternly and, having thanked him for the information, went on her way.

Now, in fact, Solomina didn't go visiting any more, but lived in the apartment belonging to the general, Miron Pavlovich Palchikov. The master of the house wasn't at home, and Nastya was resting in the drawing room, the young man was glumly playing the grand piano, and Nastya was lying on the couch by the window, in the corner of the room, and looking at the spring sky. She was as pleased to see the girl as if she were a member of her family.

"Oh yes," she said, I shall soon be getting married, in Thomas Week. I don't live badly, I don't get bored, and if things do get boring, here's my consoler."

And she pointed to the young man. The consoler blushed, got to his feet, bowed to the girl and went out

"He's shy!" said Nastya, gazing after him protectively and lovingly.

Nisa looked hard at the mistress of the house.

"What are you looking at me for?"

"No particular reason."

"You think I'm getting mixed up with my stepson. Well I swear to you that I'm not. What do you think I am, a fool or something? I'm simply friendly with him."

"What friendship can there be between a man and a woman?"

"That's right. But I assure you that Dimitry Mironovich isn't a man at all. Not at all. I'm even surprised myself."

The little girl was silent for a bit and changed the subject.

"Yes, so I'm getting married. What difference does it make? He's such a slave already, such a slave, that I couldn't ask for anything better. And if he's old, what of that? He won't be after me so much."

Glancing at Nisa, Nastya suddenly said:

"And you Nisa, you'll go far. For one thing, you're pretty, no fool, unsentimental and won't be a crybaby. You've been well brought up."

The little girl suddenly burst into tears.

"What's the matter, what's the matter, my dear? But no-have a cry. Childishness will soon pass."

"It's all right, it's over!" said Nisa, and looked about her with such dry gray eyes that not only Nastasia Alekseyevna would have realized that this little girl's education had been well begun—and she had almost finished with beginners' class.

A BLUE NOTHING

In spite of the open windows, it was as hot in the room as if bread were being baked below. It was July on the Volga, and in the dark square horses were snorting. As if kept at bay by the dense heat, the narrow circle of light cast by the icon lamp in front of the tall icon failed to penetrate to the depths of the room, where two beds and a couch, together with the women lying on them, glowed faintly pink. Every now and then came a distant rumble of male voices and, right outside, the quick drumming of heels on wooden stairs.

"Pyotr Ilich can say what he likes about the provinces of Yaroslavl and Vladimir resembling Tuscany, but I'm afraid that the bedbugs are going to make their presence felt," came a voice from the semidarkness.

"Can you feel something then?"

"No. But it would only be natural. One can't rely on good luck."

From the couch came a sleepy voice:

"What's the point of these surprise visits anyway? Zoya and Galya would be glad to see us. This shouting frightens me much more than any bedbugs."

"There's no need to be afraid of the locals. The ways here are patriarchal and unspoiled in all their barbarity."

"But why these masses of people? It's lucky we were given even this closet. I'm very cross with Pyotr Ilich."

"But this way it's turned out to be more fun, and it could have been quite delightful. But if we'd let Zoya Petrovna know, they'd have sent Dasha, Valsili and the boy to the landing stage; they'd have helped us carry our things to the ferry and then to the house. Tea and supper would have been waiting for us, rooms made ready. We can do all that tomorrow."

"Oh how hot it is, and how they shout! I won't get to sleep all night.."

"Yes you will, Katenka, yes you will. And even in your dreams you'll see a fair-headed artist with a cornflower in his buttonhole."

From the couch came the sound of soft, happy laughter, and someone rapped resoundingly on the wall. There was an immediate hush. In the adjacent room a tearful tenor voice was raised in loud complaint. It was impossible to make out the words, but every modulation was exquisitely distinct. At last one of the women shouted, as if across a river, separating each syllable:

"Can't understand a word! We're asleep."

        ❉   ❉   ❉

Nowhere in Russia are there as many urchins as there are in Uglich. It must have something to do with the special protection of Dmitriy the Tsarevich and Vanya Chepolosov, the boy martyr of Uglich. They are from nine to thirteen years old.

The older ones made the round of the sausage shops. The people of Uglich are the world's leading sausage makers. Hams you'll find in Tambov, but sausages only in Uglich, to the chagrin of the Germans. The boys aren't martyrs, they only get pulled by the forelock and the ears and given a healthy diet of slaps, that's all. But nowhere is there such a multitude of urchins as there is in Uglich.

        ❉   ❉   ❉

It is not everywhere that the Volga seems boundless. At Uglich it is far narrower than the Neva and not much broader than the Nevka. From the far bank can be heard not only the ferryman's shout of "Make fast" that reaches you even at Vasil, but the singing and music from the dacha of Zoya Petrovna Flegontova. Of course you can't make out the conversation. On certain evenings you can hear the dogs being called.

When a summer cloud dissolves, the sky seems empty, the azure as translucent as water. If you free your thoughts of booklearning and preconceptions, it's possible to imagine there's no sky, just a blue nothing.

        ❉   ❉   ❉

The travellers very soon gave up the idea of secrecy and springing a surprise, and at seven o'clock they sent the fairheaded artist to the Flegontovs to inform them that the visitors they were expecting in five days for Zoya Petrovna's birthday had already arrived.

Predictably, Dasha and Vasiliy came from across the river with a boy. The traveling party consisted of three young ladies and two young men. The servants solemnly carried the light Petersburg valises. In the marketplace all heads turned. On the river bank a crowd of urchins greeted the procession with yells and threw pancakes after the ferry. At the dacha fluttered a welcoming pink flag.

        ❉   ❉   ❉

Mousy, ginger, red, black, straw-colored, gray, flaxen, skewbald, tufted, cropped, shaven, round, elongated, smooth, cone-shaped heads bobbed around Flegontova, who was distributing honeycakes, penknives and tin whistles among the urchins. She had an irregular and charming face, covered with freckles, and wore semi-masculine attire, strong perfume and a long, dark-blue veil which streamed in the wind against the pale-blue sky. The boys were particularly enraptured with her lemon-colored gloves.

❀   ❀   ❀

Natasha Sachkova sat at the open window; her fiancé, a young exciseman, was almost indistinguishable in the twilight. From across the Volga a warm wind carried singing and the muffled tones of a grand piano. Natasha stretched out a hand, which was kissed in the darkness.

"She's singing in German," said the girl at last.

"In German?" asked her fiancé fondly.

"Only I don't know what…There, you hear? 'Es ist bestimmt…'"

"Wagner, perhaps?" suggested the exciseman still more fondly.

Natasha didn't know. After a moment's silence she asked:

"Can they hear us from there?"

"Of course they can. Sing something."

"I don't know any Wagner."

"We'll give them something Russian then. Some Chaikovsky."

Natasha lit the candles in front of her round face, but nothing was heard at the Flegontovs as sounds are carried by the wind, and the wind has never been known to blow in two opposite directions at once.

❀   ❀   ❀

The shadow of the merchant's widow, Anastasia Romanovna Kurganova, glowed sumptuously pink on the balcony awning. She had not yet finished drinking tea with raspberry jam, and the eighth cup positively steamed in the noonday heat. Propping her cheek on her hand, Kurganova fixed her pensive and somnolent gaze on the sky.

"I wish you good appetite!" the watchmaker Abram Jasminer, his face overgrown with hair to the eyebrows, hailed her from below.

"Thank you, Abram Ionych. What a marvelous cloud! I couldn't take my eyes off it. It hung there and hung there, then melted away. Right before my eyes, just like that. That's how it is with us…What is this life of ours?…"

Jasminer thought to himself that Anastasia Romanovna didn't bear much resemblance to a cloud, but he remained silent, with no expectation that the widow would offer him tea. He knew the social code and the ways of the town.

❀   ❀   ❀

The young exciseman reasoned with himself:

"I would give a great deal for my name not to be Shkafikov. For the following reason in particular. I am, unfortunately, acquainted with the dictum of a certain armchair philosopher that every country has the form of government it deserves. There are many who extend this proposition to the outward appearance of individuals. Very well, how does it apply to surnames? Clearly an absurdity results. I don't in the least resemble a cupboard, big or little. Only yesterday I looked in auntie's cheval glass. I'm not handsome, but what has a cupboard got to do with it? My stomach doesn't stick out, I'm of medium height, my hair is light brown, and, after all, I did attend St. Petersburg University for two years. As far as bad luck goes, there are far worse surnames to be found here in Uglich, particularly among the merchant class. And the Ukrainian ones are simply a disgrace. Gogol took a great deal from life. The main thing is that Natasha shouldn't guess about all this. It's so much on my mind that I could easily let the cat out of the bag. Anyway, Shkafikov or not—I'm happy, I'm the happiest of men. Nastasia has given her consent. It seems to me that Zoya Petrovna Flegontova has something to do with it, although we don't have the honor of her acquaintance. Nobody does, come to that. But she's a source of energy, like the sun. She lives far away, but she fills everything with herself.

I was out for a stroll with Natasha, and I made her a declaration, but she didn't say anything in response and was somehow indifferent. In fact, she was overcome with exhaustion and sat down on a hillock. Suddenly a cavalcade came into sight: carriages, horsemen, dust, voices, laughter. In the middle of it all, like a queen, Madam Flegontova. She's so dazzling you can't make out whether she's good-looking or not. Apparently not very—but extremely unusual. That evening a very young man was riding at her side, and he continued to speak as they drew level with us:

"But how could one possibly live without love, Zoya Petrovna?"

They rode on. Natasha sat for a long time, then suddenly said:

"Yes, it's true. You know what, Valentin Pavlovich? I'm prepared to reciprocate your feelings."

✧　✧　✧

The exciseman was right in saying that Madam Flegontova knew no one, but there was in this not the least trace of pose, no haughtiness of any kind. Somehow it came about of itself that Zoya Petrovna lived as a "distinguished foreigner," content with the society of her own household and visitors from other parts.

Nor was he far from the truth in calling her a "source of energy." Not to him alone, but also to Anastasia Romanovna Kurganova, the watchmaker Jasminer and the street urchins, life seemed much more interesting during the lady visitor's sojourns on gossip and the most elaborate speculations about what was being concocted in the Flegontov kitchen, what clothes Zoya Petrovna was wearing, what guests she received and the nature of the relationships between them, their actions seemed more meaningful, their blood circulated more briskly and each of them felt as if he were on stage or at a station during an express train halt. Everyone knows how the natives and the transient visitors strut about in front of each other at such moments, how they long to leave as favorable, as sharply etched an impression as possible in the traveling memory. And even the telegraph operator contrives a specially stylish lift of the elbow as he runs along the thunderous platform, knowing that through the steamed-up windows of the "international" car gaze the longing (and longing indubitably for him—he is as conscious of it as he is of his own stylishness) eyes of a lady in mourning. And the mourning is for him too: perhaps she became a widow just for his sake, just as for her sake he had fallen in love with a young lady at the diocesan school. And this isn't some odd kind of romanticism, the pathos of social remoteness, the Nekrasovian "Why do you hungrily gaze at the road?"—but a natural feeling of theater, of playacting, the feeling that a stranger's eyes are fixed on you.

Whether or not Flegontova paid any particular attention to the citizens of Uglich was hard to say, but her influence did not by any means come to an end with her disappearance from the scene. The mere thought that the pink flag fluttered across the river and that Zoya Petrovna breathed, moved, existed, quickened the pulse and added a piquancy to every pursuit.

✿ ✿ ✿

Let us yield place to Vikentiy Pavlovich Shkafikov (who does not bear the faintest resemblance to a cupboard).

"Some very odd things happen in this world. I think I'd be justified in calling myself the unhappiest of mortals—that is, if I felt myself to be unhappy. It's all over…between Natasha and me. And again Zoya Petrovna, I mean Madam Flegontova, was behind it all. I thought everything was following its natural course, that our feelings were gaining strength—and that after Assumption Day we would, in the ordinary way of human nature, plight our troth. Well then, who is this Zoya Petrovna? An outsider, a lady from over the Volga, the last person you'd ask to a christening—but she goes away and Natasha suddenly gets depressed. In her place I'd have been delighted, as regards jealousy, that there was less temptation around, but she got upset. You might even say quite noticeably upset. Didn't even think of trying to hide it. Once, just to distract her, I asked her to sing something. She looks at the window and says:

"Why should I sing now? For whom?"

"For me, Natasha, You weren't singing for anyone else before, were you?"

She gave a mocking smile.

"I don't know myself who I was singing for. And anyway, who needs my singing?"

"Why give way to such gloom? I need it very much, and what's more, I love you!"

"I'd forgotten all about that."

"You've got a short memory, Natasha."

"I'd forgotten all about it—and I advise you to forget about it too. It's just a lot of nonsense: I don't love you at all, and never did. It was like something blown in by the wind. Meaningless."

At first it felt like a fire or a thunderstorm, then I realized that Natasha had made the scales fall from my eyes and revealed me to myself. And that there really was no one to sing for, and no one to love either. Suddenly it seemed that a lamp had been taken out and everything had gone dark. Boring.

I said:

"Thank you, Natasha, You have given me a present."

"It's not my fault. I thought I loved you myself. I made a mistake."

"No, please don't apologize. I thanked you quite sincerely. You have opened my eyes for me. I can see now that I wasn't the slightest bit interested in you myself."

Natasha flushed, but said:

"So there you are—everything has turned out for the best."

She was silent a moment, then seemed to cheer up.

"Well, now that our romance has come apart, I'll sing something for you, if you like—informally, not for the public."

And the slyboots launched into Chaikovsky:

"Dear God, so quickly to forget

Life's gift of happiness!"

A pack of local urchins were bathing in their habitual spot right across from the Flegontov dacha. But somehow the diving wasn't going too well. The flag wasn't there. Even the dogs weren't barking. Boys will be boys, and eventually the air was filled with laughter and racket, but suddenly there was no chic in suddenly thrusting a rosy behind out of the water right in front of the gentry's balcony.

❁   ❁   ❁

Everything carries distinctly across the Volga, but there's nothing worth listening to, just dogs barking. There's no pink flag fluttering.

✿   ✿   ✿

When a summer cloud dissolves, the sky seems empty, the azure red.

✿   ✿   ✿

If you free your thoughts of booklearning and preconceptions, it's possible to imagine there's no sky, just a blue nothing.

FISH-SCALES IN THE NET
(FOR MYSELF ALONE)

Being possessed of a poor memory, I am compelled to accompany not only my writing, but also my ordinary day-to-day reading with the making of extracts. Books, meetings and conversations give rise to stray thoughts; they are not suppositions and observations that particularly concern the subjects most interesting to me, but rather organized attentiveness; one conjectures and thinks as naturally as one breathes. These lines (intended exclusively for myself) have no pretension to any dominant idea, definitive interpretation or final judgement. Complete contradictions are quite possible, since I have made selections from notes taken over a six year period, 1916-1921.

M. Kuzmin

Marot's failing was that he was a Calvinist.

◊　◊　◊

The *Heptameron* belongs with the virtuous books. The *Cent nouvelles nouvelles* are much more daring and less *fade*.

◊　◊　◊

In Shakespeare's time there was an exaltation, probably to a certain extent reflecting the society of the day, the like of which has never been seen again; in Euphuism there is more of exaltation mechanically imitated than there is of *précieusité*. This transport differs from the exaltation of the Romantics in that it is a masculine one, stemming from superabundance, and healthy, while the other is feminine, visionary and stems from thinness of the blood. The whole age is somehow bursting with high spirits.

Rémy de Gourmont makes specious witticisms at the expense of various trivialities. So it is with the professional wits: what's good the first time is bad the eighth.

✢   ✢   ✢

The *Heptameron* is perhaps the least witty and piquant of the collections of the nouvellistes. An excess of virtue, long-windedness and lack of proportion reveal a feminine hand. But everything is much more bloodthirsty than with the Italians.

✢   ✢   ✢

To what an extent the wit, the realism, the extended similes and glittering paradoxes to be found in the verse of this same Marot or the prose of Rabelais were lost or sank into obscurity at the end of the seventeenth and throughout the eighteenth century, not to speak of the beginning of the nineteenth.

The Renaissance is ardent, fleshly and full of enthusiasm, the eighteenth century is cold, frigidly licentious and stilted, although the adventurers of that age are entrancing too, but without that breathtaking sweep and brilliance.

✢   ✢   ✢

Marot's Lutheranism is terribly harmful to him, as it is, to an astonishing degree, to Milton, Schumann and others. I think that a true Protestant cannot be a true poet, rejecting as he does concreteness, sensuousness and tradition.

✢   ✢   ✢

Marot is very charming, unconstrained, lively, unexpected, but a kind of strained quality and mere versifying make him similar in places to Potyomkin.

✢   ✢   ✢

Schumann is very unpleasant rhythmically, harmonically and melodically, although original. The most disastrous of influences.

✢   ✢   ✢

Mei was and is undeservedly neglected. It is he, of course, and not Pushkin, who best suits Rimsky Korsakov.

✢   ✢   ✢

Vyacheslav Ivanov's *Children of Prometheus* recalls the *Nibelungenlied,* particularly in Pandora's narration. It is clearer than his *Tantalus,* but more superficial, a little bit obscured by psychological allegory. There is no loam in it, nor any real tenderness.

✢   ✢   ✢

Yurkun's *Misty City* is a thing that Bryusov might have dreamed of writing, but which would always have been beyond him.

✿   ✿   ✿

Wackenroder's book was historically important—unfortunately. The only interesting thing in it are the anecdotes from Vasari. Altogether a feeble and childish book.

✿   ✿   ✿

Serebryanin has already been compared to Benediktov.

✿   ✿   ✿

The more art and the age strive toward *grand art,* the more lifeless they become.

✿   ✿   ✿

In Straparola's novellas one can already sense Gozzi and the German Romantics.

✿   ✿   ✿

March 10th, the Feast of Saint Anastasia. She sought salvation in the guise of a eunuch. The usual saint's life. When at the point of death, she talked with a holy hermit, the lay-brother who attended him stood there like a blockhead, so that the hermit was obliged to lay hold of him and cast him down at the dying woman's feet. She blessed him in the proper manner. But when the hermit entrusted him with the task of dressing her for burial, he noticed her breasts "like dry leaves." He kept silent then, but on the return journey he said to the elder, "But the eunuch was a woman." "Hold your peace, my son, I know that without your telling me!"—and proceeded to whisper the whole story in his ear.

✿   ✿   ✿

Nekrasov published a series of "reasonably priced" booklets, where, under covers decorated in the pleasantly crude style of popular prints, novels—Mérimée, Grebenka, Pushkin, Tolstoi—were mixed with some trash or other. I was enthusiastic at first, then cooled.

✿   ✿   ✿

Offenbach's *Le pont des soupirs* is boring nonsense, say what you will. Lecocq never fell as low as Offenbach did on occasion. It is as if the composer were asleep and humming the most banal commonplaces from memory. The posthumous appraisals are, on the whole, just, and attempts at galvanization rarely succeed, and then only briefly. *Avis aux snobs.*

✿   ✿   ✿

A certain monotony in Yurkun's digressions and descriptions (of a street, a fog, the sun) are not repetitions, but, as it were, *ideés fixes,* characteristic of an entire period. And then he varies them with great virtuosity. But in the matter of theme his judgement is sometimes odd. A successful detail he considers to be already a theme. Fortunately he doesn't set about realizing it at once. For example: "A man reached down a star from the sky: it was wet and small, like an oyster." Fine, but he considers this a theme.

Z…remarked that illiterate people, not connecting the word with its written form, preserve a freshness of acoustic impression. In my opinion, that too becomes dulled. For that one needs a special gift.

❊   ❊   ❊

Yu. Yu. goes about asking everyone who our leading poet is, thinking they will name me; no one does, though.

❊   ❊   ❊

Skriabin's death from a pustule on the eve of his mystery is very significant. Demonism. Napoleon. Wagner. Neitzsche. Blackness. Pathos and contemplation. The struggle either with light or with oneself (Beethoven, Dostoevsky). Rozanov is always of God. Remizov is attached to little demons and all kinds of abominations: this harms him. One's own will is like a ray of the divine will. The aim: to realize the work of the Supreme Artist in all its fullness.

Happiness, gaiety, lightness.

Disaster, outward success, the divided self.

❊   ❊   ❊

Protestantism cannot give birth to genuine art—it is devoid of divine grace.

❊   ❊   ❊

Kulbin quite unthinkingly let fall the remark that taste is divine grace, our guardian angel.

❊   ❊   ❊

"If thou art tempted by vanity, do thou create some work or image before the people, that they may dishonor thee" (*Prolog*, March 25th). A theory that could lead to temptation.

❊   ❊   ❊

Hoffmann's *Kreisleriana* No. 5. Unconnected thoughts, paragraph three. The idea of the Correspondence of colors, sounds and scents fifty years before Baudelaire and the decadents. "The scent of a deepred carnation has a kind of magic power over me; I involuntarily fall into a dreamy state and hear, as if from afar, the deep tones of a cor anglais ebbing and flowing in waves."

o   o   o

When Lourier deals with the voice, he becomes simpler and sometimes even coincides with Korsakov. It's like Futurist costumes. However strange the design, when it is carried out and put on a living being, it becomes simpler and more natural.

o   o   o

"We understand words, but form our own opinion of them" (Amvrosii Mediolansk's Sermon on the Hoped-For Resurrection). In general, rather banal and rationalistic. Very western, almost eighteenth century.

o   o   o

The Muscovites have long been fond of argumentation. The Schism and Slavophilism are understandable. Now there's Futurism and Bely theorizing all the time. We have Kulbin and Evreinov, but that's *pro domo sua,* and not from love of art. Acmeism is so obtuse and absurd that the mirage of it will soon pass. In Moscow they are more serious, but, good God, what chatterboxes and argufiers, drowning in their own chatter! I forgot about the Holy Trinity of the Merezhkovskys, but what kind of theoreticians are they anyway? Peevish palace porters out of a job.

o   o   o

Under the Constellations

End of the eighteenth century—Voltaire
1800-1810—Rousseau
1810-1820—Hoffmann
1820-1830—Pushkin
1830-1850—Balzac
1850-1870—Dickens
1870-1880—Dostoevsky
Chekhov is very local, although he did foul things up. For the beginning of the twentieth century—Anatole France? I'd like that.

o   o   o

It's a pity for Yurkun personally that he's a Pole. Actually he's really a Lithuanian, though I don't know what that means. Something like a Montenegrin. Not a distinctive *universal* nation.

o   o   o

Cazotte's fairytales are long-winded, but new for the eighteenth century and delightfully romantic. The snobs don't mention him—he isn't sufficiently *galant*—but he contains Hoffmann and, at times, even France.

✿   ✿   ✿

Prussia and Germany during the eighteenth and at the beginning of the nineteenth century possess the great charm of provincialism. Chodwiecki is a fine
poet, and he is also dear to me because he is the illustrator *par excellence* of
charming things.

✿   ✿   ✿

Scarron in his novel not only felt no constraint in depicting a performance of his
comedy *Jodelet,* but even in praising it.

✿   ✿   ✿

Somov. After realistic experiments in the manner of Serov and the fleeting influence of the German decadents, how quickly he finds his own domain, and vast
it is. Almost all Sudeikin comes out of the canvasses "In Past Years" and "Liud-
mila." Our age was very cultured and well-read. The achievement of estheti-
cism—a new humanism. These days the best read is Sudeikin, but he's an
ignoramus in comparison with Bakst.

✿   ✿   ✿

In the eighteenth century verse was declaimed just as atrociously as it is today.
*Il faut observer la ponctuation des périodes et ne pas faire paraître que c'est de
la poésie, mais les prononcer comme si c'était de la prose. Il ne faut pas les
chanter, ni s'arrêter à la moitié, ni a la fin des vers comme fait le vulgaire, ce qui
a trés mauvais grâce (Roman Comique, Chapter LII).*

✿   ✿   ✿

Lafontaine is very second-rate when all is said and done. Easygoing somewhat
in the manner of Beranger. The same themes are far more piquant in his sources
than in what he makes of them.

✿   ✿   ✿

Rozanov's *Fallen Leaves*—a mass of brilliant thoughts, a first-rate writer, but terribly remote and alien. A man insensitive to many things. Sometimes he doesn't
understand even sex because of his fetishism.

✿   ✿   ✿

A monk was sentenced to death. A brother monk kept following him around.
"Don't you have any work to do in your cell?"—"Yes, but in the first place I'm very
lazy, and in the second place nothing seems able to touch my heart. But maybe
when I see your execution my heart will be touched." (*The Spiritual Meadow*).

⁂ ⁂ ⁂

Chaque terme a l'esprit ne portait qu'un image;
Un oiseau voulait dire un oiseau, rien de plus;
Et cage voulait dire cage.
La basse allusion de son impureté
N'avait rien encore infecté.

(Pirron. *Epitre pour "les courses de Tempeé"*) So there was *acmeism* even then. Amusing that Symbolism is understood only as concealed bawdy.

⁂ ⁂ ⁂

Our age is the crucible of the future. Positivism and naturalism burst like bubbles, throwing us back not to the third quarter of the eighteenth century, when they were beginning, but to a far more primitive epoch. Primitivism. Painting, Debussy, the reaction against Wagner. Every new movement, wanting to be sufficient unto itself, reaches an impasse, leaving behind whatever of value (to which no one paid any attention) it brought with it. It's like the second century, and perhaps other centuries too. Khlebnikov would have worked it out.

⁂ ⁂ ⁂

How primitive and silly *Les illusions perdues* is really. Only Balzac's genius makes it great and overwhelming.

⁂ ⁂ ⁂

For where sadness is will no good be found (*Limonar*).

⁂ ⁂ ⁂

The more I read Casanova, the less I like him. A paltry, insolent little man. The adventures are monotonous and vulgarly recounted.

⁂ ⁂ ⁂

One gets less from Sallust than from Suetonius, with his simplicity and, perhaps, lack of talent. In the work of the former the cards are stacked with oratorical pathos. It is an epic poem, and the conclusion is very fine. Caesar's speech in the Senate is evasive and hypocritical. Catullus himself is fine, although within him already sit Lorenzaccio, Adolphe and Pechorin. Cicero, of course, is an old fool and untalented intriguer. A repulsive, very modern personality, with a touch of the French academician about him.

⁂ ⁂ ⁂

How carefully matched the colors are in the *bylina* about Churilo: white snow, ermine, silver carnations, silver chessmen, a crystal chessboard. The warmth, the bed, the voluptuousness, the blood (like white peablossom)—are all pure Russian.

❆ ❆ ❆

L. Bruni spoke of Christian art, of criticism, of talent, of everything we talk about—in a confused and obscure way. The rejoinder of B…was well-organized, tolerant and convincing—but the former was right.

❆ ❆ ❆

The Chinese call inspiration that is classical and harmonious "clear" (as of water).

❆ ❆ ❆

Jean Paul Richter is heavy and monotonous. Not first-rate, but better than Sterne. Many of his paradoxes have something in common with Wilde.

❆ ❆ ❆

The descriptive parts of Aretino's dialogues are so fanciful, so well calculated and so humorous that they bring Gozzi and the Romantics to mind. In general, a master of great worth.

❆ ❆ ❆

Pypin's *History of Masonry* reveals not the slightest understanding of its subject—it's as if M.I. Semyonov were writing about Mme. Guyon. I don't even know whether it's highly regarded. There is an unamusing eccentricity and a kind of mediocrity in the incongruity between the subject and the manner in which it is investigated.

❆ ❆ ❆

At the end of *The Brothers Karamazov* there is a certain psychological "swaggering" in the speeches of the layer and the procurator; an impartiality that Dostoevsky doesn't really have and which doesn't come off. Or did he want to compel the reader to experience the *angoisse* of the public present at the trial? That isn't achieved either. The magnificent novel *dégringole* a little toward the end. The entire business with the boys looks toward the future and is often quite unintelligible.

❆ ❆ ❆

Beaumarchais's prefaces are already romantic and demagogic. The fantastic imagining of Hoffmann, but also the unbuttoned style of Heine, the watered-down journalism of Jules Janin. Part Cazotte, part journalist. Piquant, fanciful, dishevelled and rather bad form. "Hydras" and "satraps" are just over the horizon. Extraordinary boastfulness. Sometimes Balzac, but more unbottoned.

◊ ◊ ◊

I have cooled very much toward Regnier. He's positively another Auslender, un-sureness of hand and very ordinary. Conception and detail are engaging, devel-opment and psychology flabby and commonplace, sometimes beautifully written, often dry and flat. An esthetic Chekhov. Ridiculous to compare him with France.

◊ ◊ ◊

After the *Thousand and One Nights,* not only Defoe, but Dickens and Balzac are insipid. Perhaps Shakespeare, Goethe, Dostoevsky can withstand the compari-son.

◊ ◊ ◊

All the arts act on the imagination by means of external sensual feeling. Poetry alone confronts us directly. Music is the most amorphous element, like chaos, the female principle, astral and indeterminate. For this reason it is drawn toward precise, almost mathematical forms. It is the most seductive of all. Every element hungers after what it lacks (extremes meet). Germany is the land of music and philosophy (the link between them is in the unreal and metaphysical character of these arts). Germany represents the ideal of music, but not its nature. The music of the spheres is like a miracle, not an inherent quality. To create from that which exists least in the outer world. The arts are autonomous and have equal rights, but painting and in particular sculpture are, of course, simpler and more earthy, manipulating forms already created by nature.

◊ ◊ ◊

"The supreme hieroglyphs for the human heart" (page 6). "All visible things are a representation of the invisible, are a voice summoning us from the truths of Na-ture to the great Truths of Eternity." A representation, inasmuch as it is some-thing created, is no more. "Nature's truth" is unclear. It is dangerous to be carried away as the eighteenth century was and to lean too heavily on nature and natural law.

◊ ◊ ◊

"Nature is an organ of the powers flowing from the one and only Power"—is this not a deviation toward Deism? Nature is the creation of God, His handiwork and not the conductor of His power. It is a conductor only to the extent that it is instinct with "the Divine image,"—i.e. creative force which both man and art possess. All that has to do with creation is divine, the particular deification of nature is an error, and one that is characteristic of the eighteenth century.*

* Is Ekkartshausen, who so often speaks of a Nature that is material, subject to

decay, external, corrupt, to blame for the "particular deification of nature?" As far as the errors characteristic of the eighteenth century are concerned, the century of "Enlightenment" *par excellence,* is it not he who calls it "the century of illusions?"

"...Poor humankind! How far have you extended human felicity? Was there ever a century that cost humanity so many sacrifices as the present one?" (Ekkartshausen). That is not about us, but about that very eighteenth century... (Editor).

§   §   §

"Truth comes before error, clam precedes turmoil." Unclear or untrue in the second part. Oneness precedes multiplicity, of course, but "calm" and "turmoil" designate states and not qualities, and chaos precedes ultimate harmony. On the other hand, in order to move one must naturally emerge from a state of immobility. And it is impossible to imagine a primordial motion.*

§   §   §

Saint Ephrem

A pure heart	from divine love
joy	from meekness
meekness	from humility
humility	from service
service	from trust in God
trust in God	from faith
faith	from obedience
obedience	from kindliness

Root—kindliness

Hatred	from rage
rage	from unbelief
unbelief	from hardness of heart
hardness of heart	from weakness
weakness	from gluttony
gluttony	from pride
sloth	from impatience
impatience	from idle speech

Root—envy

* Just as it is impossible to imagine primordial immobility. In general, for this kind of speculation to have any precision, logical stress must be laid not on motion or the lack of it, but on the primordial, about which of course all kinds of views may be expressed, but about which the reasoning, sensual man can know nothing (Editor).

✿   ✿   ✿

Love joins. The source of love is God, and creation is the work of His love. The primal law—love. The revelation of this law—truth. Truth and love—Divine Wisdom.

✿   ✿   ✿

That which has an immortal soul is guided by inner forces.

That which has no soul is guided by external forces, but forces which have their beginning in love. Love for oneself is the primal instinct, the capacity for perfection; the goal is love toward everything in its entirety, deviation from the goals is disorder.

Virtue—the readiness to regulate one's actions according to the relationships of universal love.

Religion—the goal—is the union of our sensual with our intellectual nature, and love of self with love of God.

Christianity acts directly on the heart or the will, while philosophy acts only on the reason and neglects the shaping of the will. The will is governed by knowledge, but inclination and practice are necessary. A depraved will can know, but it cannot execute.

Wellbeing is not a goal, but the result of love or goodness. Love is the force, Good the action of that force, the result—wellbeing.

Wisdom, which is truth together with love, is attained by the union of knowledge and will.

Worldly wisdom—knowledge without will—is conceit.

Science has no foundation, as the only foundation is the human heart.

Knowledge without heart and goodwill is merely a strengthening of the passions, love without order.

✿   ✿   ✿

Is not this the secret of the Trinity? God is fullness, Creation, oneness. As soon as there is a creation, there are two: the Creator and the created. Division. But at once there is love as union and active fullness. That is why there is no Nirvana, no inertia.

✿   ✿   ✿

Christ's passion is the exertion of the Divine love. Is it not sexual? The channel of love is the cross. The Phallus. Only in the life of the flesh is there the union of creation and oneness.

✿   ✿   ✿

The miracle of the enfeebled priest, where he is carried from bathhouse to bathhouse in the rain, and the saint appears in the guise of a bathhouse attendant, abouts in fascinating detail (*Makarevskie Cheti-Minei, 1st November*).

❋   ❋   ❋

The self-engendering activity of the prime mover instilled in dead clay

1. movement
2. feeling
3. fire, or life

Then light and love, intelligence and knowledge, oneness and wisdom also began to be potentially present there.

The Sabbath is the return of all things to oneness.

❋   ❋   ❋

The Annunciation (conception) was celebrated in ancient times on one and the same day as the passion or the Resurrection. Does not this confirm my ideas about the erotic significance of the passion?

❋   ❋   ❋

Hettner has a very severe attitude toward the writers of the *Sturm und Drang* and the Romantics, but they emerge more clearly and attractively from the censure of a man of talent than the praises of a fool.

❋   ❋   ❋

It is clear that Yurkun's novel has most in common with the work of Klinger. It's new and interesting. I'm speaking of *The Fog behind the Grille*.

❋   ❋   ❋

It's time someone started a campaign against Formalism. Or is it harmless and will decay of itself? Perhaps laziness and inertia hold me back. Literary battles are ridiculous, of course, but in this little life they are also essential.

❋   ❋   ❋

In a vision Saint Mina commanded a lame man to lie with a woman stricken with dumbness. The man resisted, but at last submitted. The woman cried out with fright and that paralytic ran away. Thus both were healed. Healing by means of incubation. Dreams in the temple. Completely identical, down to the details, to the practices of the Esculapian cult.

❋   ❋   ❋

In the summer the hermit would receive visitors almost naked and wearing his cowl back to front. There was temptation. Rebuked, he replied: "Our work is not for men: let him who wishes to learn do so, and him who wishes to be tempted be so. I attend to my business—the rest passes me by." And he commanded his pupil to speak the simple truth, "If I am eating, say he is eating; if I am sleeping, say: he is sleeping (*Prolog*, May 17th).

        ✿   ✿   ✿

If I make note of something, it's usually grist to my mill, and not an argument to the contrary.

        ✿   ✿   ✿

Ephrem the Syrian's sermon on love (December 24th)—compare with Ekkartshausen. Love is the salt.
    There also: For God *named* driveth forth devils" (*Imyaslovtsy*, 2,44).
    Were it not for a certain asceticism, it would be a magnificent specimen of Platonic soaring combined with Syrian fieriness. Love is the source, the salt of all creation, it brings the Son of God down to earth.

        ✿   ✿   ✿

In Shakespeare's day everyone was mad about poetry and nobody needed prose. There is poetry in Utopian language (*zaum*).

        ✿   ✿   ✿

Wilde, almost a man of genius, strives with all his might to be an empty society chatterbox. D'Annunzio, almost a society chatterbox, has ideas and poses that are inspired. The first was almost successful in his unfortunate intention.

        ✿   ✿   ✿

What does "outer darkness" mean?

        ✿   ✿   ✿

A title: "Reading for the Edification of the Worldly, the Entertainment of the Devout."

VIRGINAL VICTOR:
A BYZANTINE TALE

To Arthur Lourier

The Holy Church commands us to take pity on orphans. In the imperial city of Byzantium a vast orphanage had been established; for both private individuals and public institutions it was held to be a great desert in the eyes of the Almighty to nourish and rear infants deprived of their parents. If nothing can restore to a child its mother's tenderness, at least there is always the possibility of providing it with food, shelter and instruction in Christian conduct.

Although Victor, son of Timothy, had lost his parents, he had no need to have recourse either to private or state charity, since he had inherited a commodious house, one of the city's finest libraries, three dozen house slaves, splendid stables and a sizeable country estate in the north. The sister of his deceased mother, the widow Pulcheria, took up residence in his household, not in the capacity of a guardian, as the youth had already reached his nineteenth year, but merely so that the management of the household should be under a woman's eye. She established her quarters in the upper part of the house, next to the private chapel, from which the gulf and the shore of Asia Minor could be seen in the distance. In her rooms there was always semi-darkness and the whisper of holy discourse. Priests in soft slippers slid noiselessly by, stopping at the drawn door-curtains to murmur a prayer, the servants were elderly women, yesterday's incense hung in the air, and through the window, instead of sea and boats, one saw painted branches, beasts and birds. Sometimes hermits would come, hulking fellows dressed in goatskins, as simple-hearted and dirty as shepherds.

Victor often listened to their tales. Pulcheria, as befitted a Christian matron, did not expose her sparse, graying hair, swathing it with a fillet sewn with the modest amethysts and emeralds of widowhood: by family tradition the widow belonged to the "Green" faction. Her face was immobile from the thick layer of ceruse, rouge and stibium, her puffy yellowish fingers were unable to bend from their multitude of rings, the folds of her robe, smoothed out by her slaves, seemed carved of stone, her neck and waist were festooned with crosses, incense pouches, rosaries, miniatures of saints, fragments of holy relics and amulets; in one hand she held a scarlet kerchief fringed with gold lace, in the other a sprig of lavender, which from time to time she would raise to her whitened nostrils to rid herself of the goat smell of some hermit. Now and then her eyebrows would quiver, and then the maid attending her would drive a somnolent fly from her mistress's face or hands with a fan. Beside her stood her household priest, explaining to her in an undertone the words of the anchorite, who mingled barbarian expressions with Greek ones, waved his arms about, sighed and stammered.

Afterwards Victor would dream of sand and trees, birds and deer similar to those patterned on his robe, for it was on cloth that he most frequently saw these things. Of course, in the nearby countryside birds flew, poppies and burdocks flourished, but the youth did not go any further from Byzantium than the Manastery of Olympus, whither each year in all kinds of weather he would make a pilgrimage in memory of the five holy martyrs of the thirteenth of December. Their house had a small garden, but the pious gardener had given all the bushes and trees the form of Christian emblems: the barberry bushes were clipped in the shape of hearts and anchors, the limes resembled fish with their tails pointed upward (as is well known, their very name is make up of the first letters of the following words: Jesus Christ, Son of God, Saviour), while close by the apple tree, the boughs of which had been lopped in the form of a cross, were placed two poles, painted in red lead, representing a spear and a stave.

The most Christian city of Byzantium wafted its fragrance to the Creator, not like a lily of the field, but like a precious oil, poured into a vessel wrought by cunning goldsmiths, stooped in their dark cells, their shortsighted eyes accustomed to envisioning sky, flowers and birds in an improved, a more brilliant, a more fantastical guise than nature, that guileless simpleton, presents them to us.

The widow Pulcheria had long been yearning for monastic life, but she was reluctant to leave her nephew until he had given the house a new young mistress. But here her intentions met with an unexpected obstacle, and the good woman had to recognize that even virtue itself can present certain inconveniences. There was no shortage of brides. Although Victor had no official post and no rank, his wealth and beauty made him a desirable husband and son-in-law for all. But the youth himself felt no inclination to marry and to all appearances his heart was free; consequently he responded evasively to all attempts at matchmaking. Enquiries made among servants and friends revealed no love affair to tie the young man, so that the lady Pulcheria didn't know what to think. At last she decided to have a frank talk with him.

When Victor entered the woman's quarters, the widow was holding in her arms a white long-haired cat, a gift from the Archbishop of Antioch, which she was combing with a small gilt comb. Having spoken of the allegedly deteriorating state of her health, of household matters, of the recent storm, Pulcheria said:

"Well, nephew, have you thought about which of the maidens I have proposed to you you would prefer as your wife, so that I may begin discussions with her parents?"

"I have, lady Pulcheria."

"Well, and on whom has your choice fallen?"

"I have decided to wait awhile yet."

"But why wait? You're a grown man, I'm growing weaker with every month, it's time to think of the future."

"My heart feels no inclination toward any of them."

The widow angrily removed the resisting cat from her knees and exclaimed:

"What nonsense! Surely, nephew, you don't imagine that life is a pastoral novel or the "Ethiopian Tales?" What's this "inclination of the heart" you're talking about? If a girl is worthy and of noble birth, and you can rely on me to see to that, it follows that the blessing of Heaven and the Church will be on your house."

But to all his aunt's arguments, Victor kept repeating only one thing—that he didn't want to marry. Pulcheria listened to his reply, knitting her brows, as far as the ceruse permitted her to, and at last announced enigmatically:

"Remember that there is no secret that will not be revealed in time."

"I have nothing to hide, I assure you."

"So much the better," replied his aunt, and with that put an end to the conversation. Afterwards, when her nephew had left, she heaved a sigh and sent for the household confessor.

On the Tuesday of the fourth week in Lent, the priest received a country gift: a clay pitcher of honey and two dozen red-cheeked apples in a golden dish. The widow wrote briefly that she begged him not to disdain her modest gift and to accede to her request. By Friday, in all liklihood, the mission had already been accomplished, since the confessor appeared in the lady Pulcheria's quarters, and as soon as the customary greetings had been exchanged and the servant sent away, said:

"He is pure in the sight of God."

A faint mocking smile parted the lady's painted lips.

"Can that be? Victor—a virgin?"

"Your nephew is a stranger to carnal sin."

"And my suppositions have proved groundless?"

"The Lord be praised, my lady, you were mistaken."

Seeing that Pulcheria expressed no particular joy, but sat frowning and motionless, the confessor went on soothingly:

"You should thank heaven for such a mercy, for without grace from above, it is hard to keep one's purity, as the young master has kept his."

Seeing that Pulcheria maintained her gloomy silence, after a pause the priest began cautiously:

"Of course, my lady, this calls for further investigation. What has not been subjected to temptation cannot be considered virtue, anger may find no external expression, but nonetheless a man who has anger in his in his heart remains privy to that sin."

"To this the lady listened attentively.

"Perhaps your nephew is too timid, has little knowledge of the world, his passions sleep that they may with greater fury gain possession of him when it will already be too late. We might put his resolve to the test."

"What can we do?"

"Neither you nor I, my lady, is likely to be experienced in these matters, but I too have a nephew, whom I have kept at a distance because of his unworthy behavior, but it would seem that the ways of fate are inscrutable. Even a muddy path sometimes leads to salvation. He has a wide acquaintance in the circles needful to us, and I am confident that he and his lady friends will willingly take upon themselves the task of putting the young master to the test."

It was clear that the priest's plans were to Pulcheria's liking; she turned the conversation to the empress, whom she had seen at a service, remarked that in her next conversation she would not fail to mention him as a loyal and devoted man, asked whether the apples she had sent had been tasty, and at last lowered her blue-painted, hen-like lids, as if to convey that the audience was at an end. Only in parting did she add, again becoming somewhat animated:

"As long as my nephew doesn't get into the gaming habit! Another thing—I don't wish in the least that Victor should remain in this company for ever."

"Set your heart at rest, my lady, set your heart at rest. It will be no more than a trial, and then we'll marry the noble youth."

The good priest had some trouble finding his scapegrace nephew, but in the end he was extracted from some nocturnal eating house. It took some time to comprehend what was demanded of him, but having grasped it, he willingly agreed to help the widow and take her nephew in hand. Among those ladies who might put Victor's virginity to the test, Pancratius (as the priest's nephew was called) moved, so to speak in the middle circles, knowing by name but having no access to those women who had already attained riches and fame, and who imitated noble matrons in their dress and manner of painting their faces, mimicking strenuous piety and occasionally turning their hand to erotic verses in the form of acrostics, which often became confused with *eirmosa* and *kontakia*. Knowing the inconstancy of fate, and meeting a great many people—courtiers, grooms, bishops and conspirators—these women dreamed of being raised up to the throne, for in this world, and particularly in the imperial city, all things are possible. Dull, ambitious and malevolent thoughts crept across the standing pools of their eyes, as they sat in state, like idols in the circus, gazing enviously at the seats reserved for matrons of noble blood. When they were born away in their litters, the dark-skinned, flat-breased flowersellers would gaze at them no less enviously.

With these ladies Pancratius was not acquainted, and besides they were of no interest to Pulcheria's virginal nephew, closely resembling those who were proposed to him as brides. But the acquaintances of the priest's kinsman were not street harlots either, lying in wait for stray sailors—they were gay, carefree creatures, mocking, sentimental and heartless. But apparently Pancratius too met with no particular success, for when he appeared before his uncle a month later he had an embarrassed and somewhat astonished air.

"What news?" asked the priest, not turning from the desk at which he was composing a sermon for the following day.

"Nothing good, uncle. The Lord Victor is in the same condition as he was on the day you acquainted us."

A learned starling called out "Peace be unto you," but the master of the house flapped his sleeve at him and inquired anxiously:

"The Lord Victor, you say, remains chaste?"

"Yes—an odd young man!"

"Perhaps you're wanting to ask more money from me so that you can carry on with your merry life on the pretext that the virtue of the respected Pulcheria's nephew has not yet been sufficiently tested?"

"You can be sure that I wouldn't refuse, but unfortunately I have to confess defeat."

Uncle gazed at nephew, not knowing whether to marvel at his moderation or Victor's resolve. In the silence the starling again called out "Peace be unto you," but no one took the slightest notice of him. That very evening the lady Pulcheria received a report of the state of affairs.

It is hard to say whether the youth himself guessed that the widow's questions, the confessor's admonitions, the sudden appearance of a new friend, so apparently attached to him and so eager to accompany him to various houses—that all these things were closely connected, and had something to do with his spiritual qualities. He did not consider his condition out of the ordinary, and lived quietly, dividing his time between library and church. Of course, the most natural thing for him would have been to contemplate the seclusion of a monastery, which, after all, differed but little from his present way of life—but perhaps for this very reason such dreams did not particularly attract him. What future prospect might have attracted him was difficult to imagine, and he revealed it to no one, not even to his favorite slave, Andrew the Hungarian, who accompanied him everywhere, and when his master read, sat drowsing nearby or with his eyes fixed unwaveringly upon him. He had recently been brought from the north and bound in service to Victor, who soon grew fond of him. He knew only about a dozen words of Greek, and so it was not possible to have long conversations with him. It was not, then, for his conversation that his young master became attached to him; perhaps it was for his quietness and piety, perhaps for his strange, wild air or for his devoted tenderness and meekness.

Andrew would always accompany his master to church, to all services, praying decorously and devoutly, looking neither right nor left, or raising his eyes to the choirs curtained at the sides, where the female parishioners were. From above, nevertheless, more than one feminine gaze was directed on master and servant, and impressions, marvellings, conjectures were passed to the opposite wall in whispers, as if in some kind of game.

One day, as Victor and the Hungarian were returning from Mass, they found their way barred by a large crowd which surrounded a tall man in a loose robe and a nightcap; the man laughed, capered about and spat, slapping his ribs and mouthing incoherently to the tune of a street song. Catching sight of the approaching youths, he paused in his capers for a moment and, leaning on his long staff, seemed to be waiting, then he began to whirl even faster. He stopped once more, wrinkled his nose and frowned. Everyone waited to hear what he would say.

"Faugh, faugh! What a stench of devils!"

They all began looking about them, wondering whether the exclamation might refer to them, but the holy fool went on:

"You think it smells of musk? Hellish brimstone, that's what! See that demon dancing—he's blowing his pipe, the foul fiend, he's pulling faces, grinning, trying to trip me up."

Suddenly the man of God buried his face in his hands and began moaning like a woman; "Oh! Oh! Oh! Woe is me, would that my eyes could not see!

> Mizra, Mizra, full of guile
> What made you journey to the Nile?"

A smiling woman's face, heavily painted and surmounted by towering ginger coiffure, looked down from an upper window. The holy fool withdrew his hands from his cheeks and yelled to the whole street:

"And you laugh, you filthy whore! I shall fight—and I shall not yield!"

And without further ado he leaped in the air, pulling up his robe, and, naked as he was, assumed an indecent pose. The green window-shutters were slammed shut, and uncontrolled laughter came from behind them, while the old man, having adjusted his clothes, suddenly began to speak in a preceptorial manner:

"Do not imagine, brothers, that this Herodias, this Jezabel, is worse than any of you. And besides, you witnessed how easily she was subdued. I tell you that those two over there" (here he pointed his stick at Victor and Andrew) "are a hundred times worse than she. There's as many devils on them as fleas on a dog."

Everyone turned toward the youths, and, flushing, Victor went up to the fool and asked humbly:

"Reveal to us, O father—by what devils are we possessed?"

The fool clicked his tongue and answered:

"What I say to you is: 'Not on your life!' Find out for yourselves!"

And again he began babbling something incomprehensible.

Victor never spoke to Andrew of this incident, but the fool's words often came to his mind, particularly during hours of insomnia to which he was subject. Meanwhile the Hungarian fell sick and as his health failed, so his piety grew stronger. Rarely leaving his narrow bed under the stairs, he was forever whispering prayers, his eyes fixed on the sombre icon in the corner. Victor spent all his time in his servant's cramped quarters, holding his dry and burning hand in his and listening to his rambling speech, which sometimes turned to outright delirium. One day he was sitting there, the sick man had dozed off, and Victor, as he gazed at the dusky, sweating brow and the dark eyes, which, for all their sunkenness, seemed to start from his head, suddenly recalled the day the fool stopped them. What had he meant, and to which of the two of them had his words been directed? As if sensing his master's gaze, Andrew opened his eyes, and, feeling his hand in the hand of the other, began softly:

"My hour has come. My soul's anguish is twofold. It is parting with the body and it is taking its leave of you; to me, sweet Victor, you were not a master but a brother and friend."

The sick man wanted to say something else, but clearly it was beyond his strength. He only signed to Victor to bend over him, twined his arms about his neck and pressed his lips to his master's lips. Suddenly his mouth grew cold, and his arms weighed more heavily. Carefully Victor unclasped Andrew's fingers, and the Hungarian fell back lifeless on the pillows.

Only after his servant's death did Victor understand how dear he had been to him. It would have been easier, so it seemed, if his right hand had been cut off, or he had been thrown into a dungeon for life. Only now did he realize how tenderly he had loved the dead man, without whom even his beloved books came to seem dull and devoid of interest. Church services alone attracted him more than before; besides, circumstances themselves compelled him to intensify his piety, for, apart from the customary memorial services, he would pray alone every night for the repose of his friend's soul, never ceasing to wonder what the fool's words of long ago had meant and what it was that Andrew had wanted to say to him before his death. He could not forget the lips grown suddenly cold, and that kiss, the only kiss of his life, apart from the casual salutations of greeting and farewell. This had also been a kiss of farewell, but for ever; a kiss of eternal separation.

One day Victor prayed for a long time before the icon-shelf in his room, as emotion, tears and heavy thoughts had kept him awake, even in bed. Turning his face to the wall, where the tiger on the carpet glowed red in the light of the icon lamp, he whispered over and over again:

"Lord! O Lord! Grant my soul peace, assuage my sorrow; if my brother Andrew cannot be brought back, then reveal to me what has befallen his soul, its wanderings and its place of rest, that I may know whether to shed more tears or rejoice."

Victor said all this with his gaze fixed on the tiger, and he felt a desire to look at the Saviour, the Mother of god and Victor the Martyr, who stood in the row on the middle shelf. Quickly he turned over on the bed and saw…

By the lintel of the door stood his brother Andrew, quite naked except for a cloth about his loins. At first Victor did not recognize him in this guise, having never seen his slave stripped of his clothes. Then he knew him; gave a joyful cry of "Andrew!" and even reached out his arms; then all at once he began to make the sign of the cross over his visitor, muttering "May the Lord rise again." Andrew did not vanish, but smiled calmly and pointed to the cross that hung about his neck.

"Have no fear, Victor, my brother, and do not turn away in horror! I am no ghost and no demon, but your beloved brother. You summoned me, you wished to learn of the sorrowful path beyond the grave, and so I have come to you. I am no ghost, you can take me by the hand if you wish."

He reached out his hand. Its shadow loomed vast on the wall and touched Victor's feet. He tucked them under the blanket, which he drew up to his throat, and said:

"I believe you and I thank you. Tell me brother, of the dark path beyond the grave."

Again his visitor smiled, and began his tale; it seemed to Victor that Andrew did not open his mouth and that his words did not echo in the room, but rather as if someone inserted them into his, Victor's ears.

"Bitter is the final hour! When noseless death appears with her spears, saws, forks, sabres, swords and deadly scythe—you don't know where to hide yourself, you rush hither and thither, you groan, you implore, but she has no ears and no

eyes—she is inexorable. She sunders bone from bone, she cuts through all your
sinews and tendons, and pierces your very heart. The angel of death waits
gloomily while the noseless one goes about her business. On either side stand an-
gles and demons with thick books, waiting. More bitter than vinegar with mus-
tard is the last hour. And bitterest of all is the last breath. And with the last breath
the soul leaps from the body, and the Angel of Death gathers it up. How it cow-
ers, how it clings, how it weeps, the poor little naked soul! The Angel of Death
turns its head about and says: "Look at your body, your envelope, your comrade.
You will enter it again at the last resurrection." And the body lies white, motionless, voiceless, like a log. Friends and kinsmen stand over it and weep, but there
is no restoring to it the precious breath of life! The soul buries its face in its hands
and cries out: "I don't want to enter it!" But the Angel of Death answers: "You
will when the time comes!" and carries it further. Fair youths and dark demons
follow them. And now they mount a long bridge, two weeks it takes to cross it.
On the far bank you can glimpse the green of meadows, fields and groves, and
little white flowers. They move about, and every now and then they fly up in a
swarm like dandylion down. These are angels and the souls of the righteous in
radiant paradise. The bridge passes above dense fog. If you look hard, you can
made out what look like fiery mineshafts with a great many divisions and subdi-
visions. Only the coarse terrestrial mind fails to see the difference between, let
us say, lying and untruthfulness, calumny and slander, hardness of heart and mer-
cilessness, pride and arrogance. But the subtle minds of heaven know all the dif-
ferences and distinctions and assign everything its proper place. You will not be
sent where you ought not to be, be assured of that. The bridge is the place of ordeals. It's a bit like our tollgates or excise houses, where taxes are collected. Angels sit at high tables; in their hands they hold the most precise scales and
measures, and everything is written in a book; your slightest thought, desires
that you yourself have forgotten, stand there as if alive, each one docketed. The
soul is filled with terror and trembles, recalling all its sins and remembering
nothing good; but the angels have everything written down, not a jot escapes
them. The demons unroll their scrolls, the angels open their books; they weigh,
they measure and either let the soul proceed or cast it from the bridge; and the
youths weep, while the demons bare their teeth, kick up a racket and cheer like
a mob at the races. In this way I passed through the ordeals of untruthfulness,
slander, envy, lying, wrath, anger, arrogance, intemperate speech, lewd speech,
idleness, sloth, vanity and came at last to the twentieth ordeal."

Here Andrew fell silent.

"Well, and what is the twentieth ordeal?" asked Victor, apparently not noticing
that his visitor was no longer standing by the lintel, but was sitting on the bed,
all rosy with the light of the icon lamp, looking down at him with starting eyes.

"What is the twentieth ordeal?"

"Do not question me, sweet brother, do not question me. I am with you now. The fire of hell has not extinguished the blood and the heart within me. I am cold…"

Victor had forgotten his fear, he was ready to cover his visitor with anything to hand, to warm him with his own breath, his own body, if only he would tell him about the twentieth ordeal. Whereas before Andrew's lips had grown cold in a kiss, now they burned, searing Victor, as if infusing him with the flame that had not been extinguished in the fire of hell. Terrible and sweet it was, and this sweetness, this terror, would have made him forgetful of Andrew's final ordeal, had the latter not said to him in parting:

"And now, brother, you too know the yearning of the twentieth ordeal—take care lest it destroy you."

Often it happens that words of warning, constantly called to mind, push us toward the very thing they would guard us against. And so now Victor thought only of his dead friend's visitation and the tale he had told; he would have given anything only to bring him back. It seemed to him that everything life had to offer him grew dim before what had been revealed to him. Not knowing how to express his longing, he prayed that he might once again hear the tale of the twentieth ordeal. But all was in vain, and he wandered flushed, vacant-eyed, distraught, exalted, not knowing what to do with himself. At last he revealed these strange prayers of his to his confessor, who having heard him out, was silent for a long time, and said at last:

"It is from meekness, lord Victor, that you resort to such prayers—you are too pure. But often meekness turns into boundless pride, and of this you should beware. I advise you always to keep to the prayers that are to be found in the prayerbook. They were assembled by the holy fathers—and, rest assured, they knew better that you or I what is needful to man."

That very day the priest hastened to the widow Pulcheria and said:

"Your nephew must be married at all costs. Use force, appeal to the emperor and let him issue the command, but marriage is essential for the lord Victor. His virginity is not from God."

Pulcheria agreed and, glancing down the list of eligible brides, said:

"I'll send matchmakers to Leucadia, the daughter of Demetrius, the chief scribe"—then she gave a sigh and became thoughtful.

"Why do sigh, my lady? It will be for your nephew's good."

"I know. As a woman I sigh for poor Leucadia, that's all."

FROM THE NOTEBOOK OF
TIBERTIUS PENZEL

The dark blue cup flashed meteor-like through the pale blue sky, leaving a shining parabola in its wake. The white gleam of a saucer's underside followed hard upon it. Clearly, a trembling hand had imparted their zigzag capriciousness, but it seemed unlikely that anyone had deliberately taken aim at the stiff headgear of the abbe, rosy as a doll, who chose that particular moment to raise his head. The smiling expression of the round and unclouded doll-face was suddenly transformed into a mask to ornament a drain, the more so as café au lait trickled from the pipes of the plush curling brim onto the pear of the nose. Having wiped his face, he was on the point of breaking once more into a smile, but instead with a preoccupied air removed his hat, in which a deep blue shard had lodged like a cockade. One could positively have sworn that Terzina had taken throwing lessons from some antique discobulos. For some time I had been about to enter the cool doorway, but on hearing the singer's voice raised as if she were rolling the roulades of some aria at the San-Cassiano theater, I had stopped to let the storm pass, knowing from experience that such storms were of brief duration. The eructation of deep blue I had not foreseen. Glancing at the witness of this scene, that it, at me, the abbe announced, in a manner both sprightly and aggrieved, "I shall go up and demand an explanation! I hold holy office, and my hat is a brand new one. What's more, I'm a poet! The Signorina is unaware of these things." "She's in a temper," I said in an attempt to dissuade him, "If you have business with her, call in forty minutes time and you'll be able to laugh together, she'll offer you fresh chocolate and, who knows, may even sing something if she doesn't have a rehearsal at San-Cassiano.

❀   ❀   ❀

The chocolate was insufficiently hot, but the weather was mild, the barber was in particularly good form, the offended abbe was a seasoned librettist, and indeed an hour and a half later (the coiffure of the abbe made my prediction as to forty minutes impossible of fulfillment) the three of us were sitting at the round table, while the maidservant, scared by the morning's flare-up, served chocolate so hot that even Signora Terzina herself seemed hardly able to swallow it, although she made an effort to conceal the fact.

✿ ✿ ✿

She's small and dimpled all over: her cheeks, her elbows, her sweet little neck; her rosebud mouth forms smiles easily; ribbons, bows, furbelows, a froth of lacy trimmings seem for ever to be fluttering in the breeze; she adores music, can-zonets, sprightly duets—and keeping accounts; the couches in her little room are upholstered in gaily patterned silk, the pet monkey and the lapdog are fed regularly; she calls me Tiburtik, herself Terzina, Terzinochka, Terzinetta, Terzinettochka, sometimes inventing diminutives undreamed of by any philologist. Sometimes I have the feeling of suffocating in all these little cushions. I've even talked to my friend about it. She became pensive for a moment, then a little smile and a patter of words; "Tiburtik, we're not living in Carpaccio's day. And why should a woman have to resemble a cow or a horse? You don't care for all this? Maybe, my sweet, you'd like to return to the old days when they used to post an official list of all the grand and golden courtesans, complete with price list? All that's for foreigners. But then, you're a German boy, after all. And that's—how shall I put it?—too solemn, too cumbersome for me. The grandiose frightens me, and I don't want to make myself a laughingstock. I can sing Sophonisba or Dido abandoned, but in life…in life I prefer a different scale."

"Like the princess who was so small that she was carried about in a pocket?"

"How disgusting! What am I—a flea, or a crumb from a dry crust?" Then she grew thoughtful; "You know, though? That's not so bad. I'd be happy if the man I loved were to carry me about in his pocket…"

And again she grew thoughtful.

✿ ✿ ✿

But in love too, it would seem, Terzina is afraid of the grand scale, preparing to invest her passions in her conversations with her maidservants and the tradesmen.

Recalling the blue cup that served to introduce us the rosy librettist, I complained that she was less fiery at our trysts. Ardently kissing her lips, her breasts, her shoulders, I asked where she was hottest. Terzina laughed as if she were being tickled; then, almost seriously, she came out with:

"You know, I think my heels are the hottest part of me, or the sole of my feet in general: I've worn out four pairs of shoes this month."

✿ ✿ ✿

Every day she scans the newspaper for wonders, and drags me to look at the elephants, or hippopotami, or an apothecary's wife who has been delivered of six stillborn babies. The apothecary's wife was modest and pious, the babies had been placed in jars filled with alcohol. Terzina thought they'd been born in the jars.

❀   ❀   ❀

Hesperus came to me in despair. Without a word, he threw open the window and breathed in the damp silvery air like a stranded fish. In the distance, against the rainy pinkish sky above the lagoon, swayed a gray airballoon, such as no one had ever seen before, and the applause and shouts of the crowd came to us like fitfully breaking surf. I was surprised that Terza had permitted me to stay at home.

In his uncertainty, Hesperus goes from one mood to another, flying up to the heavens one moment, falling into gloom the next. He is not afraid of big words and strong feelings.

Antonia remains unyielding to his arguments and doesn't leave the convent. The romance of his affair is somewhat diminished by the fact that his parents know all the details of it and that his father is almost ready to come to Venice himself in order to aid his son in matters which are not customarily looked upon with an indulgent eye.

❀   ❀   ❀

Antonia is Venetian, but she is not like my friend. More like a horse or a cow, as Terzina irreverently puts it. She is tall, slow-moving, blond. Her matt complexion, puffy cheeks and the bags under her eyes are not, of course, the results of the monastic seclusion in which she has been living scarcely two or three months. She looks half asleep, but it appears that she is not without firmness, even stubbornness.

❀   ❀   ❀

Inspecting a colossal negro, whom Terzina has decided she absolutely must have as her footman, I thought for some reason of the two Carlos, Goldoni and Gozzi, the quarrel between whom is keeping all Venice entertained. It's a fact that they close their ears to all political news here, as if the world consisted entirely of comedies and freakshows. Well—let them. In this cradle of gaiety and laughter you really can forget everything, except for masks, concerts, operas, comedies, abbes, cicisbeos, players, gondoliers, little Terzinettochkas with their chocolate, their parrots, their lapdogs and pet monkeys, except for the watery sky and the sky-like waters. And always song, song, song! Is it a *concert spirituel* at the orphanage, a cradlesong, a barcarolle—or perhaps a funereal carnaval? I look on somehow from the wings. In these amorous sighings I fancy I hear something that speaks of last things.

But I have strayed from Goldoni and Gozzi. A strange fate is theirs! One of them—a whimsical connoisseur of bygone days, a fantast in his study, a count, a poet, defends the decaying art of improvisation; the other—the product of a petty, semi-artisan milieu, a street observer, rather obtuse, semi-educated, a brilliant improviser—reforms the Italian theater, striving to give it a French and classical character. Of course I'm no prophet, but it seems to me that Gozzi writes for the common people and for children, but will survive with refined lovers of art. Goldoni, on the other hand, who aims at the connoisseur, will always be loved by the motley audience and the mob.

Today it's rain all day—perhaps that's why I'm musing about art.

From the big window one can see wet stairs and walls; the iron rings clank softly in the turbulent water, the black prows of the gondolas gleam, the lanterns creak as they swing, and the blossom of the solitary jasmine spray that has forced its way through the stones of the house opposite is falling, falling…A square of pale gray sky seems to come right into the room. On the sandbank in the distance the wooden scaffolding for spectators, knocked together on the occasion of the balloon ascent, has not yet been dismantled, people are swarming about it, as if after an execution.

❈ ❈ ❈

I understand the love that Terzina, and Venetians in general, feel for the country house on the mainland along the Brenta or in other spots. I would give a great deal myself to see our own little garden in Königsberg. The storm has passed, after the thundercloud as it creeps away the rainbow casts its seven-hued radiance, and beneath it a horseman in red gallops swiftly over the bridge. How his caftan or cloak flames! How distinct is the clatter of hooves! How distinct everything is!—as if your ears had been cleared by some deathbed luminescence! Geese cackle. The apple trees do their best to smell sweet, a queen's diamonds lie strewn in the grass. What benediction! And from the uncle's room a Mozart quartet comes like a benediction made visible, like heaven brought down on our house: on the musicians, on me, weeping in the wilderness, on Aunt, Sophia, on everybody, on everything, on the cur that frightens the frogs as they hop out onto the road; on the smoke from the chimney, on the vanilla smell of the pastries.

❈ ❈ ❈

Antonia is an orphan; her stubborn resistance to the wishes of Hesperus and his family cannot be attributed to any family pressures. In the concerts given at the convent, she plays the double bass. That's a bit odd for a woman, but there are girls who play the bassoon, the French horn and even the trombone. The wits say that after these concerts for the young ladies, no instrument is any longer to be feared, but when I first saw Antonia standing with this enormous, deep-toned fiddle, serious, unsmiling, drawing the bow confidently and powerfully across the low, droning strings, wearing a white dress and with a posy of cherryred flowers behind one ear, her long, lustrous eyes cast down, I thought I was seeing an angel. I'm not saying this because I'm a friend of Hesperus, and I haven't cooled in the least toward Terzina's charms. To tell the truth, I don't exactly know why I've become fond of this Venetian woman, with her little cushions smelling of pomade—and I don't want to know. I am lulled, dulled by her, by the town, by the sea, by the eternal singing.

⚬   ⚬   ⚬

Singing fountains, oranges that release plump living girls when cut, laughing statues, playing-card kings, cities transformed into deserts, masks, sausages, newspapers, shipwrecks, azure birds, serpents, crows—all that overwhelmed me of course, but when to the magical sounds of violins a green star slowly floated and the smell of phosphor came drifting from somewhere, I suddenly felt how dearly I loved Teresa. I turned round. Her mouth was stuffed full of sweetmeats and she was stealthily wiping her sticky little hand on the pink box-curtain. She quickly understood my gaze, and pressing her shoulder against me she softly asked:

"Tiburtik loves me?"

"I love you, I love you!" I exclaimed almost loudly, paying no heed to the surrounding crowd.

The star lowered itself sedately, the violins shrilled, and with a rustle of yellow silk Terzina put on her mask. I ceased to recognize her at once.

⚬   ⚬   ⚬

I'm probably very stupid, but I still can't get used to masks. White *bautas* simply frighten me. They make everyone look like ducks, and Terzina has to remove her mask from time to time in order to reassure me that she is herself and not an unknown apparition, even though she never stops talking and even bursts into song, so that I can hear her voice very well.

⚬   ⚬   ⚬

Although the Cupid was not wearing a *bauta* but a narrow ribbon-like black mask across his broad, pendulous, very red cheeks, the sheer bulk of the face, the roguish hazel eyes behind the slits, the curly gold perruque and the pudgy, puckered arms, creased as if they were tied round with string, inspired me with horror. He was dressed in a green camisole, a quiver jangled at his fleshy shoulders, a miniscule tricorne was deftly perched over his left ear, and in his hands he held some kind of a paper.

"Signor Tiberzio! Signor Penzel!" he shouted to me, grimacing and slapping his idiotic paper against his chubby palm. From the look of him, he was a sturdy infant, but suddenly I saw him as a swollen dwarf who might at any moment burst with a malodorous bang.

I was in front of a letter from Hesperus, and the urchin was his servant, to whom I had never before paid any attention. Nobody here has any idea what is going on in Paris. All the same, the remote subterranean tremors cannot but be reflected everywhere, even if it is all the doing of freemasons and out-of-work lawyers—failures in life—as malicious tongues assure us. I don't know, but it will probably end badly.

Hesperus asks me to go with him to his rendezvous at Antonia's convent. Terzina has invited herself to come along too, saying that visiting days are an occasion for fashionable gatherings and that she won't get in anyone's way. It's a fact that, separated by a grille from the sisters, their orphan changes; the public chatters, sings, drinks coffee, plays dominoes and cards, while dogs bark underfoot and private conversations are completely drowned in the buzz and bustle. The ringing of the bell announcing the end of reception hours is scarcely audible.

o   o   o

I was talking with Terza about old age. An unsuitable enough conversation, admittedly—and, in effect, it didn't take place. I'd scarcely opened my mouth, when my friend tapped my lips with her fan and said superstitiously:

"What kind of talk is that, dear heart? When we die, that's when we'll grow old. Do you understand? When we die, not before. Have you ever seen old people in Venice?" But evidently this conversation stuck in her mind, because at the convent she brought it up herself.

Ignoring the crowd, Hesperus and Antonia were conversing through the grille close by.

"You see, Tiburtik...you see, old age...that's nonsense, German nonsense! There's no such thing as old age! And anyway, generally speaking, all Germans are ridiculous people! I used to know two brothers, they were twins...Now don't go thinking anything bad...they were simply acquaintances...I was just a chit of a girl...and they looked so much like one another, I'd have felt awkward, I'd never have known which of them I was in love with. I'm surprised they didn't go on the stage. You know, those plays where everything's all muddled, one man is mistaken for another—they would have been priceless. And then they loved each other so much, were so taken up with each other, that everyone found it funny, and in fact it was never discovered whether either of them had a mistress. But none of that's what I was meaning to say. I know a lot of stories about them, but I've never heard of such brotherly love before. Not that I read much, anyway. Just newspapers. And do you know why? Too many new books come out, you'll never manage to read it all anyway. Isn't that true?"

The Signora stopped in mid-course, ice cream having been served. I noticed that for several minutes Antonia had been paying more attention to Terzina's story than to the words of Hesperus, who was excitedly explaining something to her in a loud whisper. When my friend fell silent, Antonia pretended not to be in the least interested in our conversation. Opposite us, a gentleman in a dark coat, who had been walking back and forth in front of us, evinced an unmistakable impatience to learn of the further fate of the twins. Raising his had, he said:

"Excuse me, madam…"

"What can I do for you?"

"I heard…quite by chance…you know…Don't jump to conclusions. But I'm terribly curious to find out what happened to those twins."

Terza wasn't offended; she continued with a laugh:

"What happened was what will in all likelihood happen to all of us, alas! One of them died."

"So that's the story!" The stranger smacked his lips.

"There wasn't any story—and if there was, then it happened after his death. The point of all this wasn't that they were twins, and both handsome, and a model of brotherly love…I was telling this to the Signor with respect to old age, as an example…'

"With respect to old age! Well I never!" drawled the dark jacket sympathetically.

It was clear that Terzina didn't care for him. Swallowing the last morsel of pistachio ice cream, she cast a sombre glance at our new acquaintance and, addressing herself solely to me, continued:

"And so, dear heart, one of the boys dies. They were still very young, hardly more than boys, and such pretty little things. His brother nearly went out of his mind. During his brother's illness—he had already lost consciousness—he kept kissing him, combing his hair, wiping his hands, whispering something in his ear. You couldn't help weeping to see such devotion! But he died. And then his brother gave way to indescribable grief and all kinds of weird behavior: banged his head against the wall, lay down to sleep in the coffin with the dead man, kissed him, shook him, thinking it would wake him, poor boy! At last he dressed him in his best suit and sent him off to the good Lord like that. I saw it all: the dead man lay there, looking like a picture, and the one who remained alive was more like a corpse. Yes…And so the little German didn't lose his youth even in death. But then he was young anyway, so my story is neither here nor there, but I've told it all the same, and there's no taking it back."

Teresa was silent for a little, and for some reason everything around her became quiet. But the Signorina, having got into her stride, could not so quickly stop.

"A strange thing! The surviving brother began to dabble in magic, trying to summon up the dead man. Whether he appeared or not, I don't know...That's a great sin, you know, Tiburtik, to disturb the dead. But he visited me once, although I swear by the Madonna I didn't dabble in magic and wasn't even thinking about him. I even forget about the living, come to that. They say you get hallucinations when your stomach is upset—but I was in perfect health, I'd taken a purgative only two days before...and suddenly...I was asleep. A clicking sound woke me up, as if someone had snapped open his snuffbox...A night-light was burning in the room...Riccardo comes in (I recall now that one of them was called Riccardo, the other Ernesto), Riccardo comes in, actually takes a pinch of snuff, and comes right toward me. I pulled up the blanket and crossed myself. Politely and softly he says: 'Pardon me, madam, for disturbing you. Please tell Ernesto that I'm very lonely.' What a strange young man! What kind of fun and games did he expect in the other world! Then he marches right back and goes out. I hadn't been asleep."

"Well, did you pass on his words to Ernesto?"

"My darling Tiburtik, you think I'm a silly little fool. They were both extravagant creatures, melancholic and eccentric. If I'd have told Ernesto his brother was lonely, he'd have shot himself."

"To keep him company?"

"Well of course. No, I'm not wicked, I kept it a secret. And somehow the very memory of it upsets me. It makes me feel quite out of sorts."

"And did this Ernesto live on happily after his brother's death then?" Antonia's voice suddenly rang out close beside us. She had flushed and sounded slightly breathless. Next to her, on the other side of the grille, Hesperus made a movement. Teresa lifted her head.

"Ernesto? I don't know...No, come to think of it, I do...He died soon after, but he didn't kill himself. Just died, of an illness."

It seemed that Antonia's decision depended on the life or death of this Ernesto whom she had never met. She listened to Teresa's answer with a certain impatience, and suddenly, throwing back the white fans of ther dress, she reached out both hands through the grille to Hesperus, who pressed his forehead and lips to them.

The gentleman in the dark coat was mincing in front of Terezina, backing away, not daring to ask a question. But she had already forgotten that she was cross with him, and gave a smile. Overjoyed, he lifted his hat and, bowing and scraping with every word, began to ingratiate himself.

"Excuse me, madam…please don't…empty curiosity…Not at all! Strict science…Who will condemn me? Three children…little angels, if only you could see…"

"What is it?" asked Teresa, having quite recovered her good spirits.

"Excuse…the indiscretion…Their age? Those young Signori, the unfortunate brothers."

"How old were they?"

"Yes, if I may ask."

"Twenty."

"And the other one?"

"But they were twins."

"That's right, that's right! Capital! Twice twenty is forty."

And he scribbled something on a scrap of paper with a pencil-stub.

¤   ¤   ¤

I couldn't get Teresa's story out of my head. What I was particularly afraid of was that I might hear the click of a snuffbox.

At home I found a letter waiting for me. Oscar von Rittich had shot himself. No one knew what had driven him to take such a step. He left no notes. They called him in the morning, but he didn't open the door of his bedroom. About three o'clock they brok down the door. He was lying there with a bullet through his brain, and on the table Goethe's novel *The Sufferings of Young Werther* lay open.

Goethe! Is his novel to be blamed for this death? And how would he react to such an accusation if he were to be confronted with it?

I saw him three years ago, by chance. What a fine, what a manly face! What a godlike air! That's true genius for you! Of course, no accusation made by short-sighted burghers can touch him!

But I'm sorry for poor Oscar. He belonged to the race of dreamers Teresa calls melancholics and fantasts. In Venice to think means to be sad; pensiveness and sorrow are one and the same thing. There's a measure of truth in that, of course.

Again the fleshy cupid, this time minus perruque and quiver, and mask, hands me a letter from Hesperus. Without his mask and dressed in his livery, the urchin no longer inspires me with horror, although I wouldn't employ him myself. It's clear that I have an aversion to plump napes and pudgy arms, creased as if they were tied round with string.

Hesperus is triumphant. Antonia has given her consent. He ascribes this change to the impression made by Terzina's story and is profuse in his gratitude, although our aid was unconscious and involuntary. All the same, it's obvious that he's quite assured of the lastingness of this consent, since he has hastened to carry off Antonia, now his betrothed, to his native land. So great was his hurry that he didn't even have time to take leave of us. Teresa brags a good deal about the successful outcome of this affair, although it seems that, in her heart of hearts, she understands and approves of neither the one nor the other.

✿ ✿ ✿

The wind tears off the translucent petals and carries them down the staircase—tulips, poppies, roses and jasmine, shot through by the slanting evening sun. And my own jasmine flower, Teresa, went tumbling down with everyone to the greenish water. A shout from the gondolier, a splash, and the whole band, swaying as if they were in a dormeuse, casts off. Shouts, laughter, squeals and singing are scattered along the canal.

✿ ✿ ✿

I cannot see the evening star now without a tremor—I keep waiting for it to slide sedately across the gray cardboard of the heavens, surprised that I can't hear the high singing of violins.

I shudder every time someone clicks open a snuffbox in my presence.

The story of the twins gives me no peace. Clearly I belong to the same breed of eccentrics

✿ ✿ ✿

Experiencing no strong emotions and passions, I am obliged to put in their place an abundance of impressions, a variegated heap, many-hued and miniscule, of needle-pricks, laughter and diversion. Teresa is delighted, and thought up a new diminutive as she caressed me. The next morning we had both forgotten it. And the gondoliers sing the stanzas of Torquato Tasso as if they were tidings from another world. All the same, the stories about the gondoliers being able to sing the whole of *Gerusalemma Liberata* are, of course, exaggerations. They remember three or four stanzas, and always the same ones. The melody has grandeur and pathos, though one must admit that it is not without a certain monotony.

✿ ✿ ✿

We played cards nearly all night. We won a little. This gives Teresa a child-like pleasure. Afterwards we went for a ride. And suddenly I remembered, as if this were the thing that had been tormenting me all the time.

"Teresa, my angel, do you remember the gentleman who wanted to know about the age of the German twins?"

"Yes, I remember him."

"How mysterious! What was his connection with them? Have you thought about that?"

Teresa gave a shrug.

"What's there to think about! I knew then what it was. He's a gambler: he was taking part in a lottery and wanted to guess a lucky number. That's all."

And here I am among the melancholics and eccentrics!

The sun was rising. It dyed the water so red that the floating pieces of orange peel were invisible—you simply couldn't make them out. A warm, warm wind assailed us resiliently; it was like thrusting your face into a woman's breasts.

Twice twenty is forty. A lucky number for someone. Teresa is sleeping, curled up in a ball. She's such a tiny little thing, so dimpled, so rosy—how could she carry the weight of strong passions and other German oddities!

POETRY

THE TROUT BREAKS
THE ICE

FIRST PROLOGUE

The stream is hankering for ice
(The wintry sky's to blame).
Its chains of sugar candy
Twang brittly as lute strings.
Thrust, trout, with a will!
The sun's aquamarine,
The fleeting bird-shadows—
Are you not weary of them?
The fiercer your convulsions,
The brighter their echo (friendship's return).
On the ice a peasant stands.
The trout breaks the ice.

SECOND PROLOGUE

When visitors come knocking
And stay unasked to tea,
A man must make them welcome
Or fail in courtesy.

Their eyes are lamps extinguished,
Their waxen fingers gleam,
Beggared the light that glosses
Each threadbare trouser seam.

Titles from oblivion,
Word that never were...
A riddling kind of chatter
That leaves the mind blur...

Stamps a capricious heel
The painter long sea-slain,
Next a hussar, a stripling,
With a bullet through his brain...

And you're not even born yet,
Dear *Mister* Dorian—
What business have you lounging
Coolly on my divan?

Well, memory's a hoarder,
Fancy a wilful boy—
This prank will cost you dearly
If ever I have my way!

THRUST THE FIRST

Winter in the streets, and at the opera—"Tristan."
The wounded sea sang in the orchestra,
The land of green beyond the azure haze,
The heart brought to a shuddering standstill.
Who saw her enter? No one. She was simply
There in serene possession of her box,
A beauty from a painting by Bryullov.
Such women live in the pages of novels,
On the screen too they are to be encountered...
Terrible crimes are committed for their sake,
Their carriages are besieged by loyal admirers,
For love of them poison is swallowed in garretts.
She sat there unselfconsciously absorbed

In the unfolding tale of fatal love,
Leaving unstraightened the scarlet shawl
Which had stolen from a pearly shoulder,
Caring not at all that she was the target
Of many an unwavering binocular…
And I, who did not know her, I too peered
(Was she alone?) into that shadowy box…
I'd just come from a spiritualist seance,
Though spirits aren't my line, and the medium,
A seedy Czech, had seemed to me pathetic.
Though the window came a flood of light,
Pallid and chill, and with a bluish tinge,
As if the moon was shining from the north:
Iceland, Greenland, ultimate Thule,
The land of green beyond the azure haze…
This I remember: my every nerve was bound
By such a languor as precedes eruption,
Expectation mingled with revulsion,
Ultimate shame, consummate bliss…
And something within me knocking, knocking,
(The thrusting tail of a fish immured in ice)…
Staggering I rose, blindly, like a sleepwalker,
I reached the door…Suddenly it opened…
From the anteroom emerged a man,
He seemed about twenty, and his eyes were green;
Taking me, perhaps, for someone else,
He shook my hand and said "Care for a smoke?"
How the fish lashed, with what wild urgency!
Who spurns the will attains a higher will!
Ultimate shame, consummate bliss!
The land of green beyond the azure haze!

THRUST THE SECOND

The horses rear in terror,
Entwined with a band of blue,
Wolves, snow and shooting, jangling bells!
What of the reckoning, black as night?

Will your Carpathians not tremble?
The honey harden in the ancient horn?

The sled-rug shakes, a wonder-bird;
Screech of runners—"Maritza, whoa!"
Halt…a footman running with a lamp…
So that's the lair you make your home in:
Madonna's gleaming at your bed-head,
A horseshoe sanctifies your threshold,

Colonnades, a snowdrift on the roof,
Behind the wainscotting mice scamper,
Shabracks, knotted lace and carpets!
Oppressive are the formal bedrooms!
A whole felled forest fills the hearth,
Resin sputtering like incense…

But why then have your lips turned yellow?
Do you not know on what you've ventured?
No laughing matter here, my friend!
It was not a Bohemian vampire—
But blood brother that you swore to be,
The world's your witness. Be a brother!

The prison laws that govern us,
Ah they are strict and wilful things:
Blood for blood, and love for love.
We're honor-bound in what we give and take,
Blood vengeance we do not need:
God alone will free us from our oath,

Cain pronounces judgement on himself…
The youthful master has turned pale,
And drawn a knife across his palm…
Quietly drips the blood into the glasses:
Sign of exchange and sign of safeguarding…
The horses are led out into the stable…

THRUST THE THIRD

Like a wing, a wing shot through,
Hangs the ship: a model sloop.
The radiance of a hothouse
Lurks in the glazing of such libraries.

Yesterday's journey and the knife,
The oaths in frenzy taken
Held seeds of falsity for me,
A parody of fearsome crime…

I felt like asking…What a shame…
But this manly kind of comfort
Hinted strongly that this spot
Was not intended for such talk.

You have just gone out, Shakespeare
Lies open, cigarette smoke drifts…
"The Sonnets!!" How the world seems simple
To the March lilt of a question!

As embroidery of snowflake
Melts at vernal rays' assault,
In such a young man's life
May follow a capricious path!

THRUST THE FOURTH

This breakfast, how it brings to mind
Those orchestrated interludes
When every sound and every thought
Awakes its loving opposite:
The clarinet and horn converse,
The flute sleeps in the harp's embrace,
Bodes the funereal trombone—
A sound appealing to the dead alone.
This breakfast how it brings to mind
A sideshow with its Siamese twins;
A single stomach, but two hearts,

Two heads, and yet a single spine...
How can such freaks of nature be?
The answer is a mystery.
Express our traffic literally—
A freakshow for the world to see.

You're awakening—I'm awake,
We are two wings—a single soul,
Two souls we are—our maker one,
Two makers we—a single crown...
But why the suitcase packed and locked,
The railroad ticket ready booked?
This breakfast, how it brings to mind
Some lie, insidious and bland!

THRUST THE FIFTH

The month of May we pass in country style:
The blinds are down, we go about in shirtsleeves,
We've dragged the billiard table to the hall.
And half the day, from breakfast time to tea,
We push the balls around. An early supper,
Then up at dawn for swimming, indolence...
You having left, it seemed appropriate
To live as parted lovers ought to do:
A life of somewhat humdrum healthiness.
I wasn't much expecting letters,
And started when I saw the postmark "Greenock."
"We're spending May in wild delirium,
The rose runs riot and the sea is blue,
And Eleanor is lovelier than ever!
Forgive me, friend—if you could see her
Dressed in her dove-gray riding habit
Of a morning in the flower garden,
You'd understand that passion conquers will."
Then that was where it was, the land of green!
Who could have thought that tranquil scenery
Could not be backdrop to catastrophe?

THRUST THE SIXTH

Red-haired, red-cheeked, the sailor left
To sail the distant main.
The years wear on, the beard grows hoar—
He did not come again.
Year in, year out, his grandam prayed
God grant his spirit rest,
And heavy lay the icy weight
On his betrothed's breast.
The table has been cleared long since,
The house cur gnaws a bone—
It lifts its head and starts to howl…
In the doorway stands a man.
A sailor he, of years two score.
—Who's master here? Come say!
I carry tidings from afar
To Mistress Annie Ray.
—What tidings can you have to tell?
My man long dead is he!—
He rolled his sleeve back, and behold
The birthmark plain to see.
—Then welcome me, your Erwin Green!—
The fainting bride sinks down…
The father weeps, the mother too,
And kisses her son's brow.
Merrily ring the bells around,
"Ding-dong" through dell and dene.
To church to wed goes Annie Ray,
And with her Erwin Green.
The skirling bagpipes pipe them home,
They're left alone at last.
Said she: I beg you, husband mine,
To set my mind at rest:
Many a strange land you saw
While I lived lonely here—
Have you forgot the holy law
Of your own land and dear?
You spurn the sacraments, I mark,
Nor do you bend the knee,

Nor with a loud amen assent
When the choir sings joyously,
From the holy font you stay your hand
And sit you down uncrossed—
O do not say your heart has banned
Our Saviour Jesus Christ…
—Lie calm, lie easy, Annie Ray,
And leave this foolish talk!
You've never seen, 'tis clear as day,
The northernlandish folk.
Green is the light that glimmers there
From earth to heaven's rim,
A flower from the water rises clear—
A heart upon the stem,
And brighter shines the icy star
To hearts that know no fear…
If you would see your plighted lord,
Gaze boldly on me here!—
She lifts her eyes and long she stares,
Her mind reels in amaze…
The mariner of two score years,
The partner of her days,
Stands tall and of a noble frame,
Smooth-skinned as any boy,
Proud temple, brow and silken lash—
She cannot look away!
As fresh as any rose he gleamed,
His cheek was rosy-red,
So fresh, so fair he had not seemed
In boyhood days long fled.
His hair is fine as finest flax,
His lips are burning fire,
His eyes are glittering and green,
Miraculous their power…
Then all at once it came to her
How many years ago
The young lord at the break of day
Had given up the ghost.
He lay a lily in the tomb,
His grieving mother by;

"How sweet it were," a soft voice came,
"With such a lad to lie!"
Soft whirrings and vibrating blue,
And lights swam all around;
Sunk in a green and icy sleep,
The dreaming house slept sound.
She burns and shakes, her salt tears flow,
To pray she has no might.
He waits upon her "yes" or "no"...
Soft whirrings fill the night...
—Ye may be the devil come from hell
My mortal soul to damn,
But devil or no, I love thee well,
Thy bride till death I am!

THRUST THE SEVENTH

The bathing lad—a stranger—
Takes a secret bath.
He cautiously looks about him
With an offended eye.
In vain you try to cover
Your bashful nudity—
You present no interest
To the village passer-by.
Crossing yourself, but lightly,
You dive down from the steep...
But were you a bit cleverer,
You'd be Narcissus' self.
And the dragonflies and midges,
The scorching village sun...
You're gazing straight into the sky,
And from the earth you're far...
Allusion or memory?
Submerged, your body
Gleams, is luminescent
With green mica-scales.
Hold your swimming to the left
And you'll swim out on a bank!..

There lashing in the water see
A trout, a silver trout!..

THRUST THE EIGHTH

Caught in crystal, the sunbeam decomposes
To its elements—you see the rainbow quicken
And points of light leap blithely round the room.
Unless we die, we cannot be reborn.
I stepped outside; roses were darkening,
Smelling of Good Friday in the flower-filled church.
The crimson-flooded sky of sunset
Was swallow-streaked, the pond was all aglow.
Dust billowed from the distant herd. Suddenly
A motorcar comes streaking like an arrow
(A sight that's most uncommon hereabouts)
A cloak of green is streaming in the wind.
Dazed by the swiftness of these happenings,
I was gazing into two green eyes,
Two other hands were warmly grasping mine
And, dusty from the road, the weary face
Aroused familiar love, familiar pain.
—Here I am…I have no strength…I'm done for.
Our transfiguring angel has abandoned me.
A little, and my blindness will be total,
A rose will be a rose, the sky the sky,
And nothing more! Mere dust, I shall return
To dust! My blood and bile and brains and lymph
Are dessicated utterly. My God!
Nothing to draw strength from, no exchange!
Walls of unshatterable glass imprison me,
I'm threshing like a fish! —And your green cloak?—
—What green cloak? —Surely you arrived in one.—
—That was a mirage. There isn't a green cloak.—
American dustocat, kid gloves, gray tie
And a cape the tender hue of *rose champagne*.
—Stay with me here! —You know that cannot be!
Each passing day I seem to sink in deeper!—
His face became a quivering net of nerves,

As if a vivesector stood beside him.
A kiss, and in a moment he was gone,
His motorcar below had long been puffing.
Five days later I received a letter
Stamped with the same odd postmark: "Greenock."
—I meant to write before, but you agree,
Laxness may be pardoned in a happy man,
And happiness for me is—Eleanor,
As a window is a window or a rose a rose.
It's ridiculous, isn't it, after all,
To maintain that behind the form of words
Some kind of "higher meaning" lies concealed.
I'm happy then—Just simply, sanely happy.—
For a letter to arrive here takes five days.

THRUST THE NINTH

I invite not friends, but "people I know:"
With them it's easier to pass the time.
Of what is past I feel no need to talk,
And what's the point of trying to tell the future?
Not revelry but orderly enjoyment,
Smooth words, words that are agreeable,
White wine does not leave a heavy hangover,
An empty head is lucid, clear.
Every hour is filled so carefully
That a single day could well hold forty,
And the epiderm is gently tickled
By that we give the general name of love.
And to keep a changing round of faces,
Not to attach oneself too much to one.
How could balderdash about a land of green
Have simply come into my head?
—You've passed out? —In a metaphorical sense.
—Greenock? —It exists. A Scottish townlet.
Metaphors cloud the atmosphere like smoke,
But vanish in a ring below the ceiling,
Sober day disperses all chimeras—
Many an example can be cited.

With waters of green the river roars,
We cannot save the small canoe.
In a kid-glove, a beckoning hand
Will summon you always from afar,
And Erwin Green the mariner
You shall not clasp yet to your heart.

THRUST THE TENTH

Sometimes the round of favorite pleasures
Becomes more tedious than sitting at a desk.
Then chance, and only chance, can rescue us,
But chance is no pet dog to come at beck and call.
The temple of chance is the gaming house.
The fervency of flaming eyes,
Parched lips and brows of deathlike hue
There's no need to describe. The croupier's rasped edicts
Became the music of my waking nights.
I felt as if I were sitting under water.
The green baize put in my mind
The land of green beyond the azure haze…
But memories I did not seek to waken,
Rather I wished to put them from my mind,
Waiting for chance's nod. One evening
A personage in heavy spectacles
Walked across to me and said: —I see
You're not a gambler, but rather an amateur,
Or, more probably, a seeker after sensation.
Admit, though, it's too dreary here for words:
Monotonous and quite uninteresting.
It's early yet. Perhaps you'd care to see
The small collection that I've put together
Of curios? I've been all over Europe,
Been traveling since I was a boy—Seen Egypt too.
Over the years it's grown to quite a museum—
You might find a thing or two to amuse you.
All collectors—and I'm no exception—
Are grateful for an audience; unshared,
This passion, like all others, is a dead thing.—

I consented at once, although to tell
The truth, the man did not appeal to me:
He seemed a bore, and a stupid one at that.
Still, it was only quarter to one,
And I certainly had nothing else to do.
Not much, you'll say, of an adventure!
We walked three blocks; the usual kind of entrance,
The usual middle-class apartment,
The usual collection of scarabs,
Arquebuses, broken telescopes,
Moth-eaten perruques, keyless clockwork dolls.
A languid web seemed wound about my brain,
Nausea came on me, my head began to spin,
And I prepared to make my excuses…
My host was at a loss, stammered and said:
—I'm afraid this isn't to your liking.
But of course it won't impress a connoisseur.
I have one final hope of pleasing you,
If you'll forgive its uncompleted state,
As yet I haven't found its other half.
One of these days I hope to bring it off.
Perhaps you'll take a glance? A twin! —A twin?!
—A twin. —One of a pair? —One of a pair.—
We went into a tiny room: in the middle
Stood an aquarium; its top was covered
With a sheet of glass, blue-tinged like ice.
A trout made melancholy curves within,
Beating melodiously against the glass.
—The fish will break the glass, be sure of that.
—But where's this twin of yours? —A moment, patience.—
He opened, smirking, a cupboard in the wall,
Skipping back behind the door. On a chair inside
Against a backcloth of green calico,
Reclined a ragged being, sunk in sleep
("Caligari!"—a lightning flash of thought):
Green translucence lurked beneath the skin,
The lips' curl told of bitterness and sin.
About the forehead clustered auburn curls
And in the dry temple a vein was throbbing.
With expectation and revulsion

I stared, unable to take away my eyes…
Softly the fish was beating at the ice…
An aery tinkling mingled with a peal of blue…
The American dustcoat and the neatly knotted tie…
The cap the tender hue of *rose champagne*.
He smote his chest and shouted in a frenzy…
—Good God, you mean to say you know each other?
And even…perhaps…I can't believe my luck!…
—Open up your eyes, your eyes of green!
I take you as you are, in whatever guise
The land of green has sent you back to me!
We are blood brothers. In the Carpathians,
You remember, Shakespeare still lies open
And radiant words dissolve in rainbows.
Ultimate shame, consummate bliss!—
The thrusting fish deals blow on blow on blow.

THRUST THE ELEVENTH

—You're breathing? You're alive? You're not a ghost?
—The first-born I of green vacuity.

—I hear your beating heart, your blood is warm…
—Those whom love has summoned may not die…

—Your cheeks are redder, and corruption fades…
—A secret interchange is taking place…

—What is it first meets your restored gaze?
—I see a trout, a trout that breaks the ice.

—Lean on my arm…And make an effort…Rise…
—Fabric given airing takes on strength…

—Will you put your green langour out of mind?
—I set my foot upon a higher step!

—And can your spirit once again take fire?
—Copper is welded by fire to gold.

—Has the transfiguring angel come again?
—Yes, the transfiguring angel has come again.

THRUST THE TWELFTH

On the bridge the horses glisten,
Caparisoned with snow,
And palm to palm tight pressing,
We swiftly gallop home.

There are no words but only smiles,
No moon, but burns a star—
Changes and mistakes
Like water flow away.

Along the Neva, round a canal
And up the carpeted stairs
You hasten as in days of yore,
Into the familiar house.

Two garlands made of porcelain,
Two sets of knives and forks,
And in your steady gaze of green
Two roses upon stems.

The hallway clock is audible
Slowly beating twelve…
And my trout resoundingly
Breaks the remaining ice.

Are we alive? We're living still.
We're dead? O enviable tomb!
Paying age-old custom honor,
The bottles pop their corks!

No place here for melancholy,
For doubting or for care!
Through the doorway comes the golden-haired,
The lunatic New Year!

EPILOGUE

You know my original intention
Was to depict the twelve months of the year,
Devising for each of them a proper role
In the carefree round of amorous diversion.
And just look at the result! Clearly
I'm not in love and not so light of heart.
Memories came flooding in upon me,
Snatched from novels read long since;
The dead joined company with the living,
And such a muddle came of it that I
Feel sorry I started the whole business.
The twelve months I've kept at any rate
And indicated, more or less, the weather.
That's something. For the rest, it's my belief
A trout can break the ice that prisons it
If only it perseveres. And that's all.

Alexandrian Songs

I. PRELUDE

1.

Like a mother's lullaby
over her baby's cradle,
like a mountain echo
answering the shepherd's pipe at daybreak,
like the remote surge
of my native sea, long unbeheld,
thy name rings in my ears,
thrice-blessed:
　　Alexandria!

Like the hesitant whispering,
in the oak's deep shade, of love's confessions,
like the mysterious murmur
of the shadowy sacred groves,
like the tambourine of great Cybele,
bringing to mind far thunder and the moan of doves,
thy name rings in my ears,
thrice-sapient:
　　Alexandria!

Like the sound of a trumpet before battle,
the scream of eagles over the abyss,
the rushing wings of a flying Nike,

thy name rings in my ears,
thrice-mighty:
    Alexandria!

2.

When I hear the word "Alexandria,"
I see the white walls of a house,
a little garden with a clump of stock,
the pale sunlight of an autumn evening,
and I hear the sound of distant flutes.

When I hear the word "Alexandria,"
I see the stars over the quieting town,
drunken sailors in shady hangouts,
a dancing girl whirling in the "wasp,"
and I hear the jingle of a tambourine, the shouts of a quarrel.

When I hear the word "Alexandria,"
I see a faded crimson sunset over a sea of green,
I see the fleeced and winking stars
and a pair of clear gray eyes beneath thick brows—
eyes which I see
even when I do not hear the word "Alexandria."

3.

The twilight enshrouding the warm sea at evening,
the beacons that flame to the darkening heavens,
the drift of verbena when feasting is done with,
the freshness of dawn after nights spent unsleeping,
the shouting and laughter of women folk bathing,
the peacocks of Juno that walk in her temple,
the vendors of violets, pomegranates and lemons,
the moaning of doves and the dazzle of sunlight—
O when shall I see thee, adorable city?

II. LOVE

1.

When it was I first encountered you
poor memory cannot tell me:
was it morning, or in the afternoon,
evening, perhaps, or late at night?
I remember only the wan cheeks,
the gray eyes beneath dark brows
and the deep-blue collar at the swarthy throat,
and all this seems to come to me from childhood,
although I am older than you, older by many years.

2.

Were you apprenticed to a fortune teller?—
My heart lies open to you,
you can divine my every thought,
my deepest meditations are not hidden from you;
but knowing this, you know but little,
few words are needed for the telling of it,
no crystal ball or glowing brazier:
my heart, my thoughts, my deepest meditations
are filled with voices endlessly repeating:
"I love you, and my love shall have no ending!"

3.

At noon I must have been conceived,
at noon I must have come into the world,
and from my childhood I have loved
the beaming radiance of the sun.
One day I looked upon your eyes
and I became indifferent to the sun:
why should I adore a single sun
now that two of them are mine?

4.

People see gardens and houses
and the sea crimson with the sunset,
people see gulls skimming the waves,
and women on flat roofs,
people see warriors in armor
and pie-sellers in the town square,
people see sun and stars,
brooks and bright rivers,
but I see only
gray eyes beneath dark brows,
the touch of pallor in the swarthy cheeks,
the form of matchless grace—
thus do the eyes of lovers see
no more than the wise heart wills.

5.

Leaving my house in the morning,
I look up at the sun and think:
"How like my love
when he bathes in the river,
or gazes at the distant vegetable plots!"
And when in the heat of noon I gaze
at the same burning sun,
again you come into my mind, my dearest one:
"How like my love
when he rides through the crowded streets!"
And when I look upon soft sunsets,
it is to you that memory returns,
drowsing, wan from our caresses,
your drooping eyelids shadowed deep.

6.

Not for nothing did we read the theologians
and studied the rhetoricians not in vain,
for every word we have a definition

and can interpret all things seven different ways.
In your body I can locate the four virtues,
and, needless to say, the seven sins;
nor am I backward in tasting these delights;
but of all words one is changeless:
when, gazing deep into your gray eyes,
I say, "I love you"—the cleverest rhetorician
will understand only, "I love you"—nothing more.

7.

Were I a general of olden times,
I would subdue the Ethiops and the Persians,
I would dethrone Pharoah,
I would build myself a pyramid
higher than Cheops',
and I would become
more glorious than any man in Egypt.

Were I a nimble thief,
I would rob the tomb of Menkaure,
I would sell the gems to the Jews of Alexandria,
I would buy up land and mills,
and I would become
richer than any man in Egypt.

Were I a second Antinous,
he who drowned in the sacred Nile—
I would drive all men mad with my beauty,
temples would be raised to me while I yet lived,
and I would become
more powerful than any man in Egypt.

Were I a sage steeped in wisdom,
I would squander all my wealth,
I would shun office and occupation,
I would guard other men's orchards,
and I would become
freer than any man in Egypt.

Were I your lowliest slave,
I would sit in a dungeon
and once a year or once in two years
I would glimpse the golden tracery of your sandals
when you chanced to walk by the prison house,
and I would become
happier than any man in Egypt.

III. THE GIRL

1.

Four of us there were, sisters, four of us,
each of us loved, but each had a different "because":
the first because her father and mother had ordered her to,
the second because her lover possessed great riches,
the third because her lover was a famous artist,
but I loved because I fell in love.

Four of us there were, sisters, four of us,
each of us had a wish, but each wished for something different:

the first to raise children and cook porridge,
the second to put on a new dress every day,
the third to have everyone talking about her,
but I wished to love and to be loved.

Four of us there were, sisters, four of us,
each of us ceased to love, but each for a different reason:
the first because her husband died,
the second because her friend went bankrupt,
the third because the artist left her,
but I ceased to love because I ceased to love.

Four of us there were, sisters, four of us,
or were there perhaps not four of us, but five?

2.

In spring the poplar renews its leaves,
in spring Adonis returns
from the kingdom of the dead…
and you are leaving me in spring, my dearest one?
In spring everyone will be at the seaside
sailing, or riding swift horses
through the parks on the edge of town…
But who's to sail with me in a skimming skiff?

In spring everyone will put on their finery
and stroll in couples to the flowery fields…
and you expect me to sit at home?

3.

Today's a holiday:
the bushes are all in bloom,
the currants have ripened
and the lotus floats like a beehive on the pond!
If you like,
we'll race each other
along the path bordered with yellow roses
to the lake where the goldfish swim.
If you like,
we'll go to the summer-house,
and sweet drinks will be brought to us,
pies and nuts;
a boy will wave a fan over us
and we'll gaze
at the distant fields of corn.
If you like,
I'll sing a Grecian song to the harp—
but on one condition:
you're not to fall asleep,
and you have to praise both singer and accompanist.
If you like,
I'll dance the "wasp"
all by myself on the green lawn,

for you alone.
If you like,
I'll give you currants—but not with hands:
you'll take the red berries
with your lips from mine,
and with them
kisses.
If you like, if you like,
we'll count the stars,
and whoever loses count will pay a forfeit.
Today's a holiday,
the garden's all in bloom—
come, dearest love,
and make this holiday a holiday for me!

4.

Is it not true
that pearls dissolve in vinegar,
that verbena freshens the air,
that the cooing of doves is soft to the ear?

Is it not true
that there is none to match me in all Alexandria
in luxury of sumptuous adornment,
in fine white steeds and silver harness,
in the length of my black tresses, cunningly entwined?
Is there any who has the art
to paint her eyes more skilfully than I
and to steep each finger
in a different fragrance?

Is it not true
that ever since I first set eyes on you
I see nothing else bu you,
hear nothing else but you,
and long for nothing else
but to gaze upon your eyes—
gray eyes beneath thick brows—
and to hear your voice?

Is it not true
that with my own hands I gave you a quince,
first having tasted of it,
sent to you adroit ambassadresses of the heart,
paid your debts
(though it cost me my estate),
and for love potions
bartered my very apparel?
And is it not true
that all this was in vain?

But no matter if it be true
that pearls dissolve in vinegar,
that verbena freshens the air,
that the cooing of doves is soft to the ear—
no less shall it be true,
no less shall it be true,
that you will return my love!

In imitation of Pierre Louÿs

5.

There were four of them that month,
but only one of them I loved.
The first was utterly ruined for my sake,
every hour he sent new gifts,
selling his last mill to buy bangles
that tinkled when I danced—he stabbed himself,
but he was not the one I loved.
The second dedicated thirty elegies to me
which were read even in Rome; he wrote
that my cheeks were like the breaking dawn
and my tresses like the darkness of night—
but he was not the one I loved.

The third, ah the third was so beautiful
that his own sister strangled herself with her braid
lest she became enamoured of him;
day and night he stood outside my door,
begging me to say, "Come!"—but I kept silent,
for he was not the one I loved.

But you were not rich, you did not speak of dawns and nights,
you were not handsome,
and when at the festival of Adonis I threw you a carnation,
your clear eyes looked at me indifferently—
but you were the one I loved.

6.

Don't ask me how it happened:
my mother had gone to the market;
I swept the house clean
and sat down at the loom.
I didn't sit by the doorway, I swear I didn't,
but under the high window.
Weaving and singing I sat there;
what else? Nothing.
Don't ask me how it happened:
my mother had gone to the market.

Don't aske me how it happened:
the window was high up.
He must have rolled up a stone
or climbed a tree
or stood on a bench.
He said:
"I thought it was a robin,
but instead I see a Penelope.
What are you doing at home? Good day to you!"
"You're the one that's like a bird, up there in the eaves
instead of sitting in the law courts
writing those precious scrolls of yours."
"Yesterday we went sailing on the Nile—
and today my head aches."
"What's the good of it aching
if it doesn't keep you from nightly carousing?"
Don't ask me how it happened:
the window was high up.

Don't ask me how it happened:
I don't think he could reach that far.

"What's in my mouth—can you see?"
"What should there be in your mouth?
Strong teeth and a loose tongue—
and nonsense in your head."
"There's a rose in my mouth—look."
"I don't see any rose!"
"I don't see any rose!"
"I'll give it to you, if you like—
only you'll have to reach it yourself."
I stood on tiptoe,
I climbed onto the bench,
I climbed onto the loom (it was a strong one),
I reached out for the scarlet rose,
but the rascal said:
"With your mouth, with your mouth!
Lips must take from lips, do you hear?"
Perhaps my lips did
touch his, don't ask me.
Don't ask me how it happened:
I didn't know he could reach that far.

Don't ask me how it happened:
weaving and singing I sat there;
I didn't sit by the doorway, I swear I didn't.
The window was high up:
who could reach that far?
When my mother got back, she said,
"What's come over you, Zoe?—
instead of a narcissus, you've woven a rose!
What on earth were you thinking of?"
Don't ask me how it happened.

IV. WISDOM

1.

I asked wise men from every land:
"Why does the sun give heat?
Why does the wind blow?
Why are men born into the world?

Wise men from every land replied:
"The sun gives heat
that corn may ripen for our nourishment,
and that men may die of pestilence.
The wind blows
that ships may be brought safely to distant ports,
and that caravans may be buried in the sand.
Men are born into the world
that they may sorrowfully take leave of life
after begetting others for the grave."

"And why did the gods ordain it thus?"
"For the same reason
that they put into your head the desire
to ask idle questions."

2.

What's to be done
if the crimson of evening clouds
in the green-tinged sky
(on the left the moon has already risen,
and the great-maned star,
the harbinger of night)
fades swiftly,
utterly dissolves
before your eyes?
If our journey together along the broad way
which runs among trees, past mills
(once they were mine, but now
they are the bangles on your feet)
should end suddenly
beyond the next winding
(even though a welcoming house await us there)?
If my verse,
which I value no less
than Callimachus
(or any other great one) his,
wherein I lay away my love and all my tenderness
and winged thoughts from the gods—

the solace of my mornings,
when the sky is clear
and the scent of jasmine drifts in through the window—
tomorrow
should be forgotten like other men's?
If I shall no longer see
your face
or hear your voice?
If the wine will be drained to the lees,
the fragrance flee upon the air
and even precious stuffs
fall to dust
as the centuries pass?
Am I the less to love
these dear and fragile things
because they must decay?

3.

Eternal gods, how great is my love
for this fair world!
For the sun, the reeds,
and the gleam of the gray-green sea
through delicate acacia branches!
How I love books (they are my friends),
and the quiet of a solitary dwelling
and the distant water-melon beds
which I see from my window.
How I love the crowd that throngs the square,
the shouts, the singing and the sun,
the happy laughter of boys playing ball!
The walk home after happy wanderings
with my friend (he is already far away),
late in the evening
when the first stars are out,
past inns where the lights burn early.
How I love, eternal gods,
a lucid sadness,
a love with no tomorrow,
death without regret

for this sweet life,
which I love (by Dionysus I swear it)
with all my beating heart
and all my cherished flesh!

4.

Sweet is it to die
to the whistle of arrows and lances
on the field of battle,
when the trumpet sounds
and the sun stands high,
dying for the glory of the fatherland
and hearing on every side:
"Hero, farewell!"
Sweet is it to die
a venerable elder
in the very house,
on the very bed
where your forerathers were born and died,
surrounded by your children,
themselves now men,
and hearing on every side:
"Father, farewell!"
But it is sweeter yet,
yet wiser,
having squandered all your wealth,
having sold your last mill
for the sake of her
you would have forgotten tomorrow,
to return from a pleasant stroll
to the house you no longer own,
to eat a leisurely supper,
and, having read the tale of Apuleius through
for the hundred and first time,
to lie in a warm, fragrant bath,
and without hearing a single farewell
to open your veins,
while through the long ceiling window
the scent of stock comes drifting in,

the sunset glitters
and the sound of flutes comes floating from afar.

5.

O sun, radiant one,
divine Ra-Helios,
it is you who brings cheer
to the hearts of emperors and heroes,
to you the sacred horses neigh,
to you they sing hymns in Heliopolis;
when you shine,
lizards crawl out onto rocks
and boys run laughing
to bathe in the Nile.
O sun, radiant one,
I am a pallid scribe,
a library recluse,
but I love you, radiant one, not less
than the sunburnt sailor
smelling of fish and brine,
and not less
than his accustomed heart
rejoices
at your royal ascent
from the ocean bed,
does my heart tremble
when, fiery still, your moted beam
comes creeping
through the narrow skylight
onto the closely written sheet
and onto my bony parchment-colored hand
tracing in cinnabar
the first letter of a hymn to you,
O sun Ra-Helios!

V. FRAGMENTS

1.

My son,
the time has come for us to part.
Long will you not see my face,
long will you not hear my voice,
and yet it seems but a short while since
that your grandfather brought you here from the desert,
and you said, gazing at me:
"Is that the god Ptah, grandad?"
Now it is you who are like the god Ptah,
and you must go forth into the world,
and you must go forth without me—
but Isis will be with you everywhere.
Do you remember our walks
along the acacia-lined paths
in the temple courtyard,
when you would talk to me of your love
and weep, your dark face growing pale?
Do you remember how from the temple walls
we would gaze at the stars
and the city would grow quiet—
near to us, and yet remote?
Of sacred mysteries I do not speak.
Tomorrow other disciples will come to me
who will not say: "Is that the god Ptah?"
because I have grown older,
and it is you who have grown to resemble the god Ptah,
but I will not forget you,
and my deepest thoughts,
my prayers,
will go with you into the wide world,
O my son.

2.

When I was led through the gardens
and through many rooms—turning now left, now right,
into a square chamber
where in the violet light which filtered through the hangings
lay
in robes stiff with jewels,
with many rings and bracelets,
a woman beautiful as Hathor,
with painted eyes and tresses of jet—
I stopped in my tracks.
And she said to me:
"Well?"
But I said nothing,
and she looked at me, smiling,
and tossed me a flower from her hair,
a yellow flower.
I picked it up and raised it to my lips,
but she frowned and said:
"Did you come here,
boy,
to kiss a flower cast on the floor?"
"Yes, Empress," I murmured,
and the whole chamber rang
with the woman's silvery laughter
and with the laughter of her handmaidens;
their hands flew up as in a single motion,
their laughter came as from a single throat,
as if they were sistra at the festival of Isis
struck by the priests in unison.

3.

What a downpour!
Our sail became soaking wet—
you couldn't even see that it was striped.
The rouge ran down your cheeks—
you might have been a Tyrian dyer.
Fearfully we crossed

the threshold of the charcoal-burner's hut;
our host with his scarred forehead
pushed aside his filthy brats
(they were covered with sores, their eyes inflamed),
pulled up a block for you to sit on,
flapped away the dust with his apron
and, slapping the block, said:
"How about an oatmeal cake, your honor?"
And an old black woman
was rocking a cradle and singing:
"If I were Pharoah,
I'd buy two pears:
one I'd give to my friend,
the other I would eat myself."

4.

Once again I beheld the town where I was born
and spent my far-off youth;
I knew
that all my family and friends were gone,
I knew
that even the memory of me had vanished,
but the houses, the winding streets,
the green and distant sea
spoke to me continually
of what was unchanging—
the distant days of my childhood,
the dreams and plans of my youth
and love that had dissolved like smoke.
A stranger utterly,
penniless,
not knowing where to lay my head,
I found myself in a remote quarter of the city
where lights shone through lowered shutters
and singing and the rattle of tambourines
came from the inner rooms.
By a drawn curtain
stood a curled and pretty boy,
and when I slackened my steps, being weary,

he said to me:
"Abba,
you seem like one who has lost his way
and has no friend to turn to.
Enter in:
all things are here
to make a foreigner forget his loneliness.
Here you may find
a gay and sportive mistress,
firm-bodied and with fragrant hair."
I lingered, my mind on other things,
and, smiling, he continued:
"And if such things do not tempt you,
wanderer,
we can offer other joys
not to be despised by a wise and courageous heart."
Crossing the threshold, I cast off my sandals,
lest I should bring into a house of pleasure
the sacred dust of the desert.
Glancing at the doorkeeper,
I saw
that he was all but naked;
together we passed along the corridor
toward the welcoming tambourines.

5.

Three times I saw him face to face.
The first time was in the gardens—
I had been sent to fetch food for my comrades,
and to make the journey shorter
I took the path by the palace wing;
suddenly I caught the tremor of strings,
and, being tall of stature,
I peered through the broad window and saw
him:
he was sitting alone and sad,
his slender fingers idly plucking the strings of a lyre;
a white dog
lay silent at his feet,

and only the fountain's plashing
mingled with the music.
Sensing my gaze,
he put down his lyre
and lifted his lowered face.
Magic to me his beauty
and his silence in the empty room,
in the noontide stillness.
Crossing myself, I ran away in fear,
away from the window…
Later, on guard duty at Lochias,
I was standing in the passage
leading to the quarters of the imperial astrologer.
The moon cast a bright square on the floor,
and the copper buckles of my sandals
glinted
as I trod the patch of brightness.
Hearing footsteps,
I halted.
From the inner chamber,
a slave bearing a torch before them,
three men came forth,
he being one.
He was pale,
but it seemed to me
that the room was lit
not by the torch, but by his countenance.
As he passed, he glanced at me
and said, "I've seen you before, my friend,"
and withdrew to the astrologer's quarters.
Long after his white robes were lost to view
and the torch had been swallowed in darkness,
I stood there, not moving, not breathing,
and afterwards in the barracks,
feeling Martius, who slept next to me,
touch my hand in his usual way,
I pretended to be asleep.
And then one evening
we met again.
We were bathing

near the tents of Caesar's camp,
when suddenly a cry went up.
We ran, but it was too late.
Dragged from the water, the body
lay on the sand,
and that same unearthly face,
the face of a magician,
stared with wide-open eyes.
Still far off, the Emperor was hurrying toward us,
shaken by the grievous tidings;
but I stood seeing nothing,
not feeling tears unknown to me since childhood
running down my cheeks.
All night I whispered prayers,
raving of my native Asia, of Nicomedia,
and angel voices sang:
"Hosannah!
A new god
is given unto men!"

VI. CANOPIC DITTIES

1.

Life's light and free in Cánopus:
there let us sail, sweet friend.
The lightest skiff shall carry us
and speed our journey's end.
See how the inns stand beaconing
along the tranquil crest—
cool terraces are beckoning
the traveller to rest.
We'll take a room together there,
as quiet as we can find,
weave garlands for each other's hair,
sit hour-long hand in hand.
To trade sweet-subtle kisses—
we're no dullards in that school.
The sacred town shall bless us
and make us clean and whole.

2.

Am I not like an apple tree,
an apple tree in bloom,
say, sweet sisters?
Are not my curls
like its leafy crest?
Is not my body as graceful
as its slender bole?
My arms are as supple as branches,
my legs as firm to the earth as roots.
Are not my kisses sweeter than sweet apples?
But ah!
But ah!
The young men stand around in a ring,
eating the apple tree's fruit;
but my fruit,
but my fruit
only one may eat!

3.

Oh we've such a lot of work to do,
we'd best get down to it, and soon:
there's the grapevine's thirsty roots to wet,
the apple's withered twigs to prune.
We've lovely blooms and luscious grapes
in our secluded little plot;
come see—the purple-clustered vine
would gladden anybody's heart.
Charged by Zeus—Celestial Host—
to be unlatched and open wide,
our shrubbery-shrouded wicker gate
beckons to him who passes by.
We'll welcome everyone to our plot
who happens by our wicker gate.
No misers we: come one, come all
and share with us the purple grape.

4.

The Cyprian ranges in pursuit
of Adonis, her beloved youth—
a lioness.
Restless, the goddess roams the strand,
weary, she falls upon the sand,
by sleep unblessed.
Adonis, spectral-white, appears,
his radiant gaze grown dark and blear—
light banished.
Scarce breathing, up she springs once more,
the weariness she felt before
quite vanished.
Swift as the wind the goddess flies
to the shore where fair Adonis lies
lifeless and cold.
Piteously Cytherea moans,
dolefully the sea-wave groans,
sharing her woe.

5.

Whirl faster, step lightly,
join hands, clasp them tightly
like this.
The hiss
of the silvery sistrum is born, is born
through the echoing groves, now faint and forlorn.
Can the Nile fisherman know
what the sea will provide
when he casts his nets wide?
Knows the huntsman
when he draws his bow
who shall slay the flying doe?
Knows the husbandman
what his care will avail
his tender vines in the beating hail?
What do we know?
What can we know?

What's to regret?
Whirl faster, step lightly,
join hands, clasp them tightly
like this.
The hiss
of the silvery sistrum is born, is born
through the echoing groves, now faint and forlorn.
We know
that all is unsure,
that naught can endure.
We know
that change alone
is to change unknown.
We know
that the body we cherish
must utterly perish.
Such is our knowledge,
such our love—
then let us the more tightly cling
to every fleeting, fragile thing.
Whirl faster, step lightly,
join hands, clasp them tightly
like this.
The hiss
of the silvery sistrum is born, is born
through the echoing groves, now faint and forlorn.

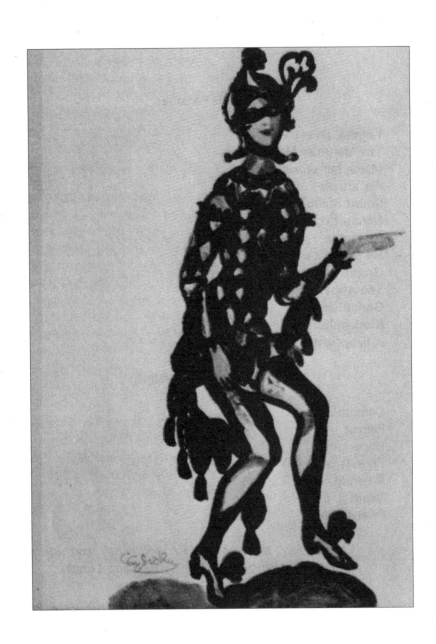

DRAMA

THE VENETIAN MADCAPS

A COMEDY

DRAMATIS PERSONAE

Finette, an actress
The Marquise Marcobruno
Maria, her servant
An actress
Count Stello
Narcisetto, his friend
Harlequin
Harlequin's apprentices
Grobuffi, the Marquise's son
The Abbe, his tutor
Gondoliers
Blackamoors
A lamplighter

PLAYERS IN THE PANTOMIME

Columbine
Pierrot
Harlequin
Friends (women)
A herald
Death
Friends (men)

The action takes place in eighteenth century Venice, the Venice of Goldoni, Gozzi and Longhi.

ACT ONE

Night. An embankment. Music.

SCENE ONE

> *(Enter servants with lanterns; two black-amoors carry on a mirror. Enter Count Stello and Narcisetto, embracing. The pause before the mirror.)*

THE COUNT

O beauty, say, why is thy hour so fleeting?
Wherefore, O love, so quick to spread thy wing?
O might a youthful heart be ever beating
Within this breast, and time's unerring sling
Not dare take aim at this inviolate brow
Until my soul shake off life's here and now.

NARCISETTO

See: cheek pressed to cheek and hand to hand,
The mirror shows us in a ghostly guise;
These shadowed forms which float before our eyes
Dwell surely in some far, enchanted land.

THE COUNT

But I have found a prize none may surpass:
A heart more true than any flattering glass.

> *(They step into a gondola.)*

SCENE TWO

> *(Enter players, Harlequin with his apprentices and Finette.)*

FINETTE

Can it be that strange man, Count Stello? The one they say is a stranger to love and tenderness for all his wealth and fine looks. As far as I can judge, he is very attractive.

ACTRESS

People here talk about nothing but his odd whims.

FINETTE

Yes, I know…The contempt he has for love is enough to make one consider him an extravagant melancholic.

ACTRESS

An actress with the troupe that was here last year did her best to seduce him—but she didn't succeed.

FINETTE

Obviously she didn't know how to go about it. Ah, that's a great art, and few have the secret of it. I'd have to do no more than lift my little finger, and he'd be at my feet.

> Finette, Finette
> Who can escape your net?
> Gray old bird or cock sparrow,
> You'll fall to my lure—
> When I loose love's arrow
> My aim is sure.
> Wise man and dullard
> Court breed and street—
> A carpet bright-colored
> For these dainty feet.
> Finette, Finette,
> Who can escape your net?

ACTRESS

You're a little bit too confident, it seems to me—and then, wouldn't Harlequin be jealous?

FINETTE

Harlequin—jealous? What an absurd notion!.. Would you like me to ask him? Harlequin, Harlequin!

HARLEQUIN

Now what is it?

FINETTE

You won't be jealous, will you, if I make the good count fall in love with me?

HARLEQUIN

For all I care, you can fall in love with him yourself.
I'd as soon be jealous of you as I would of my left foot.

FINETTE

Not a very flattering comparison.

HARLEQUIN

It's a good little beast that always comes home wherever it wanders, the way you do.

FINETTE

You're getting insufferably coarse lately, Harlequin—but you know that I love you all the same.

HARLEQUIN

Well that's just dandy!

ACTRESS

Ladies and gentlemen, time to get into our gondolas!

FINETTE

I'll attend to Count Stello en route.

HARLEQUIN

I have to warn you that I won't be coming along—I still have matters to attend to on shore. We'll meet there.

FINETTE

Another of your unsavory affairs?

HARLEQUIN

Be off with you, there's a good girl. You can kiss your precious count all you want and I won't interfere—just leave me in peace.

FINETTE

You don't love me, Harlequin.

ACTRESS

Do let's be off, Finette. They'll all be waiting for us.

HARLEQUIN

I'll stay behind with my boys, but you'd better hurry, Finette—I see just the people I need coming this way. Good-bye!

(*The players step into a gondola.*)

SCENE THREE

(*Enter the Abbe and Grobuffi.*)

THE ABBE (*boxing Grobuffi's ears*)

I'll teach you to gawp at girls, you wretched boy! I'll teach you to go sneaking into Maria's bodice. For shame, a boy your age shouldn't have the least notion of such things. (*Harlequin's apprentices laugh loudly.*)

GROBUFFI (*bawling*)

But I don't understand what you're talking about, Signor Abbe!

THE ABBE *(boxing his ears)*

I'll give you a whipping when we get home—then you'll understand!

GROBUFFI

But I thought you said I shouldn't have the least notion…

THE ABBE

What's that? I didn't say that you shouldn't have any notion at all, I was simply endeavoring to eradicate your baser instincts. *(Indicating Harlequin's apprentices).* Ask these boys whether they would dream of doing such things, even though their mothers were not, in all probability, marquises. *(The apprentices laugh.)* Take them as your example—they've never even heard of such things!

APPRENTICES

We don't go sneaking into bodices—we're not fleas!

THE ABBE

There you are, you rascal! *(Boxes his ears.)*

SCENE FOUR

(Enter the Marquise, Maria and her servants.)

THE ABBE *(changing his tone)*

You acted rashly, my son, in leaving off your scarf—it may be spring, but the nights get chilly. Of course the Lord watches over his creatures, but we should never put His mercy to the test by failing to respect the laws of nature.

THE MARQUISE

I must say I'm surprised to find you tagging along: you don't imagine we're going to take you to the pavillion with us? There'll be nothing for you to do there—you'd better stay home with the Abbe.

GROBUFFI

Mama, if only you'd let me…

THE MARQUISE

Don't argue…go to Maria.

GROBUFFI

There, you see Signor Abbe, Mama herself tells me to go to her, and you said…

THE ABBE.

What did I say? I didn't say anything…I have, however, written some verses in honor of this evening's events, and I'd be disappointed not to have the opportunity of delivering them at the appropriate time. I venture, therefore, to intercede on Grobuffi's behalf and beg that, since he cannot remain in town without my supervision, he should at least be allowed onto the balcony which surrounds the delightful pavillion of love.

THE MARQUISE

Very well, that might be possible, but only as long as you keep an eye on him—he's such an impressionable boy. As for your always charming verses, it would give me great pleasure to give them a preliminary hearing, just to assure myself that you are not too free in your expressions. You may be an abbe—but you're a naughty man all the same!

THE ABBE

I assure you, madam, that my priestly office guarantees the propriety of my inspiration. I'll be happy to read them to you this very moment.

THE MARQUISE

I'm listening. Maria, put your hands over Grobuffi's ears.

THE ABBE *(reads)*

Venus assumes her pedestal,
Freed of her last constraining fetter,
But lo, at her feet, revealed to all,
Another Venus, and a better.
Two pretty, wingless amorets
To assist love's purposes make haste,
And dazzled night, whom rage besets,
Her dusky veil o'er earth has cast.
Forget, O Venus, thy caprices,
Crease not with envious frown thy brow:
The loveliest of all marquises
Love may not boast that he doth know.

THE MARQUISE

Most touching, Signor Abbe—but why isn't Harlequin here yet? Did you convey to him my gratitude and my purse?

THE ABBE

Set your heart at rest, Marquise; indeed, he is already here, as are his diligent apprentices.

THE MARQUISE

Delightful boys! I can hardly wait to get to our pavillion. Ah, what a delicious evening is in store for us!

HARLEQUIN *(coming forward)*

Marquise, I am entirely at your service, but I find that I have somewhat under-estimated our expenses.

THE MARQUISE

Never mind, never mind, here are two more purses for you; dispose of them as if they were your own. These cupids will be coming with us, as we agreed, won't they? I have decided to bring my maidservant Maria with me so that she can stand on the pedestal in the person of Venus, the goddess of love—just imagine how poetic that will be! Our good Abbe has composed some perfectly charming little verses, which you shall hear in due course—but now to our gondolas and away! Away on our voyage to Cythera! *Allons, allons.* Ah, those boys of yours—quite, quite delicious!

HARLEQUIN

Marquise, your hand. (*To his apprentices.*) Quick march, you rascals!

GROBUFFI

Signor Abbe, don't forget to take me with you.

THE ABBE

Hurry up then, my child, hurry up!

(All get into gondolas.)

GONDOLIER *(sings)*

Over the sleeping waters
(We two in a world that's still),
The salt-breathed zephyrs waft us,
We glide at our own sweet will.

Hate is paid no heed to
And jealousy is far
When we glide toward the Lido
And love's hand guides the oar.

Now let the rower quicken
His smooth, melodious oar,
Now let love's longing waken
And bear us far from shore.

Hate is paid no heed to
And jealousy is far
When we glide toward the Lido
And love's hand guides the oar.

The salt-breathed zephyrs waft us,
We glide at our own sweet will
Over the sleeping waters
(we two in a world that's still).

> *(Finette dances in her gondola in an attempt to capture the Count's attention. The gondolas glide on, stopping at last at the two pavillions.)*

SCENE SIX

Inside one of the pavillions.

THE COUNT

Look, Narcisetto, at that amazing lacemaker, the moon! See how she spreads her golden lace over the sea's deep mourning, sewing the indigo veil of the heavens all over with golden stars. No costumer more cunning than she, Narcisetto! And what can be nobler in life than to find beauty in all things, to take delight and to lose oneself in a lover's revery? Everywhere lies hidden the most subtle beauty, to be revealed only to the eye of the elect—in night, in day, in autumn, in spring, in the fading leaf and the first violet, in the voice of the lute and the trumpet's snarl, in passionate embraces and in hopeless love…

NARCISETTO

And in death?

THE COUNT

O silent sister death, uninvited but ever welcom visitor!..

SCENE SEVEN

(Enter Finette.)

FINETTE

Excuse me, I've made a mistake…

NARCISETTO

Uninvited but ever welcome visitor!..

FINETTE.

I thought…I thought that the pavillion where my friends were supposed to land…I didn't expect to meet you here…

THE COUNT

Perhaps fate is giving us a sign, and you will consent to remain with us, all the more as there is no one to escort you to your pavillion.

FINETTE

You are too kind.

> *(Narcisetto brings up a chair for her and goes out.)*

THE COUNT

You are, I believe, one of the town players?

FINETTE

Yes, I'm their leading actress. My name is Finette.

THE COUNT

I have heard your name—it is quite a well known one.

FINETTE

You are gracious, Count, but your name is no less familiar to me than mine is to you and, to speak frankly, I am grateful for the chance, if not to make your acquaintance, then at least to talk with you.

THE COUNT

You wanted that?

FINETTE.

I can't deny it.

THE COUNT

But, tell me, what for?

FINETTE

I won't speak of your looks, your wealth and your whims, but I have heard that you are a stranger to love. Can such a thing be possible? To live without smiles, without meetings, without kisses—is that not to live without breathing?

> Were all the world's great store of riches mine,
> The privilege and power for which men pine;
> Did some great poet, crowned with deathless fame,
> Make me his muse and glorify my name,
> Yet would I count my state of little worth
> If loveless passed my days upon the earth!
> To love, I ask no more, although in vain,
> Only to feel that pleasurable pain,
> With beating heart await the appointed tryst
> When the green star glimmers through a veil of mist,
> When trembles all the drowsing, moon-blanched glade

With murmur of a distant serenade!
Can Stello, beauty's lord, unmoved move
And shun the soft captivity of love?
Nor yield his liberty to her sweet thrall
Who, like the fabled siren, lures us all?
Who can but pity, who but heave a sigh
To see a loveless traveler pass by?

THE COUNT

Very prettily declaimed. But if you imagine that any passion resembling love can be aroused in me, you're very much mistaken. I am an observer, nothing more.

FINETTE

But when you see lips and eyes that please you, when you see spring clouds and translucent leaves, a calm sea and a starry sky, surely you feel an emotion for which there is no other name than love? When you read Petrarch or listen to Paisiello, do you not experience the joy of a man in love? Do you find this hand graceful? Should it touch you, would not a delicate flame run through your veins? Can it be that you feel nothing when the gondolier sings:

> "The salt-breathed zephyrs waft us,
> We glide at our own sweet will"?

And when you kiss your friend Narcisetto—do you feel nothing then?

THE COUNT

.You're a very cunning girl—they didn't call you Finette for nothing. But I assure you that I'm no simpleton either, and quite cunning enough to resist you.

FINETTE

To resist me? You imagine that I have some sort of scheme in my head? Oh Stello, look at me: do I have the look of a scheming woman? Flighty and frivolous I may be, but I am always, always truthful.

THE COUNT

And you consider that a great virtue?

FINETTE

I'm not saying that, I'm only saying what happens to be so, without regard to whether it should please you or not.

THE COUNT

And you expected I would respond to that? I, who live for dreams and beauty and care no more for truth than I do for the stone which paves the embankment?

FINETTE

I know that, but I also know that I can make your most ardent and fantastic dream a reality, I can pour all the enchantment of love's play, love's fancy and love's smiles into this goblet like a foaming wine and raise it to your exquisite lips, as I do now.

(Pours wine and lowers curtain)

SCENE EIGHT

(Grobuffi and the Abbe tiptoe along the balcony of the pavillion to the left. Narcisetto stands on the balcony of the pavillion to the right.)

THE ABBE

Careful you don't trip up, my son—the moonlight makes everything deceptive. How dreadful if I were to miss the moment when I have to recite my poem.

GROBUFFI *(peeping through a gap in curtain)*

I don't think it's time yet, Signor Abbe: Maria is still undressed.

THE ABBE

What, she's undressed already? A wondrous sight! And are the two little cherubs ready?

GROBUFFI

But what's Harlequin going to do? Isn't he going to take his clothes off?

NARCISETTO

What's the matter with me? What's the matter with me? This woman, this actress has cast a spell on me with her beauty, her voice, her charm. I never experienced anything like it before. And what is she doing with Stello? A cloud hangs over our friendship—or can it be the beginning of love?..

GROBUFFI

Hee-hee! You should just see what those two little fellows are up to, and Maria's already got up on her pedestal. Oh, that is interesting. Signor Abbe, Signor Abbe, hurry up or you'll miss your entrance. *(Laughs.)*

THE ABBE

True, child, I think it is time we made an appearance.

(The curtain opens. Maria stands on the
pedestal, the Marquise half-reclines; one
of Harlequin's apprentices is positioned
on either side of her and Harlequin stands
behind her. The curtain descends as the
Abbe and Grobuffi enter the pavillion.)

GONDOLIER

The salt-breathed zephyrs waft us,
We glide at our own sweet will.

NARCISETTO

O cruel love, O love most fair,
I pierce your mystery at last.
All things I am, all things I dare,
Reborn, I shuffle off the past.

(Finette comes out of the pavillion
and halts.)

NARCISETTO

I love you, Finette. I love you, I love you.

FINETTE

Is that you, Narcisetto?

NARCISETTO

Yes, it is I, Narcisetto, who never knew until now what the word "love" meant,
who never smelled the smell of seaweed, never noticed orange sails, never heard
the songs of the gondoliers. You have revealed life's beauty to me. If you reject
me, I shall die.

FINETTE

You're a pretty lad, Narcisetto—it's dangerous to listen to you on a dark night.

NARCISETTO

I love you, Finette.

FINETTE

You're a great friend of Stello's, aren't you?

NARCISETTO

When you are close to me, I forget everything.

FINETTE

He's heartless and ill-bred, your Count.

NARCISETTO

What does it matter?

FINETTE

Are you listening to me, Narcisetto? Tomorrow at dawn, wait for me outside my door. Do you understand?

NARCISETTO

I understand it, but I can't believe it. Say it again, Finette.

FINETTE

Tomorrow at dawn, outside my door.

NARCISETTO

Do with me as you will, Finette; I am yours utterly and forever.

(Disappears behind the pavillion.)

SCENE NINE

(The Abbe and Grobuffi are thrown out of the pavillion, after which the curtain descends. The Abbe and Grobuffi peer through a gap, laughing loudly.)

GONDOLIER

Hate is paid no heed to
And jealousy is far
When we glide toward the Lido
And love's hand guides the oar.

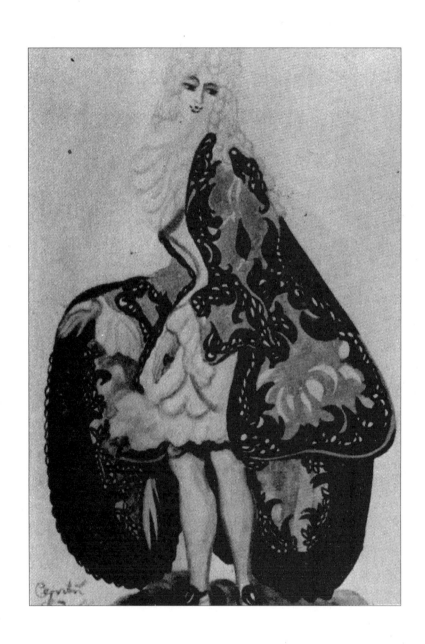

ACT TWO

A street corner. A bridge; Count Stello's palace; facing, the house where Finette lives; below, a gambling den.

SCENE ONE

(The windows of the gambling den are thrown open and laughter is heard; the window closes and all is quiet again. Harlequin enters, turning out his empty pockets.)

HARLEQUIN

Not a bad game—not a penny of the old woman's money left! The devil take the man who invented cards! I'll have to go through the comedy with the painted Marquise all over again. Another thing—I haven't the least notion of what Finette's up to—not that it interests me much; she's a woman I can absolutely rely on, after all. Of course, she's trash like the rest of them, but for some odd reason she loves me. And here she is—speak of the devil.

SCENE TWO

(Finette appears at the window.)

FINETTE

Harlequin, I'm cross with you.

HARLEQUIN

Oh, why?

FINETTE.

The old Marquise—that's why. What kind of tricks have you been getting up to with her?

HARLEQUIN.

What kind of tricks could a man get up to with her?

FINETTE.

I know what kind…

HARLEQUIN

Well that's just dandy.

FINETTE

You're a terrible gadabout, Harlequin. I'm jealous of every woman you look at.

HARLEQUIN

Quite without cause.

FINETTE.

There's another thing I'm cross with you about.

HARLEQUIN.

And what's that?

FINETTE

Why aren't you jealous of the Count, of Narcisetto? It's as if you don't care what I do.

HARLEQUIN

I care who you sleep with, but as for all the other nonsense—whispers, sighs, glances, verses, even kisses perhaps—all that, to tell you the truth, doesn't interest me in the least.

FINETTE

You talk like that because you don't love me, Harlequin.

HARLEQUIN

Just you wait, and I'll come and drag you down by the hair, just to stop you getting all sorts of nonsense into your head.

FINETTE *(joyfully)*

Just you try, just you try!

> *(She goes away from the window, and Harlequin enters the house. It begins to grow light.)*

SCENE THREE

NARCISETTO *(sings, standing on the bridge)*
O moon with bow of silver,
Dissolve the mists of night.
Reach in thy silver quiver
And put love's fears to flight.

Finette, my dove, my darling,
Wake up, you sleepyhead!
Finette, my dove, my darling,
It's time to quit your bed.
The window rattles—listen!—
The door squeaks merrily;
A foot that's light and lissom
Comes tripping down to me.

    Happy the step she touches
    As she goes twinkling by
    (Rosy with sleep, she stretches
    And rubs a drowsy eye).

But I who watch this dwelling
Am happiest of all:
Her beauty is past telling
Who lives within these walls.

    Finette, my dove, my darling,
    Wake up, you sleepyhead!
    Finette, my dove, my darling,
    It's time to quit your bed.

SCENE FOUR

FINETTE *(At the window).*
Take comfort, Narcisetto,
You have not long to wait,
Finette, your dove, your darling
Is up, and won't be late!

(She leaves the window.)

NARCISETTO

Finette! Now she's running a comb through her golden hair, losing her temper with wayward pins, pulling her stockings over her adorable feet. Now she comes running down the stairs, now she's turning the key cautiously in the lock. Oh, Finette!

(Finette enters, and Narcisetto rushes to fling his arms around her and kiss her.)

FINETTE
Darling boy—how soft your cheeks are!

NARCISETTO
At last, Finette, I can look at you, hold you in my arms, kiss you—I can't believe my happiness!

FINETTE
What would Count Stello say if he saw us together, Narcisetto?

NARCISETTO
What do I care what he would say? He's no more to me than last year's snow or the vanished moon which brought you to me, my darling, as it led away the tedious night. Why must you constantly remind me of that man?

FINETTE
Because you love him, Narcisetto.

NARCISETTO
I love no one but you, I see and wish to see no one but you, to hear of no one but you.

FINETTE
Now it's my turn to distrust you, Narcisetto. If your memory is so short, by tomorrow I too may be no more to you than last year's snow.

NARCISETTO
I shall never forget you, never—I swear it.

FINETTE
There's no need to swear, Narcisetto—oaths are the the most easily forgotten of all. Did you not swear an oath of eternal friendship to the Count?—and he's already forgotten!

NARCISETTO
The Count won't stand between us, Finette, believe me.

FINETTE
Does he stand between us then? If only he did!

NARCISETTO
Finette, Finette!

FINETTE
Don't be cross, dear boy! Though it suits you extremely well when you flush and pout and knit your brows, and your eyes gleam. One wants so much to comfort

and caress you, to do everything in one's power to bring cheer and contentment back to that dear little face of yours.

NARCISETTO

You treat me as if I were a little boy.

FINETTE

But you are a little boy—a little boy I find quite delightful.

NARCISETTO

You don't love me, Finette.

FINETTE

Love! Ah, what magic in those four—is it?—letters.

SCENE FIVE

(Harlequin appears in the doorway.)

NARCISETTO

Finette, I'll do anything you want to make you say "I love you."

FINETTE

If I didn't, Narcisetto, why would I agree to meet you, why would I come to you, why would I be speaking with you now?

NARCISETTO

Tell me, tell me that you love me, Finette.

FINETTE

Perhaps Count Stello has woken up by now and is waiting for you, Narcisetto. You know he can't bear to be without you for a moment, the good Count.

NARCISETTO

Damnation! You'll take a different tone with me this evening, Finette. *(Runs out.)*

SCENE SIX

(She rushes toward Harlequin, throws her arms about him and kisses him.)

Harlequin, my Harlequin, kiss me, hold me, squeeze me, bite me, beat me—I am your thing, a thing which will never leave you, however ill you treat it!

HARLEQUIN

Was there ever such an insane woman? Stop it, Finette, or I really will give you a beating.

FINETTE

Beat me, beat me!

HARLEQUIN.

Where did that halfwit run off to? It's true what they say—that love deprives men of their reason. Stop it, I say, Finette—here comes another madman, in love with himself or with his own shadow by the look of him. He wants to speak with us—lay off, Finette.

SCENE SEVEN

(Enter Count Stello.)

I'm pleased to see you, my friends—you can help me carry out a whim which came into my head last night. It will be both charming and fantastic.

FINETTE

As your whims invariably are, my charming count.

THE COUNT

Is it true that you are to perform a pantomime here today?

HARLEQUIN

You have not been misinformed, and I trust that we shall have the pleasure of seeing you among the spectators?

THE COUNT

Much better than that: you shall see me among the performers.

HARLEQUIN

What? The Count wishes to do us the honor of acting with us?

THE COUNT

That's exactly what I wanted to discuss with you. Naturally, you are not to know that my friend Narcisetto and I are no mean dancers—anyone who has seen us will confirm that. My idea, then, is that Narcisetto and I should take part in the pantomime—incognito, of course. We'll put on your company's masks; I would like to be dressed as Mademoiselle Finette, and my friend will be dressed as Harlequin. We shall imitate your gestures and steps, so that no one will be able to tell who are the real Harlequin and Columbine and who their doubles. That will be amusing, don't you think?

FINETTE

As is everything our dear Count contrives.

HARLEQUIN

And your friend dances too?

THE COUNT

No worse than I do.

FINETTE

A pretty lad, your Narcisetto. In your place I wouldn't let him out of my sight, I'd be so jealous. Ah, love is fleeting, so fleeting.

THE COUNT

True, but what can jealousy do about it?

FINETTE

Jealousy can do a great deal.

HARLEQUIN

Then we shall go and make some costumes ready for you and prepare for the performance in general.

(Harlequin and Finette go out.)

SCENE EIGHT

THE COUNT *(alone)*
We revel until the break of day.
The festive masks we wear are gay.
E finita la commedia,
But we must play, and play, and play.

SCENE NINE

(Narcisetto enters.)

NARCISETTO

Stello, I must talk with you.

THE COUNT

Not now, Narcisetto, not now. The day and night before us are to be given over to folly and gaiety! If you only know what an idea I've had.

NARCISETTO

Stello, I absolutely must talk with you this very moment.

THE COUNT

But what has happened? Does not my house stand where it always has, do not the pigeons coo on the Piazza San Marco, do not the gondolas glide, do not I love you as before? What is there for us to talk about?

NARCISETTO

Something very important happened today.

THE COUNT

Is it a bad dream that has disturbed you, my friend?

NARCISETTO

You seem in a carefree mood today, Stello.

THE COUNT

Indeed I am! Let's go—I'll tell you about my scheme, you'll be charmed with it!

NARCISETTO

I beg you to listen to me, Stello.

THE COUNT

Later, later!

(Goes out.)

SCENE TEN

(Enter the Marquise Marcobruno, the Abbe, Grobuffi and Maria.)

THE MARQUISE

It's absolutely essential that I see Signor Harlequin before the performance begins.

THE ABBE

I'll do everything in my power, but I doubt whether your endeavors will be crowned with success…Grobuffi, get away from Maria!…I hear music approaching.

THE MARQUISE

You are suffering from auditory hallucinations, Abbe: there is no music approaching, everything is quiet, and I absolutely must see Harlequin in order to arrange another rendezvous.

THE ABBE

Surely Madame la Marquise was not dissatisfied with the first one?

THE MARQUISE

In the first place, if I had been dissatisfied, I would not wish for a repeat performance; in the second place, certain details remain unclear in my mind.

THE ABBE

With regard to Harlequin or to his apprentices?

THE MARQUISE

I was speaking in general, you naughty man.

THE ABBE

This time I'm certainly not suffering from auditory hallucinations: I hear music
quite clearly, and I trust that you can now hear it too.

THE MARQUISE

Yes, I can hear it. How vexing that I didn't have a chance to speak with Harlequin.

PANTOMIME

*(A procession of players comes into view, followed by the crowd. Dances. The
Count and Narcisetto appear in the costumes of Columbine and Harlequin. A game
of shuttlecock. The procession moves back across the bridge. Narcisetto and the
Count make up the final pair; as they are crossing the bridge, Narcisetto silently
stabs his friend, kisses him and throws the body noiselessly into the canal. A burst
of laughter comes from the window of the gambling den and then dies away. Narcisetto runs down from the bridge and Finette runs forward to meet him.)*

SCENE ELEVEN

HARLEQUIN

Respected patrons, the reason that we are called traveling players is that we are
unable to remain in one spot even for a single performance. The prologue, so to
speak, to the play will be given here, but the pantomime itself will be performed
elsewhere. In that way, our spectators will not get tired of standing or sitting in
one place and will feel more at their ease. Silence! We are about to begin!

SCENE TWELVE

FINETTE

What have you done? What have you done, Narcisetto? Have you killed him?

NARCISETTO
Yes.

FINETTE
Did you do it for love of me, Narcisetto?

NARCISETTO
Yes.

FINETTE
You love me then?

NARCISETTO
I love nobody but the Count. I never loved anyone but him.

FINETTE
I see. So that's your great love for me, Narcisetto!

NARCISETTO
I hate you, Finette—get away from me! Stello! Stello!

SCENE THIRTEEN

(Enter Harlequin, the players, and the crowd.)

HARLEQUIN
Where did you disappear to, Finette? You and the Count and Narcisetto? We can't carry on the show without you.

FINETTE
Sssh, Harlequin, ssh! We can't carry on with the show anyway. *(Softly.)* Narcisetto has killed Count Stello—we must leave at once.

HARLEQUIN
Can that be possible, Finette?

FINETTE
It's more than possible. Let's leave, Harlequin, please let's leave quickly.

ALL
What's happened? What's happened?

HARLEQUIN *(loudly)*
Respected ladies and gentlemen, nothing at all has happened—it's simply that time is short and we have to leave for Verona at once. It had completely slipped our minds that we were due to appear there so soon that we'll hardly have time

to get there. We thank you warmly for the gracious welcome accorded to us and for all the attentions you have shown us. We hope that you will remain loyal to us in the future. Goodbye, I trust that we shall meet again soon!

FINETTE *(sings)*

Let not our deeds discomfort you or daunt,
You honest burghers, pups and poppinjays.
What is our life if not a merry jaunt?
Actors all of us in plays.

    Verona today, tomorrow Rome,
    We dance, we sing, call everywhere home.
    Clear skies today, tomorrow rain—
    Wring joy from today, lest tomorrow bring pain.

Stand not amazed at altered circumstances,
In life we all play parts, some well, some ill,
But in the giddy whirl of change and chance
We serve Another's will.

    Verona today, tomorrow Rome,
    We dance, we sing, call everywhere home.
    Clear skies today, tomorrow rain—
    Wring joy from today, lest tomorrow bring pain.

We do not forge ourselves unneeded chains
From life's encounters, be they grave or gay.
Players are we, ready to take our gains
And go our careless way.

    Verona today, tomorrow Rome,
    We dance, we sing, call everywhere home.
    Clear skies today, tomorrow rain—
    Wring joy from today, lest tomorrow bring pain.

Should our indulgent patrons be content,
Clap hands—we give you leave—and cry "bravo,"
And should tomorrow find you pleasure bent—
Come see tomorrow's show.

    Verona today, tomorrow Rome,
    We dance, we sing, call everywhere home.
    Clear skies today, tomorrow rain—
    Wring joy from today, lest tomorrow bring pain.

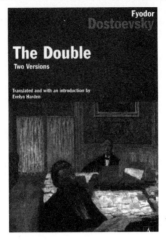
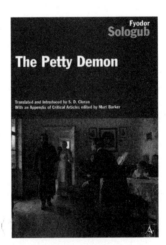